"*Too High in the Wind* is a continual thread of suspense, artfully woven by an outstanding writer."

— Ed Green, author of, *The Sapphire Prison series*, and, *The Gift*, a short story from, *Book Two*, of the same series.

"Combining intrigue, murder, quick wit, and romance into one novel isn't easy, but Lowcountry author John G. Williams has managed to do it all in his debut suspense novel, *Too High in the Wind*. As a former Marine , he plots out a murder that only someone with expert skills can convey. From the first page, Williams excites our imagination with incredible detail while capturing our hearts with his compelling characters. Truly a novel for a wide variety of readers, this is a book that I highly recommend."

— Stephanie Austin Edwards, author of, *What We Set in Motion*

"John Williams' *Too High in the Wind* is an action-packed suspense novel with compelling, well-drawn characters that you'll follow through many exciting twist and turns. Nate and Becca will win your heart just as they as they took mine, and you'll find them invading your thoughts long after you close the cover. I appreciate this former Marine writer's ability to portray Becca and her dilemmas with empathy and finesse. Plus this story offers stunning action amidst some of the most iconic locations in the South's coast and mountains."

— Estelle Ford-Williamston, Author, *Rising Fawn* and *Abbeville Farewell: A novel of Early Atlanta and North Georgia*

Too High
in the
Wind

John G. Williams

TOO HIGH IN THE WIND

© 2021 John G. Williams

Print ISBN: 978-1-66781-9-631
eBook ISBN: 978-1-66781-9-648

This novel combines actual and fictional places. I've moved rifle ranges, islands and bars (sorry, Pearl) in an attempt to provide a suspenseful story that both entertains and informs. As a former Marine and Lowcountry native this has been a work of fond remembrance.

I hope you enjoy it.

Semper Fi,
John G. Williams

To my wife, Marion:

"You are the wind behind my sails!"

ACKNOWLEDGMENTS

Thanks to all of you who've encouraged me during this novel's multi-year journey. Your comments and critiques have taught me more than you'll ever know and I deeply appreciate them. Special thanks go out to the following:

Stephanie Edwards's Lowcountry Writers' Workshop: Each of you is a contributor to this book. Your encouragement has kept me away from the shredder and I've learned more from you than I could ever give back. Thank you so much!

Jonathan Haupt, Executive Director of The Pat Conroy Literary Center, who generously supplied our writers' group with meeting space and guided us through the electronic mysteries of "ZOOM," ("Can you hear me now?")

My Pinckney Retreat neighbors, who've provided years of encouragement, patiently waiting for this long-promised book. Special thanks to Karen Sorensen who turned a series of loose-running files into a formatted manuscript ready for submission and Captain Jim Thomas for his generously shared sailing expertise. Any course deviations are solely mine.

My son Sean, a gifted artist, who created this book's dramatic cover and added much needed computer expertise to the overall publishing process.

My loving and always supportive wife, Marion. I literally couldn't have done it without her and our editing battles definitely produced a better book. Her new favorite saying is, "I'm not Becca."

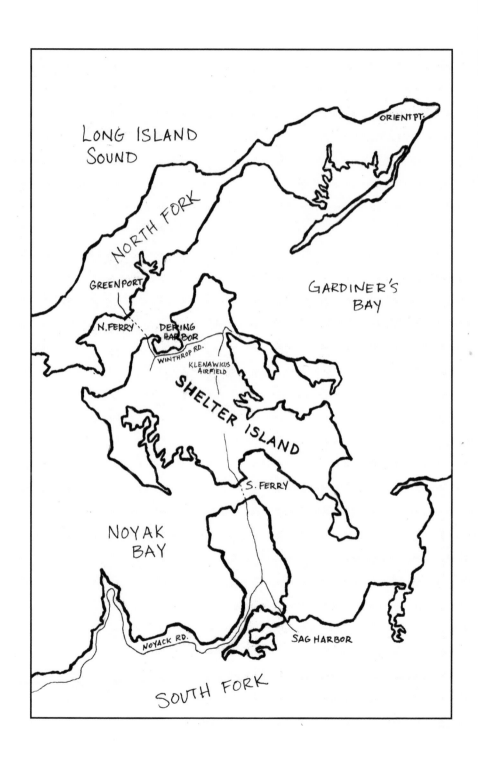

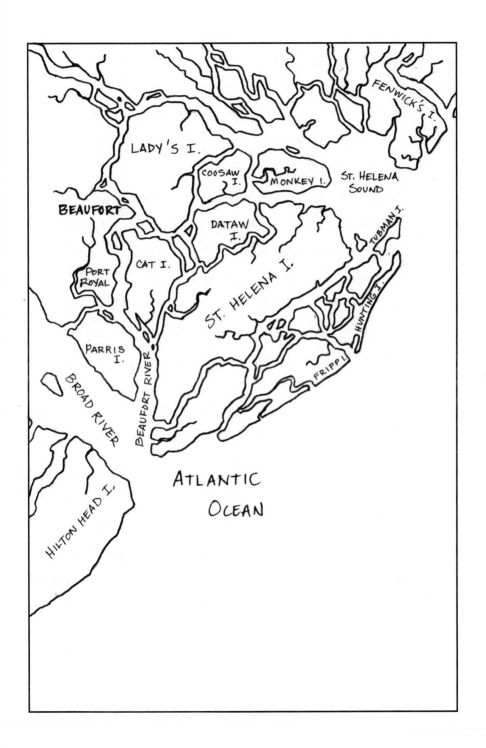

CHAPTER ONE

"MANHANSAK AHA QUASH AWOMAK," Sally Jordan mumbled to herself, looking back at Shelter Island's receding shoreline. An island sheltered by islands. Images of the Native Americans who named it floated from the darkness. She could picture them, sliding through the water, decked out in war paint, paddling their canoes across Shelter Island Sound to protect what was theirs. She felt connected. She was a warrior, too, and part Cherokee. It wasn't personal. You had to protect what was yours. By the time the Manhassets learned this, the Dutch owned Manhattan. Now part of Manhattan was hers, conquered by guts and guile, and she wasn't going to trade it for some trinkets offered by one of its original settlers.

She'd skipped the war paint. Being discovered alone in Michael's dinghy, in the middle of the sound, could be explained. Add camo paint and the explanation became more difficult. She wore black tights with a matching turtleneck and a black watch cap covered her head. If she needed more camouflage, then her mission had failed.

She'd first seen Shelter Island from the air, stuffed into a tiny Cessna 150, piloted by Michael's son, Brad. Brad flew them in across Long Island's North Fork, circling Shelter Island as he pointed out his family's compound, perched along Dering Harbor's rocky shore. Their South Fork exit proved exciting when Brad dropped the Cessna to eyeball level and scattered the rich and famous that lounged along the Hamptons' purified beaches. She smiled at the scene, but two years later, she could still picture the layout. It would help her tonight.

Michael's dinghy existed solely to shuttle him between his dock and his sailboat, not to cross open water like Noyac Bay. Underpowered and unstable, it wallowed in the swells, struggling to make headway against the currents that rushed around the island.

At least the motor was quiet. Michael had explained that the first time he took her sailing. It was a four-stroke engine like a car's, not a two-stroke like most small outboards. He'd said a lot more, but she hadn't listened. Mansplaining. The important thing was that it was quiet.

She'd sailed in the bay before with Michael and his bitch wife, Allison, but never at night, and never alone. As a child, she'd hated the darkness. She blamed her grandmother, though she'd begged to hear the stories of strange happenings along the West Virginia hollows. Mine collapses and steep mountain roads provided Granny Jordan with a never-ending supply of victims, and her vivid imagination did the rest.

At night, things always looked different. Her mind played tricks with her eyes, convincing her that her worst fears hid in the nearest shadow, patiently waiting.

Her year in Afghanistan was a game changer. "We own the night," was her team's motto and they taught her to appreciate the darkness, to wrap herself in its protective cloak and become someone else's worst fear. She'd do that tonight. Allison was about to learn a deadly lesson.

Sweat trickled down Sally's face, burning her eyes and forming a salty crust on her mouth. She licked her lips, then wiped her forehead with her sleeve. It was hot for April. Even the eternal sea breeze felt warm. The tights and turtleneck were a little much, but they were for concealment, not comfort. *Beauty and stealth know no pain,* she thought, trying to smile at her cleverness.

Getting ready mentally, psyching herself, believing she'd really do it, that was the hard part. Killing Allison would not be easy, especially with a knife. Guns were different. At least you had some distance. She'd done that herself or at least she might have. Noise, smoke, and general chaos made it hard to tell: The fog of war up close and personal.

Afghanistan was two years ago. She spent a year there, a woman doing a man's job; an Air Force Forward Air Controller. The SEALS and Rangers had another name for her: Death Angel. It was an awesome power. Sometimes she felt like God, raining death and destruction from above with a few cryptic words whispered softly into her radio mic. It was a the time to kill. The time to heal would come later or maybe not at all.

It was a sanitized way to wage war. The enemy died silently on a distant ridgeline, consumed in an orange and black ball, while she returned to the safety and comfort of her Forward Operating Base.

But one mission was different. That night, the enemy was where they landed, waiting, hidden and ready, their closeness protecting them from the planes that circled above. Here she fought, reacting, not thinking, like she was an actress playing a role. Even the enemy seemed unreal. She'd expected to face fierce, bearded warriors with sun-hardened skins. Instead she battled green video game figures that glowed in her night vision goggles, scurrying across the rocks to escape her fire.

But Afghanistan wasn't Long Island. It was someone else's world where she was a temporary inhabitant. A strange and exotic place, where rules changed as circumstances dictated; drug lords were suddenly allies and enemies became friends. She'd adapted, surprised at her moral agility, but not changed. Now she was forced to adapt again. Maybe she had changed.

She checked her watch and released the throttle. She'd used the flickering lights along both shorelines to keep her mid-channel and the aurora of the lights at Sag Harbor's marina to guide her south. Now, her final leg would take her west.

She'd been on the water for twenty minutes. Her right hand felt numb from the motor's vibrations and her back hurt from the backless seat. Shaking her hand to revive it, she removed a pair of binoculars from her mission bag and studied Long Island's shoreline.

She didn't see much. A thin mist coated the island, blurring its features, and reflecting the moonlight. She lowered the binoculars and slumped down in the seat. Maybe the fog would clear. If it didn't, she'd go further south, cross the bay and head back up the island. Either way, she'd intercept Allison and complete her mission. Sally liked the term "mission". It had a nice sound, legal and official. Murder was such a harsh word.

A rhythmic beat from the west interrupted her thoughts. Turning towards the noise, she spotted the green and red lights of South Ferry at mid-channel, heading towards Long Island's southern shore. The Hamptons' crowd had launched into the land of the twenty-dollar martini. It was time to go.

She swung the boat right, setting her course north of the ferry's route, gliding away from its lights and into the darkness. Ahead, Long Island began to reveal its shape, changing from a vague outline to a series of curves and inlets. She swung the dingy north, paralleling the shore, then released the throttle, drifting with the current.

The fog lifted slowly, clearing the land, but shrouding the trees with its gray droplets. She used a tiny penlight to light her chart. Orienting the chart to the land was the secret. Once they matched, the mystery was solved.

Sally started by identifying the point that jutted out like a waving finger, separating Noyac from Little Peconic Bay. That done, it was simply a matter of tracing the shoreline south until she found what she was looking for; a narrow inlet where the water penetrated inland, stopping just short of Noyac Road's sandy shoulders.

She'd been there this morning, picking up scallop shells and studying the terrain. "Site reconnaissance," the Rangers called it. Much better than map reconnaissance. No surprises that way. Surprises could get you killed.

Sally opened the throttle and angled towards her objective. A hundred yards offshore, she killed the engine and tossed the anchor overboard. Short oaks lined the inlet, drawing shadows along its banks. The inlet appeared empty, but she waited; watching and listening. Patience was a virtue.

An olive green ammo can lay at her feet. Sally leaned down and opened it. She flinched at its metallic pop. A jungle knife lay on top. It seemed to stare at her; its shiny surface reflecting the moonlight. She picked up the knife and drew its blade lightly across her thumb. Its sharpness tugged at her skin. She'd killed a deer with it this morning. The image haunted her. She loved animals more than people and the people she'd killed had deserved to die. The deer was innocent. Allison was guilty.

Now, Allison's image replaced the deer's. Sally could see the knife slice across Allison's long, pale neck. Bright, red blood spurted from the wound. Allison would try to scream, but she'd choke on her blood. Sally could hear the gurgling.

Trembling, she let the knife slide back into the can. Was she really going to do this? Spasms racked her stomach. She slammed the box closed, stuck her head over the side and vomited. Allison's image was gone. Sally dipped her hands into the dark water, splashed her face, then rinsed her mouth, spitting the salty water back into the bay.

She studied the shoreline. The purging had cleared her thoughts. The anchor was holding and she was in the right place. She sat down on the rubber tubing, chin in hand, and pulled out her dog tags. She fondled them like a rosary, a ritual she'd performed before and after each mission, fingering her religion and blood type as the metal tags slid through her fingers. So far, so good. No need to change for what she hoped was her last mission.

She stuffed the dog tags inside her shirt and looked at her watch. Its Ironman logo stared back at her, mocking the sudden weakness that traveled down her arms and into her hands. She had to move. Allison would be here soon and she had things to do. Everything would be in place. Once she was ready, she could still back out. No one would know.

She'd heard Michael answer the phone in the kitchen. She'd listened, then retreated. From the conversation, she'd known it was Allison.

"See you at 11:00, honey, and be careful on Noyac," he'd said. "I'm eating supper at the club." This meant Allison would pass by her about 10:30. She knew that island people were always exact with their times. The ferry waited for no one.

Sally lifted the anchor, curling the rope as she pulled—a habit she'd picked up from Michael. Neatness counted on a boat, regardless of size. She stowed the rope in the bow and began to paddle. A light land breeze combined with an outgoing tide pushed back, holding her boat in an invisible web. She was losing ground.

Reluctantly, she lowered her paddle and reached for the starter rope. So much for stealth. Her first pull produced only noise and smoke.

"Crank, you sorry SOB," she muttered to the little Honda. Sally braced herself firmly against the wooden stern and tried again. The motor sputtered, teasing her, before returning to its normal, muted growl. She slipped it into gear and headed into the inlet.

Just short of the beach, she cut the engine, tilting the motor up as the dinghy snuggled into the soft sand. Sally sat still, listening, but all she heard were small waves collapsing against the beach. She was alone.

Leaving the boat, her first objective was a small hilltop clearing. She'd stopped there before on her many trips from Manhattan to Michael's Shelter Island compound. From there you could see across Peconic Bay into Long Island Sound, and on a clear day, the Connecticut shoreline lay at the bottom of the horizon.

She'd discovered the view by accident on her first trip to Shelter Island. A small herd of deer grazing in the clearing had caught her eye. They'd scampered off when she approached, but remained nearby, observing her from the tree line.

On her next trip she'd bought six ears of corn at a roadside stand. At first, the deer scattered, but sprinkling the kernels from the center of the clearing to her hiding place along its edge brought them closer. Soon, they'd follow the corn to her feet, sniffing her clothes like the family dog, then sensing no threat, eating from her hand.

This morning, only one deer had greeted her, a small four-point buck with a scarred right leg. She remembered the scar, wondering how he'd gotten it. Probably fighting over some doe-eyed sweetie. She wanted bigger antlers, but these would do. The knife would do the real work.

"Good morning, big guy," she'd greeted him. She offered him corn with her left hand, the knife in her right, hidden behind her back. "My, aren't we hungry," she'd said when he inhaled the corn from her hand and nuzzled her for more. With his head against her, she'd struck hard, slashing across his throat, the deer's tough hide parting as the knife ripped through his flesh. Blood spurted from the wound. The deer dropped to his knees, snorted once, then rolled over on his side. She waited until he was still, then stopped the bleeding with a battle dressing. *She'd need this blood later.* Sally dragged the deer's body into the underbrush and covered it with leaves. She'd marked the position with a rotting oak stump. Now, she had to find that stump.

Sally moved across the beach and into the trees. She picked her way through the brush, winding her way uphill, grateful for the moonlight that lit her way.

Finding the clearing was easier than she'd thought. The moonlight reflected off its sandy surface like a lighthouse, guiding her to the deer. She guessed it weighed about eighty pounds, roughly the same as the rucksack she'd humped across Afghanistan. There, she'd soon learned the key to wearing a ruck was balance. The same technique applied to the deer. She leaned it against the stump, held its feet together and pulled it onto her shoulders, twisting and bouncing until her load felt comfortable. Satisfied, she grabbed her ammo can and headed downhill towards Noyac Road.

The hike took ten minutes. She'd picked her spot with care; a 180-degree loop with a cliff along its outer edge. Allison would die here; from the crash she hoped. If not, there was always the knife.

Sally dropped the deer, opened the ammo can and slipped out her Beretta pistol. She pulled the slide partially to the rear. A shiny gold casing glinted back at her; the weapon was ready to fire.

Her legs felt heavy as she retreated from the road's edge and merged back into the shadows. Carrying the deer had drained her. She propped against the hillside and stretched her legs. Once she was still, the forests noises returned, led by a choir of crickets chirping their displeasure at her unwelcomed intrusion.

Mosquitoes soon found her, buzzing her ears as they sought uncovered skin. She looked at the deer beside her. The idea came from a *Sixty Minutes* story. Its message was clear. The deer population on Long Island was out of control. Collisions were frequent; future fatalities inevitable. She'd just speed things up.

In the cottage her plan seemed perfect, but now, alone in the dark, she began to have doubts.

It had begun two nights ago at Michael's home. She'd jerked awake, trembling. It was the same nightmare. Unfortunately it was real. After the firefight, she'd lifted the poncho for a final look at her Team Leader, call sign, "Papa Goose". The SEALs tried to stop her. She wished they had. "Papa Goose" had no face.

She couldn't sleep and finding the medicine cabinet empty, she'd slipped into her bikini and headed for the hot tub.

Opening the wooden gate, she'd spotted Michael. His large frame was backed against a water jet and a silly grin spread across his face. A small clam shell perched on a compact cooler caught her eye. Light gray smoke rose from it and merged with the steam, creating an acrid cloud she quickly identified.

Smelling the marijuana, Sally instinctively retreated. People like Michael kept their drug use private. Nobody gave a pothead ten million dollars to manage and ten million was Michael's minimum account. Sober and serious, that was the image. She eased her way back towards the pool gate, but a loud squeak spoiled her escape.

"I'm sorry," she stammered. "I couldn't sleep."

"Me neither," Michael answered.

His body was now submerged beneath the swirling bubbles. He appeared larger than usual, his head floating just above the steam, his hair slicked back like a 50s gangster.

Michael's voice was gravelly from the smoke. "Come on in. This baby's better than pills."

She'd protested, too late, her hair . . . but Michael was Michael, plus he was also her boss and he always got his way. She'd entered the swirling water slowly, feeling its warm embrace as she sank onto a submerged seat opposite Michael. He gave her a slow, approving look, then reached up and lifted a magnum of red wine from the cooler.

"New York's finest," he said, removing the cork with his teeth. Michael swigged nosily, wiping his mouth with the back of his hand when he finished. "Allison would call that a waste of good wine. She says red wine can't be chilled and must be sipped." He passed her the bottle.

"To unclaimed victories," Sally said, duplicating Michael's action. She couldn't care less about how Allison drank her wine and now wasn't the time to bring up the illegal transactions. They would remain their shared secret.

Work stories dominated their conversation, starting with last night's party, deteriorating from trading strategies to office gossip as the bottle's contents shrank.

"Another dead soldier," Sally said, tilting the wine bottle to drain it. Michael floated beside her. "You sleepy yet?" she asked, reaching up to return the empty bottle to the cooler.

"Sort of," Michael answered. "I've got this kink in my right shoulder that won't go away. Probably from yesterday's golf game. Goat Hill always wears me out. He arched his shoulders. "Think you could help an old man with a little massage?"

He'd tensed at her touch. "Relax," she said. "I won't hurt you. Besides, the wine has you completely anesthetized."

She worked her way across his shoulder, starting in the back, moving forward, then coming back, going lower. He pressed his back against her breasts.

"You're sneaky," she said as Michael swayed against her, leaning his head back, arching to reach her lips. It was a moment she'd waited for. That snooty, skinny bitch, Allison, didn't deserve him.

She'd kissed him back, gentle at first then harder, feeling his heat, closing her eyes, like this was a dream. She felt him turn, sliding her through the water, his lips on her breasts, then lower. One tug and her bottoms were gone. Then he was in her, her legs around him, her hands grasping the side of the tub. The water rose and fell, beginning as slow-floating swells before ending in a violent chop, neither aware of Allison looking down from her third floor balcony.

Sally checked the Beretta again. She slid the safety on, then off, testing the tightness of the Odessa silencer. She pulled the watch cap over her ears. A new crop of mosquitos had discovered her position, their buzzing almost drowning out the sound of a car motor that droned in the distance. This could be Allison.

Sally took a deep breath then slid against a tree, steading her arm against a forked branch, lining up her sights along the shadowy road, waiting to identify the Jaguar's distinctive profile. She had to be sure. Friendly fire wasn't an option; not on Long Island. Fifty dollars and a cow wouldn't buy these lives.

The engine sounds grew louder. Beams of light penetrated the woods, forming dancing shadows as the car wound its way towards her. Her breath came in short, shallow gasps, and the Beretta made wild swings as she fought to focus its night vision sights down the narrow roadway. Soon, she and Allison would meet. Michael would never know.

Entering the straightaway, the lights gathered speed, charging towards her, hiding what lay behind them. Sally concentrated on her breathing. She forced down deep gulps of air, narrowing the Beretta's swing into a tight circle that focused on the lights, aiming for the tire beneath them.

The music startled her — its thumping bass outpacing the speeding car; its vibrations felt before they were heard. The shape was wrong. She lowered the pistol. A topless Jeep Wrangler sped by, its brake lights flashing as it slowed for the turn. Sally rested her head against the tree and sank slowly to the ground.

The deer lay beside her, its brown eyes still open, reflecting the moonlight. "I'm sorry, big guy," she said to the still animal, "but you died in vain. I can't do it."

She tried to stand. Her legs trembled at the effort, exhausted by the tension, forcing her to use the tree as a crutch. Sally pulled the bandage from the deer's wound. Dark, clotted blood formed a natural glue, which seeped bright red, as she removed the gauze. She placed the bandage and her pistol in the ammo can. Her movements silenced the insects. Only the mosquitoes' persistent droning followed her as she shuffled slowly uphill, retracing her steps. Overhead a jet airliner roared, gaining altitude as it winged its way across the Atlantic.

Her legs ached from the climb back to the clearing. She sat heavily, holding her head in her hands, squeezing her forehead as she tried to force out the memories of the past two days.

Sally replayed her conversation with Allison, reaching the same conclusion: Allison had copies of the illegal account switches she and Michael had made and she'd sacrifice them both. Allison had money and power and she'd use them to ruin her. There were two choices; she had to leave or Allison had to die. *I guess I'm leaving*, she thought. But she knew one thing; whatever happened, she'd never return to the West Virginia mountains.

She glanced out across Noyac bay. Sag Harbor's lights sparkled through the trees, dotting the green hills like monochrome fireflies. Fine restaurants and quaint boutiques lay beneath them. She'd shopped there with Michael, amazed at the prices, wandering the shaded streets, helping select Allison's Christmas and birthday gifts. She remembered the shoppers; rich, happy people; people like Allison and her daughters, Becca and Staci, who spent money they didn't earn on things they didn't need.

Her father's general store was different. There, drawn men in filthy overalls signed hand-written IOUs for food to feed their families until the mine's next payday. They were old at forty and dead at fifty, trapped in an unrelenting black cloud that stained both the town and the surrounding mountains. Few escaped. A basketball scholarship had been her ticket out. Nothing would force her back.

Behind her, a light filtered through the trees. She sat quietly, listening in the dark. The lights grew brighter. She could hear the engine now, powerful and working hard. She listened for a moment, then, rested and resigned, Sally stood up and started downhill towards the dinghy.

CHAPTER TWO

Rebecca Noble ignored the cold rain, tugging her bush hat over her ears as she twisted and dodged her way through the cars that crawled along Logan Airport's Terminal Drive.

"Come on, Robert," she yelled to her ex-boyfriend who trailed her by three lanes, "I've got to make that flight."

Becca hit the sidewalk running, and sprinted inside, skidding to a stop at the first flight monitor. A large crowd blocked her path. The crowd gave her hope. This was a big storm. She'd watched it on her cell phone, a mass of red and yellows stretching from Boston down into New York.

"I'm sure you'll be delayed," Robert said, studying the radar. "Maybe cancelled," he added, giving her a sly wink. "Wouldn't that be terrible?"

It would be terrible. She was a planner, but her mother Allison's habitual spontaneity had spawned this trip; a command performance, issued this afternoon along with a paid e-ticket. Rebecca had refused at first. Too busy: papers to grade, her own graduation, job applications, and the haircut appointment she'd finally found the courage to make. Even listing them now raised her heart rate.

"Please," her mother had pleaded in her childlike voice, "A girl only turns fifty once, plus you can work here and let the island perform its magic. Don't tell your father," she added. "You're a surprise."

Becca had relented, resisting the temptation to ask about her mother's previous "no fuss for my fiftieth" decree. She could work there and Shelter Island did have a magical property; it could slow down the world. *Island time*, she thought, picturing herself in her Mom's studio overlooking Dering Harbor.

The flight board refreshed, producing moans and an occasional clap from the trapped passengers. Another recycle and the crowd thinned. She removed her hat and stepped closer. Her flight wasn't there.

"Come on, Islip," she mumbled. "I've got to catch that ferry. Show me a delay." She looked for Robert, didn't see him, and turned back to the board. Her flight appeared, a tranquil patch of white surrounded by angry reds. "Boarding," she said out loud, rechecking the monitor. "Damn it, it's boarding." She spotted Robert propped against a wall. "C7," she yelled and began to sprint.

By the time Robert caught up with her, she was in line, stuck behind an elderly couple, watching their losing battle against Island Air's solo kiosk. An argumentative trio surrounded the sole harried clerk.

"No need to hurry now," she said, shaking her head, watching the machine reject the offerings of credit cards and driver's licenses the couple presented. "I'm doomed."

She felt Robert's hand land gently on her shoulder. "Not yet," he said, "but the old-toe-tap, lip-bite-combo won't work." He dropped his arm to his side. "You've got to use the 'deep- sigh, evil-eye move' if you want to speed up these people."

His calm voice irritated her but she stilled her foot and released her lip. They'd been unconscious movements but Robert didn't miss much. She remembered his creative writing class. "Strive to be someone on whom nothing is lost," he'd said, quoting Henry James, while stroking his mandatory Harvard grad assistant beard. She'd been a senior then, struggling to decide between an MFA and English grad school. He'd convinced her. "You're a writer," he'd said after reading the only short story that she'd let escape her well-guarded briefcase. "Your voice is unique. You have to write." Now two years later, she was finishing her MFA and she was writing.

The couple finally surrendered, sulking off to the side to regroup. She ran forward, printing her boarding pass, rechecking her gate as she sprinted towards security. Robert trailed behind, dragging her backpack. *No baggage,* she thought, bypassing the ticket agent; *nothing to check, nothing to retrieve.* That was the way to go, though it helped to be going home where basic essentials and a second if slightly dated wardrobe awaited her arrival.

The security line was short. "Thanks," she said, giving Robert an air kiss and taking her pack. "See you on campus."

"Becca," he shouted as she moved through the line. "Call me when you land."

"Okay," she mouthed back, though she wanted to say no. It'd been three weeks since their breakup. She knew he'd expected something more when she called, but all she needed was a ride. Uber was rained out. She'd been firm, nice but firm. It wasn't just him, though he was part of it. She was starting over, and Robert was part of her past. She smiled at the TSA agent and lifted her backpack onto the conveyor belt. *No baggage,* she said to herself, focusing her eyes forward.

A loud beep halted the line. The man in front of her had set off the metal detector. A giant Patriots belt buckle proved to be the culprit. She hated the Patriots.

Glancing back, Becca spotted Robert standing where she left him, his brown eyes drooping like a scolded puppy. He gave her a weak wave. She waved back. '*No baggage,*' she thought again moving forward, '*no baggage.*'

The ticket agent greeted her with a tight smile. "You're lucky," she said, scanning Becca's boarding pass. "The pilot was late too."

The plane was tiny, a Saab turbo prop with noisy engines, but her single window seat was comfortable and her backpack fit into the overhead compartment with minimum effort and no glares from the lone flight attendant who now struggled to unlock the just-locked cabin door. *Just what I need,*

Becca thought, leaning into the aisle, spotting a middle-aged woman dragging a large canvas bag, the flight attendant yapping at her heels.

They stopped at the empty seat across from Becca. "It's got to fit under your seat," the flight attendant said in a weary voice, eying the large bag. "I'll check later, but the overhead bins are full."

"It will," the woman said, sliding into her seat. Becca watched. *It'll never fit*, she thought, watching the woman compress the bag with her feet then force it forward with a series of kicks. *Divine intervention,* she thought when the bag disappeared, though its contents probably needed last rites.

The woman glanced over at Becca. "That should comply with all federal regulations," she said, rubbing her hands together. "They made me check my carry-on."

Don't be a talker, Becca said to herself. She acknowledged the woman's presence with a nod, breaking eye contact before she could speak. She looked like a talker and Becca hated long conversations with strangers. *Business woman*, she thought glancing over; *they're the worst kind.*

The plane shuddered as it eased back from the terminal, its movement keying the flight attendant's monotone spiel. Becca half-heard the standard announcements, selecting out only "non-stop" and "seventy minutes flying time" from the oxygen masks and life preserver demos. The plane began to taxi, then stopped. The intercom crackled.

"We're number three in the stack," the pilot said. His voice was youthful and pleasant. "This weather's going to follow us down the coast, but we'll beat it to Islip. Wheels up in about ten minutes."

She switched on her reading light and pulled a thin paperback from her purse. Reading discouraged most talkers. "Thank you, Holden Caulfield," she whispered. *The Catcher in the Rye* was another Robert suggestion. "Re-read it," he'd said, using his professorial voice. "Either you or Holden's changed. I'll let you be the judge."

She had changed. Grown was more like it; a two-year journey with Robert as her guide. He'd encouraged her writing, understanding what she wanted before she knew herself, transferring the words in her head to the dreaded blank page, like a magical muse. "Leave out the parts people tend to skip," he'd say, turning her masterpiece into a series of blue lines and arrows, halving her word count. She couldn't write without him, and she had to write though she didn't know why.

This gave him power; power he'd used to mold her into what he couldn't become. Her days were limited to classes and her nights filled with coffee house readings along Boston's Massachusetts Avenue.

Sexually, Robert was neither experienced nor demanding, seeming to shed his worldly sophistication at the bedroom door. She winced as she replayed the clumsy seduction scene that had played out on her second visit to his Cambridge apartment.

He'd set it up: wine, candles, soft music, and the mandatory, accidental touching that he must have read about in one of the trendy men's magazines that littered his apartment. When she'd finally kissed him, he was trembling, and he didn't undress until they were in bed. It didn't last long, and after that, many of their nights together ended with only a good night peck. *We were like an old married couple*, she thought, *without being old or married*. No, writing, not sex had provided their intimacy and a three-month scholarship to Italy had proven that she could write alone. She'd work on the sex, though her expectations were low.

Ironically, her awakening had come from one of Robert's assignments: Hemingway or rather from Hemingway's character, Catherine Barkley. "There isn't any me, I'm you," Catherine said to her *A Farewell to Arms* lover. "Don't make a separate me." That's what had happened with Robert. Her "me" had been lost. Now it had returned.

Becca turned back to her book. She stifled a laugh as Holden Caulfield explained his unsought virginity: Parents coming home, nosy girl in front seat, and the fact that he stopped when the girl said stop. She remembered her first time, on Shelter Island in the bed of Jimmy Hewer's pickup, wrapped in a sleeping bag after a cold Halloween hay ride. He was an island boy that her parents hated and she'd thought she loved. She'd said stop, too, but he hadn't, and she wasn't sure she wanted him to. She'd seen him last summer, collecting tickets on the island's North Ferry. Of course, the fact that he'd dumped her after she refused an encore performance didn't improve her self-esteem.

She kept reading, almost hearing Holden's voice, pausing her reading to reflect on her opinion of young Mr. Caulfield. *Robert's right*, she concluded. *Holden's changed. I still like him, but he's become a real wise-ass.*

Becca felt the plane creep forward. She closed the book, using her finger as a bookmark and savored the Saab's acceleration as they hurled down the runway.

She knew about wise-asses. Her Writer's Lab was full of them: A bunch of unkempt freshmen who straggled in late and snickered through her instructions. *Yes*, she said to herself, *Holden would feel right at home.*

The plane twisted as it climbed, jostling her, tilting left then right before settling on a southerly direction, away from the storm. Outside her window, traffic surged along I93 into Quincy. She watched for a moment, wondering if Robert's Prius had joined the fray, hoping it had but afraid he'd remained, his nose pressed against the window, watching her plane disappear into the darkness.

At ten thousand feet the seatbelt sign turned off, followed by a noisy sigh from her aisle mate. "I've been waiting for that," she said, rising from her seat. "It was a choice; pee or fly and I needed to get home."

Becca nodded again then returned to her book. She was reading like a writer, deeply, not for story but for style, flipping back and forth, determining what worked and why. Robert had taught her that. "It's called stealing," he'd said, "only this stealing is legal."

Behind her, she heard the woman returning, working her way up the narrow aisle in a series of stops and starts. Becca burrowed deeper into her book and resigned herself to the inevitable.

"Haven't read that in a while," the woman said. She was standing over Becca, looking down, reading over her shoulder.

"Me either," Becca answered, glancing down at the book. "Not since high school."

The woman gave her an appraising look. "Let me guess," she said, taking her seat. "That would have been last year."

Becca got that a lot, though her sharp features were anything but babyish. *Maybe it's my size,* she thought, but she was five-one and had managed to break the hundred pound threshold last year. "Thanks," she answered, "but I'm a little past that."

"Harvard? There's something in your voice, and we are flying from Boston."

"For my Bachelor's , but I just finished my Master of Fine Arts at Boston U. Harvard doesn't offer an MFA." *That's me,* she thought, all school, no life: Little Becca Noble coming home to her nest like a baby bird. She felt like a little girl.

The woman extended her hand: "Elizabeth Hardin. I live in Greenport, and everybody calls me Lizzie."

"Rebecca Noble," Becca answered, shaking hands. "Everybody calls me Becca. I'm from Shelter Island, so we're almost neighbors."

"Except for that ferry."

Becca smiled. Her life had been dominated by that ferry. "Yes, there is that ferry. My Mom's picking me up in Islip. I was afraid we'd miss it."

"Great Novel!" Lizzie said, pointing at Becca's book. "I can't remember all the details, but I loved Holden. It's almost like he's a real person."

"He is," Becca answered, suddenly enthused. *If she was being forced to talk,* at least she liked the subject. "He's every teenager's alter ego, and, of course, he's every parent's worst nightmare. Salinger did a great job. I'm working on my own Holden, though mine's female. Her name's Katherine, but she goes by Katie and she's not quite developed yet."

"So you're a writer?" Lizzie asked. "I sensed something creative, but I'd have guessed an artist. You have that arty look. Hemingway's my favorite author, so I tend to associate writing with men. He'd loved your hat."

"I love Hemingway's writing but hate the man," Becca answered. "My thesis was titled, 'Hemingway's Women' and I'm no writer, at least not yet."

Lizzie whistled. "Hemingway's Women," she repeated. "Must have been a long thesis."

"Ninety pages," Becca answered, laughing, "though I did limit it to his four wives plus the female protagonists in *A Farewell to Arms* and *For Whom the Bell Tolls*. The research was tough. You know: Key West and Italy, but I learned a lot and I did skip Paris and Spain."

Her trip to Hemingway's Key West home hadn't revealed much. She wanted a sense of the man, but a few amusing anecdotes sprinkled in by the docent and a chance to stand at the podium where Hemingway wrote didn't reveal it. The fact that his beloved 'Sloppy Joe's' now sold T-shirts didn't help. She'd bought two, a long and a short sleeve, complete with Hemingway's bearded picture stamped across the back.

Italy had proven more productive. Here she'd wrestled her rented Fiat Abarth through Veneto's northern marshes, discovered Hemingway's Suite at Venice's Gritti Palace, and downed a Montgomery Cocktail at Harry's Bar. She'd also traced the route that Lieutenant Fredrick Henry and the Italian army took as they fled the pursuing Austrians.

She could feel him there and his name was everywhere. She'd stayed a month, renting a room in an Italian farmhouse, finishing her thesis's first draft while stuffing herself with local pasta and cheeses. She'd even managed to cultivate a taste for the home-made grappa that flowed through Hemingway's work.

"Sounds positively primitive," Lizzie answered smiling, "Let me know if you ever need a research assistant."

"I will," Becca said, "though I'm pretty much done with Hemingway. I can only take so much macho, and I've given up on growing a beard."

"Poor Papa," Lizzie said leaning forward. "He's only got a few of us disciples left and we're aging fast."

"No way," Becca answered, "Too many imitators." She could see the throng of white-bearded faces she'd watched roaming Key West's alleyways and bars. "No, I think you guys are safe unless the Conch Republic sinks or prohibition is reinstated."

"Well, I hope you're right," Lizzie said. "The world needs its giants, no matter how flawed." She smiled at Becca. "Since you're a Hemingway expert, what's his biggest flaw?"

Becca thought a minute. If there ever was a love-hate relationship it was her and Hemingway. She found Robert's Hemingway crush even harder to fathom though vicarious living might fit; sort of like he'd done with her writing. She looked over at Lizzie.

"Bully, alcoholic, and womanizer come to mind," Becca said, watching Lizzie frown. *He was all those things,* she thought, but somehow they appeared necessary, part of his oversized character that were forgiven or at least overlooked. "No," she continued, "I think his worse fault was his failure to understand the complexity of women, especially how they fall in love."

"Wow," Lizzie answered. "That's deep. I always thought his writing was a case of art imitating life. You do sound like a romantic, though."

Becca shuddered and shook her head. *Her a romantic?* "Not me. I was born a skeptic, but the way Hemingway's heroines arrive on the scene to service his hero put his chauvinism on full display. I call it the 'magic penis syndrome' and it can move the earth."

"You don't think it could happen that way?" Lizzie asked, her eyebrows raised and her eyes serious. "All of a sudden I mean, especially during a war?"

"No," Becca answered. She studied Lizzie. Her voice had risen and her cheeks reddened. This wasn't a hypothetical question. "Not to me anyway," she continued, "but tell me what happened to you."

The seatbelt sign chimed and Becca felt the plane tip forward, beginning its descent into Islip. "Saved by the bell," Lizzie said, turning to refasten her seatbelt. Becca sensed this subject was closed.

"Just remember, what happens on Island Air, stays on Island Air." Lizzie said. She pulled a business card from her purse. "Give me a call when you're in Greenport," she said. "If nothing else, we could slip down to Claudio's, have a couple of mojitos, and start a fight."

Becca laughed. "Deal," she said, taking the card without reading it, "as long as there are no bulls involved and you tell me your war story."

"Okay," Lizzie said. "No bulls, and I'll tell you mine if you tell me yours."

"Any war story I tell will be pure bullshit," Becca answered.

"Then," Lizzie said, pausing as the plane touched down hard, "you'd better get busy. There're plenty of wars to pick from."

The pilot braked firmly and veered towards the terminal. Becca braced against her seat. "My brother's a pilot," she said. "He calls guys who fly like this 'cowboys.'"

"Some fellow about your age is driving this thing," Lizzie said. "I checked him out when I came aboard. Say, you like pilots? You know, I'd trade a war story for a 'mile high' story."

"I have enough trouble at sea level," Becca answered. The bitterness in her voice surprised her. She reached up and removed her pack from the overhead, then let Lizzie slip past her. They said goodbye at the gate. Becca stepped aside and texted her mother. She glanced up to watch Lizzie disappear down the escalator, wondering what stories a couple of mojitos might produce. A sense of envy crept over her. Robert flashed through her mind, then Lizzie's question. She'd lied. She did believe it could happen like that; trusting your feelings when you didn't know and there wasn't time to find out. No, she believed it could happen; it just couldn't happen to her and she didn't know why.

CHAPTER THREE

Allison Gould-Noble blipped the throttle of her Jaguar XKE. The throaty roar of its twelve cylinders made her smile. This was her second lap around the parking perimeter of McArthur Airport and, unlike the racing session she'd completed this afternoon at the new, Bridgehampton track, she drove slowly, not wanting to park, searching for her daughter, Rebecca. Both the Jaguar and the racing lesson were birthday presents. She'd turn fifty on Wednesday. The Jag was a youthful thirty-nine.

"Third time's the charm," she muttered to herself as she spotted Rebecca's tiny figure beneath an oversized bush hat. Allison forced her way through a wall of taxis and wheeled the topless Jag next to the taxi stand. A definite no-no even at tiny McArthur Airport. She was now in hostile territory.

Becca threw her rumpled knapsack over her shoulder and moved slowly towards Allison. She ambled with a teenager's calculated insolence, swaying as she walked, making forward progress like a sidewinder. Allison flashed her lights. At least she could find the dimmer switch. Jaguar had hidden the remaining controls beneath a walnut dashboard surrounded by gauges that reminded her of a 747.

Becca's pace caught the attention of the waiting taxis. Their tolerance for her intrusion was limited. Behind her a horn blew, a polite tap, followed a few seconds later by another, then an irritating blare.

Rebecca studied the Jaguar like she was buying it, pausing as she circled, ignoring the rising fray behind her. Satisfied, she opened the passenger's door, tossed her bag behind the seat, stood up on the door sill and yelled, "bite me", to the herd of taxis assembled behind her.

"Show me what you've learned, Mom," Becca said, dropping into her seat, giving Allison a brief kiss on her way down. "I think you've done something to piss those guys off and there's a rent-a-cop heading this way, ticket book in hand."

Allison stole a glance at her daughter while she guided them away from the airport. With the big hat shading her features, it was like looking in a mirror and going back in time.

"You're traveling a little light, aren't you, Rebecca?" Allison asked.

"Mom," she answered, her voice a mixture of acceptance and frustration, "Everyone but you calls me Becca."

"Okay, Becca," Allison answered, "you're traveling a little light?"

"I've got underwear and my toothbrush," Becca answered, "plus a closet full of stuff at home. Besides, a certain nameless person only gave me an hour to pack." She gave Allison an inquiring look. "Now tell me what's going on. I mean the secrecy and all. Why couldn't I tell Daddy I was coming?"

"Nothing, sweetie," Allison answered. She reached behind Becca and flipped off her hat, dropping it behind her. Becca's long, blonde hair unpiled, falling randomly to her shoulders. She reached back for her hat.

"Fashion police brutality," Becca said, returning the hat to her head.

"I wanted to make certain the hair was still there. Too many surprises aren't healthy, and there's no secret. I wanted you here for my birthday. You're just a surprise for your father."

Allison wished she could tell Becca about that awful woman but no one could know that she knew, including Michael. If someone knew, she'd have to take action. The role of forgiving wife was for someone else, not her. Perfect wife and family. Her entire adult life had been spent cultivating this image, and she had no intention of ending her performance. Michael would get over his infatuation once its source was removed, plus she had him by the balls in case he found a new distraction.

"It's a great car," Becca said, "though I'm surprised you picked it. I'd have bet on a Porsche, and I'd bet red, not white."

"You know I was driving a Porsche the day I met your father."

"I know the story, Mom. You almost ran over him and you two made love on the hood that night and conceived my evil brother, Brad."

"That's your father's version," Allison answered, "and as they say, truth is the first casualty of war and that includes the battle of the sexes."

Allison smiled as she remembered the scene, a driftwood gray lobster shack along Montauk Highway; Michael, his mouth stuffed with a lobster roll, Bass Ale in hand, stepping into the dirt parking lot, right in front of her new Porsche Turbo. She had almost run over him. Sometimes she wished she had. At least she wondered what her life would have been without him. She'd been outmatched from the start, overpowered and drawn in to his dreams. Dreams that he'd forced to come true.

The fact that her family had first disliked and distrusted Michael had only added to his appeal. Of course, they looked down on anyone who wasn't there to greet the Mayflower, and she'd used Michael to pique their snobbery. He was her first and only lover, and her surprise pregnancy with Brad ended all family resistance.

She could see Michael now, strutting around the family's East Hampton compound like he owned it; her father lagging behind him like a caretaker awaiting his orders. Her dad had succumbed to Michael's charm and energy as quickly as she had. Her mother had been a harder sell, but Brad's pink cheeks and blue eyes gave Michael the leverage required to break through her remaining barriers. *Brad's blue eyes still work*, she thought. Unfortunately, they'd brought Sally to her island and as usual, he'd left behind a mess for her to clean up.

Following Brad's birth, she'd basked in the attention granted a new mother, reveling in her role, staying at the Amagansett beach house while Michael commuted to the city. His strong Catholicism allowed for only primitive birth control, and Rebecca arrived the next year, followed by Staci, thirteen months later. The rhythm method would never work on a man like Michael. Apparently, he'd maintained his appetite.

After Staci displayed a stubborn reluctance to leave the womb, and before the cesarean delivery, she'd convinced Dr. Levine to tie her tubes and not tell Michael.

She'd done the things other women in her position did: charity drives, historical preservation, and of course she'd supported the pompous but starving artists that lined the Hamptons' beaches.

But each year the crowds grew larger, spreading eastward like giant fire ants, destroying the tranquility they sought, and forcing the natives to fortify or flee. Allison glanced outside at the Sunrise Highway traffic pouring towards the Hamptons. All of New York City wouldn't fit there, but it looked like they were going to try. She put on her left blinker, waited, then forced the Jag into a tiny opening. Out here, the meek inherited nothing.

She and Michael had fled to Shelter Island where a trundling ferry provided the only connection to the mainland and Mashomack Preserve occupied half the island. The ferry's slow pace and limited schedule proved maddening to the city dwellers, anxious to begin their relaxation. Several bought homes and began to fight for a bridge to the mainland. Soundly trounced by the locals, they either moved on or adjusted to the island's natural rhythm. Merging with the natives, they too became staunch defenders of their island sanctuary.

Finding her refuge, Allison struggled to maintain her identity. Returning to Yale was impossible, but she'd painted, written poetry, and started several novels, but each year the children demanded more of her time and energy. The island also conspired against her. It formed a living aquarium that demanded exploration, and she'd shepherded her small flock from Silver Beach to Chase Creek, searching for what the tides had deposited since their last visit.

Now she looked at Rebecca's profile. Sharp chin with an upturned nose, it hadn't changed since she was a child.

"You were always an explorer," she said, reaching over and squeezing her daughter's knee.

"I deny whatever rumor my evil siblings may be spreading," Becca answered. "Besides, I was only kidding about the safari."

"I guess I should say 'what safari' but I was only reminiscing about exploring the island with you kids. Remember our 'Noble Expeditions'? You always wanted to go farther than Brad or Staci. Of course, now you're going farther than ever."

"I'll be fine, Mom," Rebecca answered, her voice reflecting both sympathy and annoyance. "Besides, nothing's far away anymore. Two hours on the plane and I'm home."

"I know, baby," Allison answered. "I was just thinking about you kids growing up, and how'd we explore the island, and now you've all gone, and I'm all alone. A girl can only play so much bridge."

"You've still got Daddy," Rebecca answered. "There's nothing wrong between you two?"

"No, sweetie, he just lives in his own little world, and I'm feeling a little melancholy right now."

She'd taken a childish delight in the treasures of horseshoe crabs and shark's teeth the children brought home for Michael's admiration. But the island safaris were soon replaced by sailing lessons, which gave way to school events, and her world soon became a child-spawned whirlwind. Her creativity gradually dissolved, swallowed by the children's needs and the household routine required to minimize their interference with Michael's work.

Overall though, it had been a satisfying life, and her contentment surprised her. Yet, lately, approaching her fiftieth birthday, she began to feel incomplete, like she'd lived Michael's life and not hers. His life and the hedge fund he started were growing, while she was only growing old and increasingly unnecessary.

She'd actually found herself jealous of the young women who populated Michael's offices. They were all pretty, but one she'd particularly resented was Sally Jordan. There appeared to be a bond between Michael and Sally that made Allison uncomfortable. *As usual, her intuition was right.*

Sally shared Michael's love for the investment world while Staci had her art, Becca her writing, and Brad flew around the world in that big Air Force plane. Sally became a frequent weekend guest in their island compound, and Michael made no attempt to hide his fondness for her, calling her the daughter he never had. He'd even hired a voice tutor to curb Sally's jarring, Appalachian twang and had his Greenwich dentist buddy cap her teeth.

"She's Eliza Doolittle and you're Professor Higgins," Allison once said to Michael, but he'd glazed over when she'd tried to explain *Pygmalion's* twisted plot.

She'd treated Sally with polite coolness, excluding her when she could and ignoring her when she couldn't. She'd learned this technique from her mother. Passed down through generations of the old rich, it convinced interlopers that their feelings of inferiority were totally justified.

Sally's looks complicated the situation. Her raven black hair and a muscularly trim, tanned body, projected an air of sexual energy that men found impossible to ignore. Brad was among them, but his passive nature soon eliminated him from the drooling pack.

Michael had appeared immune to her charms though Allison had always sensed that Sally had never focused their full power on him; that is until last Friday night. The pool scene played on the windshield like a movie; Sally lying back in the hot tub writhing, little gasps and moans escaping from her lips while Michael splashed between her legs. Allison blinked and the scene faded, leaving her alone with Rebecca who remained uncharacteristically silent.

"Cat got your tongue?" Allison asked Becca.

"Just wondering what old Scott and Zelda would think if they could see what's happened to their playground. You know, urban refugees using the wealth their society created to escape from that same society: Wooden sanctuaries in an urban jungle."

"Sounds like something from *Gatsby*. Do you really think about such things?"

"Only when I write, but sometimes I like for people to think I do. Got to keep up the old Harvard image, you know." Becca shook her head. "Actually, I was thinking about Staci. I haven't heard from her, and you haven't mentioned her. You guys throw her out again?"

"No, she was home for the weekend, but she went back to school in Charleston this morning. Something about an art project for the Spoleto Festival." Allison hated lying to her daughter. Staci's mid-night departure was probably a coincidence. No use looking for trouble.

Allison had gone to Sally's cottage early Saturday morning. Hungover and sleepy, Sally had resisted at first but she was no match for Allision's matronly anger and the copies of fraudulent brokerage statements she'd thrown in Sally's face, ended her resistance.

Finding the accounts was pure luck. Just a glance at a few papers scattered across Michael's cluttered desk. She'd worked with Michael before. These client balances were wrong. How could an account both lose and make money? She didn't know what to do but she'd made copies. Now, evidence in hand she'd given Sally an ultimatum: Be off the island by Monday and resign from the firm by Friday or she'd report both Sally and Michael to the Securities and Exchange Commission.

She'd also tied a carrot to the end of her stick: A check for two hundred thousand dollars from her personal account, plus the promise of a job with a west coast firm. Not a bad offer, Allison thought, for a West Virginia hillbilly whose nasal twang still crept through during unguarded moments. Writing

Sally's goodbye note to Michael was the hardest part. "Word it your way," Allison had told Sally, giving her the note, "but make sure it's final."

Later, when she went to Staci's room, she found it empty. Allison never knew about Staci. Maybe she'd overheard Sally's expulsion or she'd witnessed Michael's and Sally's earlier poolside performance. Allison wasn't surprised. Staci always ran at the first sign of trouble. She'd call in a few days and everything would be fine. Once she'd expelled Sally, Allison's compound would be secure.

"Poor daddy," Becca said. "An artist and a writer for daughters, and a ne'er-do-well pilot for a son. I guess he blames you for both our sizes and our right-brained proclivity."

Allison smiled at her daughter. "Don't use that word around your father. He'll think you're pregnant." They both laughed. Michael's lack of vocabulary and his creative use of the English language had been a long-standing joke between them.

"I'm taking a different way home," Allison said as she crossed the bridge at Shinnecock Hills. They swung their heads in unison, looking first left towards Great Peconic Bay and then right into the rolling waves of the Atlantic Ocean. Sunrise Highway headed south towards the Hamptons. Allison yanked the car left onto Noyac Road. She glanced towards Becca, downshifted two gears and floored the accelerator. The Jag leapt forward.

"Now I'll show you what I learned today. You can tell your father he got his money's worth."

CHAPTER FOUR

Noyac Road between Shinnecock and Sag Harbor is a seldom used, rough mixture of asphalt and rock that dives and twists its way along Long Island's south shore. Allison had traveled on it many times. She'd always driven fast, but tonight racing terms like "apex" and "braking point" sped through her mind.

The Jaguar lightened her mood, anticipating her thoughts, reacting to her touch as they carved their way east. Accelerating briskly down a short straightaway, she stole a glance at her silent daughter. Becca was smiling.

"I'm a bad influence, aren't I?" Allison asked. "You've inherited my love of speed."

"Along with your brilliant mind and enduring good looks," Becca answered. "Now, if you'll let me drive, I'll show you some real speed. Remember, I had the driving course last fall."

Allison felt the distance between them close as she braked hard for the ninety-degree left-hander at the end of the straight. Downshifting, she accelerated hard, using the car's power to force it through the turn. Her pace was fast, but not reckless, always in control. Her instructors measured pace in tenths. "Nine-tenths" was racing, flat out, nothing in reserve. *"Six-tenths"* she thought: *Entertaining but not dangerous.*

"You also inherited your father's competitive spirit," Allison said. "That'll get you in serious trouble when you challenge a superior person."

"Okay, Mother Superior," Rebecca answered, her voice light. "You keep the wheel, and I'll try to learn something. But tomorrow I get to drive the Jag. We can take on Serpentine Drive."

Allison felt the tone in her daughter's voice. Rebecca had never been a child that you sat down and talked to. She was a creature of motion, and their closest moments had always been in the form of shared activities.

"Okay, my little driving pupil," Allison answered. She was both fascinated and confounded by the differences in her three children. She'd read voraciously, devouring the experts' opinions on birth order and personality development, acquiring only a healthy skepticism for such advice.

Rebecca, particularly, flaunted their opinions. She was no peace-making middle child. Instead, she instigated between her siblings, leading them into countless misadventures that Allison credited with producing the few strands of dreaded gray hair that so far remained unnoticed to anyone but her.

"You'll get your chance," Allison answered, looking at the challenging figure beside her, "but one scratch, and I'll have you exiled from my island."

"I almost forgot," Becca said, changing the subject without admitting defeat. "I've got something for you. It's in my pack." She unfastened her seat belt and reached back into the tiny rear compartment. "Too many zippers," she said, groping in the darkness.

"No presents," Allison said. "You weren't supposed to get me anything."

"It's for your car," Becca answered, struggling with her pack, "and besides, you once gave me one."

"Now I'm curious," Allison said. Becca hated shopping as much as Michael yet she had a knack for finding the perfect gift. Allison flipped the possibilities through her mind as puffs of fog whisked across her windshield. A Jaguar shifter knob came out on top of her wish list.

The fog puffs merged into a light mist. Allison reached for the wiper switch, unsure in the darkness, her attention focused on the strange, toggle-switched dashboard. She sensed Becca tense and looked up. They were driving in a cloud.

Almost blind, Allison braked hard, downshifting, using the engine's compression to slow the car. The tires told her what she already knew; she'd braked too late, they weren't going to make the turn.

Things happened in slow motion. The fear she felt left, overcome by the need to act. Her instructor's voice resonated in her ear, muting the roaring engine and squealing tires: "If you're going to crash, spin the car. That'll scrub off speed and the seat will absorb most of the impact." Fighting her instincts, Allison jerked the wheel left and pressed both feet on the brake.

The Jaguar responded to the slippery asphalt like it did to the track's oiled skid pad, sliding sideways first, slowly completing its arc, before traveling backward through the sand. A glancing blow off a large oak flipped it onto the driver's side, launching the unbelted Becca into the scrub oaks that lived beneath their sprawling ancestors.

Allison remained suspended in her seat, locked in place by her shoulder harness. Her chin rested on the steering wheel. Her eyes were closed and her arms draped across her lap, as though she were sleeping.

Sally stopped when she heard the crash. Further down the beach, she could see her dinghy. She was almost home. No one knew. She could just leave. She walked towards the dingy, then stopped again. *I've got to know,* she thought turning around; *I've got to know.*

The crash had happened near her ambush site. Tracing noises to locations was her specialty and the Air Force had trained her well. She gave the dinghy one last look, then broke into a slow jog heading uphill towards whatever waited, breaking into a sprint when she reached Noyac Road.

Sally saw the car's lights shining deep in the woods. *It had to be Allison.* She ran faster, the ammo can slamming against her leg. Nearing the car, she slowed to a walk. She approached from its side, not getting close, circling, studying the car. Even on its side, she recognized the Jaguar's sleek profile.

Sally dropped to one knee, using the sky for a backdrop. The car's headlights blinded her. She moved closer, almost expecting Allison to leap from the darkness. She felt her way down the steering column and switched off the lights, jumping back when she brushed Allison's face. Allison didn't move.

Sally stared into the blackened cockpit, waiting as her vision adjusted to the darkness. She placed her fingers across Allison's neck. Her skin felt warm. There was no pulse, but she'd heard too many stories about live soldiers being returned from the morgue. She wrapped her hand around Allison's throat and squeezed. A faint pulse throbbed back. She looked down at the blanched figure, picturing it hovering above her bed, jaw clinched, ordering her to leave. Now God had delivered her enemy to her. It was her duty to act. God helped those who helped themselves.

Blood dripped from Allison's forehead and her left arm lay limp against the door. How badly was she hurt? Sally squeezed Allison's throat again. The faint pulse remained. It was time. She opened the ammo can and took out the knife, studying its shape against the moonlit skyline.

Sally looked at Allison then back at the knife. The knife seemed alive, a sleek creature, beautifully efficient. It reminded her of a shark. She raised the knife slowly, circling Allison's neck, her left hand feeling for the jugular pulse. Her mood was dreamlike, as though she was watching a stranger. The pulse throbbed against her fingers. She looked down at Allison, smiled, and plunged the blade deep into her neck. Blood spurted from the ragged wound, flowing down Allison's arm and onto the sand. Allison moaned softly, stiffened, then slumped back in her seat.

Sally stared down at Allison. She'd done it. The evil witch was dead. There was no turning back now. She thought of her original plan. This was even better. There was no bullet to be found. She sprinted back to the deer.

Flies circled its crusty wound. She swatted them away, threw the carcass over her shoulder and trudged her way back to Allison's car.

Sally dropped the deer on the upright fender. Allison was still there. She smiled at the thought that she might be gone. Dead witches held no powers.

Sally glanced at the deer. "Bad boy," she said. "You just killed this nice lady and I'm about to prove it."

She picked up the ammo can and slammed it against the windshield. The safety glass cracked like shattered ice. Sally bashed out a hole just above the steering wheel. The deer was next.

She forced his head into the hole then grabbed his antlers and pulled it through. Plausible deniability —that was the term her team had used when they had a "snatch mission" in Pakistan. She'd almost built her case.

Sally shoved the small antler into Allison's wound and used a broken piece of glass to slice open the deer's. Both wounds seeped blood. It was like a ceremony she'd done as a child with her Cherokee cousins, pricking their fingers with a thorn from a black locus tree, then pressing them together in a solemn ceremony they'd conducted behind her father's store.

"You're blood brothers now," she said, looking down at her victims. "Together forever in the happy hunting ground."

She was ready to leave. The accident scene was complete. Anyone could see what happened. No investigation needed. Sally switched the headlights back on. They were too bright. Even without a search, someone would spot the car. She flipped them off. She needed time. No one could find the car, not until she was home. She debated her choices: With any luck the battery would die soon or maybe they wouldn't notice the switch. "Or maybe," she said out loud, "Allison could turn them off for me."

She reached inside and banged Allison's left knee against the toggle switch, snapping it off, grinding Allison's leg against it until she tore a hole in her white capris. Sally felt nothing. Just another mission, alone, at night in a strange land.

She released Allison's leg and looked around. She'd done all she could do. It was time to go. She pulled an oak branch from beneath the car and swept away her tracks, backing towards Noyac Road, sweeping as she moved. She crossed the road and stopped. She couldn't see Allison's car. That was good. It wouldn't be found without a search.

Headlights filtered through the darkness. The car would be here soon. She tossed the branch and began to run; something felt wrong. She sensed a presence… unseen eyes following her into the tree line. She flailed through the brush, branches slapping her face. She fell, then rolled to her feet, moving like a panicked animal, desperate to escape.

Reaching the beach, Sally raced towards her boat, glancing over her shoulder as she ran, certain that someone had followed her. When she reached the dinghy, she collapsed across its hard, rubber frame. Still panting, she dug her feet into the sand, forcing the boat back into the water. The waves were larger now. They rocked the tiny craft, throwing her to the floor, forcing her to crawl back to the motor.

"Oh, God, Oh God," she cried, using the tiller for support as she struggled to her feet. The north wind carried her away from the island. She looked at the motor then back at the disappearing land. It had to start or she was going to be washed out into the Atlantic. She thought of praying but didn't. God had done his part. She turned towards the motor, braced herself and pulled, glancing upward by habit when it sputtered to life.

Tears mixed with salt spray blurred her vision. She aligned the bow with Shelter Island's white cliffs, taking one last glance back towards Noyac. She couldn't shake the feeling she'd been seen, almost expecting the beach to be crowded with her pursuers, but the moonlight revealed only the glimmering sand.

Half-way across Noyac Bay, she opened the ammo can and tossed the knife and pistol overboard, then forced the can down into the dark water.

She felt it fill and then released it, staring back into the darkness, afraid it might resurface.

Sally cut her engine just before reaching Michael's dock. She glided in quietly. Her wake bounced the rubber boat against the worn pilings. Stepping onto the float, she pulled the boat after her, using the bowline to secure it to the ladder, just the way she'd found it.

She stood there in the shadows, studying Allison's house. It appeared to be sleeping. Only a twinkle from the den interrupted its dark outline. She guessed that Michael was still at the club.

Her legs ached as she made her way up the long walkway. She stopped again at the driveway. The house was still quiet. She slipped around the side and into her cottage. Inside, she stripped off her wet clothes and mixed them with her other beachwear. She took a quick shower then dressed in shorts and a Montauk T-shirt.

Sally paced, tried to sit, then popped up. She couldn't believe she'd done it. Tears welled in her eyes, but she forced them back. An hour passed. She turned on the TV, flipped through the channels and turned it off. Her breathing became difficult, rapid and shallow. Outside the wind gathered strength, moaning softly, shadows from the swaying limbs dancing across the lawn. A light flickered through the window. She collapsed on the floor. *They've come for me,* she thought. *Someone was there.* She fought for air, then relaxed as thunder rattled the steamy, glass panes.

Dusty books filled the open shelves beneath the window. She crawled over. One book jutted out from its neighbors. A dark cover bound its thick body. Sally pulled it out. "*Anna Karenina,*" she said to herself. She turned to the first page and read the opening paragraph, "All happy families are alike, but all unhappy families are unhappy in different ways." She thought of her family and Michael's. She smiled. *Smart guy that Tolstoy.* She began to read. The storm gained strength, roaring outside her window. The lights flickered and then went out. Not unusual for Shelter Island. She lay there, using the book for a pillow, watching the rain splatter against the window, then flow silently towards the ground. Finally, she fell into a troubled sleep, wracked by dreams.

Her mother came to her, flowing in her white, church dress, a mountain rising behind her. She recognized Mount Hope's granite cliffs. Her mother carried two stone tablets. There was writing on them. She pointed to the tablets and spoke in a slow, soft voice, "Thou shall not kill." Dropping the tablets, her face hardened and spittle flew from her clinched lips. "Vengeance is mine, saith the Lord."

Squealing tires jarred Sally awake. Sunlight streamed in, lighting the cottage, hurting her eyes. Rising to her knees, she watched Michael's black Mercedes disappear down Winthrop Road, heading towards South Ferry. She knew where he was going. Allison had been found. She replaced the book, not bothering to mark her place. Her stomach churned, but she wasn't hungry.

She felt like another shower. The next few hours would assign her either the role of a despised murderer or a sympathetic friend. Either way, she wanted to be prepared. Absently, she felt for her dog tags. Last night she'd forgotten her ritual. She gasped when she discovered her bare neck. She ran into her bedroom, checked her turtleneck, then tore through her remaining clothes. The dog tags were gone. She dropped to the floor and replayed last night, grimacing as she remembered the tug she'd felt when she'd slammed Allison's leg against the light switch. The wicked witch had cast her last spell. Her dog tags were in Allison's car or on the ground beside it. She anticipated the cop's question: Of course she didn't know how they got there. Maybe she'd left them in her room and Allison picked them up. Who knew? After all there were no witnesses. Just her fingerprints and DNA.

Her mother had a saying: "Want to make God laugh; tell him your plans." He was laughing now.

"I've heard of it happening, but this is the first time I've seen it," Sheriff Mike Watson said as the EMTs placed Allison Nobles' body in the ambulance. "We had a case over in Southhold where one went through the windshield; left its antlers in the back seat and went out the back window. I always wondered what would have happened if anybody had been sitting in that seat."

Art Sherman took quick notes as Sheriff Watson spoke. They'd grown up together and Art's paper, *The Island Times,* had supported Watson's reelection. "And now you know," he answered.

The ambulance's tires spun, catching the attention of both men as they dug into the sand before gaining traction on the rough asphalt. Behind the ambulance, two deputies replaced the yellow crime scene tape.

"Must've been pretty hard to find?" Art asked.

"Yeah, we missed it last night. Rain didn't help. Mr. Noble called and reported her missing. Thought she'd come this way, but we also checked Highway 114, just in case. Car kind of jumped off the road and her leg broke the light switch. No tracks. We drove right by it twice, then we searched by North Haven. We tried again this morning. Almost missed it, but one of my guys noticed the brush was disturbed and a flock of crows kept circling around. Almost stepped on the girl."

"How's she doing?"

"All things considered, she's pretty good. The sand and brush cushioned her. She's got a lot of cuts and bruises and a nasty knot on her head. Can't remember the accident. She's in the Eastern Long Island Hospital over in Greenport. I'll go talk to her when I finish up here."

"No sign of another car?"

"No, Art, but we'll take a good look at the scene. The state boys always come out when there's a fatality. Don't want them to find anything we've missed. Might get some big city reporters up here too, considering the family and all."

"I don't know, Mike. They were old money or at least she was. Didn't do much to attract attention."

"I called her husband. He's on the ferry right now. Real upset. Didn't know the girl was with her. Made me tell him everything on the phone. Never much cared for that guy."

"Why?"

"No real reason. Just a typical city fellow, I guess. You know the type; always in a hurry. Stock broker or something like that." Sheriff Watson looked toward the causeway, squinting as the sun's rays bounced off the wet sand. "He'll be here soon. Guess I better get my facts together. Mr. Noble will have a million questions, and he won't ask 'em slow. Want to see the car?"

Allison's Jaguar remained on its side, the deer's head resting against the steering wheel. The two men circled the car silently, shaking their heads as they walked, their feet sinking into the soft sand.

Art Sherman spoke first. "Doesn't seem like much to tell. Fast car, bad road, and bad timing. Sounds like my headline."

"Sort of strange though."

"How's that?"

"Usually it's kids. You know, teenagers."

"Well, I hear she was young at heart."

"Then she died young, my friend. She died young."

A tow truck backed towards them. Its young driver stepped out, nodded, and attached a cable. The deer slid down the hood as the driver winched the Jaguar onto the truck.

"Mind if I take this?" he asked, pointing at the deer.

"Help yourself," Watson answered. "It hasn't been dead long."

"There's one thing that's kind of interesting, Art," Watson said slowly, both men staring at the Jaguar's bloody interior. "You know those Guardian Angel clips you can get to put on your visor?"

"Yeah, why?

"Well, we found one in the girl's hand."

"Thanks, Mike. I'll mention that in my story. You think it worked?"

Watson looked at the twisted wreck. "It sure didn't hurt." He shook his head. "Too bad her mom didn't have one."

CHAPTER FIVE

Becca Noble slowed from a jog to a walk as she approached Sunset Rock. The rock rose like a volcano, erupting suddenly from Dering Harbor's sandy shore.

"You're not Gibraltar," she said, "but you've done a good job so far." She leaned against the rock and removed her shoes. She'd reached the end of her six-mile run, looping Shelter Island, saying goodbye to her favorite spots—Fresh Pond, Bootlegger's Alley, and she'd endured the brutal climb up Serpentine Drive—but her last stop wasn't a place; it was a friend she could talk to.

Becca loved this rock. It was an old friendship, born in her earliest childhood memories. The rock had aged with her, its edges now smooth, resisting the efforts of the sea and the wind to blend it into the sand. She felt small standing there, looking up, stretching her neck to take in its three-story height. It had a face. Her sister Staci's artist's eye had seen it first; hidden among its crevices, a serious face with a broad nose and flat forehead staring out to sea, a lone sentinel, gray and solemn, watching over Dering Harbor.

"Permission to come aboard," she said to the rock. She slid her fingers along its lower plateau, using a familiar fissure to lift herself onto its narrow ledge. She felt secure. The dizziness that had plagued her after the accident had gone. She ran a finger across the bridge of her nose. The scar was still there. The doctors wanted to repair it but she'd said no. Instead she wore it like a medal, a permanent reminder of a crash she'd struggled to remember for the past fourteen months. They'd tried to take her dream too, but she wouldn't let them. The blurry crash and its ghostly figure was a part of her and she couldn't let it go, no matter how hard her neurologist tried. She'd refused to see a psychiatrist. She wasn't crazy. Something else happened that night that lay hidden in her dream. Someday it would emerge.

Becca continued to climb, scampering up the rock, she grasped with her toes, before finally scaling the slim pedestal that led to the rock's anvil top.

"I know you'd disapprove, Mom," she said, looking out across the harbor, "but the view's better up here." She loosened her grip and relaxed, melding into the rock's contoured surface. From here she could see from Gardiner's Creek all the way to Dering Point. Beneath her, sailboats dotted the harbor, their bare masts wrapped with furled sails; they reminded her of a litter of puppies, tugging against their moorings, anxious to run with the wind.

A large shape moving through the mist caught her eye and she turned to watch North Ferry headed towards Greenport. Cars lined its deck. Early morning ferries were always full. The daily exodus to New York City had begun.

"I'll be leaving this morning," she said. "Going to escape to South Carolina before I'm planted here." She leaned over and kissed the rock's hard surface, tasting its salty grit. "You're a sloppy kisser," she said, wiping her mouth with her sleeve, "and I don't know what I'm going to do without you."

Cars moved along Winthrop Road. Becca watched them cross Gardiner's Creek Bridge. As a child she sent Staci beneath that bridge on a turtle hunt while she lay in wait. Her troll costume wasn't much—a horseshoe crab helmet draped in stringy marsh grass—but it had been enough to send her little sister streaking home only to soon return with a pissed-off mother and a smirking brother. She smiled at the scene, but Staci's depression had deepened with their mother's death, her once cherubic face now dull and gloomy.

Becca returned her gaze to the cars as they headed uphill towards Ferry Street. In a few hours, she'd join them. The thought made her shudder, and she flinched at the boom of the yacht club cannon.

"7:00 a.m. big guy. Got to go," she said, giving the rock a goodbye pat. "See you at Christmas."

She walked home along the shoreline, barefoot, her running shoes strung across her shoulders, wading through the cool water, before returning to shore to cross the docks that blocked her way.

She studied the moored boats that she passed. They ranged from the tiny Sunfish that flitted around the harbor to the thumping cigarette boats she'd watched blasting through "The Gut" at Plum Island on their way to Connecticut's shores.

The fleet moored at her family dock still reflected her mother's taste. Here, a lead-keeled Herreshoff Doughdish rocked beside a mahogany-trimmed Chris-Craft. Her mother had loved anything classical; the Honda-powered dinghy resting on the float was a reluctant exception.

She climbed onto the dock and glanced towards her house. There were two figures on the porch. She knew they were watching. They always were. She gave a royal wave. "I'm not crazy," she said in a voice she knew wouldn't reach them. "One day you'll know."

Becca walked to the end of the dock and plopped down on a weathered bench, relaxing to the tune of the tiny ripples that collapsed on the hard sand. She turned towards the house, looking up from the porch, focusing on the widow's watch. From here it looked frail; four spindly legs struggling to support the enclosed cupola that hung above them. She'd spent many hours there, alone and quiet, perched above the giant elms like an osprey, drinking in the harbor's views and listening to its sounds.

She'd written her first story there: a twelve-year-old's account of a serious but unrequited crush on a fourteen-year-old summer resident, Brandon Jesup. She smiled at her effort. The writing had been therapeutic, and things hadn't ended well for Brandon's character. "A woman scorned," she said out loud, glancing around before heading towards the house.

The scene on the porch looked familiar. Her father sat at a faded wicker table hidden behind, *The Wall Street Journal*. Additional papers sat stacked beside him. He'd computerized his investment business under threat of secretarial revolt, but he didn't believe anything until he saw it on the printed page. She couldn't remember a time when he was far from a paper.

A brown coffee thermos sat at the table's center. Only Sally saw her arrive.

"Becca, you're a mess," she said, rising to greet her, brushing her damp, stringy hair from her face. Becca stiffened at the gesture. The ten-year difference in their ages made Sally's attempts at mothering hard to take.

"You should cut your hair like Sally's," Michael said. He dropped his paper and walked over to join them. "She can do just about anything and not get a hair out of place."

He ran his hand through his new wife's raven black hair. The constant touching bothered Becca. Once she'd become aware of such things, she'd noticed how seldom he'd touched her mother. Now he couldn't keep his hands off Sally.

"He's pussy-whipped," Lizzie, her baggage destroying seatmate had said, downing her second Claudios mojito, "and considering her age, it's probably terminal."

"Almost anything, wild man," Sally said, leaning up and giving Michael a quick peck on the cheek. "It's real convenient when I take the Bentley on an appointment. I like to keep the top down." Becca winced. Her mother had loved that car.

"You sure you want to do this God-awful thing?" Michael asked Becca as he returned to the table. "We can still tell those South Carolina people you're not coming." He was hidden behind the paper before she could answer.

"I'm sure, Daddy," Becca answered. She pulled his paper down and gave him a big smile. "You'll love it down there. It's just like Shelter Island with a southern accent."

"That's because you went down there at Christmas. I was there in the summer during Vietnam, and I tell you there's no comparison. Hell, Vietnam was a relief from the heat and bugs of that swamp they call Parris Island."

"Daddy," Becca answered. "I'm not going to Parris Island. I'm going to Beaufort and I'm sure the Marines have a way to make their island miserable. Besides, you loved it!"

"Michael," Sally said. "She's right. You did love it. You're always talking about your Marine Corps training. Couldn't we visit Parris Island while we're down there? I'd like to see what you went through in your glory days."

"Hell, honey," Michael answered, "if they saw me they'd want me back in a recon unit."

Becca studied her father. He was a big man, tall with a barrel chest that produced a resonant voice and a deep laugh. Many hours of golf and sailing had darkened his skin and lightened his hair. Only a receding hairline and the beginning of a paunch betrayed his sixty years. He was chewing on his bottom lip, something he often did when he was thinking.

"By God I'll do it," he said leaping to his feet. Both Becca and Sally jumped. Her father laughed and pounded his chest, producing a bass drum sound that echoed off the porch walls.

"Easy, Tarzan," Sally said. "I'd hate for the Marines to see you in a cast."

"You can't hurt steel," Michael answered. "As soon as I check Tokyo and London, I'll call down there and check on a tour. Eat some breakfast, girl," he said, squeezing Becca's shoulders as he walked by. "You're as skinny as those models I see in the city."

"You know," Sally said when they were alone, "he really thinks he can control the world with that phone; God forbid if he ever learns how to text." She shook her head. "I used to watch him in the office. Sometimes I'd think he was going to pop a vein when the markets moved against him."

Becca remained silent. She'd didn't need Sally's description; she'd seen her father in action. She'd been his gopher since the accident, filling in between her substituting teaching assignments while she splattered the southeastern coast with résumés.

"It's a pressure cooker Sweetie," Sally continued. "It gradually wears most people down. Of course, your father's different. He just uses the pressure to create energy."

Becca laughed. "Well," she said, "I hope he doesn't vent too much when he sees where I'm teaching."

She'd found Beaufort by accident, a chance encounter of a day trip from Charleston following a Staci visit. She'd been lured in, riding beneath the moss-draped oaks in a horse-drawn carriage, traveling past homes where she almost expected Rhett Butler to emerge and greet her with a bow and a smirking smile. Unfortunately, her Saint Helena school wouldn't fit on this postcard but she felt lucky to be there.

"He won't," Sally said. "The Marines will keep him busy. Of course, he may die of heartbreak when he has to leave you down there. You're his favorite, you know?"

Give it a rest, Becca thought. She didn't like the feelings that Sally created within her. There was something there, hidden beneath the calm routine that had been established since her mother's death. It was too quick; a wedding nine months after the funeral. It was almost as though her mother had never existed. Like Sally had been there all along, and Becca was a guest in a familiar home.

"I doubt that," Becca answered. "It's hard to compete with a pilot and an artist and you know what Daddy says about teachers?"

"What's that?" Sally asked, rising to clear the dishes. She handed Becca the last remaining cinnamon roll.

"You know—that old saying. 'Those who can, do; those who can't, teach.'"

Sally smiled. "Yeah, I've heard that. Of course we all know that you're going to be a writer and the teaching is temporary."

"No," Becca answered. "The writing may happen, but no matter what, I'm going to bring Shakespeare and Byron to those kids even if I have to acquire a southern accent to do it."

"You know," Sally said, heading for the kitchen. "You sound just like your father."

Rinsing the breakfast dishes, Sally watched Becca nibble on the roll while she paced along the porch. *That girl's never still,* she thought. That explained her figure, though her thoughts remained a mystery. Becca had attended their wedding, breaking her family's boycott, but Sally knew this was out of love for her father and not a welcome sign. Events had somehow taken on their own momentum; propelling her into a role she'd had no intention of playing.

Sally had battled her guilt, justifying the murder, forcing herself to believe Allison would have died from her injuries. In any event, the Bible allowed for self-defense. Allison would have destroyed her. She had to defend herself. She'd prayed about it. She felt forgiven. God had special plans for her, just like her mother had always said.

After the funeral, mourners had jammed Michael's house. Sally retreated to her cottage. She couldn't stay. She'd escape in the confusion, leave Michael a note, then disappear. Allison had won. She was leaving. She'd just finished the note when she heard a light knock, followed by Michael's burly frame. He glanced at her packed bags, then back at her. "You need to unpack," he said, his voice low and serious. "We'll talk later, but I need you to stay."

"I can't," she'd said.

"You can," he answered, moving towards the door, then turning to face her. "You're too tough to run away."

She'd felt Michael's power from the day Brad had brought her to the island. Good old Brad. They'd met two years earlier when Brad flew her team home from Afghanistan. He'd seemed shy, inviting her into the C17's cockpit, serving her coffee like a VIP, while he identified the tiny villages that clung to the steep mountain cliffs. They looked different from the air. At least you couldn't see the bad guys, though she knew they were there.

"It's pretty tight up here," Brad said when she leaned forward from her jump seat behind him. "I'll let you fly the plane," he'd said when she settled back, "but unfortunately you'll have to sit in my lap." She thought back to the night patrols with the Special Ops guys; the way they'd turn their backs when she had to pee. She'd pulled her load, and they'd accepted her and now this, twenty minutes after they'd met. That's when she'd spilled her coffee into his lap.

"Turbulence," she said watching him squirm. "I'm so sorry."

A month later, she was nursing a beer at Pope Field's Smoke Bomb Grill. The letter had arrived two days earlier. She hadn't slept since.

"Thank you for your contribution," it read, "but your services are no longer required." She was being riffed, caught in a reduction in force produced by the drawdown in Afghanistan. She looked at her beer. I should be doing shots, she thought. She was about to order when Brad tapped her on the shoulder.

"You look like someone just dumped coffee in your lap," he said, sliding on to the barstool next to her.

"The only turbulence here is in my personal life," she'd answered. He ordered a beer and she told him about the letter.

"You need a break," Brad said when she finished "and I need a copilot: I'm renting a Cessna and flying to my parents' home for a long weekend." He gave her a sly smile. "One condition though," he said, breaking into a full grin. "No coffee."

"No laps," she answered, "and separate quarters."

They'd landed on a small, grass strip. "Welcome to Klenawicus International," Brad said, as they taxied across the bumpy, grass field. The only foreign object she saw was a huge black Bentley parked along the wood line.

Michael had greeted her with a gentle handshake, opening her door like a chauffeur. Surrounded by leather and wood, she'd resisted the temptation to confess this was her first ride in a Bentley.

Over cocktails that afternoon, she and Michael had discovered a common interest: Stock trading, an addiction afflicted upon her by a friend's stockbroker husband. She'd opened a small brokerage account and a couple of successful trades later, she was hooked. Her simple trading strategy had intrigued Michael while he'd confused her with a complex mixture of options and short sales.

Michael's fund sold stocks he didn't own and he swore it was legal. He'd named his firm, 'VALKYRIE'. "Allison actually named it," he said. "Seems a Valkyrie was a Norse female figure that floated over the battlefield and picked out who was going to die. That's what we do with companies," he said. "Short them until they die."

They'd been a platonic threesome that weekend. Allison was visiting their two daughters in Charleston and Michael had self-appointed himself as her tour guide. She was glad. Brad's intentions remained suspect and Michael proved to be a charming chaperone. He reminded her of a camp counselor, planning every minute. There was no down time. All he needed was a whistle.

They'd spent Saturday body surfing Montauk's west coast waves. "You can rest when you're dead," Michael said when Brad complained. "We've got reservations at the yacht club at six and we've got a 7:00 o'clock tee-time at Goat Hill in the morning." Brad groaned.

Goat Hill lived up to its name.

"Must be named after a mountain goat," she'd said, making the steep climb to the eighteenth green.

"Don't know about that," Michael answered, "but you're on top of the island. That's Peconic Bay over there," he said, pointing with his putter, "and down there's Dering Harbor."

"It's postcard pretty," she said, looking out at the blue water far below, "and you can definitely tell it's an island."

"You can tell better from my sailboat," he'd answered. "Let's grab a sandwich and we'll do a circumnavigation."

"All the way around the island?"

Michael laughed. "It's only nineteen miles and the natives are friendly, plus we've got a favoring wind."

I'm taking a nap," Brad said, joining them on the green. "I can't keep up with this old guy."

They'd launched from the yacht club, taking the club's shuttle out to the boat tied at Michael's mooring.

On board, he moved quickly, down in the cockpit, up on the deck, tightening a line here, loosening one there. "Hold the tiller," he said, when he released them from the mooring. "Just keep it straight," he said, "but watch out for other boats." It was like a poorly choreographed dance, but the sails went up and they gained speed.

Michael joined her in the cockpit. "You learn fast and follow orders well," he said. "I've been watching you all weekend. Brad told me about your Air Force problem, and I've got a proposition for you." He reached behind her and locked the tiller in place.

Like father, like son, she thought, then he offered her a job. She'd listened to the details, then politely declined.

"I can't sit in an office," she'd told him. "I've got to have some action."

"You'll get action," he'd promised and when his offer doubled her Air Force salary, she'd said, "yes." She beat the Air Force to the punch, requesting a transfer to reserve status. She'd retained her commission. It provided the guarantee that she'd never be pulled back into the West Virginia mountains. She'd die to keep it.

True to his word, Michael taught her the intricacies of using money to make money and the speed and excitement of investment banking provided the adrenaline rush she craved. She became his star pupil, suggesting trades that profited the client, the firm, and herself. She felt like a true Valkyrie.

Sally wondered if her looks had played a part, but Michael treated her like any other successful broker, bragging on her accomplishments like a proud father. He'd even let her run the firm's fixed income money. Nothing fancy——just brokered CDs and fixed annuities-finding the highest guaranteed return for his most conservative investors. *No Valkyries in this group.*

The market crash hit them like a virus, silent at first: "No contagion," the Fed said. "Just a few bad loans." Michael agreed: "How can a handful of sub-prime mortgages bring down an eighteen-trillion dollar economy?" He bought call options on big safe companies like GE and Citibank, laughing at the fools that sold them. But the virus mutated, exploiting hidden weaknesses, dropping industry giants to their knees. The further they fell, the more risks Michael took. By August, he was in serious trouble.

That's when he'd come to her. He needed the safe money she managed to stay in the game. He had it figured out. The financial stocks would collapse. He'd sell them short, regain his losses and replace her money. Everybody would win. He only needed a little time to cover his short sales. He didn't need her help, only her silence.

"It'll be okay," he'd promised, "you just trust Uncle Michael."

It was an elaborate conspiracy, swapping money from account to account; creating separate spreadsheets to track whose money went where while producing client statements that showed gains in a falling market. There were withdrawals; people running for cover as their world collapsed around them.

"You sure you aren't in cahoots with Madoff?" was a frequent if joking question. Michael responded by buying Bernie's yacht, *Sitting Bull,* from the Feds and anchoring it in Dering Harbor. It provided a reassuring image of Michael's solvency, floating serenely near his Dering Harbor dock. The withdrawals stopped.

"It's almost like stealing," Michael said one night in December, as they settled their short accounts with worthless paper and exercised their "put options" for pennies on the dollar. She looked at the spreadsheet. For once it glowed green, not red.

"You declaring victory?" she'd asked.

"Yes," he'd answered, giving her a high-five, "but the war's not over."

It had been a war, she thought: They'd been in danger, facing an uncertain outcome and they'd fought it as a team. "Battle buddies," the Rangers called it and just like real combat, the shared dangers had drawn them closer. She could feel it. There was something there. He felt it too. She could see it in his eyes. The night at the pool was late but inevitable. Somehow, they'd fallen in love.

Her thoughts turned to Allison. A snitch, not the SEC had nailed Bernie. Allison was their snitch. Michael had made her job easy. He'd brought everything home, covering his desk with incriminating documents; the same documents Allison had thrown in her face. Their gray, shredded ashes now lay at the bottom of Dering Harbor.

She watched Becca finish her cinnamon roll and bounce down the porch steps, turning left towards the pool. Becca remained a question mark. What had she seen and what would she remember? Finding Becca, alive at the crash scene, along with Sally's missing dog tags were puzzles she couldn't finish. She'd just have to wait but she couldn't wait forever.

A year afterwards Becca still couldn't recall the accident, but she had reoccurring dreams, "visions," she called them, that revealed facts Sally knew were real. In them, an obscure figure slammed something into Allison's windshield. Michael dismissed them, and Sally hoped the dreams would fade with time.

Leaving the island would help, Sally thought, especially leaving that Lizzie person Becca had met on the plane. "Elizabeth Hardin, Life Coach and Spiritualist" her card said. The cops had found it in Becca's pocket. Sally had watched Lizzie at Allison's funeral, listening as she spouted her psychic garbage, encouraging Becca to pursue her vision. Lizzie was Becca's only confidant. They met weekly at Claudio's Greenport bar. Separating them would help.

The dog tags remained a mystery. They had to be in Allison's Jaguar though she couldn't imagine how they remained undiscovered. She'd searched the accident scene yard by yard. There was nothing to be found.

A loud splash broke her thoughts. Becca was using the high dive. Sally took a deep breath. She actually liked the girl, but she'd do what had to be done. Becca had wanted her Beaufort move to be a father/daughter outing. Michael had agreed, but Sally had lobbied Michael in a currency Becca couldn't match. She had to be there to see what effect Becca's new surroundings had on her memory. She'd planned for the worst; studying Becca's apartment layout and plotting a nighttime route there from her hotel. An internet search revealed a local hardware store had her climbing equipment in stock. She was ready but sad. Sally closed her eyes and tilted her head up. "Please, God," she prayed softly, "for both our sakes, don't let her remember."

CHAPTER SIX

The early Friday morning ferry line was short. North Ferry was running extra boats. Becca counted the cars. There were fourteen. The ferry carried twelve.

"Second boat, Dad," she said to her father. She'd done this since she was a child. Part of her mother's teaching opportunities that Staci and Brad had somehow escaped. Becca relaxed into her seat. She could have flown alone, but she was glad her father had come. She'd tried to exclude Sally but apparently she still had her whip.

"And they say an MFA is useless," her father answered. He reached back and ruffled her hair. "I'm sure going to miss having you do the ferry calculations. I might even miss the boat." He laughed at his joke. Sally moaned from the passenger's seat.

"I sure won't miss this," Becca said. She watched the ferries scurry across the harbor. "At least in backward old South Carolina they have bridges."

The second boat came in fast, bouncing hard against the padded slip, its side-thrusters fighting to slow its momentum.

"Rookie driver," Michael said, glancing up at the narrow pilot house. "That's Joey Milano's daughter up there, and she handles this boat like a bumper car. Guess the boss's daughter has a different set of rules."

A wind-tanned deckhand directed them to the center of the front row. He gave Michael a quick thumbs-up. "Good-old, Bubbie," Michael said. "He takes good care of me. We'll be the first one off." He lowered the windows and switched off the Mercedes's engine.

"Wow," Becca said, "a whole twenty-foot head start. Let me know when the checkered flag drops."

"Twenty feet can get you to an exit when the expressway turns into a parking lot," Michael answered. "I've got this thing down to a science."

Sally laughed. "Old habits are hard to break, Sweetie. Your dad's just an old Long Island Expressway war horse and you can't rein him in. He'll be on auto-pilot until we reach LaGuardia."

The ten-minute ferry ride to Greenport was smooth and Becca watched the boat slide into its slip with only slight rumbles from its thrusters. A set of metal teeth locked the ferry to the ramp.

"Don't lose the lead, Dad," she teased, as Bubbie removed a wooden chock and waved them forward.

"I won't, honey," he answered, accelerating hard, turning left on Front Street, only to be stopped by Greenport's solo stoplight.

Becca turned, straining to see over the worn pilings at Claudio's dock. Shelter Island's white, sand hills slipped slowly below the horizon. She'd be back, but it was no longer her island. In the past year, she'd surrendered her claim to Sally. She reclined her seat, took out her iPhone and opened her game app. There was nothing left to see. Her sanctuary was gone.

Two hours later Michael looked at his beeping GPS. Exit seven was backed up. He picked a small opening and forced his big Mercedes into the traffic line.

"Almost a record," he said, braking hard to merge with the exiting traffic. Becca lowered her phone, stretched, and gazed blankly at the metal herd that surrounded them.

"We should have flown from Islip," she said. "This place is a zoo, and we're the animals."

"It's a fine and historic airport," her father said. "It's just a little overused, and it's got no room to grow." He took the exit for long-term parking and flagged down a departing shuttle.

"It's just like the airport," Becca said, sitting down. She ran her finger along a tear in the crowded shuttle's seat and stirred the paper wrappers with her foot. "Why can't they clean this?"

"They do," Sally answered, "but only when they change shifts. Besides, a little dirt's good for you. It makes you tough."

"You're tough and extremely clean," Becca said. She knew Sally considered her spoiled and protected.

Sally smiled. "Once you get through your dirty stage, you can clean up, but your toughness remains."

"Forever?"

"It won't stay the same forever, though it never completely fades. It's like your father being in the Marines. He'll always have part of that in him."

"Once a Marine, always a Marine," Michael added. He was relieved to speak. Things between Becca and Sally got heated pretty quickly.

"Well," Becca answered, "I can't wait to see you at Parris Island. Maybe they will keep you."

The terminal greeted them with a dull roar. "I told you it's a zoo," Becca said. She watched the ticket lines twist their way across the terminal in random patterns. How anyone knew where to go was beyond her.

"This way," Michael said, moving away from the crowd. "We're going to 'Flagship Check-in'. There'd better not be a line there."

There was no line. "Gate C34," the smiling gate agent said, handing back their tickets. "If you're interested," she added, "we're serving a complimentary brunch buffet in our Admirals Club. It's on the way to your gate and you've got a little time."

"Sounds good," Michael answered. "It's nice to be appreciated."

"It's like a cave," Becca said, leading them into the lounge. "Dark and quiet." She scanned the room. A horseshoe bar dominated, its stools filled with middle-aged men in rumpled suits, their eyes focused on two muted televisions that flashed stock tickers across their screens. Becca spotted an empty table and headed towards it; Sally and her father followed.

A waitress almost beat them there, arriving with a coffee thermos and a platter of fruit and pastries. Sally reached for the coffee.

"It's delicious," she said, taking a sip. "I think it's Starbucks." Without asking, she filled Michael's and Becca's cups.

Becca eyed the platter. "I'm having carb withdrawal," she said. "This morning's run took a lot out of me."

"Me, too," her father said, handing her a large crescent roll. "That was one tough drive."

Becca inhaled the roll. Her father handed her a cheese Danish. "You trying to fatten me up, Dad?" she asked, taking a big bite.

"Tried all my life… never could. You were born to be thin; just like your mother."

"You know every woman on this planet hates you," Sally said. "If I ate that, I'd just skip the middleman and apply it directly to my hips."

"You seem to apply things very well," Michael said. He gave her an appraising look, then patted her thigh. "Yep," he said smiling, "mighty well."

Becca cut her eyes at her father then reached down and pulled a book from her bag. It was going to be a long trip. She thought of Lizzie's "mile high" trade offer. She'd miss their Claudios rendezvous, but she'd keep in touch.

"What are you reading, Sweetie?" Michael asked, eyeing her book.

"*Lolita*," she answered. She looked back at her father then opened her worn copy of *Romeo and Juliet*. It was her favorite play.

"Sounds familiar," her father said. "What's it about?"

"Just a love story," she answered. "You wouldn't be interested."

The flight to Savannah took almost two hours. Michael had navigated them down the East coast, pointing out Atlantic City and the naval base at

Norfolk before they climbed through the clouds. Now as their plane circled, losing altitude and waiting for its turn to land in Savannah, he continued to narrate.

"There's Hilton Head. You can tell because it's shaped like a foot. Parris Island's right across the sound."

Becca pressed against her window while Sally leaned across Michael. "If you look a little north, there's that awful island that Becca's going to. What's it called?"

"Saint Helena," Becca answered, trying to orient herself. To her, the islands were a confusing collage of creeks and lagoons.

"Saint Helena," Michael repeated, looking back at Becca. "Isn't that where they sent Napoleon to die?"

"Different Saint Helena," she answered. "It's even pronounced differently."

"Probably named after it though," Michael said. "Wonder what it means?"

"It means Becca's Paradise," Sally said. "I bet it's covered with palm trees and beaches."

"I bet it's covered with mosquitoes and leeches," Michael answered.

"You're both wrong," Becca said, pausing as the plane touched down. "It's covered with farms and shrimp boats and I'm going to love it there. By the way, Saint Helena's the patron saint of new discoveries. My Karma must be good."

Michael stood up. He pulled their luggage from the overhead and placed it in the aisle while the plane taxied to their gate. Becca never understood his rush. They were deplaning first and the flight attendant would save them from the economy class hordes. It was just like the ferry; he had to be first.

"This airport looks just like Savannah," Sally said, as they entered the terminal. She pointed at the fountains and trees that divided the airport into a set of squares.

"I flew into here once with a platoon of Rangers from Fort Stewart. Downtown looks just like that—a bunch of squares that hook together. It's really pretty."

"Maybe we can check it out next time," Michael said, glancing at the squares but not slowing down. "Right now we need to stay on schedule."

"What color Cadillac did you rent this time, Daddy?" Becca asked, as they approached the baggage area. "Let me guess." She looked at her father and smiled. "I'd bet black. Those poor Beaufortonians are going to think the Mafia's arrived; especially when they hear you talk."

Michael shook his head. "You're wrong on three counts, Sweetie. It's not black, it's not a Cadillac, and it's not rented." He winked at Sally. "Let's just say that I'm borrowing a very special car from a very special person."

Becca's thoughts turned to her father's taste in cars. Anything was possible. He once picked her up at Harvard in a borrowed limo, complete with a chauffeur's hat. He liked making a statement, and "understated" wasn't in his vocabulary.

"Daddy, please tell me you didn't borrow some Rolls or other monstrosity." She stomped her foot and turned to face him. Her hands rested on her hips. "We can't go down there looking like we came to buy the island."

"Relax, honey," Michael said, in a fake southern accent. "I'll offer those boys a fair price. Besides, I think you'll like this car."

Becca grimaced. "I can hardly wait."

Michael laughed and grabbed her hand, leading her down the empty corridor. Sally trailed behind them.

"Don't we need to pick up our bags?" Becca asked, as they hurried past the spinning luggage carrousel.

"Wouldn't fit in this car," Michael answered. "Barely fit in the Mercedes. I had everything shipped to the hotel. You had too much stuff; almost as much as Sally."

"You do want me to look pretty for those Marines?" Sally asked, catching up and wrapping her arm around her husband's waist.

"I could tell you something about what Marines like," Michael answered.

"Spare us, Daddy."

"You might find this interesting," Sally said, "especially since you're going to live near their island."

"They can stay on their island and I'll stay on mine," Becca answered. "Now let's see this land yacht Daddy's commandeered."

"Damn, it's hot," Michael said as they left the terminal, heading towards the rental cars. "It's just like I remember it."

"You'll survive, Daddy," Becca said. "You just need to acclimate."

"I hope she likes it," Sally whispered to Michael as Becca increased the distance between them.

"What's not to like? A girl like her with a car like that?"

Becca reached the end of the cars and turned to face them, her face crinkled with curiosity. Michael smiled broadly. "It's in there," he said, pointing with his chin towards a large canvas tent that sheltered the car detailers from the Georgia sun.

Becca stepped through the tent's rolled-up side. It couldn't be too bad, she thought; not if it can't hold our luggage. She strained to see in the darkness. The car sat facing her. She recognized its familiar outline first and its color became clear as her pupils dilated. They'd met before. "A red BMW convertible," she said, glancing back at her father before moving closer. "An M6," she added, her voice rising as she spotted the fabled M label in its oval grill. A white banner stretched across its windshield. "Congratulations, Becca," she read, "our favorite teacher."

Becca shook her head. He'd done it again. She wasn't mad, just disappointed. He wouldn't let her grow up. To him, she was still his little girl.

"Oh, Daddy," she said, "it's perfect and you were sweet to buy it for me, but I can't keep it." Her voice hardened slightly. "You know I'm going to live on my salary and that car cost more than I make in two years. Besides, we're supposed to pick up the Jetta I ordered on Hilton Head."

"Becca, honey," Michael stammered, as he searched for the right words. He liked to be prepared for any argument, but he hadn't anticipated this. She'd practically drooled over this car in Southampton; now she was turning it down?

"I know you want to do things by yourself," he said. "I admire you for that. But I can still buy you presents. Besides, I already cancelled the Jetta."

Sally stepped forward, joining Becca beside the car. "It's awfully pretty." She looked inside. "Six speed too. I hate it when people put an automatic in these cars." Becca remained silent, her arms crossed, her attention focused on her father.

"Why don't we drive it to Beaufort?" Sally asked, filling the silence. "Then you two can work something out. I bet your father can cut you a real good deal."

"Real good," Michael said in the salesman's voice he'd used many times to persuade reluctant clients.

"There's nothing to work out," Becca said sharply.

Michael cringed at the exchange. Becca overreacted to Sally. *Probably natural,* he thought. Becca and Allison had been so close. Looked alike too. When he glanced at Becca, he saw Allison.

"Well," he said, his voice deep, expressing a confidence he didn't feel. "We need a car and I like this one. We'll take it to Beaufort, and if Becca doesn't like it, I'll give it back to the dealer." He pulled the key fob from his pocket and tossed it to Becca. "You drive, hot-rod, I'll navigate. Neither woman moved. "Let's go," he said, opening the passenger's door and motioning Sally in. "We've got stuff to do."

Becca slid behind the steering wheel. She'd drive the car to Beaufort, but she wouldn't keep it. She adjusted the seat then hit the start button, smiling at the subdued rumble that slipped from beneath the hood. "You were right, Mom," she whispered, "I did inherit your love of speed."

Beside her, she watched her father battle a map he'd pulled from the glove compartment; folding it until the route from Savannah to Beaufort lay on top.

"Which way, Dad?" she asked.

"Just start moving," he answered, wiping perspiration from his forehead. "I've got to get some air." He traced his finger along the map. "We're okay for a little while then we need to take a left"

"Okay, Magellan," Becca said. "Just tell me when."

"Go left here," Michael commanded, when they reached the first light.

"Yes, sir, Captain," Becca answered. She glanced around. She'd been here in December for her job interview. "Last time, I used the GPS and it took me straight down I-95." She looked over at her father, watching him twist the map. "I didn't have any trouble," she continued, "Besides, there're signs all the way."

Michael looked up from his map.

"Signs," he said. "Signs are for sissies that can't read maps. Besides, you went way out of your way and you missed some great scenery. We'd be in deep shit if Columbus couldn't read a map."

"Didn't he think he was in India?" Becca asked, battling down a giggle that hung in her throat.

"Okay wise-ass. Bad example but anyway he discovered us and that's that."

Michael continued to trace their route with his finger. "Take your next right," he said, twisting the map again, "Looks like there's a straight shot right into Beaufort." He tapped the map and whistled.

"What did you find, Michael?" Sally asked from the back seat. "From the look on your face, I'd bet you discovered a southern stock exchange."

"Better than that," Michael answered. "There's nothing but swamps and water along this road. I feel like I'm leading a patrol down Highway One in Vietnam." He pointed straight ahead. "Here comes our first river crossing. In Vietnam, this would he the Tourane River and Hill 327 would be behind us."

"Well, Dad," Becca said, "we seem to have missed Vietnam and leaped straight into South Carolina." She read the 'Welcome to South Carolina' sign that greeted them as they crossed the Savannah River. The bridge was narrow and rust stained its spindly girders. She looked down, watching the brown water swirl past the remains of trees it had torn from the riverbank. Two large alligators lay sunning on a sandbar. "Looks creepy," Becca said, shuddering at the scene below her. "I sure wouldn't want to be down there."

"Me either," Sally said. "I'll take the desert any day, scorpions and all."

Becca took a deep breath, inhaling the musty smells that drifted up from the river. She felt free, like she'd crossed the border into another country rather than from Georgia into South Carolina. She flipped on the radio. A soft southern voice gave her the temperature, "ninety-six with a heat index of one hundred five. Time to head somewhere cooler," the voice added, "and here's the man to take you there."

Willie Nelson's raspy voice poured from the custom Nokia speakers. She listened, then began to sing. *On the Road Again* was one of the few songs she knew by heart.

"I love this song," Sally said joining in the chorus. "Come on, Michael," she said. "We need a baritone."

Becca glanced over at her father. She'd never heard him sing, not even in church, but now he was singing on command. Lizzie's right, she thought, listening to her father's faltering voice; *He is pussy-whipped. What a descriptive term,* she thought, still singing along with Willie. *Maybe I'll use it in my novel.* She'd write things she'd never say out loud. She owed that to Robert.

"I'm glad to see you're happy," Michael said. "I've been worried about you, especially about your weird dreams."

Becca's fingers tightened around the leather steering wheel. She sensed the doubt in her father's words.

"They're not just dreams and they aren't weird," she said, raising her voice. "They're visions." They're blurry right now, but they're getting clearer. I really believe that something happened that night that nobody knows about but me." She pounded the wheel. "I won't stop until I find out what."

She watched her father and Sally exchange knowing glances then stared straight ahead. She'd overreacted; she always did. They didn't believe her. No one but Lizzie did and sometimes she didn't know if she believed herself.

Her father glanced at her then back down at his map. The car was quiet. Swamps dotted with tiny, fern-covered islands replaced the marshes as they headed north.

Several tense minutes later Michael turned to face Sally. "Don't tell Becca," he said in a stage whisper, "but the scenery's going to improve real quick."

Becca glanced at her father then focused back on the road. The Chechesse River Bridge seemed to leap from the trees. It lifted them gently above the sand flats surrounding it, exposing the hidden coastline that hugged the surrounding islands.

"It's beautiful," Becca said. Her mood lightened with the expansive scenery. She pointed to the right. "Port Royal Sound, right, navigator?" she asked her father.

"There's hope for you yet," he answered. "You know," he said, twisting his head, "it reminds me of Peconic Bay. Water just keeps going until it runs right into the horizon."

"That's almost poetic," Becca answered, "though a writer would say the sky and water merged."

"I'm sure they would, honey," he answered, "but the only mergers I care about happen on Wall Street. It is pretty, though." He winked at Sally. "You know," he said, "maybe I could open an office on Hilton Head. That's where all the rich Yankees go to hide from our taxes."

"That's sweet," Sally said.

"What's sweet?" Michael answered.

"That you want to be close to Becca." She leaned forward and kissed his cheek.

"You're crazy," Michael answered. "Any decision I make is based purely on financial data."

Becca concentrated on her driving, sensing the car's smooth power as she guided it across an S-shaped causeway.

Her father would never leave his island compound. She'd miss him, but she had to go. Right now, the memories hurt too much and the visions were too real. At times she felt like she was abandoning her birthplace to Sally but that was a done deal. For the coming year, she'd concentrate on her teaching and do some writing. After that, she didn't know. She needed a new island. Maybe she'd found one.

Becca listened to the banter between her father and Sally. Carrie Underwood replaced Willie on the radio. Crossing the Broad River, she turned at a sign that said, "Beaufort, eight miles." She was almost there. Soon she'd be in charge of her own life. She felt both happy and alone.

CHAPTER SEVEN

"Follow me," Becca said, as she led her father and Sally from the hallway and onto her apartment's upstairs porch.

"You're going to love this," she said, turning to face them. She walked backward as she talked. Her intro to Beaufort was going well. She felt happy. Her upstairs apartment with its exposed brick walls and ancient, wooden floors had won instant approval, but she'd saved the best for last; nobody could resist this porch.

"The shops and restaurants are to your right," she said, gesturing with her left hand like a tour guide, "and the historic district is to your left. Straight ahead for your viewing pleasure is the Beaufort River complete with a historic waterfront park, guarded by three Yankee cannons."

She turned to her father. "What'd you think, Dad?"

"You done good," her father said, stretching out his words. He walked across the porch and placed his hands on the banister. Sally followed.

"Thanks, Dad," Becca said, sliding in next to him at the railing, "but that accent's got to go."

She was glad he approved. Not that it really mattered; she'd stay anyway, but seeking his approval was a life-long habit she found hard to break. This was a first step but she was glad he'd come.

"What'd you think?" she asked, "Million dollar view for a thousand bucks a month?"

"It beats the crap out of that dump Sally had in Midtown." he answered. "Three thousand a month for a studio. Hell, I had to give her a raise."

"I was still underpaid," Sally said. She winked at Michael. "I mean considering the wide variety of services I provided."

Becca winced. The comment was for her benefit, one of Sally's hidden body blows intended to fortify her position in their battle over Michael, a fight she'd already conceded.

"Doesn't it remind you of home?" Becca asked her father.

Michael stretched and leaned out over the railing. "Well," he said, pivoting his head, "it's the same ocean, but we don't have cannons and we sure as hell don't have horses and buggies."

"What?" Becca asked, then she heard the clomping hooves. "Beaufort Carriage Company," she read, looking down at the horse-drawn carriage parked beneath her porch. "We're part of the tour."

The guide's voice drifted up to them. "I took this tour last winter," Becca whispered, as the guide explained the houses' histories.

"Planters' homes," the guide continued, "cooled by the sea breezes, away from the heat and mosquitoes of the inland plantations."

He pointed at the cannons. "These old guys were as fickle as Scarlett O'Hara. They fired on both the French and Spanish, before the colonists turned them on the British. The last time these cannons fired from here was across at Port Royal during that period of unpleasantness that the rest of the country calls the Civil War." He snapped the reins and the carriage moved forward.

"They're part of the charm," Becca said to her father, watching the carriage continue down Bay Street. She punched his shoulder, "and the cannons are to repel bad Yankees like you."

"That didn't work too well last time," Sally said. She pulled a brochure from her purse. "I picked this up at the hotel. It says here that the Confederates abandoned Beaufort without a fight, and that's why so many antebellum homes are left." She flipped through the brochure then looked at Michael. "What does antebellum mean?" You'd think they'd have that in here."

"I don't know," Michael answered, "but they sure are pretty." He turned to his daughter. "Okay, hotshot, show me what I got for my money."

"The Latin was free." Becca answered. "I took it in high school. Mom made me." She looked at Sally. " '*Ante*' is Latin for 'before' and '*Bellum*' is Latin for 'war,' so *Antebellum* means 'before the war'. Of course, the war we're talking about here is the Civil War."

"I don't know how you keep so much stuff up there," Michael said. He patted his daughter's head. "If that teaching job doesn't work out, you've got real potential as a tour guide."

"No," Becca answered. "If something happened to my teaching position, my dream job is right downstairs. It's a bookstore," she continued. "You didn't notice it because we came up from the back."

"Let's see," Michael said. He walked to the side of the porch and looked down. "By the Bay Books," he read from an open-book shaped sign that hung from a rusty chain. He looked at Becca. "All you reading people try to be so cute." Becca knew he divided people into two groups: Those who did things, and those who read about them. "That's not even original. They stole that from that old TV show about that lesbian."

"Gay. The correct term is 'gay, Sally said. "Besides, her store was called 'Buy the Book.'"

"Close enough," he answered. "I sure hope those people down there aren't gay. That's all Becca needs."

"Aw, Daddy," Becca said, "It'll make a nice change." She hooked her arm through his. "I mean once I get tired of all those macho Marines, I can come home to a nice soft woman who'll know just what I need."

She knew he was serious. His morality was inconsistent: Greed got a pass, but personal conduct was strictly by the book.

She blamed this on his strict Catholic upbringing. She'd learned early on not to share any misdeed with Granny and Papa Noble, but sometimes she could bring her father around, teasing him into seeing the contradictions of his positions.

"Joke if you want," Michael answered, withdrawing his arm, "but things are different now."

"Who else lives here?" Sally asked. She looked at the second set of windows. "I saw two bathrooms at the end of the hall so someone must live across from you."

"Some guy's supposed to move in this weekend," Becca answered. Sally's discovery annoyed her. She didn't need anything to add to her father's worries. "I think he's a Marine."

"Very interesting," Sally said, "and convenient. I can smell the romance already."

"I'm not looking for romance," Becca answered sharply. Sally was quick to step into her personal life. "I don't need a man to complete my life. I'm totally self-sufficient."

"Totally?" Sally said.

"Totally," Becca answered, louder than she meant. "Sex's not all it's cracked up to be."

"No comment," Michael said. He turned to Sally. "We need to get to the hotel and check in. We're leaving on Sunday and we haven't even seen Becca's school."

"We could skip the school," Becca said. "Give you more time to see Beaufort." She wasn't real crazy about the school tour. The building was old, a product of the fifties, planted in the middle of a field beneath a stand of oaks, and landscaped with sand and gravel and whatever else chose to sprout there. Her father would not be impressed.

"No," Michael said. "I want to have a picture in my head when I think about you. Pick us up in an hour. We'll do a drive-by then eat supper at that Crazy Frog Restaurant you talked about."

"Foolish Frog," Becca corrected. She hugged her father. "See you at 4:00," she said, "and try to stay out of trouble."

The next morning Becca awoke early. She'd fallen asleep in the living room, stretched out on her couch, listening to the waves lap against the tabby seawall. She felt refreshed. She'd slept deeply, tired from the trip and unpacking the boxes that now lined the hallway. She stretched, then bounced to her feet. She checked her phone: six-thirty. The Parris Island bus tour would leave her father's hotel at nine. She had time for a run.

Becca slipped into her shorts and T-shirt, then headed across the hall. She hated the bathroom's location but at least she didn't have to share. She remembered Harvard: *eighty grand a year and stuck in Pennypacker dorm.*

She splashed her face with cold water. It jarred her awake. She replayed her father's school visit. His reaction had been muted. She felt relieved. At least he wasn't going to try and drag her back home. She didn't need another battle and the memories were too strong. They'd compromised on the car. She'd keep it and give him the money for the Jetta. Not perfect but she could live with it.

Glancing in the mirror, she thought of her mother. Everyone said they looked alike. She agreed, especially without makeup. She leaned towards the mirror. Her scar was fading. She hated that. The scar was her proof, and she wore it proudly.

It's my freckles, she thought. They're covering it up. She traced the scar's jagged outline with her finger. She'd done that the night of the accident, right after the stitches. She remembered the doctor pulling her hand away while the policeman kept asking her questions she still couldn't answer. What happened?

She squeezed her eyes closed. She could feel the pain of the stitches and hear the frustration in the policeman's voice.

Suddenly she felt a presence. There was something there. She opened her eyes slowly, afraid of what she might see, but she was alone. She checked the hallway. It was empty. She checked again then dashed across to her apartment, locking the door behind her before dropping to a kitchen chair: Then, she remembered the dream.

It came tumbling out, hidden in last night's heavy sleep. It was the same dream, but gradually the figure became clearer, like her mind was bringing it into focus a frame at a time.

She forced herself to concentrate. The dream had changed. A figure still slammed something into the Jaguar's windshield. The difference was its form. Before, it had been almost ghost-like, wispy with no shape, floating above the car. But now it was human, small, dressed in black, and strangely familiar. The only feature it lacked was a face.

Becca laced up her running shoes. Running was her therapy and right now, she needed a long session. Her dream had changed. She needed to know why. A few endorphins would help and, hopefully a long, slow run would produce them.

She skipped down the stairs and onto the sidewalk. Warm, wet air greeted her as she headed towards the river, looping the waterfront park before heading deep into the historic district. She ran for an hour, listening to the mantra of her footsteps echo along Beaufort's narrow streets, waiting for the secret to unlock her dream. As usual there was nothing. She'd have to remain patient. She plopped down on a park bench and watched the early morning twilight merge into a gray, splattered sunrise, then walked across Bay Street to her apartment.

Despite the results, the run lifted her mood, leaving her with a pleasant fatigue that softened her thoughts. She felt ready; ready for Parris Island and ready for a day with Sally and her father.

Becca arrived early at their motel and headed straight for the restaurant. Her father would be there, coffee cup in hand. Maybe they could grab some alone time. She frowned when she spotted Sally.

Their backs were to her. Her father wore a camouflage jacket with USMC embroidered across its slanted pockets.

"I thought you were a tree," she said, leaning down to kiss him. "Plus you don't have a paper."

"I couldn't pry him out of that jacket," Sally said.

"And they've only got the local paper," Michael answered, ignoring the jacket comments. "Plus the TV doesn't have a business channel and the internet's down."

"I told you it's a plot, Michael," Sally added. "You know, to halt the Northern War of Aggression."

"It's not a plot," Michael answered, "but it's a damn inconvenience." He turned to Becca. "So, honey, how was your first night in your apartment?"

Becca hesitated. Telling him about her new dream would accomplish nothing. He'd only worry, and he didn't believe the dreams had any meaning. But, she'd waited too long to answer. Her father's face drooped and he emitted a heavy sigh.

"It's the dream, isn't it?" he asked. "You had another dream?"

A waiter approached. "Let's order," Sally said. "We can talk about this while we eat."

Michael and Sally ordered oatmeal. Michael frowned. Sally insisted. Becca settled on the buffet. She was hungry from the run and she told them about the dream between bites of scrambled eggs, bacon, and pancakes. She skipped the grits.

"So what do you think this means?" her father asked when Becca finished her story. He snitched a bacon slice off her plate.

"I still think," Becca answered slowly, "that something happened that night. I think that I saw it and that I only remember it in my dream." She studied their faces. Her father's was skeptical; Sally's was blank. "I also think," she continued, "that soon the vision would be clear. Then, I'll be able to identify the figure."

"And what'll that prove?" Sally asked. "I bet it's some mythological character from all those literature courses you took, you know, like *The Headless Horseman.*"

"This isn't in my mind," Becca answered. She pounded the table. She was being dismissed again. Before, she'd doubted herself, but not now. "It's real," she said, "and someday I'll know who it is. Then we'll all know what happened that night."

"Okay, honey," Michael said. "We'll just have to wait and see." He glanced at his watch. "We better get moving. That bus will be here in five minutes and I don't know where it leaves from."

They headed outside towards the parking lot. The bus was easy to spot. Its bright blue body straddled a dozen parking spaces and its washing machine idle produced a black exhaust that clung to the spreading palms. A line had formed by the bus's closed door. Michael headed towards it.

"God, I hope this isn't ours," Sally said, eyeing the bus. "Not even the Taliban would ride in that thing."

"Come on," Becca answered. "It'll make you strong." She caught up with her father who'd joined the line. "See anyone you know?"

"They must be from another war," Michael whispered. "They all look old."

Becca did a quick survey. "Sorry, Daddy," she answered, "but they're your age. They just aren't as well preserved."

A slim black man dressed in a gray uniform and carrying a covered coffee mug walked up behind them. He moved to the head of the line and opened the bus's door.

"Good morning, folks," he said from the top step. "I'm James." I'll be driving you today on your Parris Island adventure where you'll observe the training of America's finest warriors." A course of Oorahs rose from the line. "Sounds like you guys have been here before," James said. "Thanks for coming and welcome aboard. We'll have you back in the Corps in about twenty minutes."

Inside the bus, the line moved slowly, passengers taking the first empty seat, forcing the following passengers to navigate the narrow aisle towards the rear.

"Excited, Daddy?" Becca asked from her seat behind him.

"Yeah, baby," he answered. He looked around. "I just hope the excitement's not too much for these old guys."

Becca patted his shoulder. "Sorry, I got a little carried away back there. It's like I'm being teased by some evil spirit that won't let me forget, yet he won't let me remember. Plus I sensed Mom this morning. I've never felt that before. I think she's trying to warn me."

"Just keep trying to remember," her father answered. His voice was tired. She knew this wasn't his favorite subject. He always listened, but he didn't believe her. "Doesn't seem like much else you can do."

The bus started forward. "I'll try to give you a little history on the way over," James said over the mic, "but everything is pretty much like you guys left it including these narrow streets that sure weren't built for this big, blue bus." He turned left onto a four-lane road.

"This is Ribaut Road," he said, fitting the bus into a narrow lane. "It's named after a French sea captain, Jean Ribaut. He built a fort on Parris Island. Long story short, he got captured by the Spanish and executed down in Florida for being Protestant." James smiled into his large rear-view mirror. "I guess some people take their religion mighty seriously." A slight chuckle rose from his passengers. "Tough crowd," he said, "but now we're getting ready to meet Sergeant Rock."

They crossed an elevated bridge over Battery Creek and exited onto a palm-lined causeway.

"What does MCRD stand for?" Becca asked, as they stopped at the Parris Island gate. A poster-perfect Marine dressed in khaki and blue blocked their path.

"Marine Corps Recruit Depot," Michael answered. James opened the door and the Marine stepped inside. He stood silently for a moment, his harsh eyes passing from seat to seat.

"You people didn't get enough last time," he growled. He shook his head. "Well, you'll be sorry you came back. You'll never make it off this island again." He looked at James. "You know what to do."

The bus was silent. Wives turned to husbands whose eyes were locked to the front. A smile eased onto the Marine's tanned face.

"Just wanted to bring back some memories, folks," he said. "Thanks for what you did and enjoy your day." He gave a quick salute. "*Semper Fi*," he said softly, before stepping off the bus.

"*Semper Fi*," the men answered in unison.

"I thought he had you for a minute," Sally said to Michael. "You looked a little worried."

"You know," Michael answered. "He did have me going for a minute. These guys can get away with murder out here."

The bus followed a narrow causeway onto the island, crossing Archer's Creek before entering an oak-shrouded park complete with grills and picnic tables.

"Are you sure we're on the right island?" Becca asked. "Where's the barbed wire and guard towers?" She turned to her father. "We've paid good money to stay in resorts that weren't this pretty."

"You'll see in a minute," Michael answered. "Besides, a lot of guys died trying to escape across that marsh. They'd hide in those trees and go into the water at night. Pluff mud got them before they reached open water. Sometimes, they didn't even find the bones."

"That's true," a drawn man in the next seat added. "It's like quicksand. The more they struggle, the deeper they sink and the crabs don't leave much." He turned back towards his window.

"See," Michael said. "I told you this was a tough place."

Palm trees replaced oaks as they travelled further inland, gliding past old brick barracks before turning onto a narrow, asphalt road. James picked up his mic.

"We're coming up to Leather Neck Square," he said. "It's named after an area the Marines controlled in Vietnam. It's used for hand-to-hand combat and the Confidence Course is straight ahead."

Outside, camouflaged Marine recruits squared off against each other, tossing their opponents into the soft sand, before finishing them off with lethal blows to the throat.

"I love it," Michael said "They can have me back." He looked at Sally. "Aren't you pretty good at this stuff?"

"I could take you," she answered.

"Confidence course coming up," Michael said. "I'll settle up with you later."

"Promise," Sally said. She let her hand run down his leg.

"Pay attention," Michael answered. "You might learn something."

Ahead, other Marine recruits climbed rope and log obstacles that disappeared into the tall Carolina pines. One recruit clung to a crossbar, four stories up, frozen in place. Three Drill Instructors waited beneath him. "Get your ass up there, maggot," one yelled, "or I'm coming up there to prove that chickens can fly."

"Why do they call it a 'Confidence Course'?" Becca asked. "That poor guy sure doesn't have any."

"Because it gives you confidence that you can overcome your fear of heights," Michael answered.

"Suppose he can't?"

"Then they'll give him something else to be afraid of." He laughed. "Like those D.I.s. He's more afraid of them than he is of going up. Fear's a strong motivator."

"It's cruel," Becca answered. The bus began to move, circling back around. She turned to watch the struggling recruit. "It gives that sadistic pack an excuse to abuse the weak."

"Becca," Sally said. "He came here to test himself; to overcome his fears. Those sergeants are just helping him. You'd be surprised to see what you can do when you have no choice."

"You always have a choice," Becca answered.

"Not always," Sally said. She looked out at the recruit and back at Becca. She shook her head slowly. "Not always."

"Heading for some shooting," James said turning onto a gravel road, past a line of open, white sheds stuffed with recruits. "These guys are learning how to hit a man at five hundred yards," James said. "There's no misses allowed, but if you do, a lady named Maggie will embarrass you real good." A wave of laughter passed through the bus. "Don't worry, ladies," James said. "Any of these gentlemen can explain Miss Maggie. She's probably the first lady they saw on this island."

They rolled past the white huts to where a set of metal bleachers faced each other across a grassy field. James pulled the bus behind the first set of bleachers and stopped.

"This is the 'Combat Shooting Range,'" he announced through the mic. I'll be leaving you here for now." He opened the door. Distant popping noises rode in on the humid air.

"M16s," Sally said, as they worked their way down the aisle. "An AK's louder. You learn to tell the difference. Now tell me about Maggie."

Michael smiled. "It's actually called 'Maggie's Drawers,'" he said, stepping down from the bus. "Maggie's Drawers is a red flag they wave if you completely miss your target. Nobody wants to see Maggie's Drawers."

CHAPTER EIGHT

Marine Sergeant Nate Forrest tugged at his cammie's tight sleeves. His shoulder wound had healed and the doctors had allowed him to begin lifting. The results showed. He liked the effect. *Got to look the part*, he thought, flexing his biceps, *even if I am an imposter*. He glanced at the Sergeant's chevrons pinned to his collar. He had them fooled. He wore the same uniform, spoke their lingo—a strange mixture of profanity and acronyms—but he was different. They didn't know. No one did.

He'd done well, promoted to Sergeant, had a chest full of medals; Purple Heart, Bronze Star, and a handful of "I was there" ribbons that hung from his Dress Blue blouse, where they invited the caress of gentle hands who softly asked, "What's that one for?" He never answered, *"That's for killing people,"* though that's what he wanted to say; not for the shock value but because it was true.

He looked at his nametag. It said Forrest. *It should say Imposter*, he thought, like the novel he read last semester in French Literature; a story about a priest that lost his faith but continued to perform his duties. That's what he'd done, but he'd had enough. Today was his last day.

His lost faith had been hate, blind hate, produced on command, mixed with a crusader's faith that allowed no doubt. *Necessary*, he admitted, but his was gone; spent in a sniper's perch in Fallujah on a cold November morning. It wasn't his fault. They kept coming; he kept shooting. "Sixteen" they told him later. He hadn't counted, but it had been enough.

Beside him, a squad of Marine Recruits awaited his command. They didn't know. He was good at his job. They'd seen him in action, showing them how it was done, instinct shooting, willing your bullet to its target, not thinking, just doing, the way a quarterback hits a wide receiver. He never missed.

He'd been a sniper too; different shooting, calculated and slow, the distant target dying silently, a red mist filling his scope, confirming his kill. He'd served two tours; the first in Iraq, then a second in Afghanistan that ended in a rocky field near Marjah, where his talents were not enough to save him or his best friend.

His skills came naturally, a country boy from the South Carolina swamps. He'd grown up in the woods, stalking squirrels, graduating to deer, watching his father and grandfather hunt, moving patiently, then finishing the job.

By twelve, he could shoot with the men, the shooting matches held after the hunt, the backstop an old tree, the cross-shaped target carved with the knife that skinned the deer. A secret brown bag was passed around before the shooting, skipping him though, and his grandfather. It was his heritage, they said, watching him shoot. That was what did it. It was in his name, Nathan Bedford Forrest, his great-great-grandfather, whose harsh eyes peered down at him from the wall of his grandmother's parlor.

It was a burden, the family name; the others felt its warrior call, his grandfather in Korea and his father in Vietnam. Now he'd had his war. Part of the tradition he'd broken; the preparation at the Citadel with its gray uniforms and Friday parades. He started, maybe he hadn't tried. It wasn't much . . . an Ashley Hall girl, a few beers, the motorcycle on the bar at Big John's. He'd been scared, but he'd ridden it anyway. He wasn't hurt bad, but between the cops, the fake ID, and the girl's father, he'd proven a little high profile for the Citadel. "Maybe he could come back next year his advisor said. Maybe, but now he needed redemption.

He'd told them on the ride home. His father didn't say much. He understood. His mother understood too, but she cried anyway. He hadn't needed a sales pitch. He knew he'd enlist when he walked in the door. It had to be worthwhile. He wanted infantry; the Marine Recruiter made him a better offer: Scout/Sniper, MOS 0317.

Nate was waiting for the tour bus. It came every Saturday morning, waddling in across Leatherneck Square, depositing its cargo of former Marines. Gunny Kearns called it a pilgrimage, a pilgrimage to the God of Eagle, Globe and Anchor, the Marine Corps emblem they'd worshipped here before being sent forth to carry out the Corp's commandments. 'Thou shall not kill' wasn't among them.

The bus was coming. Nate could hear its ancient diesel, straining in the soft sand before easing as it reached the gravel, heading towards Gunny Kearns' hideout; a shed filled with targets and computers, whose plywood walls smelled of the coffee of four wars.

The bus flushed Kearns. He exited slowly, straightening his DI hat as he walked. His pace was measured, balanced, his arms swinging evenly, a march he did by habit. Kearns strode to the bus, halting, then pivoting, a parade-ground left face, directing the passengers to the bleachers like a traffic cop.

Nate watched the unloading, nothing unexpected; always older guys, no kids, only wives or girlfriends, no trophies here, not in the three months he'd been watching, not until today.

The trophy came first, pretty, coal black hair, steered by her captor: big, older, camo jacket, trailed by a blonde girl, young, skinny, tanned, and frowning. He watched her climb, her faded canvas shorts and white shirt moving upward, reaching the top, poised like a princess surveying her kingdom, joining the camo king and his queen. He named her "Princess White Shirt."

Kearns' briefing started with history, Corps history, two hundred forty years of tradition. Nate listened. He wanted to add, "unmarked by progress". He whispered it to himself then checked the recruits. They were true believers: Pure, cleansed, and ready for sacrifice. Such comments were not for their ears, not yet, not from an imposter.

Kearns' voice was strong, yet soothing, the kind cultivated by airline pilots, calming passengers down while describing the flames roaring outside their window. He'd heard it before; Kearns' voice, rising over the hell of Fallujah, calming him, steadying his hands as he outdueled the minaret sniper.

Iraq was two years ago. The advance was stalled when he reported in.

"Go find Gunny Kearns," the XO screamed, three radios barking. It was a surreal moment, a history question from the company Gunny. Bullets whistled, chipping stone, spraying dust, then skipping away. Kearns pulled him inside. The stone walls muffled the angry sounds. It was his first day. There was no welcome, just, "I see you're a college boy?" It seemed a challenge, both intellectual and physical. All he could say was, "three years."

Kearns nodded. "Know what Churchill said about getting shot at and missed?" he asked. Nate didn't know, but the distraction helped.

"Said it was the most exhilarating feeling on earth," Kearns said. "Your experiences bear that out?"

"I don't know, Gunny," he'd answered. "I'll get back to you on that."

He was in hell. The terrifying ride, the up-armored HUMVEE, dodging tracers, fifty-caliber chugging above him, returning fire. Now here, bloodied Marines, radios screaming, chaos epitomized and a crazy Gunny.

He had a duel to fight. He knew about duels, Stalingrad, Carlos Hathcock; there was history, sniper history, fed to him by both family and Corps. They gave him maps, one official, colorful like a tour map, others dirty, hand drawn, sketched by men who'd fled from where he was going.

"X" marked the spot. The sniper was in the minaret. Nate studied the maps, playing them across his eyes like a movie, then he stepped outside.

Kearns followed. "I'm your spotter," he said. Nate nodded, focused now, the maps coming in line with the city. They moved forward. "Well", Kearns said, pivoting around, checking the rear then facing him, "was Churchill right?"

"Maybe, Gunny," he'd answered, his back against a stone wall, Kearns behind him, the minaret visible now, rising above the smoke. He saw movement, the black keffiyeh creeping through the gray smoke; a three-hundred meter snap-shot that produced his first kill. He turned back to Kearns. "Churchill was right," Nate said, "but only if 'exhilarating' and 'scared shitless' mean the same thing."

Kearns finished the history. Nate watched the recruits, thirteen men, just like a regular squad, all camoed up, weighted down with web gear and helmets, M16s resting across their laps. They looked ready, but he knew they weren't. You could only teach so much. The rest they learned when they got there. That's where the Corps's Gunny Kearns came in.

Nate listened as Kearns described the course.

"We call it the John Wayne Course," he told them, "because John Wayne played a Marine in a couple of movies and because in the movies, every Marine shoots from the hip. That's what we do here." Kearns paused and pointed towards Nate. "Sergeant Forrest will lead our patrol." Nate removed his cover and waved towards the bleachers, waiting for Kearns to finish. "We'll follow him," Kearns continued. "On this mission, I'll serve as your guide." Kearns was silent for a moment, pacing, then turning back to face his audience, chin in hand, like there was something he'd forgotten.

"You know," he said, his voice at its most folksy, "considering this is a live-fire exercise, our civilian casualties to date have been remarkably low."

Nate watched the group. The casualty remark always caught them by surprise. They looked at each other, eyes questioning, knowing Kearns was kidding, yet not quite sure; distant rifle fire added fuel to their doubts. A few seconds passed, then Kearns laughed and they laughed with him, like they'd known all along.

Princess White Shirt didn't laugh. She shook her head and frowned at Kearns. Camo King reached over and ruffled her hair. She straightened it with a head flip, gave him a big smile, and they started down from the bleachers.

Nate took a deep breath, ready to make his last trip downrange. "Squad, Ten-Hut," he yelled, and twenty-six boots hit the deck. They were eager to begin; ready to be tested and afraid of failing. He could see it in their eyes. It wasn't combat but it was close, going into the bush against a hidden enemy.

He told them what he'd told them all week. "He who shoots first, wins. React, don't think; put the first round low." A white patch slipped into his peripheral vision. She was leaning against the shed, looking back towards the bleachers where Kearns was handing out earplugs. Nate focused back on the recruits. "If you aim low," he said, "sometimes you get a lucky ricochet, and if you don't, he'll duck, and you'll have an aiming point."

Nate looked towards the firing line. The red range flag flew beside an ambulance manned by two Navy Corpsmen: Marine Corps requirements for live-fire training. Kearns had his group in position, the target control box in his hand. Nate didn't see Princess White Shirt. Probably back on the bus. He turned back to his recruits. "Any questions?" he asked. No one spoke. "Good," he said, "fall in at the head of the firing line."

Nate followed the chorus of "Oorahs," positioning himself behind the first recruit, Private Cash. A path cut by a thousand boots formed the firing line. It traveled across a clearing where sand-bagged bunkers hid their cardboard enemies. "Lock and load," Nate ordered, and Cash slapped a magazine into his rifle and chambered a round.

The clearing was a warm-up. They'd practiced there yesterday and uncovered dirt, freshened by their bullets exposed the targets. Kearns hit a switch, the target rose; the lead recruit fired twice, then ran to the rear of the squad. Nate studied their techniques. Overall, they were good. A couple were slow, not trusting their instincts, aiming instead of pointing. He made mental notes for later. Cash returned to his position.

"Follow the trail into those woods," Nate said, pointing towards a clump of oaks that grew along the marshes of Archer's Creek. Cash moved towards the trees. Nate knew how he felt. It was like walking through a House of Horrors—something was going to grab you, you just didn't know when. It was the same way in combat: No warning, "a killing event"—the manual called it—bullets or explosives blasting you into hell before you had a chance to say your prayers or cry out for your mother.

Beneath the oaks the trail grew wider, following an old logging road kept clear by the Marine boots that stalked its sandy surface. Nate glanced behind him, checking each rifle. He didn't like being in front of twelve weapons but at least they were all pointed in the right direction. Kearns trailed the last recruit with Princess White Shirt close behind. *Bet camo king made her come,* he thought; otherwise, she'd be on the bus.

Kearns had options. Nate knew Kearns was watching Cash, making him sweat, waiting for a mistake. Cash moved forward, his head dipping, then rising, pivoting from left to right, scanning close then far, the way he was trained. The trail curved left, then dipped towards a wooden footbridge laid across a tidal creek. Cash stopped. Sweat rolled down his neck and darkened his jacket. Keeping his eyes forward, he removed his right hand from his rifle and reached for his canteen.

It was quiet. Even the civilians were still. A slight breeze slipped across the marsh, cloaking them in a salty vapor, masking the target's swoosh as it rose from its hiding place. It seemed to strut, swaying in the grass, mocking Cash, who dropped his canteen and fumbled with his rifle. He had four seconds. It wasn't enough. The target fired first. Explosions tore through the air, their noises trapped by the natural canopy.

Nate charged towards Cash. "You're a dead man," he screamed, slapping Cash's rifle on safe and spinning the trembling recruit towards him. "Report your death in action." Cash stared at him, his eyes blank. "Like on the booby trap course," Nate said, "or did you forget that too?"

"Sir," Cash said, his voice loud but shaky, "Private Cash reports his death in action as a direct result of his own stupidity."

Nate grabbed Cash's canteen and slammed it into his chest. "Died for a drink of water." He pointed back down the trail towards the recruits. "They're dead too. An Al-Qaeda patrol just wiped out a Marine squad because you were thirsty. I can see them now; searching the bodies, jabbering among themselves, and God help any poor devil who's still alive." He stared at Cash. "You happy now, Private?" Cash's lips trembled and his eyes welled with tears.

"Get to the rear, crybaby," Nate said, shoving Cash back down the trail. "I don't need you up here, screwing up my Marine Corps."

Nate followed Cash. Behind them recruits lay sprawled along the trail. The civilians clustered around Kearns. "That's far enough," Nate said, when they passed the last recruit. Cash turned to face him but Nate pointed towards the wood line. "Look in the bushes," he said, "that's where the bad guys are."

Nate glanced at Kearns. He thought he detected a slight smile but he wasn't sure. Kearns was hard to read. Not so Princess White Shirt. Her green eyes cut through him like a laser. Jogging back to the front, he could still feel the wound. He wondered how she'd look if she saw Private Cash's bloody body lying along the trail. He wanted to ask her. Instead, he yelled back over his shoulder, "Next man up."

Nate watched the next recruit double time towards him. He was a tall, skinny kid from Tennessee named McCoy. Yesterday, Nate had been impressed by McCoy's relaxed, natural shooting, but now McCoy looked anything but relaxed; his knees trembled and his breathing was rapid and shallow. Nate glanced back at Kearns, then turned to McCoy.

"You know who Sergeant York was?" he asked.

Nate watched McCoy's breathing slow. The question had surprised him.

"Yes, sir," McCoy answered, "he was from Tennessee and the best shot in the whole Army."

"That's true, Private," Nate said, studying McCoy. "The question is, could he outshoot a Marine?"

McCoy hesitated. Nate crossed his arms and waited. "Well, Private?" he asked when McCoy didn't answer.

"No, sir," McCoy answered, "nobody can outshoot a Marine."

"Good answer, Private," Nate said, "now lock and load and let's give Tennessee another reason to be proud."

Kearns popped a target, just as McCoy's foot hit the bridge, forcing him to fire off balance. It didn't matter. McCoy fired first, dropping the target and another one Kearns popped closer in. Nate eased up behind McCoy. "Sergeant York would be mighty proud," he whispered, "now clear that weapon and send the next man up."

Cash's screwup and McCoy's performance calmed and inspired the remaining recruits: Targets popped, M16s fired, and targets dropped. Kearns rationed the targets, leaving two for Cash, who dropped both. Nate walked over to Cash. "Nice shooting, Private," he said. "Now wipe that silly grin off your face before you give away our position."

When they reached the bleachers, Nate waved Kearns and his group by, waiting for them to be seated before bringing the squad forward. Salt and cordite hung in the humid air. Nate felt almost high. He inhaled deeply. A line from *Apocalypse Now* crept into his mind. He'd watched it with Kearns in Iraq's "Green Zone". It was Kearns' favorite movie.

"I love the smell of napalm in the morning," he whispered to Kearns.

"You're smelling the crap you scared out of those recruits," Kearns whispered back. He nodded his head and gave Nate a half-smile. "I'll tell you something else, college boy. You're going to miss it."

Nate turned the recruits over to their Drill Instructors, and Kearns took charge of the tour. Rifle fire from adjoining ranges continued to echo as he slipped away from the bleachers and across the parking lot to his car.

His Miata's top was down. Nate unbuckled his pistol belt and tossed it on to the passenger seat. Sweat soaked his cammie jacket. Only the thought of being hassled by the gate MPs made him keep it on. He didn't need that; not on his last day.

He turned to watch Kearns herd his charges back to the bus. Camo King's trio had him surrounded. The big guy was telling war stories. Nate could tell by the way he held his arms; left arm out with the right one by his side. *That's how you hold an invisible rifle,* he thought. An invisible rifle to kill the invisible enemies that followed you home, no matter where you fought your war.

Gravel crunched behind him and he turned to see a classic, mustard yellow Toyota Land Cruiser pull into the parking lot; the type you see on *National Geographic,* herding rhinos, not wheeled through grocery store parking lots by frustrated soccer moms. He knew its owner well; Sergeant Charlene Stone was the vehicle's soul mate. She named it "The Yellow Peril".

"You kill any bad guys today? Sergeant Forrest?" she asked, climbing out from the doorless Toyota. She wore her Sam Brown belt and a 9 millimeter Beretta covered her hip.

"Fourteen bad guys and one recruit. Your end of the island secure?"

"Yep. No invasion today. The taxpayers should be happy."

"We need to stop the tourist invasion," Nate said. "Makes it hard to train."

"Lighten up, Marine. The American people need to see how we waste their tax money."

"That's just it, Charlie," Nate answered. He could still feel the hate in Princess White Shirt's eyes. "They want us to treat these privates like Boy Scouts, lead them into the depths of hell against the world's worst monsters and bring them back unhurt. Is it just me, or is there a contradiction there?"

"Man, you're entirely too serious," Charlie answered. She patted the Beretta. "Besides, you'll feel better when you pay off your debt."

Nate shook his head. "If I'd known you made the Olympic tryouts, I'd never let you talk me into a shooting match, especially with a pistol."

"Just be at 'The Yankee' with a fat wallet and you can probably buy my silence." She removed her campaign hat. It hid a mass of tightly curled brown hair. A line of sweat rolled down her forehead. "A cold beer's going to taste mighty good," she said, wiping away the sweat with the back of her hand.

"Isn't that hot?" Nate asked. "The hair, I mean. Even my high and tight feels like a blanket."

"Not as hot as when it's down."

"You ever wear it down?"

"I will tonight," she answered, reaching for a strategically placed pin that dropped her hair to her shoulders.

Nate stared at the transformation. "Wow," he said. "That's a major change."

"I'll take that as a compliment," Charlie said, "now tell me something; are you really getting out?"

"Afraid so."

"To teach history?"

"So we can fraternize."

She punched him on the shoulder. "Fraternize is male code for sex, and I wouldn't fraternize if you were the last Marine on this island. School teacher!"

"You make it sound like a crime."

"It is. What kind of a wimpy job is that for a guy like you? I'll come by that school every day, eat your lunch, and fart in your classroom. Where're you going to teach anyway?"

"If I tell you, I'll probably go hungry, but it's not far from here. A little island out towards the beach called Saint Helena."

"Shouldn't be too hard to find." She looked at her watch. "I've got to go. I guess you could give me a good-bye hug. You know, in case you don't make it tonight. I know how delicate history teachers are."

"I'll be there, Charlie," Nate answered, "but I'll take the hug." He stretched out his arms and she walked into them. Her tight grip surprised him, then he felt her hips twist and found himself lying at her feet.

"Every day, history teacher, and it better be good." She helped him up.

"The lunch or the sex?"

"The lunch. You'll have to find some sweet, little schoolmarm for the sex, and I bet it won't be good."

The bus lumbered towards them, its diesel roar ending their discussion. They waved at the departing tourists who waved back from behind their tinted windows.

Becca looked down at the two Marines. "Daddy," she said seriously, "you don't think they mate and multiply?"

"No," he answered, listening to the D.I.'s cadence as they marched their recruits back to their barracks. "If they did, Superman would be out of a job."

James took them for a quick ride around the island, stopping at the rappelling tower and the Iwo Jima statue before heading back to Beaufort.

"Ready to shop 'til you drop?" Sally asked Michael, as they pulled into the hotel parking lot.

"Nope. I've got to make some money. Why don't you and Becca go spend some?"

"I'll pass too," Becca said. "I've got tons of work to do at my apartment." She paused at the door. "I'll see you guys for dinner tonight."

"Seven, okay?" Sally asked, following her out.

"Great," Becca answered. "Anywhere but a mess hall is fine with me."

Sally watched Becca walk away. She'd tried to spare her, but God must have had other plans. Her prayers for the dreams to stop went unanswered. Now they were growing clearer

She wanted more time, but she didn't have it. Hurried missions often failed, but it had to be tonight. She and Michael were leaving in the morning. Later, might mean too late. She'd reviewed her plan at the rappelling tower, complete with backup. All she needed was a little luck.

Sally window-shopped her way down Bay Street. She bought a sailing book and chart for Michael and a jean hat for Becca, moving slowly south towards her ultimate objective.

She'd checked the hardware store online and spotted it from Becca's porch. With its brick columns and cluttered windows, it would have looked right at home in West Virginia.

Inside, it was just like she expected: tall shelves that rose above wooden floors, a mixture of hardware for the locals and toys for the tourists. She wandered over into sporting goods. Hidden between the hunting supplies and camping equipment, she found what she came for: A climbing section complete with ropes and hookups, just like its web page said. Things were looking up. She made her selection quickly and walked to the register. She paid with cash. "No bag," she said, opening her purse, "I'll just stuff them in here." She placed the climbing rope under Becca's jean hat, not that Michael ever paid any attention to what she bought, but attention to detail was an ingrained habit.

"Not many places to climb around here," the elderly gentleman remarked, as he rang up her purchases. She guessed him to be the owner.

"There are, if you're a Marine," she answered in her best southern accent. "They're for my husband out at Parris Island. He likes to practice on his own."

"Ambitious fellow."

"No," she answered, giving him a wifely smile, "he's just crazy like the rest of them."

CHAPTER NINE

Sally slipped silently out of bed. The sound of Michael's snoring comforted her. She paused to listen, then dressed. Next she checked the climbing rope, gloves and seat harness hidden in her purse.

Sally looked over at Michael. His mouth was locked in a tight oval, while his lips vibrated in a series of snorts that rose and fell with his breathing. The big steak dinner, complete with three drinks would have probably done the trick, but her double cowgirl performance was better than Ambien. He'd never wake up.

Their plane left Savannah at 6:15 tomorrow morning. They'd said their good-byes to Becca at the restaurant. Tomorrow was her first day at school and she'd wanted to turn in early. She'd been quiet during the meal. Sally sensed she was ready to be alone. She'd help Michael remember this in the morning after the body was found. It would be sad. Becca had so much promise, but her mother's death had haunted her and the dream with its ghostly figure kept the wound fresh, not allowing it to heal.

Alone, in a strange town, it had proven to be too much. Maybe, Sally thought, the figure ordered her to jump. It was a thought worth considering, especially if she found Becca's computer unlocked. She'd try anyway. A note would provide closure and Michael deserved that. She really did love him and after Becca was gone, their marriage would be complete. *What God has joined, let no man cast asunder.* God was on her side. She could feel it.

Sally eased the door closed, glanced around, and headed away from the lights of Bay Street. She'd memorized a tourist map of downtown Beaufort. She was a block north and a mile west of Becca's apartment.

She fought the urge to hurry, keeping her pace deliberately casual, pausing occasionally to read a historical plaque. Her dark jeans and green shirt merged into the darkness. "Blend in," the Special Ops guys said. "Look like you belong."

Nothing about her stood out. She was just a tourist taking a late stroll on a hot summer night. At the corner of Port Republic and West Streets, she nodded to an elderly couple walking a frisky golden retriever. *Two blocks,* she thought, glancing back at the couple. "Two blocks to Operation *Dream Killer.*" She smiled at the name. Her life was full of dead dreams. Tonight, that would change.

Nate Forrest propped his feet on the railing that lined The Yankee's deck and leaned back in his chair. Beneath him the Beaufort River gurgled, forcing its way around the barnacle-covered pilings. He wished Charlie would hurry back with his beer. His mood was perfect, not drunk, not sober but light, in control but only loosely, like skiing on the edge. If he didn't get a beer soon, he'd crash.

He turned towards the lighted bar. Charlie was stuffing a bill into the tip jar. He watched her pick up the drinks, one dark, one light, a beer for him and a coke for her. She hesitated at the screen door. He started to get up, but she opened it with a twist of her hips, rotating through, letting it close softly behind her.

"You okay, Nathan Bedford Forrest?" she asked, sliding onto the bench beside him. "I'd hate for anything to happen to the descendant of a true Confederate hero." She handed him his beer and dropped his change on the table. "Of course, we did kick you guys' asses."

"Yankee propaganda perpetuated by an inferior northern school system," Nate answered. He took a sip of beer. "If you don't believe we won, look over there." He pointed across the river where the lights that lined eastern Bay Street created an abstract of yellow and gray as they danced across the choppy water.

"Those aren't the homes of a conquered people," he said. "They're a living museum defended by the original invaders. Now, I'd call that a victory."

"Wow," Charlie said. She slid up onto the railing. "You really are into that history crap. What else turns you on?"

"You do," he said. It was an automatic response to what he considered to be a flirting invitation. Except with Charlie, you never knew. He liked her, but there'd never been any attraction. She was different, direct, and she didn't play games. The range instructors nicknamed her "Attila the Nun".

Charlie sat silently, not responding, her back to him, staring out over the river. She wore faded jean shorts with a pink cotton top and her thick, brown hair flowed across her shoulders. She looked soft sitting there and strangely vulnerable. He had trouble picturing her back at the range, shouting orders to trembling recruits.

Charlie swung back around, pushed off the rail, and landed beside him with a thump.

"Let's get you home, wimpy boy," she said, grabbing his hand and pulling him to his feet. His body was relaxed. *I'm in neutral,* he thought. *I'll go in any direction I'm pushed.*

He staggered slightly. He'd drunk more than he thought. He squeezed her hand as he regained his balance. She squeezed back. Her skin felt soft but her firm grip steadied him.

"I'm driving," she said, still holding his hand, "and don't give me any shit."

"So, you're just like the other Marines," he said, "get a guy drunk, drive him home, and take advantage of him."

She jerked her hand away. "Listen, teacher man, in your condition there's nothing to take advantage of. Now chug that beer and let's move. I've got an island to defend in the morning."

Nate slipped the almost full, plastic beer cup under his T-shirt. "Liquid courage," he said, watching Charlie frown, "for the ride home in the 'Yellow Peril.'"

Sally stood in the shadows next to the park's cannons. She wasn't hiding, but she'd be invisible to all but the most observant eye. Across Bay Street, Becca's porch lay shrouded in darkness, shielded from the street lights by the tall palms that swayed beneath it. She turned to watch the traffic trickle in across the Lady's Island Bridge. Most of it continued straight, though a few cars turned left on Bay Street. No cars turned right toward her. That was good. The fewer people that saw her, the better.

She waited until the traffic cleared, then crossed Bay Street. She scurried through the light, and through an open iron gate before returning to the darkness. She looked up at Becca's porch. It was only two stories high. Three would be better.

Sally removed the rope and climbing harness from her purse then stuffed the purse behind a brick column. She felt the rope and carabiners. She could rig a climbing harness in the dark, but the dim street light helped. She thought about Becca as she worked. She was no longer a person but an object—an obstacle that had to be removed. Her dreams were becoming clearer. It was only a matter of time. *Becca was wrong*, Sally thought, remembering their Parris Island talk: *Sometimes you don't have a choice*. Becca had left her with no option.

Sally debated another choice: break Becca's neck before tossing her from the porch or wait to see if the fall did the job. Her thoughts were calm; no emotion, weighing her options: Just a job that needed doing. How she had gotten this way, she wasn't sure. Afghanistan had played a part, but she suspected something else: a survival gene formed in the harsh West Virginia Mountains, a gene that remained dormant until needed. *Kind of like The Hulk*, she thought, *only I don't turn green.*

She looked back up at the porch. Best to wait, she decided; leave things natural. She'd have time to check the body. If Becca survived the fall, she'd do it then. It wouldn't take long; just a quick snap. She looked back up at the porch and took a deep breath. It was time to begin.

She uncoiled the rope, freeing just enough to clear the banister, then tossed it towards the porch. A bumping noise shocked her. *The rocking chair!* she thought. How could she have forgotten that? She froze, listening, watching for lights in Becca's apartment, cursing to herself, listening to the rocker's motion slow before finally stopping.

There were no lights. She retrieved her rope, shortened it and threw again, watching the rope clear the railing. She pulled the rope towards her before running it through her carabiner. She tested the anchor with her weight. It felt solid. She checked Bay Street. No one was there. H-Hour had arrived. She looped the rope around her leg and began to climb. A few seconds later, she swung her leg over the banister and pulled herself onto Becca's porch.

She stuck her landing like a gymnast, softly with no extra steps. She looked around, then tied the release rope to her knot. She walked silently across the porch. The surrounding houses were dark. She studied them, searching the windows and alcoves, scanning the shadows, assuring herself that no one was there. She didn't need another Becca.

Lights from an unseen car flickered through the trees. Sally eased herself to the porch floor. The lights grew brighter, then faded as the car began its descent from the bridge. She high- crawled across the porch towards Becca's door. She knew from her visit it wasn't locked. No need to lock an upstairs door with no outside stairs. She reached up and twisted the handle. It turned stiffly, releasing with a soft click.

Sally pushed against the door. It felt stuck. She pushed harder. The door loosened, then reluctantly opened. Sally stared into the dark hallway. Becca's door was on the left. Sally paused, picturing the layout. Becca would be in bed. She'd use a sleeper hold, grabbing her from behind, controlling her with her legs. There'd be a brief struggle, but in eight seconds Becca would be asleep. She'd never wake up. *There're worse ways to die*, she thought, moving forward. She'd seen a few.

She'd reached Becca's door when the spotlight hit. She closed her right eye, conserving her night vision, and turned to watch. The light danced across the banister, lingering along her rope, following it to the yard below before fading to darkness. She opened her eye and waited. It had to be cops. Who else rode around shining spotlights? Beneath her she heard two car doors slam. Someone was coming. They'd spotted her rope. She looked at Becca's door. She was so close. It was like Afghanistan: Her position had been compromised. It was time to abort.

Sally backed out the door and crawled across the porch, grabbing her rope before giving the hallway a parting glance. She looked up into the darkened sky. God was watching. For some reason he'd given Becca a second chance. How many lives could this girl have?

"Sleep tight," she whispered to Becca's door before stepping off into the darkness, "and no dreams."

Charlie's Land Cruiser bounced and groaned crossing the Lady's Island Bridge; slammed by the connectors that pieced together the concrete slabs.

"Damn, Charlie," Nate said, as the last connector sent them airborne, soaking his shirt with beer. "I've ridden in smoother riding tanks." He gulped the remaining beer and tossed the cup on the floor. "I could've driven, you know."

"Wuss," Charlie answered. "You'd be fish food, if I'd let you drive. Next week you'll be taking a leak sitting down, and I bet it goes downhill from there."

"I love it when you talk dirty to me," Nate said. He leaned across the console and put his head on her shoulder. Her long hair felt soft against his cheek.

A firm elbow forced him back across the console. "Then you should love the ass-kicking I'm about to give you." Charlie pulled her Toyota sharply against the curb. "I believe this is where you get out."

Nate stared at the girl across from him. She looked impatient, almost angry, ready for him to leave. "Thanks for tonight, Charlie," he said. "If you helped me out, I could get that goodbye hug."

"I don't do doors," Charlie said. "Not even for school teachers. And you got your hug."

"That was no hug," Nate said, pushing against the bare-metal door. "That was a body slam, and besides, your door's stuck."

Charlie leaned across and twisted the handle. The door refused to budge. "I usually leave the doors off," she said. "Try putting your shoulder into it."

Nate hit the door twice without result. "Pretend you're a man," Charlie said.

"It's your door," he answered. He coiled his body and slammed against the door knocking it off its hinges and dumping him on to the sidewalk.

"Charlie," Nate called out from his sitting position, "I think I need a little help."

"I think you need a lot of help," Charlie answered, climbing out her door. She bent down beside him and looked up at the stairs. "You live up there?"

"Afraid so," Nate answered. "Somehow it seems higher."

Charlie laughed. "The sidewalk's high to you right now. Come on, I guess I'll have to carry your sorry civilian ass."

They struggled up the stairs, Nate holding on to the railing with one arm and Charlie with the other.

"You're almost home," Charlie said. She dropped Nate on the platform at the top of the stairs. "At least it levels off from here." She pulled him to his feet. "You got a key?"

Nate rummaged through his pockets, finally producing a large, two-pronged, iron key. He held it up for her to see.

"Looks like a brig key."

"It's the key to paradise, my sweet Charlene. Now if you'll allow me."

Nate stepped in first. The hallway was dark and narrow. He ran his hand along the wall, feeling for a light switch. He'd only been here twice: once to look at the apartment and this afternoon when he had dropped by to throw in a few things before meeting Charlie.

He tried to visualize the hallway. The other apartment was on the right, just inside the door. The hallway went straight for a few feet then turned right. His door was about halfway down on the left. He felt Charlie's hand on his shoulder. "Can't you afford any lights," she whispered.

"I can't find a switch," he whispered back. "Just use your night vision. I'm down on the left." He started slowly, picking up the pace as his eyes adjusted to the darkness. He was at full stride when his right foot hit a stack of shipping boxes. Nate stumbled forward, his arms flailing against the wall before catching a door jamb and sliding to the floor

"Nate," Charlie called out. "You okay?"

"Yeah," he answered, resting his back against the door. "Why'd you attack me?"

"I didn't attack you yet," she answered, "but I might when I find you. Remember what I did to you in the fighting pit?"

Nate watched Charlie move towards him. It was like lying in a foxhole and using the sky as a backdrop. You always saw the enemy first. When she was just above him, he pounced.

"Payback time," he yelled, wrapping his legs around her waist, attempting to pull her down.

Charlie braced herself against the door. Nate pulled harder. The door groaned, then released, dumping them both inside.

Nate heard a scream. *That's not Charlie*, he thought. *Nothing could make her scream.* He remained still. Across the room a white-robed figure moved towards him. A butcher knife protruded from its right hand, its large blade reflecting the ambient light like a circling firefly.

"It's okay," Nate yelled. He rolled off Charlie and bounced to his feet. The fall had carried them halfway across the room. The figure retreated several steps but the knife continued to sway back and forth across its body. "I live across the hall," he continued. "We just fell through your door."

He yanked Charlie up. "We're leaving," he said. "Sorry to bother you." Pulling Charlie, he backed towards the door. The figure remained still and silent. Two beams of light trickled down the hallway, growing brighter as they came closer. They appeared in the doorway like two disjointed headlights.

"I don't know what's going on here," a deep southern voice said from behind the flashlights, "but I want everybody on the floor with their hands out front until we get things sorted out."

Nate's eyes swung from the flickering knife to the blinding lights. "Who the hell are you?" he asked over his shoulder. A hand came out of the darkness. It lifted him into the air by his collar before dropping him to the floor.

"Keep still, boy," the same voice commanded as Charlie dropped to the floor. The lights turned towards the robed figure.

"Princess White Shirt," Nate whispered to himself. He'd never forget those green eyes. It was like a drunken dream except now he felt sober.

"Now, little lady," the voice said, "I need you to drop that knife and join these other folks. I think you're the one that called, but from my point of view, things are a mite confusing."

Nate could now see the figure clearly. He watched Princess White Shirt lower the knife to her waist then let it fall, blade first towards his head.

"Damn it," he yelled, feeling the blade slice across his forehead. Blood flowed down his face. The figure by the door switched on a light and Nate saw two Beaufort police officers, guns drawn, standing over him. He read their name tags: Bennett and Welford.

"Everybody just relax," Bennett said. "Miss," he said to the girl, "if you could get a damp washcloth we might save this young fellow from bleeding to death."

"I'm Becca Noble," she said, rising to her feet and backing towards the kitchen, "and I called you." She looked back at Nate. "Sorry about the knife," she said. "I thought the police might think I was dangerous and I just wanted it out of my hands." She moved towards the kitchen then turned back towards Nate. "You look familiar," she said. "I've seen you somewhere before."

Charlie lifted herself from the floor. "What brought you guys out?" she asked, facing both officers. "You must have been in the hall when we fell through the door."

Bennett gave both Nate and Charlie a quick glance, then holstered his pistol. Welford did likewise.

"Miss Noble here called us," he answered, nodding towards Becca as she returned with the washcloth. "She thought she heard somebody on her front porch. We rode by and saw a rope, so we looped the block, came up and found this." He opened his arms in an expanding arch that encompassed the entire group.

Becca held the washcloth out to Nate. Her motion was slow and hesitant, like she was reaching out to a snarling dog.

"Thanks," Nate said. He leaned forward and snatched the washcloth.

"We're going to check the porch," Bennett said. "I'm sure we scared off anybody who might have been out there." He started towards the door, then paused. "It's probably nothing. A lot of people in these old buildings used rope ladders for fire escapes. Sometimes they fall on their own. I'd bet that's what we've got here: A case of the escaped, escape rope."

"Can we come?" Charlie asked. "I'd like to see what caused this ruckus."

"You and your friend caused this, as you say, ruckus," Becca said. She pointed her finger towards Nate, her thumb raised like a revolver's hammer. "I finally remember where I'd seen you. It was you on the rifle range abusing those recruits."

"Nate?" Charlie said. She stepped between Nate and Becca. "He's the biggest softie on the island." Becca stepped back, dropping her hand. Charlie reclosed the distance. "Something else, China doll; if you hadn't left enough boxes in the hall to outfit a battalion, we wouldn't have tripped, and I wouldn't have had the pleasure of making your acquaintance."

Bennett stepped between the two women. "Look," he said, "we need to check out that porch, not stand here squabbling amongst ourselves." He looked at his partner. "Welford, why don't you take the car back to the station? I'll walk back when I'm done. I don't think there's anything else to see."

Bennett led the group down the hallway and onto the porch. A sea breeze blew in across the river, swaying the rope against the banister. Bennett walked over to the rope, examining it from a distance, then approaching it slowly, shaking his head the entire time. Finally he picked it up.

"There won't be any prints," he said. "Too much friction. Got to wear gloves or the rope will fry your hands." He pulled the slender rope through his fingers. "Tell you something else: this is no escape rope. No, sir, this is a fine piece of climbing equipment. We use it on the SWAT team." He held the rope up for the others, moving it into the light that shone from Becca's apartment.

"Look at this; a carabineer and opposing figure eights. Whoever put this together was an experienced climber. He planned to rappel off here when he was done." He held the rope above his head. "See this," he said, pointing to a smaller rope that was looped over the larger one. "This is a release rope.

When our guy finished his business, he'd just pull this and get his rope back. You'd never know he'd been here. Must have left in a hurry."

Becca gasped. Her legs wobbled and she grabbed the porch's column for support. "I know this sounds crazy," she said, "but whoever killed my mother came here to kill me."

Bennett dropped the rope and stepped past Charlie and Nate towards Becca.

"Hey," he said. "Nobody's going to hurt you." He glanced quickly at Nate and Charlie. "Let's go back inside," he said to Becca, "and you can tell me what happened." He nodded towards Nate and Charlie "Why don't you two join us?"

"That an order or a request?" Nate asked.

"It's a request," Bennett answered, "but I'd take it mightily unkind if you refused."

Becca led them into her living room and sat on her couch. Bennett did a quick look around and sat beside her. He pulled a pad and pen from his shirt pocket. "Okay," he said to Becca, "Tell me your story and don't leave anything out."

Nate listened as Becca spoke. The whole thing didn't make much sense, yet, somehow he believed her. One thing was certain; she believed every word.

Bennett summarized when she finished.

"So," he said, "you think your mother's death wasn't an accident and that the figure in your dream is a real person who's trying to kill you?"

"I know it sounds crazy," Becca answered. "I never thought about anybody trying to hurt me until tonight. It was like I knew when I heard that noise that he had come for me. I think my mother warned me."

"Well," Bennett began in his slow drawl, "somebody that's pretty serious tried to get in here tonight. Now that doesn't make much sense from an economic point of view. I mean we got jewelry stores and all kind of other businesses almost next door. Why'd anybody go to all that trouble to climb up on your porch?"

"How about rape"? Nate asked. "You had several rapes near here last year, over by the university." Becca gasped and Nate felt Charlie's elbow dig into his side.

Bennett fixed Nate with a harsh stare. "You're a Marine, right, son? I mean with that haircut and all. It's funny though; most Marines don't know nothing about Beaufort, but you seem mighty well-informed."

"I'm from here," Nate answered. "My father's N.B Forrest. He's an attorney." He held Bennett's stare. "By the way, I was discharged today."

Bennett's face relaxed. "I know your daddy pretty well. He's not a bad fellow for an attorney. Knows lots of lawyer jokes. Keeps us laughing while he gets the guilty bastards off." He turned back to Becca. "Those rapes were solved last month and none of them involved a second story entry. Nope," he said running the rope through his fingers, "whoever belongs to this rope is a serious dude." Bennett formed the rope into a tight coil. "Real serious," he finally said, then glancing up, he tossed the rope to Nate. "You ever see one of these?"

"It's a climbing rope," Nate answered. "We use them on the rappelling tower out on the island." He passed the rope to Charlie then turned towards Bennett. "You think this guy's a Marine?"

"Could be," Bennett answered. "Could be." He looked back at Nate. "Might even be you two?"

"Us?" Nate asked. "You followed us down the hallway and the rope's on the front porch. Plus, I have a key."

"Well," Bennett answered, "I've got to start somewhere." He turned towards Becca. "We'll keep an eye out tonight, Ma'am, but I doubt whether he will come back. Remember, we're just around the corner." He looked at Nate and Charlie. "You two are free to go. Call me if you think of anything."

Nate turned to Becca. "Tell me your first name again?" he asked, as they watched Bennett walk down the hall.

"It's Becca, Mr. Forrest," she answered, "but I don't think we're going to be on a first name basis. Besides, tomorrow I'm going to look for a new place to live."

"You don't need to do that," Nate said. "You heard the cop. That guy probably wasn't after you. Even if he was, you're as safe here as anywhere; lots of people around and almost next door to the police station. Plus, I could help you turn this place into a real fortress, complete with overwhelming firepower."

Becca shook her head slowly. "You just don't get it, do you?" Her voice was low but its tone was harsh. "I don't need your protection or your advice. Furthermore, I don't like forts, I don't like guns, and after watching you bully those recruits, I don't like you."

"Okay," Nate answered, looking into the same harsh, green eyes he'd felt on the range. "It's your life. Come on, Charlie. Let's leave the princess in her tower."

"She's a princess all right," Charlie said, "a royal pain in the ass." She grabbed Nate's hand and pulled him towards the door.

"Come on," she said, "Let's check out your apartment. I hear the neighborhood's going to improve real soon."

Nate opened the thick, wooden door that led from the hallway to his bedroom.

"It's kind of an unusual layout," he said as they entered. "This partition separates my bedroom from the kitchen and the living rooms through there." He pointed towards a door on his right.

The room was empty except for an unmade iron bed with peeling white paint. Nate's seabag and two weathered suitcases lay beside it.

"You need a decorator," Charlie said, walking towards the bed. "I've seen prison barracks with more personality."

"Hey, Martha Stewart, I've only been here for a few hours. Besides, I need your professional, military opinion: Where should I hang my Eagle, Globe and Anchor?"

"Civilians can't have a Marine Corps emblem," she said. "You'll have to make do with a fishhook and a map." Charlie patted the bed. "I haven't seen one of these since we sold Granny's house." She patted it again. "May I?"

"Help yourself."

Charlie leaped backward on to the bed. A smile slowly crept across her face. She bounced again, going higher this time, laughing now as the bed groaned in protest.

"You're easy to entertain," Nate said, landing beside her, catching the rhythm and bouncing with her.

"I saw the bed and it reminded me of when I was a kid," Charlie said. "I always wanted a trampoline, but Granny's bed was as close as I got. I finally learned how to do a flip."

Nate looked at the girl beside him, trying to picture her as a child. He'd gotten a little info from Kearns when she'd first reported in: Oklahoma farm girl with an abusive father; raised mostly by her grandparents. Kearns knew everybody's history. Nate felt a sudden sadness.

"Hey," Charlie said, sitting up. "You look weird. Don't you go getting sick on me."

"Were you sad when you couldn't get a trampoline?"

Charlie laughed. "Look, there were a lot of things I couldn't get, but it all worked out." She reached up and grabbed a pillow, holding it above his head. "Besides, I never lost a pillow fight."

"I need a pillow."

"Here," she said, slamming the second pillow into his face, "not that it'll do you any good."

Her first blow sent him sprawling backwards across the bed. He tried to sit up but she forced him down, falling across him, her pillow smothering his face.

"Uncle Charlie," she said. "Say 'Uncle Charlie' if you want to continue to breathe."

Nate began to laugh, softly at first, then louder. Charlie pressed harder.

"Okay, Charlie," he muttered from beneath the pillow. "You win. I've put up the good fight. Take me, I'm yours."

"I don't want you, teacher man," she said, pressing harder. "Last chance: 'Uncle Charlie' or I feed your bones to that man-eater across the hall."

"Then I want you," he said suddenly, flipping his legs up and rolling her beside him. She grabbed for the headboard but he pulled her back, sliding his arms beneath her and pulling her close. She squirmed, her back arched like a horse trying to throw its rider. Her arms were pinned. She tried to worm her way upward, twisting, feeling for any looseness in his grip.

"Okay, Nate," she finally said, "you win, let me up."

"I don't think so, Charlie. To the victor go the spoils. I'm the victor, and that makes you the spoils."

She resumed her struggle, freeing one hand, pounding his back with her fist, twisting to free herself from his grip, exhausting herself in the struggle.

"Uncle Nate," he said, when she was still. "Say 'Uncle Nate' and I'll let you up." They were lying face to face and he felt her breath; hot, slow, and deep. She squirmed again briefly, then relaxed, pressing her head against his chest.

She took a deep breath.

"Your shirt smells like day-old piss."

"You're the one that spilled my beer." He ruffled her hair. "You know the difference between beer and piss?"

"Fifteen minutes," she answered. She tugged his shirt. "This thing's got to go." He raised his arms and she pulled the shirt over his head, running her hands across his bare chest. "You know," she said softly, pulling his head down to her, "I really don't want to get up and contrary to what those range assholes say, I'm not a nun."

The kiss surprised him. He tried to kiss back, but it felt wrong, like he'd walked into a dark room and mistakenly kissed his sister; plus there was that performance thing. You shouldn't promise what you can't deliver. The urologist said his plumbing was fine and his therapist said his impotence would resolve when he forgave himself for his best friend's death. Nate didn't think so. He'd done all he could to save Danny. It wasn't his fault, conscious or subconscious, Dr. Price was a bearded quack that had never been shot at. Somethings have to be experienced. He hadn't told anyone and he wasn't going to start with Charlie. His fellow Marines weren't exactly an understanding audience. Their prescription would be a Hilton Head strip club, complete with a lap dance.

"What's the matter?" Charlie asked. "You never kiss a Marine before?"

"No, I've never kissed you before, and somehow for some stupid reason, I'm sure I'll regret later, I don't think I should start now."

He felt her go limp. "Uncle Nate," she said, sliding off the bed and dropping to the floor. "You win." She leaned back against the bed and placed her head in her hands. "I guess now would be a good time to tell you about the transfer."

"What transfer?" He reached down and rubbed her shoulders. "You'll never leave your island."

"Wrong answer: I put in for a transfer to Quantico after you left. I'm taking that slot on the pistol team. Gunny Kearns says I can leave as soon as my orders are cut."

"Because of me?"

"Listen, Nate," she said, "I like you, but you're different. You've got options. Your family's got money and you're educated. To you, the Marines was something to do until you got your head out of your ass. To me, they're all I've got. We're going in different directions. I just decided to speed things up."

"Then why'd you come here tonight, if you're so hell-bent on leaving."

"I don't know. It wasn't planned. It's just…" He felt her shudder. A tear trickled down her cheek. A sharp slap rejected his attempt to wipe it away.

Charlie stood up. "Thanks for tonight. I'll talk to you soon." She headed for the door. Nate followed.

"Wait, Charlie," he called out as she opened the door. "Why are you mad? What did I do?"

"I'm not mad," she said, continuing down the hall, "and you didn't do anything."

Nate heard a door squeak and looked across to see Becca staring at him. She wore the same white robe, but the knife was missing.

"Something wrong in the animal kingdom?" she asked. "You guys are sure loud when you rut." He noticed her eyes. They were staring at his shoulder. The bullet had left a jagged scar when it entered and the surgeons had left a smooth one when they took it out.

"No," he answered. "All's well in the animal kingdom, but if you get your kicks by listening, you need to learn the difference between pillow fighting and lovemaking: it's all in the groans." He made a soft grunt. "Now that's a pillow fight."

"No," she said before he could finish, "That's a Neanderthal saying goodnight before he slinks back to his cave." She slammed her door.

Nate heard the lock click. *Rough night*, he said to himself, turning around. *Now if only somebody could tell me what happened.*

Back inside, he dropped onto the bed and pulled his clothes around him. Charlie's scent lingered on the pillow. Could he have missed something? Probably not, he thought. Nobody could predict Charlie.

Nate closed his eyes, but the girl across the hall filtered into his thoughts. He'd seen her type before, spoiled, little rich girl, headed south to educate the masses. Probably a teacher. They usually lasted about a year.

He knew she was afraid. He could picture her, wrapped in her white robe, holding the knife, waiting for something to happen.

Nate dropped into a troubled sleep that ended when the dream started. He jumped up before the bad guy's head exploded, managing to squelch a scream before it left his throat. Fallujah's number sixteen had returned. *Becca's lucky*, he thought. *I'd trade my guy for a faceless figure any day.*

He lay there in the darkness, listening to the old house settle in for the night. Charlie raced through his mind, followed by Becca. He felt protective. Suppose the cops were wrong. What if someone did come back? He pictured a shadowy figure, the faceless one from Becca's dream, creeping down the hallway towards her door. It seemed almost real; too real to just lie there.

Nate slipped out of bed and placed his ear against the hallway door. The old wood felt rough, but the hall was quiet. He eased the door open and slipped silently into the empty hallway. A stream of light flowed beneath Becca's door. He moved towards the porch, his left hand forward, his right hand cocked, ready to swing. He checked the porch first, ducking below Becca's window, finding nothing but a huge cockroach that scampered away into the darkness. He reentered the hallway, moving silently, taking care to avoid the boxes that lined the left side. Another trip wouldn't do. "Princess White Shirt" would have his head.

He found the back door locked and both bathrooms empty. *Perimeter secure*, he said to himself, moving back down the hallway towards his room. *Time to make sure it stays that way.*

Nate turned on his light and dumped his seabag on the bed, producing a pile of boots, uniforms, and his shaving kit. He removed a new roll of dental floss—his last PX purchase—from the shaving kit and slipped back into the hallway. He tied the floss to both doorknobs then retreated to his room. Once there, he cut the floss and laid it across his bed. Lying down, he tied the hall door floss to his right big toe and the porch door floss to his left. Satisfied, he pulled a wrinkled Marine Corps raincoat from the pile and wrapped himself in it.

"Do what you can, with what you have, where you are," he said out loud. It was one of Gunny Kearns' favorite quotes. He looked down at the floss that trailed from his toes. *I guess this qualifies*, he thought. He pulled the coat tighter. Feeling secure, he drifted off to sleep mumbling, "right toe-door, left toe-porch."

CHAPTER TEN

The next morning, Becca Noble stretched slowly, embracing the sun's warmth as it filtered in through the palm trees that lined her porch. She arched her shoulders then rolled her neck, feeling her muscles resist, then loosen. Her body demanded relief from last night's contortions.

She'd fallen asleep in the Queen Anne chair, her feet propped on its slender stool; the knife resting on her lap.

She shook her head, trying to jar her brain awake, replaying last night, looking again at the knife. She focused on a dark red line that ran across its tip. It hadn't penetrated far. *Thick skulls, those Neanderthals, and my neighbor's definitely one, right down to his cave woman companion.*

An interesting night, she thought, examining the knife. She pictured it falling, clinching her teeth as she remembered Nate's surprised cry. The picture of the three of them lying outstretched on the floor made her smile. It seemed like a silly movie, a strange mixture of Rambo and the Keystone Cops.

"Rambo, aka, Nate Forrest." *He should be named Primeval*, she thought. *Primeval Forrest. What a great name.* She remembered him last night in the hallway, shirtless, trim and muscular with scars that ripped across his right shoulder. His deep tan accentuated their redness. Where would they have come from? she asked herself. But somehow she knew: Only a bullet could leave such a wound. She winced at the thought of a bullet tearing into his flesh, then thought of him last night with cave girl, visualizing her tracing his wounds with her fingers while he made love to her. *They were definitely loud*, she thought. *Quick, but loud. She'd never been loud.*

Becca slapped her forehead. *What are you thinking?* she asked herself. Her last words echoed in her ears: *Neanderthal saying goodnight.* She smiled. *That was good, Becca,* she told herself, *but hardly conducive to a long-term relationship.* Lizzie's story exchange slipped further into the future.

She looked around her apartment. The first time she'd seen it, it had appeared like a coastal magazine picture, drawn to perfect proportions, everything in place, needing only her to complete it. That wasn't going to happen.

"Paradise lost," she said out loud, "but I can't stay here."

She eased out of the chair, stretched, and checked her watch: 6:15. Her father and Sally should be boarding. She was glad they were gone. Tonight, she'd call home, but last night's events would remain her secret, at least for now.

A loud beep from the kitchen interrupted her thoughts. Coffee. She'd made it last night keeping one eye on her door and the knife on the counter.

Shipping boxes lined her kitchen counters. She checked their labels, opened a small box and pulled out a Shelter Island mug. She took a sip. Not too bad, she thought; sort of a weak expresso that'll taste better on the porch. *Coffee on the porch.* She'd dreamed of this moment since she'd rented the apartment, gazing out at the river, beginning her day with a caffeine-fueled spurt of creativity. At least she'd have today.

She opened her door and peeked into the hallway. The sun shone in over the transom, lighting the upper walls but leaving the floor a twilight gray. She paused a moment then headed towards the porch. A white string trailing down the hallway stopped her. She studied the string. It looked harmless, but it hadn't been there last night. The string looped around the doorknob before disappearing onto the porch. She slipped off the loop and followed the string outside, reeling it in as she walked. She gasped when she saw its path across her window. She'd slept only a few feet from here. She inched closer, tugging the string loose from the window.

A fuzzy, gray spider popped out to investigate. "I hope you didn't spin this," she said, holding up the string for the spider to see. "I'm having enough trouble with ghosts and humans."

Becca reentered the hallway. It was lighter now. She followed the string, stopping briefly at her door before continuing. She traced the string to Nate's door, saw where a second string merged with the first, then followed the second string to the back door. It was like being on a scavenger hunt without clues.

Retracing her steps, it came to her. *Dental floss*, she told herself. He was protecting me with dental floss. She dropped the two piles of floss and stared at Nate's door. A warm smile lit her face. *An alarm system needed testing*. She stifled a giggle with her hand. *This is crazy*, she thought: It's either sleep deprivation or caffeine overload. She stood there, alternating her eyes between the floss and Nate's door, then reached down and picked up the floss.

"What the hell?" she said, giving the floss a hard tug. "*Let's see how alert Nate Forrest really is.*"

A muted scream followed by not-so-muted cursing slipped through the door. She heard his feet hit the floor, feeling the vibrations as he ran towards her. Maybe this was a bad idea. His door flung open and there he was, his face grimaced, teeth bared, in full fight mode, and she was his target. It was definitely a bad idea.

"It's me," she yelled, dodging to her right, seeing his expression shift from anger to surprise just before he hit her. It was only a glancing blow, but it sent her stumbling backwards into the wall. She slid to the floor like a cartoon character, landing in a sitting position still focused on his startled face.

"Well, that answered my question," she said. "Your alarm system worked. No further tests required." She reached out her hand and he pulled her to her feet.

"You okay?" he asked.

"I'm fine," she answered. She looked down at the pile of floss still attached to his feet.

"Sorry about your toes. I just wanted to test your alarm. I didn't expect such a violent reaction. Maybe you could get a bell or something."

"Maybe," he said. "Sorry about the tackle. I was asleep and instinct just took over. I couldn't stop myself."

"Well," she said, "I had a little instinct problem of my own last night." She studied his forehead. A dried line of blood ran from his eyebrow to his hairline. "Sorry about the knife and some of the stuff I said. My survival mode just kicked in, though I still don't like guns and forts, and now I'm a little concerned about alarms."

A slight grin crept across his face. His default face was harsh. This was the first time she'd seen him smile. "Well," he said, "at least I got off your dislike list. Maybe we can agree to disagree on the rest, especially with your moving and all. Any idea where you'll go?"

"Towards the beach," she said. "My school's that way, and I love the ocean."

He gave her a questioning look. "You teach at St Helena?"

"English. How'd you guess?"

"Local knowledge. It's the only school between here and the beach. I hear it's got a great faculty, especially the guy that teaches Honors History."

"You know him?"

"Yeah." His smile got bigger. "So do you."

"No, I don't. The only people I met were the principal and my department head."

"You'd remember this guy: brown hair, about six feet; former Marine with a scar on his shoulder. Kind of charming in a primitive sort of way."

The primitive gave it away. "You," she said. "You teach at my school?"

"Either me or my evil twin," he answered.

"That would be your good twin." She concentrated on his face ignoring the scars that were only half-hidden by his raincoat.

"Did my father hire you?" Becca asked. She studied his face, looking for a resemblance to one of her father's friends. *Daddy's got a long reach*, she thought and his old Marine buddies occasionally turned up.

"Hire me?" Nate asked, his voice rising. "Hire me for what?"

"To protect me. You seem to be everywhere I am." She watched his face crinkle.

"Yeah, right. We faked the whole Parris Island scene. Hired actors and everything. Then I created a teaching job and your dad paid the guy who lived in my apartment to leave." He looked down at her, shaking his head. "Yeah," he continued. It's just like a movie, except you and me are the stars."

"You and I," she said. "The correct pronoun is I, and if you knew my father, you wouldn't think I was crazy."

"Well," he answered, "I don't know your father, so I do think you're crazy."

"What about the dental floss?"

"Look, I know what it's like to be afraid, especially at night. Thinking about how scared you were was keeping me awake, so I rigged an early warning system."

"Worked, too," she said lightly. His face remained solemn. "I guess I should be grateful."

"Well, I didn't do it to earn your gratitude. I did it so I could get some sleep, but I'd be grateful if you gave me a ride to my car. I left it at The Yankee last night. It's right on the way." He paused a moment, and added, "It's a bar."

"Somehow, I would have guessed that," Becca answered, "all things considered." She looked at Nate's raincoat. It had gradually opened, its wide, green belt hanging down both sides. "You wearing your flasher outfit?"

"No," he answered, pulling the coat around him. "I only wear this after dark. Kind of like Dracula."

"In that case, Count, meet me at the back door in thirty minutes. Wear a hat because I'm putting the top down."

Becca dressed quickly, brushing her teeth in the kitchen sink before grabbing her Red Sox cap. She smiled at herself in the wall mirror. *This should be an interesting trip.*

He was by her door when she came out, propped against the wall, dressed in faded khaki pants and a bright, blue polo shirt. He looked almost preppy. A desert camouflage hat sat cocked on his head. Brown splotches marred its brim. She wondered where it had been.

"Nice hat," she said, "but you're not in the desert."

"It's all I've got," he said. He thumped the bill of her Red Sox cap. "We're not in Boston either, but I like your hat."

"Thanks. It's dangerous to wear this in New York, but I'm guessing that South Carolina's neutral in the Red Sox-Yankee war."

"South Carolina's never neutral," he answered, holding the door open. "It's written in our constitution."

Nate whistled when she reached her BMW. "So this is yours?" He gave the car a quick glance and looked back at her. "We must be on different pay scales."

"Probably," she answered. She unlocked the doors with her remote. "I hear they pay by ability levels."

"Ouch," Nate said, sliding into the passenger seat.

"Sorry. You seem to bring out my snarky side." She gave him her sweetest smile, the one she used on her father, then hit the starter button.

"Nice engine," he said. "It sounds almost eager."

"She's a girl and she is eager. Her name's Scarlett."

"Like in O'Hara?"

"Like in her color, though I'm a big fan of your Scarlett. She glanced at the dashboard. "Now where's that button?"

"The one that makes Scarlett topless?"

She fought back a smile. "Yes, that one."

"Lower center of your console. The one with the top diagram."

"Now, who's snarky?" She pressed the button, watching the top lift then fold itself into the trunk.

"That why you bought the car?"

"No," she answered. "Scarlett's beauty is more than skin deep." She yanked the car away from the curb and accelerated hard towards Carteret Street. Scarlett definitely felt eager.

"Not many girls can drive a five-speed," he said. "My sister burned out the clutch in my Miata."

"It's a six-speed," she answered, "and you don't know the right girls." She blipped the throttle, balancing the engine's RPMs with the next gear, then turned left on to Carteret Street.

"Where's everybody?" Becca asked, as they climbed the Lady's Island Bridge. She looked around. Except for a few scattered runners trudging their way up the pedestrian walkway, they were alone on the bridge. "There's not another car on the road." She slowed down to take in the view. It reminded her of Greenport.

Nate shifted in his seat. "They heard you were coming," he said. "I saw the headline in this morning's paper. 'Crazy Yankee girl begins march to sea in German car. Deadly combination of Sherman and Blitzkrieg. National Guard mobilized. Locals warned to flee.'"

Becca glanced at Nate. "You're very creative," she said. "That sounds like a front line dispatch."

"Only repeating what I read, Miss Daisy. By the way, Scarlett's original name was Pansy."

"I slowed down to enjoy the view," she said, "but if you're in a hurry, then Scarlett's your girl, and she's no pansy." Becca downshifted and accelerated into the sharp left turn that marked the beginning of Lady's Island.

"Damn," Nate said. He braced with his legs. She kept the throttle floored, her hands busy making short, quick correction, as centrifugal force carried the car to the right, towards the railing.

"You're not your typical Bimmer driver," he added when she dropped back to the posted forty-five mile per hour speed limit.

"Is that good or bad?" Becca asked. She kept her eyes focused straight ahead. Scarlett felt strong, like she'd enjoyed her little morning workout.

"It's good," Nate answered. He turned his head towards her, raising his voice to be heard over the wind. "Most people who drive these cars don't appreciate them. They buy them for the logo and waste their performance."

"Well," she answered, still looking straight ahead, "at least we agree on one thing."

"That's scary," he answered. He pointed towards a grove of oak trees on their left. "This is where I get off."

"The Yankee," Becca said, reading the faded, red and white sign that hung crookedly from a rusting post. "Must be an enemy outpost deep in rebel territory." She swung the car into the dirt parking lot. "Where's your car?"

"It's the silver Miata over by the dock." Becca punched the throttle and aimed Scarlett towards the Miata.

"It's the one without any body damage," Nate added, when she launched them on a collision course with his car.

"Looks like Confederate Gray," Becca answered. "Remember, Sherman and that other thing?"

"Blitzkrieg? It means lightning war." He raised his hands. "I'm ready to surrender, unconditionally."

"I accept," she said, "now hang on." Becca yanked the handbrake and spun the wheel hard left. She'd learned this technique at the Bridgehampton track. So had her mother. It was her last conscious act and it had saved Becca's life.

Scarlett complied, lurching around, as the soft sand absorbed her momentum. She slid to a stop two feet from Nate's bumper.

Nate opened his door, checking the distance between their cars. He closed her door before opening his, dropping down into the Miata's sunken seat. "You know," he said, "you drive pretty well for a girl."

"Thanks," she answered. "I'd have gotten closer, but I was afraid you'd wet yourself."

He gave her a hurt look. "I thought you were working on your snarky side."

"I am," she said, "but you're an enabler."

"No," he said, "I'm a catalyst."

"Whatever," she said. "Don't be late for class." She popped the clutch, trailing twin dust vortexes as she sped across the parking lot.

CHAPTER ELEVEN

"Gone with the Wind," Nate said. He pulled out of The Yankee's parking lot and searched the long straightaway that led to St Helena. No Becca. Scarlett's cardinal red hue had vanished into the island mist. He searched again when he pulled into the school's driveway, spotting Scarlett hidden among the Buicks and Fords that dominated the oyster shell parking lot. Only a worn Volkswagen bus broke the domestic monopoly. *Nobody here under fifty*, he thought, unfolding himself from the Miata.

Nate studied the building. It was a collection of bricks, shaped like a block, completely functional and totally uninspiring. A billboard dominated the front. A large black panther lurked on top. Beneath it, weathered, once-black letters spelled out, "St. Helena Panthers." The message board read, "Welcome back teachers and students." Very creative, he thought as he walked towards the building. Same guy must have designed the school.

A small crowd gathered outside the main entrance, mostly middle-aged women, sprinkled with a few younger faces with an even distribution of black and white. He didn't see Becca but one face caught his eye. It was thin and pale with a scraggy beard surrounded by long, brown hair. Charles Manson eyes sparkled beneath brushy brows. Its owner stirred the air with weak gestures that Nate somehow thought were directed at him. A tall black woman stepped forward to greet him.

"Good morning," she said, "and welcome to Saint Helena. I'm Dorothy Robinson, and I'm the librarian." She had a big smile.

"Nate Forrest," he answered, unsure if he should offer his hand. "I'm going to teach Honors History."

"Well, Mr. Forrest, then I'm certain I'll see a lot of your students." She looked back at the group. "I'd introduce you around, but there isn't time. We're meeting at my place in about two minutes."

"Your place?" Nate asked, before he realized what she meant. She clasped his arm with both hands.

"I mean the library, sweetie. But for the next nine months you're going to think it's my house, just like you're going to think your classroom's yours. Dorothy stretched out her arms. "Let's go, children," she said. "We don't want to get Dr. Newberry off to a bad start."

The group trudged forward. "Like herding chickens,".Dorothy said bringing up the rear. She flapped her arms, shooing them along. "You know how he gets when you don't let him think he's in charge," Dorothy said, addressing the group. "Remember, last year he hung a root on a teacher."

"What's a root?" Nate asked. He was just in front of Dorothy.

"It's the part of a plant that grows into the ground," his new, bearded friend answered. There was a group snicker.

"But in this case," Dorothy said, "it's a spell cast by a root doctor." She shook her head. "You know, that poor man's still trying to hide from that haint. Even painted his porch haint blue."

The library followed the design of the building; essentially a box inside a box. A tall desk sat at its center. Round tables were evenly spaced around the room. Books lined its green walls and one section by the windows that looked out over the parking lot was reserved for magazines. The tables near the room's center were filled with teachers and cheerful, animated voices rose from them.

Nate followed Dorothy Robinson through the maze. He felt like his first day in kindergarten, alone in a strange environment, looking for a friend.

He searched the collage of faces as Dorothy led him to the front of the room. He didn't see Becca.

"You come sit with me, Mr. Forrest," Dorothy said, patting a chair next to the desk. "Must be a bunch of Baptists. Nobody wants to sit up front." She stood for a moment, taking a long, appraising look at the group assembled behind them.

"You taking attendance?" Nate asked, when she finally sat.

"More like inventory," she answered. "Seeing what the merchandise looks like this year. By the way, she's over there by the back wall next to the door."

"Who?" Nate questioned. He glanced toward where Dorothy had looked and spotted Becca. Apparently, his new friend had spotted her too. He watched her mouth move and her eyes smile. She seemed completely engaged, oblivious to his presence.

He felt a tap on his shoulder. "In case you're interested," Dorothy said, "his name is James Riley. Everybody calls him J.R."

"What's he teach?" Nate asked, "and please call me Nate."

"Art," she answered, "and please call me Dorothy. He's been here about six years, and everybody loves him, especially the women."

"Really?" Nate answered, glancing back at J. R. "He sure doesn't look like a lady killer."

"Oh, but he is. He kills them with kindness and sensitivity, but he does have a dark side."

"What's that?" He continued to watch Becca and J.R.

"Well, I don't like to talk out of class, but once Mr. Riley," she paused, clearing her throat, "kills them, if you get my drift, he totally loses interest. He's like that with his art too. He's done some great murals around here, but once he's finished, he never goes back. It's like the doing's the thing and the feelings afterwards don't matter. You aren't like that, are you, Mr. Forrest?"

"I don't know," Nate answered seriously. "I don't draw and no woman ever fell in love with me."

Dorothy looked at him, keeping him in the foreground as she studied the room behind him. "I don't believe that," she said. "I don't believe that for one minute." She leaned in closer to him, her voice low. "I'll tell you something else. There're several ladies in this room that have their eyes on you."

"You a root doctor too, Dorothy?"

"No," she said, pointing towards the desk. "Doctor Newberry's the only root doctor we've got."

"I heard that, Mrs. Robinson," Dr. Newberry said, taking his position behind the box desk. He was a hulking man, not particularly tall but with broad shoulders and a barrel chest. His small, brown eyes sparkled with curiosity and humor as he surveyed his assembled faculty. Satisfied, he pulled a portable podium from beneath the desk. Quiet whispers spread from table to table and heads turned in his direction. When it was quiet, he cleared his throat and began to speak.

"Good morning to the best faculty in the state of South Carolina," he began. Loud applause followed and Newberry waited for it to end.

"You're here because I hired you or I allowed you to stay. If you failed to notice, my initials spell: CAN. Calvin Arnold Newberry. Can's a word I believe in. I believe these island children can learn, and I believe you can teach them." He had a rich and deep voice that achieved volume without effort. *He'd make a good Drill Instructor*, Nate thought.

"If you keep these two things in mind, everything else will fall into place. Forget them and nothing else will matter." Newberry paused and looked directly at Nate. His eyes were powerful and intense. "Some of you are new," he continued, "like my friend Mr. Forrest here. You're full of energy and ideas. Some of you are not so new." He waited for the ripple of laughter that spread across the room. "You have knowledge and experience that only time can bring. I ask that you share that knowledge with these young people." He looked at Nate again. "And you, young people," he continued, "I want you to share your energy and ideas with these veterans. Without you, a faculty becomes stale and stagnant. With you, Saint Helena becomes a perpetual learning machine, educating an unending line of productive students who serve as a living memorial to your dedication and talent."

Small beads of sweat appeared on Newberry's forehead. He pulled a burgundy handkerchief from his breast pocket, unfolded it carefully and mopped his brow.

Applause filled the silence, softly at first, accompanied by whispers, then louder as the assembled teachers rose as one, ignoring Newberry's raised arms, quieting only when they were ready.

"I was once told," he said, "that no speech can be too brief. And I've also been told to quit while you're ahead." He smiled when light, hidden applause arose from the rear. "I guess that means I'm briefly ahead, so I'm going to let you report to your respective departments. If anyone doesn't know where their department head is located, see Mrs. Robinson." He pointed at Dorothy. "She's the experienced one right in front of me."

The group rose as one and the flood of movement trapped Nate in his seat, his vision blocked by the wave of torsos that flowed past. When he turned around, Newberry was beside him.

"Good morning, Mr. Forrest," Newberry said, extending his large hand. "I see you've found our own Mrs. Robinson, who I'm sure has filled your head with various and sundry untruths regarding both me and our island culture."

Nate was uneasy. He never knew how to treat civilian authority figures. In the Marines, it was clear. Who you were was sewn on your sleeve and there was a book on how to treat each rank. He always liked to know where he stood.

"No, Sir," Nate answered, rising to take Newberry's hand. "She's been very helpful."

"Good, good," Newberry said, looking at Dorothy. "She's been known to scare some new teachers with her voodoo island tales." He looked back at Nate. "You know," he said, lowering his voice, "if I didn't need her so badly, I might hang a root on her."

Nate smiled uncertainly. Newberry gave him a friendly shoulder pat. "You're going to like it here, Mr. Forrest," he said. "I can tell. I'll tell you something else."

Dorothy waved her arms, pointing towards a small group that had gathered behind them. Newberry paused in mid-sentence. "My most creative teachers," he said. He shook his head and smiled. "I'll bet you're lost. English teachers are always lost because their minds are so full of beautiful words that there's no space for the commonplace. Isn't that right, Miss Noble?"

Nate strained his neck to see. Becca was at the group's rear.

"Well, Dr. Newberry," he heard her answer in a clipped, precise voice. "I've learned to proportion my brain so that the practical and the abstract remain in balance. Now I'm lost because nobody told me where to go, not because I live in a fantasy world of sonnets and soliloquies."

Newberry rolled his eyes. He looked down at Nate. "You know her?"

"Slightly. Why?"

"Because you're going to work with her on the Accreditation Committee to develop a school mission statement." He winked at Nate. "Word is you got volunteered." He turned back to the group. "Now come on, ladies," he said before Nate could respond, "and I'll take you to Miss Denton's classroom."

"Miss Noble's one of them," Dorothy said, watching Newberry lead the group into the hall.

"One of whom?"

"One of the ones that's got her eye on you."

"Not that one, Dorothy. The only way she wants her eye on me is through a rifle's sights."

"You're wrong, sweetie. You just listen to Dorothy. Now, are you lost?"

"Go left out of the library. Take the next right then straight out the double doors into the annex," Nate answered, repeating the directions Newberry had given him last week. "Fulton's room is the first one on the right."

"You got it, baby. Check your closet when you get to your room. I hear there might be a surprise in there."

"Not a root."

"Too early for a root." She formed an "X" with her index fingers. "See you at lunch."

Nate walked slowly down the empty hallway. He glanced into each classroom, examining the artwork that decorated the doors and the academic posters that lined their walls.

Everybody had a head start. Most had stuff from last year. He thought of his room. Its bare walls and empty bulletin boards wouldn't sit well with his peers. Teachers were as competitive as Marines, especially when it came to their classrooms. He'd learned that from his practice teaching at Beaufort High, but his one-day transition from Corps to classroom couldn't be helped. His position had only opened up last week. He'd be ready tomorrow.

Nate found Fulton sitting at his desk. He was a heavy-set white man with short crewcut hair. He chaired the History Department, and he'd been present when Newberry interviewed Nate; a strange interview, where Fulton interspersed details of administrative daring from a Marine Corps' career spent in aviation supply with a series of "Yes, Sirs," directed at Newberry.

Fulton introduced him to the two other history teachers; Tina Shirley, a tiny black woman with perfect features, and Doris Haley, an older white woman, who quickly informed Nate that she was retiring next year. "I don't see how you young people are going to survive," she said, taking a seat beside Nate.

Fulton handed out grade books, attendance rosters, and a thin policy manual.

"Y'all can go to your classrooms now," he said when he was finished. "Remember, us history teachers got to stick together this year." Nate flinched at the grammar and thought of Becca. The next faculty meeting should be interesting.

Nate's classroom was at the end of the annex. It looked like all the others; a large, wooden desk at the front dominated long rows of metal desks that radiated the length of the room. A narrow closet jutted out from the back wall. Inside, he found a collection of news magazines, a pile of *National Geographic* magazines and a stack of neatly folded maps. A blue sticky note was attached: "Thought you could use these," it said. "There's a loaded stapler, scissors, and tape in your desk." It was signed D. Robinson. He smiled at the note and went to work.

He started with the news magazines, cutting pictures to create a timeline of international stories on one wall and doing the same with domestic stories across the front. Maps were interspersed to show locations. His "newshound" personality slowed him down. He couldn't display a story without skimming its contents and he was reviewing his work when Newberry's deep baritone voice boomed through the intercom.

"Lunchtime, boys and girls. Our PTA is treating us in the cafeteria. Don't be late." Nate looked at his watch. He couldn't believe it was noon.

The intercom clicked off and Nate heard rapidly moving footsteps in the hall. He turned to see Fulton, his arms pumping, hurry past his room. He met Miss Shirley in the hallway. They both turned to watch Fulton's wide body disappear through the annex door.

"Whatever happened to women and children first?" Nate asked.

"Rules are different out here, Mr. Forrest. Rule one is never get between that man and food."

"What's rule two?" Nate asked, as they walked down the hall. Miss Shirley hesitated. "Now this isn't very nice," she said in a soft voice, "but rule two is don't get between that man and a bathroom after he's had food. He's been known to clear the teacher's lounge."

They entered the lunchroom which doubled as the school's auditorium. A section had been carved out for the teachers, its perimeter defined by plastic chairs draped with red tissue paper. A serving line ran through the kitchen and back out into the dining area. Nate turned and found Miss Shirley gone. From what he remembered of the morning meeting, most departments sat together. He looked for Becca and found her in the serving line. J.R. was behind her. That figured. Their conversation seemed serious. J.R. was doing most of the talking with Becca nodding in agreement. He watched her move through the line. Their morning together had proved interesting, but it was probably the last time he'd see Becca alone. It's for the best, he thought as he joined the end of the line, but somehow he wasn't quite sure.

"Excuse me. I don't believe we've been introduced." The voice came from behind him. Nate turned to find an offered hand. It belonged to a tall brunette. "I'm Jackie Denton."

"Nate Forrest," he answered, taking her hand. "So you're the English Chairperson with the missing faculty."

She laughed. "Well, it has been a source of conversation around here that I don't possess all my faculties, but I didn't know it was universally known." She spoke slowly, mixing southern speed with a slight British lilt.

"I meant your new teachers," he answered, but her tone told him she knew what he meant.

"Yes, they're quite a group. I believe you know Miss Noble?"

"Slightly," Nate answered. He was curious how she knew that. His name must have come up. He felt her study him as the line moved forward.

"You know," she said, "Not many men of your background come to Saint Helena. May I ask what attracted you to our fair school?" He estimated that she was around thirty, though somehow she seemed older.

"I wish I had a profound answer, but the truth is that I wanted to teach history and there was a late opening here. That's pretty much it." It's the questioning, he thought. She sounds like someone's mother checking out her daughter's friends.

"So how long have you known Miss Noble? She seems like quite the young lady. We've never had anyone here from Harvard before."

Nate smiled. "A couple of days." His thoughts flashed back to his first glimpse of Becca at Parris Island. "Somehow," he said, "it seems longer."

They moved slowly through the serving line. Friendly faces filled his plate with homemade casseroles, fresh vegetables, and baked ham. Exiting the line, Jackie Denton slipped past him and headed towards Becca's table. He started to follow, then spotted Dorothy waving him over.

"You don't want to sit over there," she said, as he joined her. "You've got to play hard to get." She glanced over at Becca's table. "Besides, J.R.'s like arsenic; deadly but slow. The way I figure it, you've got until Thanksgiving."

Nate spent the afternoon fine-tuning his displays and flipping through textbooks. The heavy lunch made him sleepy and the reading didn't help. He needed a nap. That a good grunt could sleep anywhere was a Marine axiom. He was headed towards the closet when Newberry walked in, trailed by Fulton.

"Looks good," Newberry said, studying Nate's displays. "Real good. Problem is, kids today don't appreciate history. I hear it all the time. They always want to know why they need to learn about things that happened so long ago." He turned toward Nate. "You got an answer?"

Nate glanced at Fulton and saw a smug smile. "I think George Santayana said it best," Nate answered. "What do you think, Mr. Fulton?"

Fulton's smile faded. "I guess so," he said. "There are so many reasons."

"What did Mr. Santayana say?" Newberry asked. Fulton turned towards the wall and began to study a map, tracing along it with his finger, excluding himself from this conversation.

"He said that those who fail to learn the mistakes of the past are doomed to repeat them," Nate answered.

Newberry nodded. "Wise man," Newberry said; "Both you and Santayana." He looked around the room and turned back to Nate. "Leave whenever you're ready, but remember that your students arrive in three days." He turned to leave with Fulton following, then paused at the door. "Don't forget to get with Miss Noble. The Accreditation Committee takes the mission statement real seriously and I need it by Thanksgiving."

"Let me know if you need any help," Fulton added. "I know what it's like being the new kid on the block."

Alone, Nate walked slowly around his room. Newberry's words rang in his ears. In three days, these empty desks would hold real, live students. His students, entrusted to him by their parents to be educated and enlightened, then returned to them at the end of the day, wiser for having been there. He closed his eyes and imagined the room full of students, their fresh minds striving to answer questions that had plagued mankind since its existence. Was he ready? He didn't know, but they were coming anyway.

Nate walked over to the blackboard and wrote his name. It looked strange. Mr. Forrest was his father. He erased it and wrote it again, neater, larger, carefully forming each letter. Neat handwriting was an expected teacher skill. He was a natural scribbler. Neatness required concentration. He didn't hear the door open behind him and he jumped when she spoke.

"You write quite nicely," Becca said, then added, "for a man."

"Thanks," he said. He turned to face her. "It's easier than driving."

"Safer too," she said, "and it's gender neutral." She glanced around. "I just thought I'd drop by and see how your day went." Her voice was relaxed, like that of an old friend accustomed to dropping by at the end of the day, like the past two days hadn't happened.

"I'm okay," he answered. "I started from scratch, but I got a lot done. Thursday's D-Day though. I just hope I'm ready. I bet you could start tomorrow."

"Probably," she said. "I had a bunch of stuff ready so I had a head start. Those boxes you attacked held more than clothes."

She gave the room a quick look then slid past him. "Now let's see what you've been up to."

She walked slowly along the wall, her hands behind her back, examining each map and picture. "You're very innovative," she said, when she reached the end. "I never could get into history. It's just so…," She paused for the right word. "Extraneous," she finally said. "Like it doesn't matter anymore."

Nate flinched. "That's the second time I've heard that today," he said, "though I'm surprised to hear it from you."

"Why me?"

"Because you teach literature and most great literature is based on history."

She turned to face him. "Well, Messrs. Dickens, Hawthorne and Melville might disagree with you, but go ahead and make your case."

"Well," he said, "my first exhibit would be *War and Peace*, followed by all of Shakespeare's Histories. Then there's. . . ."

"What's your favorite history?" she asked, cutting him off. Her tone was challenging, questioning, like a professor doubting the depth of a student's knowledge.

Henry IV. He paused to elaborate but she fired another question.

"Favorite character?"

"Falstaff, though Hot Spur's a close runner-up."

"Why?"

"Hey," he answered. "I've already passed English Lit."

"Did you learn anything?"

"A lot, mainly about English teachers. They're a serious group."

She smiled and her tone relaxed. "So just between us, why'd you like Falstaff?"

"Well, first of all, he's funny even after you sort through all that archaic language. That means 'old,' by the way."

"To be precise, it means old-fashioned." She walked towards him, her hands still behind her back. She reminded him of a drill instructor ready to pounce.

"What else?"

"Well, he's every soldier of every war. Afraid, not filled with lofty ideas about God and country. Just an ordinary guy, trying to do his job and not let his buddies down."

"Have you read *War and Peace*?"

"Last summer. It was my beach read, though I'm not up for a quiz. Those Russian names give me fits."

She laughed. "That's okay. You've already passed, and besides, J.R.'s taking me out to Fripp Island. He lives there and it's close and very safe. You have to go through a security gate to get on the island and J.R says there's a condo near him that I might be able to rent." She checked her watch. "Got to scoot." She twirled around and sped towards the door. "See you tomorrow," she said over her shoulder.

Nate moved towards the door and watched Becca walk down the hall. Her steps were small and quick, one foot moving before the other planted, her pony tail swishing evenly from left to right. He wanted to say something, preferably something brilliant, but at least something. "Okay," he finally said, just before she reached the annex door. "History test's at 11:00 tomorrow morning. We'll start with Neanderthal Man."

"Let's not go back so far," she said, maintaining her pace and not looking back. "I've just promoted you to Cro-Magnon."

CHAPTER TWELVE

There were only two cars in the parking lot when Nate left school; his Miata and an ancient Volkswagen van. He guessed that the van belonged to J.R., and that they had taken Becca's BMW out to Fripp Island. Scarlett would be right at home among the Audis and Mercedes that lived there.

He'd planned to drive out to the beach at Hunting Island, but decided against it. Hunting Island was on the way to Fripp and if Becca saw him, she'd think he'd followed her. He didn't need that. He wasn't sure what he needed. Her visit had surprised and confused him. What he needed was time to think.

Nate lowered the Miata's top and started home, tasting the salty air as it swirled around him. It was an easterly wind—a typical afternoon sea breeze that could be counted on to stir the stagnant August air.

The salty wind, fresh off the ocean, also blew in thoughts of Becca and J.R., then Becca alone.

He replayed her visit. She'd ignored him all day. Why the visit? Why'd she care if he knew Henry IV from Henry Kissinger? More importantly, why did he care? What was the attraction?

It wasn't her looks. She was more pixie than pretty; cute, though, with eyes that would doom a poker player. Today they'd remained neutral, no emotion, cool and focused.

Crossing Chowan Creek, from St Helena on to Lady's Island, he inhaled deeply, savoring the musty bouquet that seeped from the pluff mud below. "*Low Country perfume*" his grandmother called it, though he admitted it was an acquired taste.

The smell stayed with him as he passed The Yankee. He hadn't been there since the night with Charlie and his next visit would have to wait. He rendered a parade-ground salute.

"You can't tempt me," he said, not slowing down. "I'm on a mission to organize and civilize."

His apartment would come first. Four years of deployments and ship-board living had left him immune to many creature comforts. If they were available, they were furnished. If not, as was often the case, you did without. Things like toilet paper and cleaning supplies came from the guarded shelves of surly supply sergeants like Fulton, not from friendly supermarkets.

Arriving at his apartment, he dug an old notepad from his seabag and began a list. He started in the kitchen. He needed everything though his mother was putting together a care package of dishes and silverware, and of course, she'd make sure he didn't starve.

He worked his way through the two adjoining rooms before heading down the hall to the bathroom. He'd almost completed his list when he heard a car door slam.

Nate walked to the back door. Becca was leading J.R. up the stairs. She climbed with quick, light steps, barely landing on one step before launching for the next, swinging a tote bag as she climbed. Her face glowed and a light sweat reflected the sun. Her hair was down and windblown. *She was almost pretty.*

He retreated to his bathroom, timing his exit with the opening of the back door.

"Fancy seeing you here," he said, as Becca bounded in. She froze in mid-stride, then smiled in recognition.

"Well," she said, "not for much longer. I found a condo out at Fripp Island."

"Right next to my complex," J.R. added, panting as he came through the door. "Of course, she still has the option of moving in with me."

"Now you tell me," Becca said to J.R. She pursued her lips in a pout. "Too bad I already signed the lease." She turned towards Nate. "Do you two know each other?"

"Only by reputation," Nate answered. He extended his hand. "Nate Forrest."

"James Riley. Yeah, I saw you at school today." He looked from Nate to Becca and back; his eyes were curious, feeling for a connection. "I guess Dorothy had you going with that root doctor story. She's a funny lady but she's got a big imagination. By the way, everyone calls me J.R."

"J.R's been a big help," Becca said. "He knows this Marine who's deployed until next June, so I'm leasing his place."

"That's great," Nate answered. "I hope you find better neighbors."

"Me too," Becca said. She looked at him and shook her head. "Actually, I think my old neighbor might be okay once you get to know him."

"Too bad you won't get the chance," Nate answered. His words came out harsher than he'd intended.

"Life goes on," she said, her tone cooler. "I'm going to have a beer. You guys care to join me?"

"Sounds great," Nate said. His shopping trip could wait.

"Just water for me," J.R. said. "Beer makes me sleepy, and I've got my talk tonight."

"Oh, I forgot," Becca said. "You told me about the Art League. Speaking of art," she said to Nate, pulling a drawing from her bag. "Look what J.R. drew out at my new place." She handed him the drawing. "Doesn't this look great?"

Nate examined the picture. It was a pencil sketch of Becca. She sat perched on a balcony, her eyes-half closed and dreamy, her hair tousled by the wind. Behind her, the ocean foamed beneath gray clouds. In the bottom right hand corner, the initials J.R. leapt from the page.

"It looks just like you." He handed the picture back. "Good job," he said to J.R. "I can feel the storm brewing."

"Thanks, man," he said. "I had the perfect model." He nodded towards Becca. "Look at that hair and that skin. She was born on the beach, and that's where she belongs."

"Actually," Becca said, "I was born in Greenport, and I'm thirsty from all this beach talk. Come on in, and I'll get your drinks."

"It looks different in the daylight," Nate said, as he and J.R. passed through the kitchen and into the living room.

"Less crowded too," Becca said from the kitchen. She flashed a quick smile and pulled two beers from the refrigerator. She handed Nate both beers and poured J.R. a glass of ice water.

"Red Hawk," Nate said, reading the label. "Never heard of it."

"It's my favorite," Becca answered. She handed him an opener. "I brought a few bottles with me. It's a New York micro-brewery."

Nate took a large swallow. "That's good." He wiped his lips with his hand and read the label. "New York? Must be brewed with imported water."

Becca sighed. "I've changed my mind about my former neighbor. He's a victim of stereotypes and stuck in an environment that perpetuates them."

"Hey," Nate said. "I was only kidding, and the beer's great." He held out his bottle. "Truce?"

Becca clinked her bottle against his.

"For old times' sake," she said, then turned to J.R. "So, what's your talk about?"

"Abstract versus Realism." He glanced down at Becca's sketch. "Art's not photography, though that's a losing battle with the Art League audience."

"Why bother?" Nate asked.

"Because these old biddies fund ninety percent of our art programs, including the ones they don't like. We just try to broaden their horizons." He took a couple of sips from his glass. "I've got to go," he said. "Can't keep the flock waiting." J.R. looked at Becca. "Sure you won't change your mind?"

"I can't. I've got to start packing and get some school work done: maybe some other time."

"I'll hold you to it," he said.

Becca slipped her arm through J.R.'s and walked him to the door. "Thanks for the sketch and the condo," she said. "I can't wait to settle in on my new island."

"I can't wait to get you there." He turned to Nate. "Take good care of my model." He gave Becca a long, possessive look. "I might do a series of her if she'll let me."

Nate watched J.R. amble down the stairs and disappear through the gate. He turned towards Becca.

"Sounds kind of cynical," he said. "Sort of like selling your soul."

"Not really," Becca said. "My sister Staci's an artist and my mother always supported the arts." She lowered her head. "Staci's been depressed since my mom died. She can walk in a room and sense everything there; feelings, smells, everything. She got that from my mom."

"Was your mom an artist?"

"Frustrated writer, but I think writers are like that, too—sensitive, I mean. That's why so many destroy themselves. They adopt other people's feelings, and they can't stand the pain. Same goes for musicians." She looked up at him. "Sorry, I've got a case of the negative nellies."

"That's okay," Nate said. She looked vulnerable again, almost fragile, like she had last night. Her features seemed to soften with her thoughts.

"I'm sorry about your sister," he said. "That must be rough."

"It is," she answered, "though as Garrison Keillor says, 'Nothing bad ever happens to a writer. It's all material.'"

"So you're a writer?"

"I used to think I was or that I would be. I've always written. Now, I don't know. It's like I've got nothing to say. I mean, who am I and what have

I done?" She took a long swig of beer. "And yet it's a curse. I feel like I've got to write, but I don't know what?"

"That takes us back to history," Nate said.

She shook her head. "Too much research. It destroys my creativity."

"I don't mean the big stuff. I'm talking about the little, quirky stories. Every small town's got some. Beaufort's full of them."

She looked up. "Such as?"

"Well, take your newly occupied Fripp Island."

"What about it?"

"Well, one of its first inhabitants was a rather interesting guy named Edward Teach."

"Never heard of him."

"Sure, you have." Nate walked towards the window and looked out at the river. When he turned around, Becca was on the couch, chin in hand.

He took a swig of beer. "You look like 'The Thinker.'"

"I'm the learner. Finish your story." She sounded impatient.

"Well," Nate continued, dragging out his words, "Mr. Teach even traveled to your part of the world. You just know him by his nickname."

She pulled her feet under her. "Okay, you're toying with me. What's his nickname?"

"Blackbeard."

"The pirate?"

"The same, though he didn't live on Fripp alone."

"Well, he must have had a crew."

"He had a lady."

"Okay, I'm a sucker for a love story. Who was she?"

"A young, pretty Charleston girl, who went down in history only as Miss O. It seems that one day Blackbeard walked by her house and she flirted with him. Being the pirate he was, he threw her over his shoulder and carried her back to his ship, *Queen Anne's Revenge*. Then, he slipped out of Charleston and sailed to North Carolina. Blackbeard had certain arrangements with the governor there who married them over Miss O's rather vehement protest." He paused, waiting for her reaction. It wasn't what he expected.

"You use big words," she said, "and your pacing is distracting."

He sat down on a stool facing her.

"I'm sorry," he said. "It seems I've slipped into in my lecture mode. I borrowed it from a Citadel professor and it requires a pretentious vocabulary and reflective movement. I'm still working on my gestures."

She nodded. "Well, I'm sure your students will be impressed; but does this particular lecture have a point?" She emphasized the word 'lecture'.

"Several," he said, "but let me finish. Anyway," he began, "Blackbeard took her out to Fripp with only him and a treasure chest full of jewels for company. Long story short: She eventually came around and they ended up in the West Indies."

"So the first point is that money can buy love. What's the second?"

Nate hesitated. "That J.R. isn't the first bearded pirate to shanghai a girl to Fripp Island."

"I see," Becca said, uncoiling before sliding her feet to the floor.

Her tone told him he'd made a mistake. He stood and stretched his shoulders. *One foot's in the Rubicon*, he thought; *might as well complete the crossing.*

He told her about his library conversation with Dorothy.

"Anyway," he said, when he finished, "I just thought I'd give you a heads-up: A friendly shot across the bow, so to speak."

Becca stood and walked towards him. Her face was taut and her green eyes were narrow and focused.

"So," she said, when they were face to face, "you think I'm just some little airhead who fell off the turnip truck and you've made it your business as to whether J.R. may or may not be after my. . ." She hesitated a moment. "Treasure," she said, "in keeping with your pirate vernacular."

Nate fought back a smile. "Treasure," he repeated, "now that's an interesting term, though not one I'd personally choose." She took a deep breath, biting her bottom lip, turned away, then turned back.

"You know," she said, "I'd be interested in what term you would choose."

"Well," he began slowly, but her laughter stopped him.

"I'm sorry," she said, holding her hand over her mouth. "I can't believe we're having this conversation and I don't think I want to hear your answer."

"That's good," he said, "because I don't have one, though 'booty' might do."

They both laughed. "You know you don't have to move."

"Yes, I do." She looked at him, her eyes serious now, the laughter gone. "You see, I've got this crazy neighbor."

"Crazy's like beauty," he said. "It's in the eye of the beholder."

"Not in this case," Becca said, opening the kitchen door. "Now you need to set sail because I've got to get this place shipshape."

Becca started by tossing the beer bottles into the trash. *It's different here*, she thought. At home, these bottles had big deposits and even those that didn't were recycled.

Her moving boxes still lined the hall. She needed them to repack but retrieving them would send Nate scurrying to help. She didn't want to see him. For now, she wanted to think and work on her lesson plans. Packing could wait.

Becca dug into her book bag and removed her planning book and teacher's guides. J.R.'s drawing slid out. She could see him sketching it, remembering the way his eyes flipped between her and the sketch pad while his hands moved in short, quick strokes. "You just flowed from my pencil," he'd said, when he finished. "Almost like magic, like there's a connection." He gave her a sly wink, "You know," he said, "I may have just captured your soul."

She'd felt something too. Nothing serious, just a slight flicker of interest that quickly flamed out. Becca picked up the sketch and walked to the porch window. Her reflection looked back at her—a ghostly figure etched into the faded glass. She compared her image to the drawing. J.R. had softened her features, rounding her sharp nose and eliminating the freckles that lay sprinkled along its bridge. Her scar was gone. She took this as an act of kindness. *Nate's wrong,* she thought. *J.R.'s harmless.*

Becca sat on the couch and opened her planning book. She'd start with her first period grammar class. Bad grammar grated on her like fingernails on a blackboard. At Harvard, Robert had called her his "grammar Nazi". She'd inherited this trait from her mother: no dangling modifier or double negative escaped uncorrected in her house.

Teaching grammar was another matter: Too many rules and exceptions. It was a tedious, first-year teacher task she'd try to avoid next year.

Her literature classes were different. She was excited for her students. She'd already made plans to take them to see *Romeo and Juliet* performed in Charleston. Shakespeare was her favorite. Nate had surprised her. *Henry IV* showed Shakespeare's versatility: history to tragedy.

Nate was versatile also; almost too versatile, like a chameleon, changing his color to match his environment. In the few days she'd known him, he'd evolved from a screaming, sadistic bully to a soft spoken, well-read intellectual. Too much, too soon, she thought. The evolution might not be permanent. Maybe her promotion had been premature.

She glanced around her apartment, focusing on the hall door that Nate and Charlie had burst through earlier.

Charlie was a question mark. She might be the original Nate's soul mate. It depended on which Nate was real. The original Nate was gone, at least in her mind, replaced by the unknown Nate.

Her plans were almost complete when she heard Nate in the hall, followed by the back door's distinctive squeak. She slipped over to the window, and watched him walk to his car. He wore green cargo shorts topped with a gray muscle shirt. USMC was stenciled across its chest. This morning's camo hat sat cocked on his head.

"No butt and great legs," she told herself, watching him slide into his Miata. A smile creased her face, then vanished.

"Bad girl, Becca," she said out loud. She took a final peek before slipping into the hallway to retrieve her boxes. She considered updating Lizzie but decided against it. There was really nothing to report.

The next morning, Nate woke early. The Marines had stenciled 5:30 onto his brain. He'd slept well, content with the progress he'd made in his apartment. Of course, the three beers he'd drunk with his dad hadn't hurt.

Drinking beer with the old man was a new experience, though once he'd joined the Marines, his father had adopted a new motto: "If you're old enough to die for your country, you're old enough to drink a beer."

They'd discussed sports and politics; subjects they generally agreed on though Becca's break-in had dominated the conversation. As Nate expected, his father had a copy of the police report. "Just be alert," he'd said when they'd finished reviewing it. "I don't think a repeat performance is likely, but you never know." Nate knew. His father was wrong. Becca was too convincing; this thing wasn't over.

Nate looked down at his running shoes. He'd laid them out last night and they were doing their job, calling out to him, preventing him from falling back asleep.

"Okay, okay," he said sleepily. "I'm coming."

He started his run slowly, waiting for the stiffness to leave his legs, and his body to adjust to the effort. No need for speed, he thought. PT tests were a thing of the past.

He turned towards Craven Street, following it to the river, then swung north, hugging the shoreline as the river wound its way inland.

A pearly mist floated in from the river, a waist-high fog that wrapped him in its droplets, separating from him as his legs churned through the air.

He turned west, away from the river only to meet it again as he reached Bay Street. Beaufort, after all, was an island.

Nate grew stronger as he ran. He finished his three miles with a sprint, enjoying the effort as he gulped down the moist air.

It was lighter now, the sun just breaking across the horizon. Nate leapt up the stairs. He wanted to run further but there wasn't time. He opened the door quietly and eased down the hallway. He was unpinning the key from his shorts when he heard the back door open, then quickly close. *Did he lock it?*

Nate stood silently listening, waiting. Becca's back door rattled. He hesitated. It could be her. The door rattled again: Somebody was trying to force the lock.

He sprinted down the hall and stopped at the corner. His heart rate leaped and his breath came in shallow gasps. *Was anything there?* Becca's story raced through his mind. The door rattled again. He took a deep breath then leapt around the corner, landing in a fighting stance just above Becca's door. She screamed.

Nate took a step back. "I'm sorry," he said between breaths. Becca gave him a curious look, then shook her head.

"I thought we removed that floss." She wore shorts and a sleeveless T-shirt. Sweat dripped from her arms and forehead. Her shirt was drenched.

"I thought you'd be barricaded in," he said, "and I sure as hell didn't know you were a runner."

"You either," she said. "You're just full of surprises."

"You too. So how was your run?"

"The end was exciting." She wiped her forehead with her arm. "I usually can't get my heart rate to this level without moving." She pushed the door with her foot. It creaked open.

"This old lock was stuck," she said, "and the door sticks too." She shook her head. "You sure we removed that floss?"

"Positive," he said, "I just can't believe that you'd go out running alone in the dark."

"It's funny," she said. "I don't feel afraid. It's like I know before something's going to happen. Sounds crazy, doesn't it?"

"Not to me. I've seen guys like that in combat. They just knew."

"Well," she said, opening her door, "I've got to get moving." She started inside and then turned back. "It's not like it's over. I'm still having my dream. There's something out there. It's just not here right now."

Nate finished his workout: push-ups, sit-ups and stretching, then took a cold shower. Breakfast consisted of instant coffee, a banana, and a protein bar. A lazy man's smoothie. No blender required.

Footsteps on the front porch caught his attention. Looking out, he saw Becca standing by the banister. She was wrapped in a gray hoodie. Steam rose from her coffee as she stared out across the river.

"You're going to miss this," he said, joining her on the porch.

"I know," Becca said softly, "but I'm trading it for an ocean."

"Not a bad trade, I guess." She was looking at the spot where the rope had hung. "Not if you like that sort of thing."

"I do," she said, "and I especially like islands. I was brought up on one and it made me feel safe."

"Water works both ways: barrier or highway. One if by land, two if by sea."

"I don't think this guy's British." She pulled out her cell phone. "Got to run." She looked down at their cars. "Want to race?"

"No thanks," Nate answered. "I know when I'm outmatched."

Becca arched her eyebrows. "Are we talking skill or equipment?"

"Equipment," he answered. "Your skills so far are gender-rated."

"You mean that I drive pretty well for a girl."

"Right," he said, "but you've got world-class equipment."

She walked over and stood beside him. He felt her bulky sweatshirt brush against his hip. She tilted her head.

"We are still talking about cars?"

"I hope so," Nate answered, "otherwise I'd have to call J.R. for advice."

Becca took a step back. "So, you're a pirate too?"

"No," Nate answered. "I just don't know much about treasure hunting, but I hear J.R's got a real foolproof technique."

CHAPTER THIRTEEN

At school, Nate's next two days were spent in meetings and classroom preparation. Class rolls were distributed, checked, then redone. Office supplies were allocated with strict warnings about budget shortages. It reminded Nate of a Marine Corps deployment. The only thing missing were the weapons.

Becca was also missing. At school, they traveled in different directions. Each department attended required meetings on varied schedules. Classroom times were scarce and jealously guarded.

J.R. proved to be an exception. His one-man department escaped the scrutiny of the administrators, and he floated effortlessly among the scurrying teachers.

"Did J.R. help you decorate?" Dorothy asked during one of Nate's many library visits.

"He asked but I didn't need anything. Why?"

"He's giving lots of help to your friend. I thought maybe you two were sharing him. Sort of a platonic *ménage a trios*. Her room looks like a southern Avalon."

His throat tightened. "You trying to stir something up, Dorothy?"

"Not me. I just don't want a *Romeo and Juliet* ending between you two."

"There is no two."

"Okay, but if there was, I'd watch out. J.R. seems to have picked up speed."

Nate returned to his room. Everything was in place. He thought of the old military saying, "No battle plan survives the first shot." The first day would be like that, but he'd adjust.

He felt restless. He wandered down to Fulton's room, but Fulton wasn't there. Probably at another meeting. Nate took a quick look around, spotting a completed seating chart on Fulton's desk. He'd already decided to let his students choose their seats, but a chart would help him learn their names and create a sense of control.

Nate returned to his room and drew a blank seating chart, then walked to the office and made five copies. While he was in the area, he decided to check out Becca's room.

The English Department was clustered along the hallway that led to the gym. Jackie Denton's room marked the start of their enclave. Nate glanced in and saw her seated at her desk, her head buried in a teacher's manual. He walked by, glad that she hadn't looked up.

Becca's room was the last one on the right, next to the gym. Giant cardboard castles covered its closed door and laughter filtered out into the hallway. He knocked lightly and opened the door. Becca was sitting on her desk with her back to him.

"Hi neighbor," he said, surprised that she was alone.

"Hi," she said. She pointed towards her feet. "You remember J.R?" J.R. rose slowly, his hand on his back.

"I'm getting too old for these garden scenes." He looked at Becca. "I guess you'll have to rehearse on your own."

"My class is going to perform *Romeo and Juliet*," she explained to Nate. "J.R. was kind enough to help me."

Nate looked around the room. Shakespeare and Dickens dominated the left side, peering from opposite sides of a wall-length curtain.

On the right, adverbs and adjectives formed ladders, supporting nouns that dangled from plank labeled sentences.

"Very animated," he said.

J.R. slid onto the desk next to Becca. They shared a conspiratorial smile. Nate felt like he'd walked in on two lovers. He forced his eyes back to the artwork, taking in its detail and complexity.

"Whose idea was all this?" he finally asked.

"Becca had the ideas," J.R. answered quickly; "I'm just the mechanic that put them together."

"Right," Becca said, elbowing him in the side. "All I said was that I'd like to show visually what we'd be doing this semester, and J.R. did the rest."

Nate looked back at the artwork. "Well, you guys did a great job." He turned to J.R. "Maybe I should have taken you up on your offer."

"Still not too late," J.R. answered. He looked at Becca. "I won't charge you what I'm charging her."

Becca slid off the desk. "He doesn't come cheap," she said, looking at J.R. "I guess I'm going to have to dig deep into my treasure chest to pay him. I buried it out on Fripp."

She was looking at Nate now. He saw the dare in her eyes though her expression remained flat.

"Thanks, anyway," Nate said. "I'll stick with what I've got for now."

"Your room looks great," Becca said. Nate detected a slight smile. "A little understated," she added, "but very subject appropriate."

He wasn't sure if he'd been complimented or insulted. "Thanks, I think," he said. He looked back at her room. "Well, I've got to run. Even understated takes a little preparation."

That afternoon, Nate left school early, convinced he was ready for the onslaught. The parking lot was half empty, and though he tried not to look, he saw that both J.R.'s and Becca's cars were still there.

The trip home was a blur. Images of J.R. and Becca blocked his vision and crowded his thoughts. The Miata drove itself while he battled the images and himself.

He couldn't figure it out. What did he feel? He was jealous of someone he didn't even like. Maybe he just felt protective. J.R. was definitely making progress. What Becca saw there he couldn't imagine. It must be the art. What did J.R. want besides her treasure? He laughed out loud when he said it, flashing back to their conversation, remembering how suddenly her mood could change.

He reached The Yankee without remembering the drive. Instinctively, his foot lifted off the accelerator. He scanned the parking lot. Each corner held a car. Two work pickups held down the far side while next to the bar, a Range Rover and Charlie's Land Cruiser shared an aisle. Nate glanced in his mirror, braked hard, and swung into the parking lot.

Charlie was at the bar. Her back was to him. She was surrounded by two guys that Nate assumed belonged to the pickups. Both wore ragged jeans and muscle T-shirts. Charlie also wore jeans, but hers were new and pressed. A half- empty beer pitcher and three full mugs lined the bar. He spotted the bartender on the deck, talking with two men dressed in suits. He placed them with the Range Rover.

The men at the bar watched him in the mirror. Their reflections were hard and questioning. Charlie's head was down, contemplating her beer.

He slid between her and the man on the right and tapped her shoulder. "Hey, stranger," he said, "I thought I ran you out of town."

Her head jerked up and she treated him to a big smile. "Teacher man," she said, "I thought I told you to stick to those schoolmarms."

Her words were slightly slurred, and he guessed this wasn't the first pitcher. Before he could answer, the man behind him spoke.

"He bothering you?" he asked Charlie. "Me and my brother was having a nice time with Charlene. We wouldn't want anybody to upset her."

Nate turned around. Even seated, the man looked powerful. "Charlene and I are old friends," Nate said evenly.

"Marine buddies," Charlie said. "We taught marksmanship out at Parris Island. Nate, this is Bobby," she said, pointing with her chin to the man behind him, "and this is his brother, Jesse."

"You're too pretty to be a Marine," Bobby said, casting an appraising look at Charlie, "and so's he," he added, smiling at Nate.

"Well, we can't all be ugly," Nate said, returning the smile. He turned to Charlie. "Let's talk before you leave," he said. "When you're not with your friends," he added, glancing over his shoulder at Bobby.

"Let's walk outside," Charlie answered. "I need some air."

Nate stepped back, allowing Charlie room to dismount from the tall stool.

"Hey," Jesse said, blocking Charlie with his arm. "We didn't buy all them beers so you could take off with pretty boy here." He looked at Nate. "Did you call my brother ugly?"

Nate dug out his wallet and tossed a pair of twenties on the bar. "This should cover your bar bill."

"You didn't answer my question, boy," Jesse said, "and we don't need your fucking money." He tossed the twenties on the floor.

"Suit yourself," Nate said. He reached down and picked up the bills, then looked closely at Jesse. "Are you two twins?"

"You're a funny little bastard," Bobby said from behind him, "but your manners suck."

Nate felt him slide off his stool. Charlie pivoted to her right and stood, leaving Jesse holding the back of her stool.

"Let's go, Nate," she said. She started toward the door, but Jesse grabbed her arm, pulling her to him.

"We ain't through talking," he said. "Pretty boy here owes us an apology." He looked at Charlie, sliding his hand down her back. "Plus," he said to his brother, "I need a few minutes in the bathroom with this one." He glanced around the empty room. "Might be better though if we used the pool table. Then pretty boy could watch. Might learn something."

Nate could feel Bobby behind him. They weren't going to let him leave without a fight.

Both men were now standing. Nate looked at Charlie. Her hand was on the pitcher. He saw the bartender on the deck, cell phone in hand, waving his arms as he spoke. The faint wail of a siren waffled in.

"Well," Jesse said, "we're waiting."

"Okay," Nate said. "I'm sorry you're both ugly."

Jesse lunged forward. Charlie swung the pitcher dropping him hard to the floor. Nate took a deep breath and planted his elbow deep in Bobby's gut. He spun to face Bobby only to be greeted by a fist to the face. Bobby stepped backwards, then launched a roundhouse kick at Nate's groin. Nate blocked the kick, twisting Bobby's leg, wrenching him to the floor.

Nate bounced to his feet, shaking off the blow. The sirens were louder now. Jesse remained sprawled on the floor. Charlie hovered over him, pitcher in hand. Behind him Bobby groaned, struggling to stand. Nate was afraid to let him up. He grabbed Bobby's collar, using his bulk to slam his head into the wall. Bobby dropped into a limp heap.

Nate looked around at the body count. Time to leave. He grabbed Charlie's hand and pulled her towards the door.

"Damn, Charlie," he said, as they burst through the door and into the parking lot. "Next time pick some smaller drinking companions."

They sprinted towards their cars. "Meet me at my place," Nate said. He listened to the sirens grow louder. "I'd rather not talk to those guys, and my dad hates to see my name in the paper."

Charlie stood still. "I don't think you've got a choice." She pointed across the parking lot. A white police cruiser sat sideways across the exit. A female deputy stood by its open door; a shotgun cradled in her arms. Behind her, an assortment of police cars lined the highway.

"I'll kill both of you," Jesse screamed, charging out the door behind them. He held the beer pitcher but he'd smashed it until it was only a piece of jagged glass with a handle. Bobby limped behind him, unholstering his box cutter as he ran.

"Talk about self-incrimination," Nate said. He looked at Charlie. "Come on," he said, "I'll race you to the cop."

It was over in a minute. Bobby and Jesse surrendered peacefully. "They started it," Bobby yelled, as he and Jesse were cuffed and lead away. "I've got witnesses."

"So," the female deputy said, when the prisoners were loaded into the squad car, "you two were just minding your business when these guys assaulted you? I mean you didn't do anything to rile them up?"

"Nope," Nate answered. "We tried to leave, but they wouldn't let us. Ask the bartender."

"I will," she said, "but we've dealt with these guys before." She looked at Nate's face. "You need a doctor?"

"No, thanks," he answered. He licked his lips. The blood tasted salty, but his mouth didn't hurt. He knew from experience that would change. The deputy took their names and phone numbers and told them they could leave.

"You always block with your head?" Charlie asked, while they walked to her car.

"Anybody can swing a pitcher," he answered. "You fight like a girl, and that's the second time you've doused me with beer."

"I saved you from that gorilla, teacher man."

"Whatever," he answered. "Anyway, what brought you to The Yankee?

"Just slumming. I had the day off to clear the base and I got through early." He felt her eyes question him. "And no," she added," I wasn't looking for you."

"I never thought you were," he said. "When do you leave?"

"Probably tomorrow. I get three days before I have to report."

"Can you stop by my place? I'll buy you a beer."

"You don't have a pool table?"

"Not yet, though I've still got my bed springs. Come on. You'll be impressed."

Nate parked on Carteret Street and Charlie pulled in behind him. He was surprised to see Becca's car parked on Bay Street. She must have left school right after he did.

Nate walked back to Charlie's car. His mouth tasted salty and his head was beginning to hurt. He ran his hand across his lips. They were covered with blood.

"You're bleeding," Charlie said. She pulled a tissue from her purse and pressed it against his lips. The world began to spin and he felt Charlie wrap her arm under his and move him towards the stairs.

"Seems like I've done this before," Charlie said, when they reached the door. She slid her arm out. "You can make it from here."

"How about the beer?"

"The only alcohol you need is antiseptic, teacher man." She kissed his cheek softly. "I'll let you know where I am."

Charlie walked down the stairs without looking back. Nate continued to lean there after she'd disappeared, his mouth aching and his head swimming, wondering if she'd turn around, not sure what would happen if she did.

Nate heard Charlie's Land Cruiser crank. She wasn't coming back. He opened the door and stepped inside the hallway. He moved slowly, not trusting his balance. Using the wall for support, Nate eased down the hall, but the wall began to move, rocking like a ship making its way through a rolling sea. He tried to counter the movements, knowing they weren't real, but they overwhelmed him, dragging him hard to the floor. He lay still for a minute, waiting for the rolling to stop. Becca's door opened.

"You smell like a brewery," she said from above him. Her voice was harsh and judgmental. "It sure didn't take you long to get wasted."

"I'm not wasted," he said. "I got hit in the head."

"I saw you with those cops and I saw your girlfriend carry you up," Becca said. "You two make quite a pair."

"It's not what you think and we're not a pair." He reached out his hand. "Could you help me up?"

She took his hand. Her hand felt warm and soft, but her grip was firm.

"Thanks," he said, when he was standing. "I couldn't have done it without you." He was still holding her hand.

"You know," she said, examining his face, "the kids are going to think you're a real, tough guy." She withdrew her hand. "Does it hurt?"

"Only when I kiss."

Becca nodded. "That's good," she said, "then I guess you'll remain pain-free for the foreseeable future." She turned towards her door. "Now if you'll excuse me, I have stuff to do."

"When are you moving?" he asked her retreating figure.

She turned back around. "Saturday. You trying to get rid of me?"

"No. I just thought you might need some help."

"Thanks, but J.R.'s going to help. His van will hold most of my stuff."

"You'll need a truck for the furniture."

"I know. I tried to rent one, but nobody will hold one for me for a local move. I'll have to recheck in the morning."

"You can use my dad's. It comes with free labor."

She walked back towards him. "Thanks." She was close now, scrutinizing him, her eyes questioning.

"You know," she said, "I'm going to miss my crazy neighbor, the schizophrenic one that I can't quite figure out."

"Schizophrenia's also in the eye of the beholder."

"No," she said. "In this case it's in my neighbor's brain, but I do believe it's curable."

"So, you're abandoning him in his hour of need?"

"No, I'm giving him the opportunity to self-medicate in a sterile environment."

"You're not afraid he'll self-destruct?"

"No, I think he knows where his reality lies. He just needs time to adapt."

"Suppose he doesn't?"

"Then," she said walking away, "he'll meet the fate of his Neanderthal ancestors."

Nate watched the door close behind her. "Cro-Magnon," he whispered to the closed door. She always forgot. He stood there a moment. The walls quit moving and he walked slowly between them to his apartment.

CHAPTER FOURTEEN

Nate eyes swept around his classroom. Was there anything else he could do? Friday was the last half-day for teachers. They'd had three days to practice. On Monday, they'd run the full schedule. Nate's desk was piled with class changes and memos.

There were two basic types of memos: One covered student changes, and the others covered assigned teacher duties. He made two piles, and then began to update his class rosters. The paperwork was overwhelming, and the school year had just begun.

Nate's doorknob rattled and he looked up to see Fulton's ample frame.

"You doing okay, new guy?" Fulton said. He slid a chair around and flopped down. "First week's kind of confusing."

Nate held up the memos. "I thought the Marines had paperwork. When do we teach?"

"Get the paperwork done right," Fulton said, "the teaching doesn't matter." He laughed at his joke. "Seriously," he said rising from the chair, "let me know if I can help. Every year starts like this one, but by the end of next week, we'll be on cruise control."

"Thanks," Nate said. He was glad to have Fulton, despite his shortcomings. There were so many questions. If nothing else, Fulton was experienced.

"By the way," Fulton said, when he reached the door, "Newberry ordered chicken from the Frog Shack. Sort of a tradition to start the year." He looked at the wall clock. "It won't be here for half an hour, but you need to get there early. Some of these teachers are real chicken hawks."

"Thanks," Nate said. "I'll be there in a minute." He got back to work, rewriting the marked-over grade books and reading the memos. Teacher assignments were listed by last name and first initial.

There were two lunches. He had outside duty during the second one. He scanned the list with the idea of dividing the school grounds into sections. Two names below his, he read 'Noble, R.'. They'd hardly spoken all week, and he wondered how Becca was doing. He tucked the assignment sheet in his shirt pocket. He'd probably see her at lunch.

Arriving at the cafeteria, Nate found that Fulton was right. Everyone was already there. Newberry stood by the door. He waved Nate aside using a crusty chicken leg as a pointer.

"My spies tell me you're doing okay," Newberry said. He took a big bite from the chicken leg, swallowing it quickly in the manner of a man accustomed to eating on the run. "Is that right or do I need to send out my support troops?"

"Actually, I think I'm pretty good. I'll let you know on Monday."

Newberry clasped Nate's arm and turned him towards the food.

"Monday will be fine. Now get something to eat before Fulton sprouts feathers."

"That's funny," Nate said, watching Fulton rejoin the line. "He already warned me about the chicken hawks."

Newberry nodded. "Dorothy told me you were an instigator. If Fulton messes with me, I'll turn him into a chicken."

Nate filled his plate and joined Fulton. He didn't see J.R. Becca was sitting with Jackie Denton.

"The new and the old," Fulton said, motioning in their direction. He ate in a crouched position, his hands never resting. His eyes were on Jackie and Becca.

"What'd you mean? Nate asked.

Fulton swallowed. "Those two," he answered, nodding towards Becca and Jackie. "Come on, I know you've heard about J.R."

"A little," Nate answered, "though I didn't think there was much to it."

"Oh, it's true," Fulton said, cleaning a bone with his teeth, "and Jackie was the first one."

"Really," Nate answered. He looked at Jackie. *No way*, he thought, *not with J.R.* If he were to use one word to describe J.R., it would be "scruffy". His word for Jackie would be "elegant".

"Funny thing," Fulton continued, apparently sensing Nate's doubt, "is that she still fills in when he's not cultivating something new." He looked up at Nate, then back across at Becca and Jackie. "You got any designs in that direction?"

"Not particularly," Nate answered. "Why?"

"Just curious: If you did, I thought you'd like to know that J.R.'s kind of territorial. If some other guy comes on the scene, he moves real fast to lock up his trophy."

Nate laughed. "We talking about the same guy?"

"Yep," Fulton answered. "And when he locks one up, she won't be running free until he's through with her."

Nate looked at the two women and back at Fulton. He needed to discuss the playground assignment with Becca.

"Excuse me," he said standing up, "I'm going to invade J.R.'s trophy case."

Jackie and Becca were heads down in a teacher supply catalog when he approached. Jackie looked up first.

"May I?" he asked, pointing towards an empty chair.

"Please," she said. She glanced towards Becca. "I hear you two had quite an adventure."

"We did," Nate answered, taking a seat, "and I'll never ride with her again."

"I didn't hear about that," Jackie said. "I meant the cops and the rope and all that."

"He knows what you meant," Becca said. "He's just being cute." She sounded tired.

"Ready for the big move?" Nate asked, "or did you come to your senses?"

"I'm exhausted, but I've got to do it. Were you serious about the truck?"

"Like a heart attack," he answered. He winced at his remark. Bad time for a dad joke. "What time are you planning to start?"

"Nine, if that's okay with you. J.R. said he'd be there." Nate watched Jackie for a reaction. There was none.

"You need any help tonight?"

"No, thanks." She stood up slowly. "I'll see you in the morning."

Saturday morning Nate woke early. The sweet tropical air that slipped through the old building's walls settled around him, putting him in a pleasant mood.

He started the coffee, making only enough for one mug, waiting for the initial burp before heading down the hall for his shower. He wore his sweat pants and carried the clothes he'd wear; a pair of old cargo shorts and a marine T-shirt that said, 'Don't Run from a U.S. Marine: You'll just die tired'. He'd picked it to annoy Becca. He wasn't sure why.

Becca's apartment was quiet and no lights shone under her doors. He debated knocking but decided against it. It was still early.

He planned the day while he showered. Arrival at his parent's house was predictable. His mother would have breakfast ready. She'd expect him to eat, and his Dad would offer to help with the move. He'd discourage that. That would make two teams: J.R. and Becca and his father and him. This wasn't the way he wanted the day to work out. Not that it really mattered. He was just doing "what if" scenarios.

Nate gulped down the coffee and headed out. The sun was just rising above the buildings when he reached the back porch. He glided down the stairs, slipped through the gate and out to the sidewalk, breaking into an involuntary jog as he headed towards Bay Street. Only assorted sea birds and a traffic light's continual clicking broke the silence.

He slowed to a walk when he reached the corner, angling across the street towards his Miata.

"Good morning, Quick Silver," he said out loud, "you look ready to run." He searched for Becca's BMW, spotting Scarlett parked almost half-a-block away, where Bay Street ended in a hard left turn. He wondered why she parked there. There were several closer spaces. Rounding the turn, he saw the answer.

J.R.'s van greeted him with a smile. Its upturned headlights, narrow grill, and peeling paint formed a perfect caricature of its owner.

The van's appearance hit him like an ambush's sudden violence. One minute you're happy and content and the next you're knocked on your ass, wondering what hit you and if you'll survive. He felt betrayed, like a trusted local had given away his position.

He put the Miata in reverse. His heart pounded and his hands felt weak, barely able to grasp the wheel. He stopped when he reached their porch and looked up at Becca's windows. They remained dark.

Images of J.R. and Becca swept over him. He forced them away, gritting his teeth until the images disappeared. *None of my business,* he told himself, slipping the Miata in gear. Nobody here has any obligations and Becca and I are way too different for anything to ever happen. He'd be glad when she was gone. He liked his life simple.

Arriving at his parents' house, he found his father's truck parked out back by the garage. He pulled in beside it. His mother's Jeep Cherokee was missing. A sheet of yellow note paper fluttered beneath the truck's wipers. He took the note down and read it: "Gone to yard sale; keys in truck, breakfast in fridge. Bismarck's been fed no matter what he tells you."

Relief swept over him. His mother had psychic powers. She'd sense something was wrong and in five minutes she'd had him spilling his guts.

Bismarck barked a greeting from the back porch door.

"I'm coming, big boy," he yelled at the unseen animal. Nate walked across the deck and opened the porch door. The big shepherd ran towards him, and sat at his feet, too disciplined to jump but his long tail had a mind of its own, pounding the floor like a drum. Nate knelt down and pulled Bismarck against him. Nobody gave better hugs and he welcomed the soothing, wet kisses that accompanied them.

He wasn't hungry, but he microwaved the ham and eggs and shared them with Bismarck.

"Stay here, boy," he said, when he finished. "I'll tell Dad to bring you out later." He left a note, telling where they'd be and when he thought they'd finish, suggesting Bismarck would enjoy a ride to the beach.

He role-played on the ride back. He'd act like nothing had happened, like J.R. being there was no big deal. He rehearsed as he climbed the stairs, giving his words just the right tone and cadence. Convinced that he could play the role, he knocked on Becca's door.

She opened the door quickly, like she was expecting him.

"Hi," she said, "I heard the truck." She wore ripped jean shorts and a crimson Harvard T-shirt. Her hair was pulled back in a ponytail and she wore no makeup. Her eyes danced but her smile seemed forced. She ignored his shirt.

"Yeah," he answered. "It's a diesel. It's my Dad's toy. Kind of gives him status with the redneck crowd."

"Well, it's sure big enough," she said. "Between it and J.R.'s van we should only need one trip."

Nate hesitated. He'd parked the truck beside the apartment and hadn't gone past J.R.'s van. It could be gone and Becca might not know he'd seen it. After all, it had been parked on a back street far from the apartment.

"You can get a lot in those vans," he finally answered.

"Sure can," J.R. answered, coming out of the bathroom behind Nate. He was shirtless and a large, pink towel lay draped around his shoulders.

"I hope you're ready to work," he said to Nate, "I'm not much good after a hard night."

He slid between Nate and Becca, pausing to stretch when he reached the kitchen.

"I guess I'm getting old," he said, side-stepping the boxes that lined the counters and stopping at the bedroom door. He tossed the towel to Becca. "Thanks. I'll be ready in a minute." He closed Becca's bedroom door behind him.

Nate took a deep breath. J.R.'s familiarity was like a follow-up punch. He had to leave.

"I'm going out on the porch," he said. "Holler when you're ready to start."

"Holler?" Becca asked, smiling up at him. "I thought that was a mountain valley in West Virginia?"

He felt something in her voice, a forced lightness designed to temper an awkward situation.

"Actually," he said, "it completes the name of some local contests; Like Hog Hollering, for example."

"So it's a synonym for 'call'?"

"Exactly, and by the way, West Virginia's an illegal state." Why he thought of that he didn't know.

"Because everybody's got the same DNA."

Nate laughed. "No, because it was created from another state without the consent of the state, which is forbidden by the constitution."

"Come on," Becca said. She reached out and hooked his arm. Her touch surprised him. "Let's continue this fascinating conversation on the porch. I need to say goodbye to my river."

"It's my river," Nate said, allowing her to drag him, "but I'll let you visit."

Becca released his arm when they reached the door. Nate followed her across the porch and stood behind her at the banister, looking out across the river towards Lady's Island.

"Where's Saint Helena?" she asked without turning around. He moved beside her.

"You can't see it from here." He reached down and took her hand. He could touch too. "It's over there," he said, using her hand as a pointer. "Lady's Island reaches out and blocks your view, but it's not far." He aimed her hand further south. "See those water towers?"

"Yes," she answered, looking away from the towers and up at him. "Is that where they make the river?"

No," he answered, catching her mood. "They make it at the river factory. That's Parris Island."

She looked back towards the towers. "It seemed a long way when we took the bus."

"That's because your bus couldn't float."

She slid onto the banister, turning sideways, resting her back against a column.

"You seem better," she said, turning back towards him. "Why were you so nervous when you knocked on my door? You looked like you'd seen a ghost."

"You've got a ghost. I was afraid it would show up." Nate tried to keep his voice light, but he knew he didn't quite pull it off.

Becca slid off the banister.

"Nope, I don't buy that. You're not the type." She stepped towards him, leaning in, her fist raised, crowding him like a boxer trying to intimidate his opponent. "You going to tell me or do I have to beat it out of you?"

Nate laughed and retreated towards the door. "Come on, killer," he said. "Let's check on J.R. so we can get started."

"That's it," Becca said, lowering her fists. She turned towards the banister, then spun back around. "You think I slept with J.R.?"

Nate threw up his hands. "None of my business," he said, "but the evidence would support that conclusion."

"The evidence is circumstantial," she said, "and it isn't any of your business." She turned back around, her hands rested on the banister.

"That's what I said."

"But it's not what you meant." She turned to face him. "Look, last night I went with J.R. to an art reception. He had a lot to drink, and it's a long way out to Fripp Island. He slept on my couch and he was a perfect gentleman." She smiled at him. "Not that it's any of your business."

Nate sighed deeply. "Come on," he said. "Let's get you moved, so I can find a sane, southern woman to move in next door."

They met J.R. in the hallway. "That was a long goodbye," he said. "Did you cry me a river?"

"That's cute," Becca said, reaching out and pinching his cheek.

J.R. flinched. "Ouch," he said. "You're too rough." He looked at Nate. "Did he buy the couch story?"

"Hook, line and sinker," Becca answered. "Now, let's go," she said, leading them down the hall. "I want you guys to earn your beer."

Becca had everything ready: Taped cardboard boxes with white labels lined each wall. Her clothes were stuffed in plastic bags and stretched across her bed. The several pieces of furniture she owned were labeled "mine".

They started with the furniture, disassembling her kitchen table first, then wrapping it in sheets before carrying it down.

"It's sure gotten quiet," Nate said, completing his third trip down the stairs.

"I can't breathe, much less talk," J.R answered, starting back up. "I feel like Sisyphus with a square rock."

"Just think," Nate said, "when we get it loaded, we're half-way through."

"Thanks," J.R. said. He took a deep breath. "I feel better now."

"Just look at the worker bees, serving the queen," Becca said from the stoop above them. "Now get busy or I'll have to use my stinger."

"Okay," Nate said. He broke into a sweaty smile. He wasn't tired. Sandbags were heavier. "But for the record, queen bees only use their stingers to sting other queens. It's sort of a bee nuclear option."

They worked quickly, moving like a conveyor belt, up and down the stairs. Becca's strength impressed Nate. She handled large boxes easily, and seldom took breaks. Following her up the stairs, he reached around and squeezed her arm.

"With muscles like these, you don't need a stinger."

She turned to face him. "Only if another queen tries to steal my worker bees."

"Worker bees are all female."

"That figures. So what does that make you and J.R?

"Drones."

"What do drones do?"

"Mate with the queen, but they only do it once, then they die. It's not pretty. The queen flies off with their reproductive parts."

"Sounds like a Harvard divorce," Becca said. "You a bee expert?"

"My grandparents are beekeepers," Nate answered.

"You're still full of surprises. Now let's empty this hive before I lose you to another queen."

By late morning, the truck was loaded and they started on the van. At noon, they stood on the porch stoop, dripping with sweat, and admiring their work.

"You guys did great," Becca said, looking down at the loaded vehicles.

"Your gratitude overwhelms me, madam," J.R. said. His voice was deep and forceful. "Now if you'll provide me with mead and substance, I'll prepare for the second half of our crusade."

"Let's keep going," Nate said. "If we stop now we'll never get started. We can get a sandwich and beer on the way out." He glanced at Becca. "The Yankee's open."

"I can't drive and eat," J.R. said. "It's a right brain affliction."

"Baby," Becca said. "I'll drive; you eat, but you'll have to bring me back for my car."

Leaving The Yankee, J.R and Becca took the lead. Behind them, Nate battled the big diesel, steering with his knees while he ate. From his perch, he watched J.R alternately pass Becca her beer, then her sandwich. Their actions seemed strangely intimate, choreographed, like an old married couple that no longer needed to speak. *He wished she'd ridden with him.*

Nate's topless Miata greeted them in Becca's condo's parking lot. His father and Bismarck were nowhere in sight.

"Let's go," Becca said, following J.R. out of the van's passenger side. "Door's broken," she said to Nate's unasked question. "That your car?"

"Yeah, my dad drove it out. He's probably on the beach, walking my dog."

"That's nice," Becca said. "Now don't get any ideas about escaping."

"Aye, Captain Bligh," J.R. muttered, chugging his beer.

"I can't wait to live here," Becca said, spinning in circles. She stopped, facing the ocean. "Isn't this great? When we finish, we can cool off with a swim." She looked back at Nate and J.R.

"Break's over, boys," she said. "Time to put the queen in her castle."

Becca did less lifting and more directing on the move in, inspecting each box's label before sending it to its appropriate destination.

Her unit was ground level. That cut the walking distance in half, and a sliding glass door further sped things along. By mid-afternoon everything was inside if not in place.

"I'm going on strike if I don't get another beer," J.R. yelled to Becca. He and Nate were sprawled across the lounge chairs on the front patio.

"Get your own beer," she yelled back. "I don't need you anymore."

J.R looked across at Nate. Beads of sweat wound their way through his beard before dropping from his chin. "I think we've been used."

"No doubt," Nate said. He stood up and looked towards the beach. "You going swimming?" he yelled to Becca. "I need to find my dad."

"Great minds," she answered, stepping onto the patio in a black cover-up, flashing it open to reveal a white bikini. Both men whistled. "Exhaust them, fill them with beer," Becca said bowing, "and they'll follow you anywhere." She looked at J.R. He still wore his clothes from last night. "You'd need a permit to go on the beach in that outfit."

"I'm going to lie here and drink beer until the urge to move goes away," J.R. said. "I'll be here when you get back."

Nate stripped off his shirt and laid it across the lounger. He placed his wallet and keys on the shirt and wrapped it like a hobo bag. He liked his things in order. "Okay," he said to Becca. "Let's go catch the perfect wave."

They followed a wooden walkway that curved its way across the dunes, winding past golden sea oats whose swollen pods looked ready for harvest.

"Which way, Captain Teach?" Becca asked when they reached the beach.

Nate looked at the sand. Bismarck's padded prints stood out among the sandal markings.

"That way," he said, pointing in the direction Bismarck was heading. Becca walked ahead, wandering across the soft sand to a tidal pool left by the retreating ocean. She stopped at its edge. Nate followed.

"I'm surprised you remembered my Blackbeard story," he said, when he reached her.

"I found it fascinating," she said, "especially how you related it to the present."

"You didn't take its lesson too seriously. Pirates can be dangerous." He stood behind her, watching her reflection. It stretched across the pool, the tiny ripples wrinkling her skin. "You looking for something?"

"An answer," Becca said, sliding her foot across the pool's surface, shattering her image. She started to walk. "You think I'll find it?"

"I think so," Nate said, following her. He knew she was talking about her mother. "You've just got to look in the right place."

"I'm sorry to be a downer," she said, turning to face him, then looking down at the sand. "It's just that beaches always remind me of my childhood and the times I spent with my sister and mother. Now, Mom's dead and I feel guilty enjoying them."

Nate was silent. Her mood swing had caught him by surprise. She'd been so happy all morning. Becca doodled with her foot, then looked up. "Think J.R. would be impressed?" He looked down. She'd drawn a smiley face.

"It doesn't look like anyone I know," he said. A sudden ocean breeze lifted her hair and wrapped it around her face, dropping it over her eyes. He reached out and brushed it away then dropped his hand to her mouth and lifted both corners.

"Perfect match," he said, looking back down at her drawing. "Now J.R.'s got some competition."

They walked without speaking, threading their way through the umbrellas and coolers that lined the dunes, stopping when Bismarck's tracks ended in the packed sand and debris of the high-water mark.

"I've spotted our quarry," Nate said, pointing seaward. He watched Bismarck charge into the surf, bobbing like a furry cork, his favorite orange tennis ball protruding from his jaws.

"I never said thanks for all you did today," Becca said, as they headed towards the swimming dog.

"You're welcome," Nate said. "Anything to get you moved."

She laughed. "You know you're going to miss me."

"I'm afraid you're right," he said, "but I'm going to work on that."

"Why?" She was suddenly serious. "Am I that bad?"

"You're fine," he said. "It's just that you don't really like people like me."

She stopped walking. "I like you. You've got some weird ideas, but you're very likable."

"Entertaining would be a better word. Sort of like a sideshow in your real world of Ivy League schools and New England brogues. I won't even bring up politics." He kicked the sand. "Look, we're different, and that's okay." He extended his hand. "Friends?"

She hesitated before taking it. "Friends," she said. She was smiling again. "I hope your dog likes me too."

"Ahoy there," Nate yelled, when they were closer.

"Ahoy yourself," his father yelled back.

Bismarck sniffed the air, then broke into a gallop, spraying sand with each stride. He skidded in beside Nate.

"Bismarck, this is Becca," Nate said. "She talks kind of funny but she's okay." Bismarck sat at Nate's feet, his giant head cocked in Becca's direction. His tongue hanging from his mouth, like a purple popsicle.

Becca stuck out her hand. "My, what big teeth you've got," she said, as Bismarck lifted a giant paw. "I'm glad you're friendlier than your master, or I'd be in big trouble." She knelt beside Bismarck and hugged his neck.

"Dogs can tell who likes them," Nate said, watching Becca. "It's an instinctive thing."

She reached her hand up and he pulled her to her feet. "I wish people could do that," she said, "though it would take the fun out of certain situations." Nate looked back down the beach. His father was jogging towards them. The orange glow of Bismarck's ball shone through his fingers.

"You've got to get this straight," Nate said, when his father reached them. "You throw, he fetches."

N.B. flipped the ball to Bismarck who snapped it from the air. "Thanks, I'll try to remember that." He looked at Becca. "So, Miss Noble, you're the one abandoning our fair city for this tropical isle?"

"I'm afraid so," Becca said, "though I don't think I'm going to suffer too much."

"No, I don't believe you will." He pointed his chin at Nate. "At least you won't have to put up with N.A. there."

"N.A.?" Becca asked, raising her eyebrows. "Not applicable?"

"No. No Ass. That's what his Marine buddies called him."

Nate shook his head. "Come on, Bismarck," Nate said, taking the tennis ball and tossing it down the beach. "Let's get out of here before Dad starts showing my baby pictures."

He ran with Bismarck; his father and Becca trailed behind. His father was a natural ambler and slow talker. The distance between them quickly increased.

J.R. was gone when Nate reached the condo. He wasn't sure if that was good. He regarded J.R. as a snake. Snakes were only dangerous if you didn't know where they were.

Nate turned to check Becca and his father's progress. They were wading through the surf, his father's dramatic courtroom gestures providing a strange contrast to their slow movement.

"Beaufort's fortunate to have such a lovely and educated import," N.B. said when they returned.

"And your father's an intelligent and witty man," Becca said. She slipped on her cover-up then turned back to Nate. "You must be adopted."

"No," his father said, wrapping his arm around Nate's shoulders, "we just haven't had him back long enough to work the Marines out of his system."

"When do you think that might be, Mr. Forrest?" Becca said. "After meeting you, I think he might have potential."

N.B. gave his son a quick glance. "Thanks," he said. "I think with a little luck he might be ready to present to society by Christmas."

Becca looked at Nate. "Well, I'm planning on feeding him tonight. You think I can trust him with sharp objects?"

"Probably," N.B. answered, "though his mother is expecting him for supper."

"Oh," Becca said. She sounded disappointed. "I guess it'll just be J.R. and me." She smiled at Nate. "Maybe we can compare notes."

"Dad," Nate said, "you think I could cancel out on Mom?"

"Well, son, that's up to you, but she did ask Mary Beth."

"The E.R. nurse?"

"One and the same." N.B. looked at his watch. "Matter of fact, we need to get going."

"Mom's a nurse," Nate said to Becca. "She's always trying to fix me up. Sorry about supper."

"Dinner," Becca said. "We call it dinner and that's okay. Goodbye, Mr. Forrest," she said. "I hope to see you again."

"I'm sure you will," N.B. said, opening the door for Bismarck, who leaped into the Miata's passenger seat. "Nate, you prefer the manly truck or the wimpy car?"

"I'll take the car," Nate answered. Bismarck sat in the passenger's seat like a tall person, his head rising above the windshield. Nate slid in beside him, waiting while his father fired up the diesel. Becca walked over and rested her elbows on the Miata's door.

"You know," she said, "I've heard that nurses make the best lovers. They just know how everything works, and they're trained to sense feelings." She ruffled his hair. "Makes sense, don't you think?"

"Maybe," Nate said. He watched his father pull away. "But I've heard that writers hold that honor."

"I assume there's a reason?"

"Sure," he said. "They're accustomed to getting inside their character's minds, so they do the same thing with their lovers. They become their lovers so they know everything they want and feel."

"Sounds reasonable. What about artists?" Her green eyes glimmered. She was teasing him. He almost repeated his J.R. warning but said instead, "Too self-absorbed. Worse than pirates."

Becca laughed. "You've sure got a pirate hang-up."

"Well," Nate said, starting the Miata, "history does have a way of repeating itself."

CHAPTER FIFTEEN

On Monday, Becca awoke in her new Fripp Island condo to the shrill cries of circling seagulls. She buried her head beneath her pillow to escape their morning chatter, finally surrendering when the alarm added its electronic buzzer to the outside serenade.

She dismounted slowly; her legs felt heavy and her shoulders ached. Moving in had taken its toll. She grabbed her robe and headed for the shower, anticipating its warm water on her achy muscles. At least here, she didn't have to walk down the hall.

After her shower, she poured a bowl of cereal and carried it onto the patio. She felt safe and content.

Across the street, she watched gray clouds dance along the waves. They rose and fell like a wind surfer, carried seaward by the prevailing winds. *It's not home,* she thought, but at least it's the same ocean.

The weekend had gone well and she felt settled. On Saturday, she'd cooked for J.R. Her beef stroganoff had turned out well, mating perfectly with J.R's boldly-textured Cabernet Sauvignon. J.R was a wine snob, right down to sniffing the cork.

He'd been an attentive and complimentary guest, but she sensed the beginning of a long-term seduction. He reminded her of Robert, only faster with more focus.

He was charming though, sensitive with an urbane wit that would have played well at Harvard. As far as the future went, she didn't know, but a serious relationship wasn't on her bucket list. She'd sent him home early, pleading fatigue, allowing only a goodnight cheek peck and a no-contact hug.

Sunday, she'd spent alone, organizing, hanging pictures, making the condo hers. Sunday evening, she'd pampered herself with a TV movie.

She thought about Nate, wondering about the nurse. It wasn't a real date; not that she cared, just dinner with his parents that his mother had arranged. She laughed at the idea of comparing notes. "Never kiss and tell," would be her answer assuming that he asked. What would it have been like if he'd been there? His father had impressed her. *He must be a great lawyer,* she thought. In five minutes, he'd dug out her life story, right down to her father's occupation.

Of course, she'd found out some things about Nate. He'd been a troubled teenager, dropping out of college to join the Marines. A detention center with pay, according to N.B., but it had worked on Nate and he'd managed to complete his degree while recuperating from his wounds. *He's still growing up,* his father had said. *You'll see a different man in a year.* Somehow, she thought, heading back inside, she didn't think he was right and she wasn't sure she wanted him to be.

Back in her bedroom, she dressed quickly then hurried to the kitchen to make her lunch: Tuna fish on whole wheat. "You'd be proud, Mom," she said. "It's a perfect mix of protein and carbs just like you made me back in high school."

Last night she'd packed her school materials in a canvas bag along with her laptop. She carried them into the den and dumped them out, creating a messy pile in the middle of the floor. She had time for a brief review.

She flipped through each lesson plan, highlighting as she went. She then re-marked her textbooks with index cards and carefully repacked them. She'd update her computer later.

The review lifted her spirits and her legs felt lighter as she strolled to her car. She was ready. Backing Scarlett out, she smiled at herself in the mirror.

She was on her own and earning a living with words. Tonight, she would write. Her novel was beginning to ripen.

Kate had to fly from Rome to Valletta to meet Roberto. She needed to check the airline schedules and do a Goggle search on Malta. At least Kate led an interesting life.

At school, the morning disappeared, absorbed by a series of blurred class changes and hurried instruction. Everything took longer than she'd anticipated, and she was already behind her lesson plan schedule. The lunch bell's numbing buzz caught her by surprise. She checked the wall clock to make sure it was right before dismissing her class, giving tomorrow's assignment while her students streamed out the door.

These students were different than the professors' children she student taught in Boston. Just as bright, but less-structured; more verbal, with a stimulating curiosity that she found inspiring. She couldn't wait to see what the afternoon would bring.

Her classroom was a mess. She walked up and down its empty rows, straightening desks and picking up paper, stopping at the old refrigerator that held her sandwich and water bottle. The refrigerator was a relic of the Home Economics class that had previously inhabited her room. Its unauthorized existence provided a convenient alternative to the crowded teacher's lounge and Jackie Denton had already threatened Newberry with a departmental revolt if it were removed.

She ate at her desk, changing her lesson plans to reflect the day's events and making notes to condense lessons she considered less important. At 12:15, she headed out for her school yard duty, battling her way down hallways crowded with students hurrying to their lockers.

She spotted Nate propped up against a small oak near the gym, his body folded into the tree's contours like an additional limb.

"Right on time," he said, without looking around.

"Would you court-martial me if I was late?"

He unwound himself from the tree. "No," he said, "I'd exile you to an island with a pirate." He smiled slightly. "And speaking of pirates, how was your weekend?"

"Well, most of it you know, though I did see a fascinating movie that was filmed in South Carolina." She deliberately omitted J.R. If Nate wanted to know about J.R., he'd have to ask.

"*The Big Chill?*" Nate asked, before she could name it.

"No," she said, "but I liked that one too. I watched *Deliverance*. It's about four guys from Atlanta who go into the wilderness in canoes." She watched his face as she talked, trying to gauge his interest. Normally, she ranked movie descriptions right up there with vacation stories, but this movie had captivated her and the Burt Reynolds character, Lewis, reminded her of Nate.

"Civilized man versus nature and uncivilized man," she continued. He seemed interested. "The character growth was beautiful and so was the scenery."

"That movie's drowned a lot of people since it was rereleased," Nate said, when she finished. That wasn't the response she'd expected.

"Really," she asked, "stuntmen?"

"No, mostly kids who saw it and tried to take on the river. Its real name is Chattooga, which is Cherokee for 'bad-ass river'. One rapid drowned twelve people last summer. It's called 'Bull Sluice.' He was silent for a moment, "Bull Sluice," he said again. "You don't go down that river without Mister Bull's permission."

"You seem to know a lot about it."

"I should," he answered. A hesitant smile slid across his face. "I was almost lucky thirteen." Nate paused and looked out over the playground. "It was a great movie, though."

She thought back to the movie. "Did they really dam the river and turn it into a lake?"

"No," he said. "It's a protected wilderness area so it's just like it was. They did have to dynamite a couple of rapids to free up some bodies."

"Really?" she asked. "Why dynamite?"

"Because some rapids have a current called a 'hydraulic'. It'll keep a body for weeks, and it's too dangerous for divers to go in and pull them out. They use dynamite to break the current's flow and the rapid spits out the body."

She grimaced. "In one piece?"

"Usually," he answered, "depends on the rapid."

"Is it fun?" she asked, "I mean running the rapids; not the dynamite."

"Sure. It's like an all-day roller-coaster. It's a lot of hard work, though." He looked down at the ground and back up. She felt his eyes question her. "Chattooga is actually Cherokee for 'rocky river'," he finally said. "It's located in the northwestern part of South Carolina. He was quiet for a moment, then he said, "You want to run it?"

The question surprised her. It was almost like a dare. Her answer surprised her too.

"Sure," she said. She felt like she was calling his bluff. "When?"

Nate became quiet again. Becca thought he'd retract his invitation. She wasn't sure if she were happy or disappointed.

"Labor Day," he said. "We've got a three-day weekend."

"That's weekend after next."

"You scared?"

"No," she said. Things were moving too fast. In ten minutes, they'd gone from a movie to a wilderness trip that actually killed people. He was playing a game. She'd see how far he'd go. "Okay," she said, "what do we do next?"

"I'll call an outfitter and set everything up." He seemed suddenly serious, his eyes shifting across the playground and then back to her. "You sure you're not afraid?"

"Hey," she said, "I'm a big water sailor." That wasn't quite true. Her father was the sailor, but she'd crewed in some pretty rough seas.

He laughed. "That's not what I meant."

"What did you mean?"

"It'd just be you and me, way up in those mountains. You never know what could happen."

She pulled up her sleeve. "Remember that," she said, pointing at her bicep, "and we won't be alone. I'm going to ask J.R. and Jackie." He frowned. She knew he'd object, especially to J.R. but he surprised her again.

"Okay," he said. "I'll rent a bigger raft."

"I thought we'd use canoes? They had canoes in the movie. They look like a lot more fun than a lumbering old raft."

He shook his head. "Canoes take skill and special racks, neither of which you guys have. On a raft, you only need one skilled person and a crew that can follow directions."

It was her turn to frown. He was so cocky.

"Let me guess. You'd be the expert?"

He smiled, really it was a smirk. She hated that. He had a special talent for annoying her, just when she might be starting to like him. "Were you planning on being the expert?"

"No," she answered just as the fifth period bell rang. "I'm going to be the captain; sort of a nautical queen bee."

"Aye, Captain," Nate said. "We'll talk later." He saluted her and angled away towards the annex. He was almost there when he turned around. "Glad you didn't watch *The Titanic*," he yelled before he disappeared into the building.

Becca thought about the trip for the next two weeks. She replayed the movie. This time, she concentrated on the river, sensing its violence as it smashed men and boats against its jagged rocks. Some fear crept in, but she wasn't really afraid. More like apprehensive and even that she'd never admit to Nate. Something else she wouldn't admit: When he was around, she always felt safe.

She talked to Jackie, surprised at her willingness to go. She didn't seem the type. She had more trouble convincing J.R., especially when she told him the boy-boy, girl-girl tent arrangement she had planned.

"You'll change your mind when you see me in my Speedo," J.R. said, before he agreed to the trip.

Nate took his duties seriously. He made a list of supplies and clothing they'd need and scheduled a meeting after school in the library. Of course he'd shown up wearing a T-shirt that said, "Paddle faster, I hear banjo music." She smiled in spite of herself. This was proving to be an interesting experience.

Nate passed out a one-page map he'd copied off the internet. The map had paddling directions for each rapid and she couldn't believe it when he arranged their chairs to simulate a raft and conducted paddling drills. She'd felt silly, sitting on a chair, pretending to paddle an imaginary raft while Nate yelled out commands: "Back Paddle left, paddle right, back paddle right, forward left, back right. We want to be able to spin in a circle if we have to," Nate said, and remember, if you fall out, float with your head down and your toes up."

J.R. proved directionally challenged and bored by the drills. "Better to learn here than on the river," Nate told him. "Nobody ever drowned on carpet."

"We'll take two cars," Nate said, after the drills. "We're going to leave J.R.'s van downstream since the raft will already be strapped to my Jeep."

Watching Nate generated an air of excitement and the planning made her feel like part of a military operation. If her writing didn't work out, the life of a foreign correspondent had a certain rakish appeal; an appeal inspired by Hemingway's third wife, Martha, in a literary seed planted by Robert. She'd reread her thesis, recapturing the thrill she'd felt watching Martha and Hemingway cavort across the Spanish Civil War battlefields. When Nate mentioned he needed to go up a day early, she'd volunteered to go with him. That's what Martha would have done.

"We'll be setting up our camp," Nate said, his voice indifferent. "I'll bring the tents but don't forget your sleeping bag."

She'd expected a high five and a welcome aboard, but he'd become more distant since she'd moved, like he was deliberately disconnecting himself from her. Their lunchtime banter had deteriorated into banal exchanges about school or the weather. She missed the battles. She tried to prod him, voicing opinions certain to launch him into orbit. His low-key responses disappointed her. He'd mellowed. She had two suspects: Mary Beth and Charlie, but she never asked and neither one came up in conversation.

Her life consisted of school and preparation for school. "Prisoner in paradise," she told her father during one of their weekly chats. She did find time for afternoon runs along the beach and an occasional text to Lizzie, but that was about it. Even J.R. had quit pestering her.

She wasn't homesick though, and her dreamless nights reinforced the wisdom of her island move. The kids were great, but the energy required to spark their attention drained her. Weekends were spent catching up on things she was too tired to do during the week. Exciting things like laundry, grocery shopping, and house cleaning.

Kate was getting bored too. Her Trevi Fountain sex scene with Roberto was mechanical. Becca needed to do some research, maybe read a porno novel. Write what you know wasn't cutting it.

Becca was prepared to lie to Newberry when she asked for a personal day, but he approved it with a smile, noting that Nate had requested the same day.

"I don't want to know," he said, when she started to explain. "Besides, it'll be the lounge's hot topic by Tuesday, and I'm sure the rumors will be much better than the truth."

They planned to leave early Thursday morning. They'd take Nate's mother's Jeep Cherokee. Everything would be ready for J.R. and Jackie, who'd drive up Friday in J.R.'s van. They'd shuttle the cars Friday night. Saturday they'd run the river, camp Saturday night and drive back Sunday. Monday would be a recovery day. "You're going to need it," Nate said after the meeting, "but the pleasure will be worth the pain."

Her dream had a separate plan. It returned on the Tuesday before they left. This time it was different. Her role changed. She became an active participant, screaming at the dark figure as it pounded the car. The figure turned towards her, its features blurred in the shadows. It became clearer as it moved closer. Its right hand held a knife. She lay on the ground, paralyzed. The figure hovered over her, lifting the knife, showing her the blade before plunging it downward. She awoke screaming, amazed to be alive. She fought to draw the dream back into her consciousness, straining to see it only to have the figure disappear into a murky darkness. "Who are you?" she yelled. "Come back. Show me your face."

"I'll be fine, Daddy," Becca told her father on Wednesday night. She tried to shift the subject from the dream to the trip, telling him all the details. "Nate knows what he's doing," she said. "After all, he's done this before, and he was a Marine."

"That's what I'm worried about. Marines are brainwashed. They're too stupid to be afraid." She could sense the tension in his voice. "I don't guess I could offer a little bribe to talk you out of this thing? Say an expense paid trip to the Bahamas?"

"Sounds tempting," she said, "but I live on the beach. I'll be fine, and I'll call you Saturday when we finish."

Michael put the phone down, sighed, and looked up at his wife.

"That girl hasn't changed a bit. She's always done stuff like this except now it's bigger stuff, and I can't stop her."

Sally Noble leaned over her husband's chair and rubbed his shoulders. She'd listened to every word, especially the part about Becca's dream. Becca had seen her kill Allison. The memory wouldn't fade. Now it was becoming stronger. It was only a matter of time. Becca was like an IED with a faulty fuse. It might not go off, but you couldn't take the chance. You just blew it in place and moved on.

Sally's missing dog tags sealed Becca's fate. They must be in Allison's car. She'd combed the accident scene. They weren't there. Michael had locked the Jaguar in a storage shed, complete with an electronic lock and security system. It was his personal shrine. No visitors allowed. Becca's dream could end all that. God had given her a second chance. She had to act.

"Becca will be fine, Michael," Sally said, continuing to work his shoulders, "though I hate to leave you alone that weekend."

Michael shifted in his chair. "Where are you going?"

"You never listen to me," she said. "I told you that I'm going to see my mother. She wants me to look at some of Daddy's old papers, plus I haven't been home for a while."

"I must have forgotten," he said, relaxing back down into the chair. "This market's been running me crazy. It won't go down."

"You could come with me. Nothing like the West Virginia Mountain air to clear your head." Sally knew his answer. There'd been little contact between Michael and her family since their marriage. He'd never go there, and more importantly, he'd never call her there.

"No thanks, honey," he said. "I better stay here and keep an eye on things. Besides, that's not exactly my favorite part of the world."

She slid into the chair beside him. "Okay, if you're sure. We do need to plan a trip down there someday."

He pulled her close. "I know," he said. "Maybe this winter when things slow down. Besides, I'd be bad company worrying about Becca."

She nuzzled his neck and slid her hand up his leg. "Let me help you relax a little, then afterwards we could Google this river and see where Becca's going. It might make you feel better."

He slid his hands along her waist and lifted her onto his lap. Sally rocked against him. "You know," he said, lowering the recliner, "I'm starting to feel better already, cowgirl."

"That's quite a river," Sally said. She sat at the computer while Michael lay propped up in bed, straining to see. "Look at all these articles. There's even a map with instructions for running each rapid, plus it shows the approach roads and camping areas. Says here you have to register to camp and file a float plan to raft. It's got the ranger phone number and website."

"Print me a copy," Michael said. "I'll analyze the terrain and maybe give that young Marine some advice."

She made two copies, leaving one at the computer, bringing the other one to Michael, giving him a long kiss before snuggling in beside him.

He twisted the map, holding it up to the light, squinting to read it. She handed him his reading glasses.

"Thanks," he said. "Becca said they're camping at Bull Sluice, but putting in at Earl's Ford. I don't see either one."

"Northwest corner of the map. You Marines are always lost."

He ran his finger down the map and shook his head. She knew what he was seeing. The rapids were rated by difficulty one through six. Bull Sluice was a five. "It looks rough," he said, "real rough. Bet it scares the piss out of her." He lowered the map. "Might do her some good though. Hell, it might even get rid of those damn dreams."

CHAPTER SIXTEEN

Thursday morning Nate watched Becca's arrival from his upstairs porch. She was early. That figured; she'd been gung-ho all week. Why he'd let her come with him, he wasn't sure. Of course, he didn't know why he set up this little adventure in the first place. It sure didn't jive with his plan to put some distance between them. It just sort of happened; like she had some sort of mind control that he was helpless to resist.

He took a sip of coffee and watched Becca make a U-turn and park in front of his mother's jeep. Scarlett was topless as usual. Becca wore a bush hat straight out of *Indiana Jones*. She bounced out of Scarlett, glanced towards the river and headed across Bay Street.

Nate watched her walk; all energetic with a slight wiggle in her non-existent hips. Her steps were quick and short, like someone in a hurry. When she reached the half-way point, he cleared his throat and raised his watch to eye level. Becca looked up. "Hey," she yelled. "I'm early."

"You sure are," he said. "I'll need a minute. Come on up."

Becca crossed the street heading straight towards the porch. "I'm afraid you'll have to use the stairs," Nate said when she was directly beneath him, "the cops kept the rope."

She continued around the corner. It had only been a month since that night. Nate grabbed his coffee and headed down the hall. He wondered what she felt coming back here but he wouldn't ask. For now, that subject was closed.

Becca had just reached the stair's landing when he opened the back door.

"Wow," he said, "you look ready to raft. Water shorts, Tevas, bush hat. All you need is a river. LL Bean would be mighty proud."

Her green eyes sparkled beneath her hat's wide brim. *He remembered them from Parris Island,* aimed at him like a flashing rifle.

"I'm just following your expert orders," she said, "and I packed light." She leaned over his coffee cup and inhaled. "What would a person need to do to get a cup of that?"

"Let's see," he said. He took a sip. "This is mighty fine coffee, plus we've got to consider the law of supply and demand."

Becca crossed her arms. "There's a coffee shop around the corner."

"Oh," he said, surprised that she knew that. "In that case and in the interest of road trip solidarity, I think fair payment would consist of helping me roll my sleeping pad" he said, opening the door. "And," he added, as they walked down the hall, "agree to become a loyal crew member who obeys orders without question."

She followed him into his apartment. "I accept your terms on loyalty but reject blind obedience," she said, looking around. "I also reserve the right to mutiny if the coffee's bad."

Nate's luggage consisted of an internally-framed backpack with a detachable CamelBak. The newly rolled sleeping pad was strapped on top. He slung it across his shoulders. It was lighter than the ruck he'd humped across Afghanistan, despite the two tents stuffed inside. The pistol was an afterthought. It didn't weigh much and you never knew.

Nate carried his pack down to the Cherokee. Becca lagged behind, gulping her coffee as she walked. She opened Scarlett's trunk with her remote and raised the top. Nate lifted out her pack and two small duffle bags and tossed them in the Jeep.

"I thought you packed light?" he said.

"I did." She slid her pack beside his. "If you compare the total volume of our luggage, you'll find that I have less than you. You just have a bigger pack."

He closed the Cherokee's hatch. There was nothing he could discuss with this girl without arguing. It should be an interesting ride.

"Hop in, Einstein," he said. "We can discuss volume on the way up."

"Einstein was concerned with energy," Becca said. She climbed into the front seat. "Charles was the volume guy. His thing was the effect heat had on expansion."

Nate fought back a smile. "So size does matter?"

She shook her head. "Not as much as energy."

He started the Jeep and pulled on to Bay Street. Traffic was light.

"You know a lot of science for an English teacher," he said. Are we talking biology or physics?"

"Physics," she said. "If we were talking biology, this conversation would be loaded with sexual innuendos and we wouldn't want that."

"I hadn't noticed. Innuendos are in the eye of the beholder." Becca smiled and shook her head. He smiled back. He couldn't help it. Her sparkling eyes pulled him in. He was glad she came. Not that that meant anything serious. She was just entertaining in an irritating sort of way.

They drove through downtown Beaufort. Bay Street was empty with the exception of Luther's RXs' breakfast crowd.

Becca's head twisted from side to side, taking in the little shops that lined both sides of the street. She focused on Luther's. "Why the Rx?"

"My dad says it used to be a pharmacy with a tiny restaurant out back. All of Beaufort's shakers and movers met there for breakfast. The guy that bought it closed the pharmacy and expanded the restaurant. He kept the name and the same group of guys still meet there."

"Sounds like the good old boys still run things."

"Sounds like a group of successful people like to meet for breakfast," Nate answered. He anticipated her next question, and replied, "And no I don't have the demographics handy."

"Sorry," Becca said. "I do tend to get a little political." She kicked off her Tevas and propped her feet on the dash. "Besides," she said, "I'm on assignment and by the time we get to that mean, old river, I plan to know all about you. Your father already gave me the *Reader's Digest*, condensed version. You'd make an interesting character."

"Okay," he said, "as long as the coffee was good and you remain obedient."

"The coffee was great and I pledged loyalty, not obedience. There is a difference."

She questioned him as he drove: general family questions; brothers, sisters, what he was like as a child. By the time they reached the crossroad in the little town of Yemassee, he was in high school.

Nate pulled into Harold's Country Club for gas. A gray-haired man wearing a faded, green Texaco hat filled their tank.

"Country Club?" she asked, looking at the sign, then at the oil-stained concrete.

"I'll explain later," he said, "but they pump your gas and they've got the world's best steaks. Even Martha Stewart eats here."

Becca looked around again. "Only photographic evidence would convince me of that," she said, as they pulled back onto the highway. "Now, let's get back to your story. I believe you were a geeky, high school freshman." She gave him a quick glance. "I just can't visualize a geeky Neanderthal."

"Cro-Magnon," he corrected, "and I was geeky: straight As and a real teacher's pet. High school changed that. I'm not sure what, but something flipped on my rebellious switch. Mostly I cut classes and did some stuff that I shouldn't have done."

"Like what?"

"Like sneaking out in my Dad's boat or stealing beer from the Piggly Wiggly. Dad really got pissed when I combined the two." Nate smiled as he pictured his father, charging up from the dock, yelling his name, waving the forgotten Pabst Blue Ribbon can like a murder weapon.

"Sounds like you had a rough adolescence," Becca said, when he paused. "Perfect student to parents' nightmare in one year."

"I guess. I just wanted to escape from this little town. I didn't know what I wanted to do, but I knew I wanted to do something and it wasn't here. I really did want to see the world."

"So that's where the Marines came in?"

"Sort of," Nate answered. I got into The Citadel on my SATs and a little family influence, not my grades, but it was high school all over again. Anyway, The Citadel decided that a motorcycle-riding cadet with a fake ID in the company of an underage girl in a Charleston bar somehow violated the Cadet Code of Conduct. They told my parents to come get me, but I joined the Marines before Mom and Dad got there."

Becca shook her head. "I bet that was a fun day."

"Well, my mom cried, but my Dad was okay. He'd done the same thing, though he waited until after he graduated."

"And now you're back, perpetuating the same boring system that you hated?"

"I'm not like those teachers." He looked over at her. "And neither are you."

"Thanks," Becca said. "For now, I'm going to take that as a compliment."

"Look," Nate said; "I know I'm young, but in the last few years I've lived history and I've watched it being made. I understand how things in the past created the future and how war compresses that process. Standing on the banks of the Euphrates gave me a special perspective. After all, soldiers from Alexander the Great to Lawrence of Arabia stood there and I started thinking about whose footsteps I might be standing in. I do the same thing in Beaufort; wonder who's been there and what they thought?"

Nate paused for a moment. He'd talked too long but she had a way of reaching him, of finding the hidden path that led to his deepest secrets. It was time to wrap up.

"You know," he said, "history's not just a bunch of dates. If it's taught right, it's more like a novel, only the characters are real people. Kids need to understand that." He gave her a sly grin.

"Sorry," he said, "I guess I got carried away."

"Don't be." She turned towards him. Her chin rested on her hand.

"I'm pleasantly surprised. I never suspected that you had a real passion for teaching." Her face crinkled in a thoughtful frown. "I see you as just hanging around until something interesting comes along."

"Well, you did promote me to Cro-Magnon."

Becca laughed. "I keep forgetting. Keep it up and you'll make it all the way to 'Homo sapien.'"

They headed north, trading the Carolina coast for its interior's swamplands before climbing into the southern Piedmont's rolling hills. At noon, they crossed the Savannah River into Augusta. Nate drove through "Old Town". Augusta's famous azaleas were well past peak, but the Spanish moss dripping from the sprawling oaks fused a gray canopy above the narrow avenue.

"It's like driving through a tunnel," Becca said. "And look how the moss makes little swings."

Nate looked up. "Now don't tell anybody this," he said, "but when I was little I used to think that those were elf swings."

"Wow, super Marine believed in elves?"

"Didn't you?"

"No, we don't have moss, but my sister believed in trolls." She told him about her sister, Staci, and the bridge trolls.

"You were a tough little girl," he said, when she finished.

"Right now, I'm a hungry little girl. Whatever happened to that famous southern hospitality?"

"It's alive and well. Did you know that most of the South's gunpowder was produced right here in Augusta?"

Becca frowned. "I thought we were talking about food."

"I'm getting to that. Augusta also ginned much of the South's cotton until the boll weevil ruined the crop."

"Can you eat cotton?"

"No, but you can eat at Boll Weevils." He turned towards the river.

"Isn't that a bug?"

"Yes, but in this case, it's a restaurant in an old cotton warehouse down on the riverfront. I'll take you there, if you promise to eat fast and not talk funny." He glanced at his watch. "I want everything set up before dark."

"Deal," she said, "but for the record, it's you that talks funny."

Boll Weevils was crowded, but the service was fast. They ate quickly, gulping down a 'Cotton Burger,' drinking in the view of the Savannah River and passing on the thirty desserts that called to them from behind a curved glass wall.

"I never knew cotton could taste so good," Becca said as they pulled away from the restaurant. She yawned and patted her stomach. "Don't you people take siestas or is that another third world country?"

"We take power naps," Nate said, "but never when we're exploring unknown territory. Next stop, Bad Creek Outfitters."

Becca looked around. Augusta's lunch hour traffic swirled around them. She reclined her seat and yawned.

"Wake me in twenty minutes or when we run out of concrete roads and fossil fuel vehicles." She pulled her hat down over her eyes. "I'm saving my strength for the unknown frontier."

Nate drove north, recrossing the Savannah River into South Carolina, battling the afternoon sun as the road angled west. Becca fell asleep quickly, tossing a moment before twisting sideways. Her hat slid down, coming to rest on the seat beside her. Tousled blonde hair tumbled freely across her shoulders. Her face lay towards him. Her features were soft and relaxed, her lips turned upward in a Mona Lisa smile. Occasionally her eyelids fluttered.

He wondered if she might be dreaming. Asleep, she looked tiny and delicate, both childlike and womanly. A tender, warm feeling crept over him and he forced himself to turn away. There was something about her, an attraction he didn't understand but that he sensed best left alone, especially with his impairment, not that things would ever get that far. Nate noted the time on the dashboard clock. In twenty minutes he tapped Becca's arm.

"It's you," she said, opening her eyes slowly and stretching back against her seat. A sleepy smile crossed her face. "I was expecting Bradley Cooper."

"Sorry to disappoint."

She piled her hair and replaced her hat. "You know," she said, "I'm not really disappointed. He's a fake expert, but I've got the real thing." She stretched again, languid like a cat warmed by the sunshine, then glanced around. "And speaking of experts, where are we?"

"Northwest of Augusta," he answered. "This road follows an old Cherokee hunting path that they used to escape to the mountains. Not that it did them a lot of good. They still ended up on an Oklahoma reservation."

"Sally's part Cherokee," Becca said, "and from what my brother, Brad, says, she's a real warrior."

"I bet she is," Nate said, "but, tell me, how did an Air Force special ops, part-Cherokee female end up married to a rich Irish guy on a New York island?"

Becca raised her eyebrows. "Well, you're only allowed one stereotype per question but here goes: My Air Force pilot brother, Brad, flew Sally to the island; Daddy practically adopted her, and Mom hated her like a lioness finding an intruder snuggled in with her pride." She nodded. A quick smile slid across her face. "That's my Hemingway version," she said. "No wasted words and it even includes a lion."

"Not bad. Ernest would be proud. Now pretend you're Billy Faulkner and waste a few words on your island history. You're up to date on mine."

"Mine's boring," she said "You'd fall asleep at the wheel. After all, I haven't chased bad guys all over the world."

"Well, if your recent history is any example, I believe I could stay awake."

"Okay," she said, "but if I see one eye droop, I'm stopping."

Becca started with her childhood, describing daily trips around her island. "We'd go from creek to creek," she said. "Low tide was best. We always found something new. Mom called these trips, 'Noble Expeditions'. She herded us around the island like a brood of ducklings." She laughed. "Brad and Staci pretty much walked the straight and narrow, but I had a tendency to wander. Mom threatened to put a leash on me after she found me on top of Sunset Rock."

Nate could feel the excitement in her voice as she chased blue crabs up creek beds and raced her Sunfish across Shelter Island Sound. He could picture her there, a tiny version of herself, mischievous and energetic, instigating among her siblings.

She was class valedictorian and yearbook editor. "Twenty- two students," she said. "Not much competition, and we had to multitask." She threw in a couple of boyfriends, "local boys," she said, who never escaped the island. She told him about Harvard and about how she'd been amazed at the wealth, but disappointed in the academics.

"I felt like the smartest person there."

"Maybe you were," he said. Becca laughingly denied that. She described her mother's death and Sally's arrival. Stories about her father made them both laugh. Finally, she replayed her dream.

"So you still don't think it was an accident?" he asked, when she finished.

"That's the problem. I was there. I know it was an accident." Her voice rose. She'd defended this position before and she was dug in deep.

"It's like something else happened," she said, her voice lower, "maybe after the accident. I saw it and I keep seeing it in my dream." She pounded the console. "It keeps getting clearer and one day I'm going to know who it is."

"So this figure's a real person that you're going to be able to identify?"

"I know he's real and I know that somehow I know him. There's something there. It's like a puzzle. The pieces are all there. I just can't put them together." She told him about Lizzie and their Claudios Mojitos. "She's the only one who really believes me."

Her eyes looked pained. Their sparkle gone. He wanted to help but he wouldn't encourage her. Something happened that night. What, he had no idea but he had trouble believing a dream with fuzzy figures was the answer. That's what he'd say if she asked. He hoped she wouldn't.

Becca became quiet. The dream talk seemed to drain her and she turned away, her eyes focused on the changing scenery outside her window.

The road climbed steeply before beginning a winding descent towards the Sumter National Forest. The jeep wallowed through the tight turns, its tires emitting a low, protesting squeal. Nate dropped his speed. This would be a fun drive in his Miata but the Jeep was not happy.

Behind them a blue Corvette convertible gained quickly. Nate pulled over at a National Park plaque viewing area. He hated being held up. The Corvette roared by with a toot and a wave.

Nate studied the plaque. "Thomas Sumter, signer of the Declaration of Independence," he said, reading out loud.

Becca turned back towards him. "Oh, I'd forgotten. You guys used to be part of the Union."

"Still are," Nate answered, "though if youse guys aren't careful, we'll secede again. We've already got most of your money and we're holding all your Kamikaze Cadillac drivers hostage down in the Conch Republic."

Becca laughed. "Not all; my grandfather Noble's still running loose." She grabbed the dashboard and leaned forward. "I can see him now, heading down to Florida, fedora pulled down over his ears, scrunched over the wheel of his big Lincoln, blasting down the interstate at eighty."

"I've seen him," Nate said. "Those old guys travel in convoys. They spread out like fire ants and build condos like anthills. It's like Sherman on steroids, running amuck across our tranquil land."

Becca settled back in her seat. A slight frown slid across her face. "Sounds like you've been overrun."

"Don't worry," Nate said, "my cousin Willie and I came up with a plan to turn back the invasion."

Becca let out a deep sigh. "You and Cousin Willie? I can't wait to hear this."

"All right, I'll tell you, but you're sworn to secrecy."

"I took a loyalty oath."

"I guess that'll do," he said. She crossed her arms and assumed a "this better be good" pose.

"Well," Nate began, "our first step would be to capture an invasion group at a Welcome Center, fill their cars with kudzu and grits and send them back north."

They both laughed. "Two questions," Becca asked. "Why kudzu and grits, and how many beers were sacrificed to develop this strategy?"

"Well," Nate answered, "between Willie and me, the body count was around twelve." He flipped the plan through his mind. It'd been hatched on a low tide sandbar in reaction to a traffic-jammed road and an overcrowded river. Like many of his plans, it'd sounded better with beer.

"It's simple," he said. "Kudzu wipes out native plants, so it would destroy your crops. Grits would become your only food source. It's a well-known fact, documented by the *National Inquirer,* that eating grits has certain personality-mellowing properties that your countrymen would gradually adopt. They would in effect become southerners and leave us in peace." He glanced over to gauge Becca's reaction. Her face was neutral. "That's phase one," he said. "What do you think so far?"

"I don't know," she said, "I'm still digesting your plan's logistics. What happens in phase two?"

"Phase two is a gestation phase. It might take a few generations, but eventually the grits would work its magic and you'd all become southerners and we'd have won a bloodless rematch."

She nodded. "So this is a rematch?"

"Well, not exactly. The way I see it, future historians will refer to it as the 'great agricultural assimilation'. Word is that the CIA's planning to try it on North Korea, turn them into South Koreans. Problem is those guys might eat the kudzu."

Becca shook her head. "I think the only thing agricultural about your theory is its fertilizer potential." A brown, hand-painted sign caught her eye. "Of course, if you were part of a superior civilization, you wouldn't have missed your turn."

Nate braked hard. He saw the Bad Creek Outfitters sign in his mirror.

"You might have mentioned it," he said backing up, then heading down a narrow dirt road.

"Sorry," she answered. "I was overcome by manure fumes."

The road led to a log cabin surrounded by a trio of tin-covered sheds enclosed with chicken wire walls.

"Almost looks abandoned," Nate said. He tapped the horn and stepped out of the jeep. A bearded middle-aged man in faded overalls emerged from the nearest shed. Two overweight hounds wallowed behind him. One plopped down at Nate's feet.

"You must be Mr. Forrest," the man said. He stuck out his hand to Nate but his eyes were on Becca. "I'm Curtis," he said, shaking Nate's hand and nodding to Becca. "Your raft's in the shed and you're all paid up. Got all your other stuff too; helmets, paddles, life jackets. I cleaned them helmets real good."

"Thanks," Nate said. "You ready to load?" Curtis looked towards the shed then back at Nate.

· "Yes, sir. Y'all wait here. I'll go fetch your equipment."

"Helmets," Becca said walking beside Nate. "Do we really need helmets? They're so uncomfortable, and they didn't wear helmets in the movie."

Nate forced himself not to smile. "Not if you can pass the rock test."

Becca sighed and shook her head. "Okay, I'll bite. It can't be any worse than the kudzu. What's a rock test?"

"It's pretty straight forward," he said. "You hit yourself in the head with a big rock. If the rock breaks, you don't have to wear a helmet." He knelt down and petted the dog. "I used to offer it to my sniper section when they wanted to swap their Kevlar helmets for boonie hats. It's optional, though it's pretty accurate."

She folded her arms and nodded. "I bet you could pass."

"Let's be nice now," he said. "You know, the snarky thing we discussed."

"Sorry," she said, "I am working on it." She tilted her head up. "Sometimes you make it easy." Her eyes seemed to glow and a sly smile slid across her face. Their lips were inches apart, their shoulders touching. Was he supposed to kiss her? He always misread these things. There should be a manual. Lips or forehead? Hug or no hug? Suppose he was wrong? That would make for a long weekend.

Curtis saved him, emerging from the nearest shed dragging their raft. Nate helped him lift it onto the Jeep.

"You've got some pretty high water," Curtis said, when they'd finished lashing the raft to the Cherokee's roof rack. "Sure you don't need a guide? Those river rocks are mighty sneaky."

Curtis glanced at Becca and then at the cell phone on Nate's belt. "You're on your own up here." He shook his head. "Those things won't work. No towers and too many mountains."

"We've got an expert," Becca said. She patted Nate's shoulder. "If not, we'll be back for dynamite."

From Bad Creek Outfitters, the road wound its way lower into the river's valley. Car-sized, striped gray boulders lined its narrow shoulders like half-finished statues, abandoned by their creator. Deeper into the valley, the elms and maples gradually gave way to the shiny green leaves of mountain laurel.

Nate watched the raft's shadow dance across the jeep's hood. Overhead cargo made him nervous. He liked to see what he was carrying. The shadow helped.

"Are we almost there?" Becca asked, when the road leveled off. She seemed the same. Maybe he'd misread her signal. Maybe there'd been no signal at all.

"I don't think it's much further," Nate answered, "though it's been a while since I was here, and I don't usually take this road."

"You could have asked Curtis."

"Not Curtis."

"Why not?"

"Wouldn't want him to know where we're camping. He seemed to take a liking to you and some strange things happen way up in these mountains."

"You're paranoid, you know." She gave him a questioning look. "Plus you're scaring me."

"As they say, a little paranoia is a healthy thing." Nate braked hard for a sweeping left turn. "There it is," he said. He pulled into an empty, gravel parking area on the right.

"It's spooky," Becca said, looking around. "Where's everybody?"

"Working or in school. Saturday it'll be packed. That's why we needed an early start."

"Okay," she said. "What now?"

"Let's grab our stuff and get set up. I'd like to do some exploring before dark."

"That river's sure loud," Becca said, as they hiked their way from the parking lot up to the campground.

"It's calling for a sacrifice," Nate said. He cupped his hand to his ear, dropped his pack and surveyed the area. The campground was located on a plateau, carved from the river's granite banks and topped by green-covered mountains. Above them hundred-foot hemlocks dropped a soft cushion of needles and fire pits, formed from sun-bleached river stones, dotted the area.

"It wants a virgin," Becca said, lowering her pack beside his. She mimicked his ear cupping. "No," she said, "it wants an expert. Novices are too easy."

"Let's get setup, and then I'll introduce you to Mr. Bull," Nate said. "Maybe I can work a deal for old time's sake."

He picked a spot on the far side of the plateau near a fire pit. "Perfect location," he said to Becca, "Level with no rocks." Nate pulled a tent bag from his pack.

"We'll start with your tent," he said. "Ground cloth first, then we'll connect the frame and drive the stakes."

He laid the poles and stakes across the fire pit, grouping them by size. Everything was there, just like his father had promised. Becca stood behind him as he worked, handing him poles, which he bent, then clipped to the tent.

"That was way too easy," Becca said, when they finished. She'd been strangely quiet. No comments or advice, just a focused effort on what he was doing. Now, she stood back and looked at the tents. Twenty minutes ago they were a puzzle of crumpled nylon and mismatched poles. "Looks like we're ready for a real expedition." She turned to Nate. "Maybe you are an expert."

"You had doubts?" he asked, joining her by the tent's front flap. "Of course I couldn't have done it without you. See what happens when you follow orders."

"Politely stated requests," she said. "Besides, a tent's one thing; that river," she said, pointing downhill, "is another."

Nate shrugged. "Tomorrow, you'll be kissing my Tevas and worshipping the water I walk on." He ducked inside his tent and emerged with his pistol. Becca's eyes followed the weapon. He stuffed it in his shorts' cargo pocket. He knew she'd react. It only took a second.

"What's that for?" Becca asked. Her voice was loud and demanding. "You think that mountain man's going to attack us?

"No," Nate said. He kept his voice calm. "If I did, I wouldn't be here."

"You don't make any sense."

"Sure, I do. I don't think there's anything here to be afraid of, but the pistol's insurance in case I'm wrong; which I'm not."

"I guess you're a pistol expert?"

"I'm almost as good as Charlie, and she's going to the Olympics."

Becca looked at the bulge in Nate's shorts pocket. "I'm afraid of guns. They kill so many people."

"Have you ever fired a gun?"

"No," she answered, "I wouldn't fire one if my life depended on it."

"What about the night we met? Deep down, didn't you wish you had one?"

Becca was silent for a moment. Nate could sense her replaying the scene. "Yes," she finally said. "Of course, if I did, you'd have been shot. That's one of the problems."

"If you were well-trained, you wouldn't have fired."

She shrugged. "Let's discuss disarmament later. Right now, I want to see that rapid that's going to keep me up all night."

"The river's 'white noise'," Nate said. "You'll sleep like a baby, all snuggled up in your own tent. If you get scared you can always crawl in with me and my pistol."

"That's comforting to know. Now, I want to ask you something."

Her tone sounded serious. "Fire away," Nate answered, "and yes, I meant that to be funny."

She smiled. "You almost succeeded." She sat down on an elongated rock. Nate sat beside her. Becca stood back up. "Never mind," she said. "It's not important." She sat back down.

"Shoot," Nate said. "Go ahead and ask your question."

Becca sighed. "Cease-fire," she said. "What I wanted to know was if you started to kiss me at the raft place?"

So she'd noticed. He should have expected that. He wasn't sure how to answer but for now he'd tap dance around the subject.

"I think you're mistaking me for Curtis," he said. "I could feel a real attachment there." He smiled up at her. Becca's face remained relaxed but her voice was serious. "That's not an answer," she said.

"Suppose I had—kissed you, I mean?

"You can't answer a question with a question."

"You've never seen my dad in court. Anyway, I plead 'Nolo Contendere'." Nate stood up. "Court dismissed," he said. "Now let's go see Mr. Bull."

Nate led Becca down a narrow footpath that twisted its way along the Chattooga's rocky bank. A stand of mountain laurel lined the trail, its tortuous roots clinging to the scarce soil. Nate grabbed an exposed root. "Built-in handholds," he said, tugging on the root. "You'll appreciate them on the way back up."

He hoped the kiss thing was dead. It wouldn't happen again. She'd placed herself in his power. Nothing else would happen.

They moved downhill, stopping, where the campground and river trails merged. "We're going upstream," Nate said, when they reached the river. "Listen to that bull roar."

They followed the trail's narrow footholds. A light mist drifted up from the river, muddying the trail, and darkening the mountain laurel that migrated towards it. Nate looked down at the brown water, hurrying beneath them. Curtis was right about one thing; the water level was high.

"End of the line," Nate said, when a rocky outcrop blocked their way. "From here on, you pick your own path." He pointed across the river at a building-sized rock that jutted from the bank. "That's Georgia," he said. "North Carolina's a little further up river."

"Which one's Bull Sluice?" Becca asked. "They're two rapids and they both look mean."

"They both are," Nate answered. He moved up the riverbank. The wet rocks provided the traction of melting ice and he dropped to his knees when he reached the edge. Body surfing Bull Sluice wasn't on his agenda. He'd tried that once.

"We just call them 'First Drop' and 'Second Drop'. First Drop has the hydraulic." Nate pried a piece of driftwood from between two rocks.

"Watch this." He tossed the stick into the river just below First Drop.

The driftwood moved upstream, against the current, pulled like a death star into the rapid's froth before being shot out heading downstream, almost escaping before being pulled back into the rapid. Last summer, he'd been the driftwood, hurled from the raft and into the rapids. He could still feel the churning water bouncing him along the river bottom before it spit him out downstream, just as he ran out of air.

"That's why we use dynamite," he yelled up to Becca. "Come down here. I've got something else to show you."

"We're heading upstream," Nate said, when Becca reached him. "You're about to witness some of nature's ancient power."

They followed the river, leaping across boulders that collected like giant marbles along the water's edge. The cliffs narrowed as they moved north, funneling the water into a rocky flume that eventually blocked their way.

"Looks like a dead end," Becca said, "unless we're going for a swim."

Nate pointed to an opening in the otherwise solid granite wall. "We're going up there."

Becca looked at where he was pointing.

"I thought you planned to drown me, not drop me off a cliff."

"No dynamite required for climbing victims." Nate placed his foot in a narrow crevice and swung up onto a low ledge.

"Give me your hand," he said, reaching down. Becca hesitated, looking up at the top and back at him.

"I lied," she said. "The coffee was horrible."

Nate lowered his hand. "The coffee oath only applies to the raft and this isn't as high as it looks. Give it a try. We'll stop when you say to."

She put her hand in his. Her grip was strong. "Grab my wrist and I'll grab yours," he said. "You'll get twice the grip."

"Okay," she said. "I'll take all the grip I can get."

He pulled her beside him. She looked down at the river then up towards the top. Her breath came in short bursts. Nate sensed her fear. "Just go where I go," he said, "and tell me if you need to stop."

"Sounds good." Becca took a deep breath, then exhaled slowly. "But if you stop, I'll go right on past you."

Nate shook his head. She was different. No doubt about that. He looked up at the cliff and back down at Becca. How high would she go? Everyone else had quit.

"Okay," he said, "Let's climb, but stay a little below me in case I kick a rock loose. We never did that test." He turned around. A small stone slammed into his back. He looked down. Becca was smiling. He smiled back. He couldn't help it.

Nate grabbed a narrow ledge, feeling the rock's cool gritty surface against his fingers. He checked Becca, anchored his feet, and began to climb. He'd discovered this route on his last trip, a natural path that followed a series of ledges and crevices across the cliff's face before heading up.

Nate stopped at the first ledge and watched Becca climb. Her moves were deliberate, yet fluid, checking each handhold before moving her feet. She had guts. He'd give here that. He took a drink from his CamelBak and waited.

"You okay?" he asked, when Becca climbed up beside him.

"It's just like Sunset Rock, only a little taller." She looked down. "Okay, it's a lot taller." She shook her head. "Mom would definitely not approve."

Nate offered her his water pouch. She took several gulps and handed it back, wiping her mouth with the back of her hand. "Thanks," she said. "I'm ready if you are." He stored the pouch and started climbing. She'd fooled him again. He'd have bet she'd stop here.

Fifty feet higher, he found what he was looking for; a small crack that evolved into a deep fissure, zig-zagging its way to the top like a lightning bolt. "HOV lane ahead," he yelled down. "It gets easier from here."

Nate moved faster, confident in his grip, negotiating the fissure's twists like a curvy mountain road. He stopped along a natural terrace near the top. Becca was just below him, resting against a partially buried rock. Strands of blonde hair escaped from beneath her hat. He lowered his hand and pulled her up.

"You're a brave girl," he said. "Not many people would make this climb."

She laughed. "Sometimes my excessive visceral capacity expands into my cranial region." Her normally clipped speech was slow, and her breath came in short bursts.

"You'll need to explain that one to me," he said. "I'm no Charles Einstein."

"Well, Albert, in colloquial terms, it means I have more guts than brains." She looked down at the river. "Kind of like Cro-Magnon."

"Old Cro could scamper right up this thing," Nate said. He stood on the narrow ledge. "Come on. We're almost there and we don't want to climb down in the dark."

"At least I wouldn't have to look down," Becca said. She followed him to the wall's top.

"Well?" Nate asked, "Was it worth the climb?"

"OMG," Becca answered, looking out across a grassy meadow rimmed with giant spruces and enclosed like an open room by the surrounding mountains. "Looks like we've found Shangri-La."

"I think it came from up there," Nate said. He pointed to a hollowed out area on a cliff above them. "Probably loose soil that broke off and carried the vegetation with it. It's like a volcanic crater with one side open."

"It's so great," Becca said. She stood for a moment then made the short drop from the wall's top into the meadow. Nate followed. "It's almost magical," she said. "How'd you find it?"

"I spotted the opening on a rafting trip when we stopped to scout Bull Sluice. I hiked back upriver after we ran the rapid. Nobody else would come with me."

"So I'm your first visitor?"

"Sure are." Nate pulled out his phone. "We need to record this for posterity."

Becca held up her hand. "No cameras," she said. She removed her hat and ran her hand through her hair. "Not when I look like this."

She wiped her face with her arm. Dirty sweat beads flowed down her forehead, dividing at her nose before continuing across her cheek.

"You look like you should look after a climb like that; sweaty, dirty, and content." He resisted adding "radiant" and "glowing."

"You're an easy man to please."

"Well," Nate said, "my tastes are pretty primitive." He unbuttoned his shorts pocket and pulled out his pistol. "Anyway this is my shooting gallery, so I get to set the dress code."

Becca looked at him and shook her head. "How could you do that? It's so peaceful here."

"This is my peacemaker," Nate said. He raised the pistol and pointed it towards a dangling pinecone. Becca covered her ears. Her eyes flashed. It was Parris Island all over again. Nate lowered the pistol.

"It's just a .22. It's no louder than a handclap." Becca dropped her hands. "I hate loud noises," she said, "even fireworks."

Nate fired before she had time to react. The bullet ripped the cone off the limb scattering its seeds like feathers from a wounded bird.

"That's how we get new growth," he said. "I think Daniel Boone started the program." He fired twice more. Two cones fell. He lowered the pistol and turned towards Becca.

"Want to try? It's fun and you're helping the environment."

Becca looked at the pistol. "I don't know. I've never shot a gun. Suppose I do something stupid."

"We'll do a dry run: no bullets." Nate stepped beside her. "The pistol's on safe." He dropped the magazine and cleared the chamber. "It's empty." He extended the gun towards her. "Now it's just an expensive paper weight."

Becca took the pistol. "It feels light," she said, "more like a toy than a real gun." She pointed it towards a tree. Nate watched her aim.

"You look like Annie Oakley." He said. "At least you've got the hat." He slipped behind her, extending his arms, careful not to touch. "Right hand around the grip, left hand underneath, helping to support the gun's weight. All you have to do is center the front sight in the rear sight and squeeze the trigger." He reached around and flipped the safety off. "You may fire when ready. Remember, it's not loaded."

Becca aimed towards a tree across the meadow and pulled the trigger. The pistol jumped before the hammer fell. "You jerked the trigger," Nate said. He wrapped his hand around hers. His heart rate jumped at the touch. He wondered if she could feel it. "Slow and easy," he said, pulling her finger against the trigger. "Breathe, relax, aim, and squeeze," he said in a soft, low voice. "We call it BRAS."

"That's sexist," Becca said, aiming the pistol, "and your voice sounds like my gynecologist when he's got me in the stirrups."

Nate laughed. "It's an easy-to-remember acronym that refers to a common undergarment," he said, "and I was doing my best Marvin Gaye. Now let's get you ready to shoot. I need to clear that image out of my memory bank."

Nate shoved in a new magazine, chambered a round and handed her the pistol. "Two things," he said, louder than he intended. "Never point a gun at anything you don't plan to shoot and every gun is always loaded."

"Okay," she said, "but you're using your Parris Island voice. I find Marvin's more relaxing."

"I'll work on it." He stepped back. "Shoot when you're ready."

Her first shot slammed to the ground at her feet. Nate stepped up beside her. At least she hadn't dropped the pistol.

"You're anticipating the gun going off," he said. "Squeeze the trigger and you won't know when it's going to fire."

"Okay, coach." Nate watched her aim at the same cone. The pistol swayed, steadied, and then fired. The cone flew airborne.

"Well done, grasshopper," Nate said, from behind her.

She swung the pistol towards another tree. "Make my day, you big birch," she said firing twice more, dropping another two cones. Becca lowered the pistol and handed it to Nate. A surprised smile crossed her face.

"How'd you know I'd like it?"

"By the knife thing. You didn't roll up in a ball and wait to be killed. You were willing to defend yourself. You just needed a better weapon. The first rule of gunfighting is to bring a gun."

"You're very analytical in a psychological sort of way."

"I've seen it happen in combat," Nate said. "Some guys prefer the certainty of death to the anticipation of being killed. They'll stand up right in the middle of a fire fight." He handed her the pistol. "Let's empty this," he said. "I've got another box of ammo in my pack."

CHAPTER SEVENTEEN

Sally unfolded the rental company's map before leaving the Greenville/Spartanburg airport. She aligned it with the map she'd printed off her computer. Bull Sluice wasn't named on the big map. Only a narrow, blue line crossing Highway Seventy-Six marked the river. Her first stop was a pay phone in the Winn Dixie parking lot. She'd located it, courtesy of Google Maps. It was out of her way, but there'd be no cell phone records, and she'd declined the rental company's GPS. She put in her fifty cents and called the ranger station number listed on the map. A soft, southern, male voice answered. She told him she was Becca's sister and that there'd been a family emergency. She matched her accent to his. He'd resisted telling her but quickly gave in. Everybody trusted a southern damsel in distress.

"You won't have much trouble finding them," the Ranger added. "The campground's right off the main road, and they're the only ones registered."

Locating Becca was a plus. She'd have found her anyway, but having a specific location and learning the campground was empty gave her time and flexibility. Her next stop was a shopping center parking lot on Wade Hampton Drive. She'd found the gun on Craigslist and she was right on time. The truck matched the seller's description; a grey F150 crew cab with raised letter, mud tires parked by a garden center. She slipped on her newly acquired Clemson hat and polaroid sunglasses, then glanced at the freshly-printed South Carolina driver's license she needed to make the transaction legal. Not bad for fifty bucks, whoever Catherine Marie Hicks was. Ten minutes later, she'd purchased the perfect weapon for a night mission at close range; a twelve-gauge pump shotgun, complete with a box of buckshot. The extended magazine was a bonus. Eight rounds were better than five.

Rush hour traffic had eased by the time she pulled the black Ford Taurus back onto Interstate 85. She'd loaded the shotgun in the parking lot and locked it in the trunk next to the backseat pass through. No need to open the trunk. That's why she chose the Taurus.

Sally reviewed her plan as she drove. She estimated her driving time at about two hours. By then it would be dark. The map showed a parking lot just below the campground. She'd do a drive-by recon just to look things over; turn around and coast back, lights off. She'd use the hand brake. No brake lights that way.

A full moon was forecast. That would help. At night, noise was the important thing. The more light she had, the quieter she could be. She watched the moon rise on the northern horizon. The setting sun dulled its brightness. In a few hours, it would be glowing.

She visualized walking up the path, moving slowly towards Becca's campsite. Sally estimated the distance at five hundred meters. She'd fire into the tent head first, working her way down, emptying her gun. She wouldn't look inside. Even with gloves, she didn't want to touch the tent and she didn't want to see Becca's shredded body. Shotguns were brutal at close range.

She thought of Becca as she drove. Despite her hatred, killing Allison had been hard. Killing Becca would be different. Calculated and necessary, but without feeling; the knife's intimacy replaced by the shotgun's impersonal blast. Becca's friend, Nate, would become what the pilots referred to as, "collateral damage".

Nate followed Becca as they worked their way along the river, back to their campsite. She'd surprised him with both the climb and the pistol. He watched her walk. She moved quickly across the slippery rocks, stepping from boulder to boulder without breaking stride. She had runner's legs, skinny thighs with muscular calves that flexed as she walked. He realized he was staring and returned his focus to the river. There were two accepted routes for running Bull Sluice—three, if you counted portaging around on the Georgia side with your raft over your head and your tail between your legs. He'd give his crew that option. He'd used it himself. Somedays, you just don't feel brave.

Becca stopped when they reached the campground trail. "You're awfully quiet back there, No Ass," she said, turning around. "You sure you aren't checking me out?"

Her face was flush from the hike and flecks of mud speckled her cheeks. Her hat sat cocked back on her head and her hair flowed to her shoulders.

"No," he said, "but if I were, you'd pass."

Becca smiled. "You, too." She turned back around and started up the trail, "though I can see where you got your nickname."

The sun had slipped behind the mountains by the time they reached their tents, casting their campsite in shadows while still lighting the peaks above them.

Becca dropped to the ground by Nate's tent. "Killing pinecones makes me hungry," she said. "What gourmet feast do you have planned for tonight?"

He'd told her he'd provide the food. He crawled into the tent, opened his pack and took out two plastic, brown packets.

"Up here we always eat what we've shot," Nate answered. He removed a small, propane stove from its case. "Tonight's special is stewed pinecones, laced with cordite. That's 'gunpowder' for the uninitiated among us."

"I'm initiated," she said, "and I could eat a bear, so you'd better reload and start hunting."

Nate crawled out with the packets. "We'll save the bear for J.R. and Jackie. Tonight," he said holding up the brown pouches like trophies then dropping them in her lap, "we'll feast on these."

"MREs," Becca said. She examined the packages. "Hot dogs and beans or meatballs in tomato sauce."

"The brass says MRE stands for 'Meals, Ready to Eat,'" Nate said, "but the Marines in the field say it stands for 'Meals, Rejected by Everyone.'"

Becca laughed. "I guess I'm going to have the chance to cast my vote but excluding kudzu and grits, there's not much I'd reject right now."

"They're really pretty good. All you do is add water." Nate lit the stove, reaching back into the tent for a small pot that he filled with water from his hydration pack. "That's hot water for entrees and cold water for fruits and desserts. We'll make coffee in the morning."

"What can I do?" Becca asked. "I like to feel useful."

"You can reload my Colt and the extra magazine. It holds ten rounds. He handed her the pistol and a box of fifty bullets.

"Just push down from the top and slide the bullets in like this." He loaded two bullets. "After that I've got to secure the perimeter before it gets any darker."

"Are we at war?" Becca asked, loading the magazine. She looked around. "I always wanted to be a foreign correspondent." She handed the pistol and the loaded magazine back to Nate.

"Not that I know of," Nate answered, "but nothing coming out of Washington would surprise me." He put the pistol in his tent and pulled two small cardboard boxes from his pack. He handed one box to Becca. "We'll be using these."

"Booby trap, explosive, training," she read out loud. She shook her head. "What could possibly go wrong?"

"Nothing if you know what you're doing. Come on," he said, "we're going to set up a mechanical ambush along the trail to the parking lot and on the trail we took up from the river. You can pretend we're at war, but you'll have to make up your own dispatches unless your boyfriend attacks."

Becca followed Nate down the trail. "We're like Robert Jordan and Maria heading out to blow the bridge," she said from behind him. "You know... *For Whom the Bell Tolls?*"

"Didn't he get killed?"

"Yes, but they became lovers first. Remember, he finally confessed that the earth moved." She thought back to Lizzie. No story on the horizon and the earth remained unshaken.

"I remember," Nate said. "I guess Roberto died happy." He stopped where a stand of mountain laurel narrowed the trail. "We'll set the first device here," he said, "then place the other one where the two trails intersect."

Nate felt Becca's eyes as he carefully armed the explosives. "They aren't powerful," he said, without looking up, "but you wouldn't want one to go off in your hand. I borrowed them from the range's ammo bunker."

"Kind of like the dental floss," Becca said, as Nate attached a wire that became invisible when he stretched it across the trail.

"Better," he said. "This time I won't have to sacrifice my toes."

He finished arming the second device and gave her a thumbs-up. "Let's eat," he said. "I can relax now."

"Okay," Becca said. She gave him a long, curious look. "But for the record, you're more than a little paranoid."

The water was boiling when they returned to the tent.

Nate held the two MREs out to Becca. "Name your poison."

"You choose, you're the cook."

"You're the guest."

"How do a bunch of Marines choose?"

"They take them from a box turned upside down so they can't read the labels."

"Okay," she said. "I'll close my eyes; you mix them up behind your back."

Becca chose the meatballs, emitting a closed fist "Yes" when she saw her selection.

"Beginner's luck," Nate said. "Yours even comes with a chocolate bar." He poured hot water into the clear pouch, watching as two meatballs emerged from the solid red glob.

He handed her a plastic spoon. *"Bon appetite."*

"Merci beaucoup." She sniffed the pouch and took a small bite, holding it in her mouth for a moment before swallowing. "This isn't half-bad," she finally said. "Sort of like a TV dinner without the TV." Becca sat down on a rock by her tent.

Nate took a bite and sat down facing her. "I hate TV," he said, "but I always miss it for the first couple of days."

"Then what happens?"

"The numbness wears off, then I get comfortable with myself and my thoughts. My brain engages and I think about things that I never have time for."

"Such as?

"I don't know." He picked at his food and looked around watching the tents and trees fade into the approaching darkness. He flashed back to Afghanistan. The Taliban often attacked at dusk. He looked back at Becca. She was waiting for his answer. He'd start with the real one. How far he'd go he wasn't certain.

"The meaning of life," he finally said. "My place in the universe. Why I exist. If my existence makes a difference. How all people are alike, yet different. You know, the typical sitcom stuff."

"You confuse me," Becca said. She rose slowly to her feet, "and sometimes I'm not certain who you are. One day you're Atilla, and the next day you're Gandhi."

She stepped over the stove and stood above him. He strained to see her face.

"I'm nothing special," Nate said. "Just a guy who's seen a lot and tries to deal with the world the best he can. Sort of like old Falstaff but younger and better looking."

Becca sat down on a rock next to him. Only the sun reflecting off the river gave them light.

"I think you're like a marshmallow that's been cooked on an open fire," she said. "Burned and hardened on the outside, yet its core is still soft and sweet. Your 'tough guy attitude is just a facade."

"I think you're suffering from a case of fresh-air poisoning," he answered without looking up. "The mind's the first thing to go."

"Or, I could be wrong," she said, squirming to fit the rock's hard contours to her body, pushing against him in the process. "And you could be the insensitive Fascist I thought you were."

Nate laughed. "I'd prefer the marshmallow analogy if you don't mind."

"Well," she answered. "A marshmallow crown must be earned."

"What Herculean task do I have to perform?"

Becca stood up and returned to her rock. She looked over at Nate. "Well, you could begin by telling me what produced the charred shell. No more skipping the bad stuff."

"I've already told you."

"No, you gave me the PG version. I want the uncut, R-rated version with all the gritty details."

"You know what they say?"

"No," she said. "What do they say?"

"The devil's in the details."

"Well," she said, propping her chin in her hands, "let's find that devil."

He started with his sniper training at Quantico, setting the stage, taking her to Iraq first, followed by Afghanistan. Words seemed to flow. He told her things he'd never told anyone, not even his VA-provided shrink who thought he was crazy. Things no one else could understand, things about fear and hate and what it felt like to study a man before he died, holding a picture of him framed in your scope as you squeezed the trigger and watched the life leave his body in a cloud of red mist that might contain his soul.

Sometime during the telling, she moved beside him, settling against him as she sat. When she was still, he told her how he killed his best friend.

"Danny Ashley was on his first patrol," he said. "We were buddies at Quantico. He was my spotter. Danny wanted action but we were attached to an Afghani recon patrol, slipping undetected in and out of Pakistan from the Korengal Valley. We were hunting a HVT—a high-value-target—and we thought we'd found him holed up in a farmhouse. We waited until dark, then slipped across the border."

He could picture the farmhouse. It belonged on a Hollywood set. No sane person would venture up there. Not at night. Its squat form dominated the hilltop while its stone walls reflected the moonlight down into the valley the Marines called the Valley of Death. He glanced up. The same moon rose above the mountains, painting them with a soft, yellow glow. Seven thousand miles away, it looked down on a different scene, a scene where men stalked men in a desperate struggle, that no one could explain.

He could see the patrol, huddled together in the moonlight. Major Akmal's large white teeth smiled at him. He was sending a four-man patrol up the hill to watch the house until morning. Danny pleaded with Nate to let him go. "That's not going to happen," he said. "A sniper team sticks together."

The next morning, Nate woke to a clamor of rushing feet and excited voices. Akmal's soldiers formed a hasty perimeter. Five men were coming down the hill; Danny and the four-man patrol.

Their faces were bruised and bloody, their hands bound, their weapons gone. A narrow black wire unspooled behind them. Their movements were slow and rigid, like they were remote- controlled robots on a pre-programed mission. An olive-green plastic rectangle was strapped to each waist. With his scope, Nate could read the writing on the claymore mines. "'This side towards enemy." They were five self-propelled bombs. "The Taliban was giving us a choice," he said. "Kill our own men or let them kill us."

He'd cursed Danny as he traced the wire with his scope. He followed it back into the brush, finding the wire then having it disappear. He kept scanning, guessing, until he found its source, a tanned, blond man, probably Chechen, sprawled across a flat rock, partially hidden in a patch of scraggly brush. A cigarette dangled from his lip. He smiled as he watched the drama play out beneath him.

The clothespin-like detonator lay loose in his hand. It wasn't a hard shot, 300 meters with no wind. The heavy bullet would tear through the wiry brush undisturbed. He'd aimed at the top of the man's nose.

Nate took a deep breath and exhaled slowly, wondering if he could finish. The hard part was coming up. "Head shots don't always kill instantly," he told her, "but they produce an immediate, involuntary relaxing of the body's muscles.

"Sniper Biology 101," he added, fighting to control his voice. "The detonator should have dropped to the ground and blondie should've shit his pants."

Shouts rose from Akmal's men as the patrol drew nearer. The doomed men stopped. Machine gun fire kicked up dust behind them. They began to move. He heard Danny's voice. "Don't shoot. They won't blow them." He was crying. Other desperate pleas in a language he understood only by its tone reached him.

Smoke rose from his target. The Chechen was taking bigger puffs. Nate flexed his hand. The patrol was too close. If he didn't fire, Akmal would. The trigger gave easily, then tightened as he pulled. The rifle exploded, rising slightly then settled back on its target.

Things moved slowly; the soldier slid down against the rock, the detonator dropping beside him. His body jerked, refusing to die. Nate fired again. The man staggered, then fell forward; his final move punctuated by the explosion that ripped Danny in half.

He was trembling now, his voice cracking. Becca rubbed his shoulders. "Danny's legs kept walking," he said, when he could talk. "They kept coming towards us, keeping the same pace, like they hadn't gotten the message."

"What about you?" she asked, when his trembling stopped. Her fingers traced his scars through his shirt. "Is that where you got these?"

He told her the rest. About charging forward, how the bullets tore the air around him. How Major Akmal followed and died. About the four terrorists who leaped from the brush. He could see them, their dark features hidden by bearded faces, their weapons spitting flame and smoke.

He flinched, feeling the bullet, jerking from the recoil, seeing them fall at his feet. He kept firing, emptying his weapon before he crumpled beside them.

His body shook. Tears filled his eyes and spilled down his cheek. "I'm sorry, Danny," he whispered. "I couldn't wait."

He felt Becca's arm wrap around him. Her fingers moved slowly across his face. She wiped his tears, then softly traced his lips, exploring his face like a blind man.

He turned to see her. Their eyes locked. There was no question this time. She held his gaze as she bent forward. She kissed his forehead, moving down to his nose, nibbling his lips, her mouth warm and moist. He kissed her back, exploring her lips, tasting her, then harder, feeling her tongue as he twisted to pull her against him. Her eyes reflected the moonlight. They studied his face, asking him questions he couldn't answer.

She whispered in his ear, "Your tent or mine?"

He struggled to breathe. "Mine," he finally answered. His voice felt hoarse. "It's closer."

He lowered her to the ground, crawling, battling the mosquito netting as they wormed their way through the narrow opening, still locked together, and onto his sleeping pad.

She broke the kiss. Her head moved down his chest. She tugged his shirt upward. He squeezed her head to him, rubbing her neck, then her back, reaching lower, not wanting to let go.

She tugged his shirt again. "You going to cooperate or do I have to rip this thing off?" Her voice was husky but light. He relaxed his arms. She slid up him with the shirt as she stretched to free his arms.

He pulled her to his face, burying it, lifting her shirt then sliding his hands down. He unbuttoned her shorts. She squirmed, arching to help, tugging at his belt as her legs flailed. She kicked her shorts free then reached for his, surrounding him with her legs before rolling him onto his back.

"I learned that move in judo," she said. She straddled him, kissing him hard, squirming against him. He felt her dampness, arched for it, entering her slightly, lost her, then rolled her over. Everything worked.

"I learned that move in the Marines." He felt her tense, then relax. Her legs tightened around him.

"That's my capture move," she said. She locked her ankles. Her body was a muscle, taut yet pliable, melded against him. She moaned softly, squeezing him tighter, rocking him with her body. "Resistance is futile."

"Okay," he said, matching her movement. "I know when I've been licked."

She giggled softly. "You haven't been licked yet."

Afterwards he lay silently, her head pressed against his chest, their legs still entwined, her breathing soft and deep. She'd fallen asleep. Role reversal, he thought, lightly stroking her hair. He didn't want to wake her. He needed to think. Something had happened. More than just the sex. They'd both dropped their guard. They were no longer sparring partners. How she'd react to their new roles he didn't know. He didn't even know what their new roles would be or where they would lead. One thing he did know; he couldn't lose her. That thought surprised him. It had been a long time since he'd really cared. Danny had set him free in more ways than one. He owed Dr. Price an apology.

"I need to move," Becca said, breaking the silence. He unwrapped his leg from around hers. She slid towards the center of the tent. He waited silently for the words, "we shouldn't have done this," but she stretched then rolled back.

He pulled her to him, spooning against her, relieved there was no resistance. A moonlit sliver slipped through door, silhouetting her against the tent wall. He watched her shadow for clues.

"Becca," he said, "You still think I'm a marshmallow?"

She rolled over to face him. "I think you have soft hands and gentle thoughts."

"My thoughts are a little confused right now." He felt her breathing quicken, then grow deeper. She was thinking.

"Mine too," she said, "though Lizzie's going to banish me from my tribe."

He laughed. At least part of the old Becca was still there. "Okay," he asked. "Which tribe?"

"The Ferry Queens. Lizzie started it and I joined after dumping my last boyfriend. Its bylaws say you can't like men, forbids penis-inflicted orgasms, and bans anything that remotely resembles a gun." She ruffled his hair. "I think I'm three for three, though I did join before you introduced me to these forbidden pleasures."

She sighed deeply then sat up. He raised himself up beside her, his hands resting on her shoulders. "You plan on escaping?"

"Too late for that. You've already ruined me. What I really want is some of that chocolate from the MRE. Chocolate's my cigarette."

"You left it by the fire pit."

"I know," she said. "I'll get it. Besides, I think better with my clothes on."

"Hang on," he said. "Let me find a light." He pressed his lips against her shoulder. "I think better with your clothes on too." He felt for his pack. The light was in an outside compartment. He shined it towards the door where their clothes lay piled together.

Becca untangled them. "Boy," she said. "Some people can really mess up a tent."

"I had help," he said. "Some wild woman attacked me."

She handed him his clothes and sat down beside him, leaning against him as she pulled on her shorts.

"You coming with me?" she asked, patting his shorts, then slipping on her shirt and shoes.

He slid into his shorts and pulled on his Tevas. His shirt was missing. "Okay if I go topless?" She nuzzled his neck.

"I guess I could resist you as long as it's dark."

He flicked off the light and pulled her against him. "You afraid of the dark?" she asked.

"No," he answered. "Only you."

"Why me?"

"You could reveal my marshmallow secret."

She kissed his cheek. "I won't." She snuggled against him, burrowing her head into his chest. "If you got any harder, I couldn't penetrate your perimeter."

"I thought I penetrated your perimeter."

"Maybe so," she answered. She wrapped her leg around his and squeezed. "But you had inside help." Her hand slid slowly down his chest, then lower. He was ready.

"I thought you wanted chocolate?" Her hand slid back up, slowly caressing his face.

She kissed him softly. "I do," she said, "but once I'm refueled I just might want a crispy marshmallow, but this time I want it slow-roasted." He was so ready. He pulled her against him.

"Becca," he asked, "you think that chocolate could wait?"

Sally moved slowly up the trail. Her Cherokee ancestors had stalked these grounds. She felt their spirits in the thin mist that floated up from the river. That was a good omen. The more Gods the better. She stopped to listen as she climbed, counting her steps. At four hundred, she'd be near the campground. It was an easy stalk. The moonlight reflecting off the rocky trail lit her way and the gurgling river masked the light crunch of gravel beneath her feet.

At three hundred paces she spotted the tent's outline, lit like a dirty lantern against the wooded backdrop. She stood there, listening. Muted voices drifted from the tent. She couldn't hear the words, but the tone was calm. She smiled. Death Angel was in full stealth mode.

Sally moved forward again, more slowly now, securing one foot before lifting the other, like an egret stalking a minnow, her eyes locked on the tent. She halted when the tent darkened, listening for any changes. The voices remained low and calm. She was almost there. Her hands shook. She wasn't afraid, just anxious for it to begin. Waiting was the hard part. She picked up her pace.

The wire's light touch was like the shoulder tap of an old friend. Her mind raced as her foot slid forward, recognition arriving with the blinding explosion. Instinctively she backed off the path and sat. She wasn't hurt and she could do nothing until her night vision returned.

"Come on," Nate whispered. He grabbed Becca's arm with one hand and his pistol with the other. He wanted to be free of the tent. Whoever had tripped the wire would be along the path and knew where they were.

He slipped through the tent's netting and moved uphill, away from the river, and towards the forest's deep shadows. Becca was behind him, her hand clutching his shoulder.

The campground formed in Nate's mind like a battle position. Once they reached the woods, they'd have the advantage. They'd be looking downhill from concealment across the open campground.

Sally tracked the scampering noises, swinging the shotgun's barrel with them, relying on her ears, seeing nothing but a veil of solid gray. The noises stopped. She had them. They were trapped between the cliff and the river. The only way out was over her. She started forward, then changed her mind. Another tactic was called for: reconnaissance by fire. No need to get too close. She might get lucky. If she missed, they'd start running. She aimed into the darkness, sure of the direction, guessing at the height. Her night vision had returned. She closed her left eye, protecting it from the flash, and fired twice. The recoil slammed hard into her shoulder. Sally opened her good eye. Screams rang out above her. She started forward.

The pellet felt like a fist to Nate's chest. It drove him back and slammed him to the ground. His head hit first, followed by his shoulders. A sharp rock drove the air from his lungs. He heard himself moan and Becca scream. He was conscious, but he couldn't move. Becca was over him, touching his face. He tried to talk, but nothing came out. Below him, the pine needles cracked. Their assailant was coming to finish the job.

Sally didn't hurry. The booby trap made her wary. She moved forward, then sat, scanning the darkness. Rocks and trees teased her with their shapes, appearing human, moving when she stared at them, then blurring again. One outcrop seemed different. She brought the shotgun to her shoulder.

Nate felt Becca open his hand and remove the pistol. He was breathing now. He tried not to gasp. Any sound would draw fire. "He's coming after us, but he doesn't know we're armed," he whispered to Becca. "Lie on the ground and look up. You'll see him first. Aim at the center of his body, shoot twice then roll away. You've got ten rounds."

"Okay," she answered. Her voice broke. "How badly are you hurt?"

"I'm getting better. I hit my head and got the breath knocked out of me. I don't think the bullet did much damage. I just can't move. Probably a spinal bruise."

She lay down beside him. He felt her tremble. Her head was flat against the ground, the pistol extended. Below them, it was silent. He wondered what time it was. They could stay put all night. Tomorrow this area would be overrun with hikers. Their attacker couldn't wait.

Nate wanted to tell Becca. He forced his hand to move and tapped her ankle. She jumped at his touch, kicking a loose rock that began a noisy trip downhill. Three shots shattered the darkness, illuminating the shooter as they followed the rock's bouncing path.

Becca fired twice, rolled to her left, fired, and rolled again. Fire spewed at her from below, tearing into the hillside above her, showering her with rocks. She fired again and rolled, pressing her head into her arm. The rocks gnawed at her elbows and knees. Her arm was beneath her. She curled tighter; feeling the form stalking her, sensing it in the blackness. She now understood what Nate said: Men preferred the certainty of death to the horror of anticipation.

She raised her head. The woods remained quiet. A rock loosened behind her. She rolled on to her back. Another rock moved. It was closer. Crawling noises slipped from the darkness, close but shrouded in the shadows. She sat up, extending the pistol towards the trees. She felt a presence. Hands reached out from the darkness beneath her. One grabbed the pistol and the other covered her mouth. "It's okay," Nate whispered, pulling her against him, "it's okay."

They sat silently, shoulders touching, waiting, staring into the darkness as they strained to hear over the river's murmuring gurgles. In the parking lot, an engine roared to life.

"That's our boy," Nate whispered, as the car raced past. "You either hit him or scared him off." He patted her back. "You did good work, grasshopper."

She burrowed her head into his chest. "Thanks. I was trained by an expert."

He stood up, then pulled her to her feet. "Let's make sure we're alone and ride into Seneca. The cops need to get after this guy before he hurts somebody else."

"I don't think he'll hurt anybody else," Becca said. Nate felt her tremble. "It's him," she said.

"Curtis? The raft guy?"

"No, not him. I can tell by the shape. It's the figure from my dreams. He came for me."

"Well, we found five shells just like you thought," the Oconee County Deputy said. He shined his flashlight into the trees. "Your guy stayed pretty much along the trail. No sign of blood." He turned to Nate. "You sure you're okay? That's a mean-looking bruise. Looks like you caught a ricochet."

"I'm good," Nate answered. He held a small, propane lantern that cast monster shadows across the trees. "We'll leave in the morning, and I'll get it checked out then. Got any idea who we're looking for?"

"Nobody from around here."

"Why not?"

"Occasionally, some of the local boys take it upon themselves to sneak through the campgrounds and snatch some of the tourists' stuff, but from what you said, this guy came to kill. Nobody up here knows you."

He pushed his hat up with his flashlight. "Plus, a local boy wouldn't use the trail. Too afraid of running into somebody. They'd come across country and sneak in from behind." He looked hard at Nate. "No sir, I think you brought this one with you."

Nate glanced towards Becca. He debated mentioning her dream. Her head was down and he decided against it. Besides, Becca could be wrong. He turned to the deputy. "Thanks for coming out. We'll be out of here in the morning. I called our friends and cancelled the rafting trip."

A light mist cloaked the forest as they walked slowly back to the tents. Nate took the lead, his lantern swung in rhythm with his steps, its rays bouncing off the mist. He stopped and sniffed the air. "Smells like a battlefield."

"It was a battlefield," Becca said. She moved up beside him and wrapped her arm around his waist. "My first, but I don't think it'll be my last."

Nate kissed her lightly on the forehead. "Well," he said, "I'll always have your six."

"My what?"

"Your six," he said. He patted her butt. "Your six is your backside. The saying comes from the way numbers are positioned on a clock face."

Becca looked up and nodded, her face reflecting the glow from the lantern light. She snuggled back in. "I hate to admit it," she said, "but I find that both comforting and sexy." She patted his butt. "Not that I can't protect myself, and besides, you don't have a six."

CHAPTER EIGHTEEN

Michael Noble's face grew redder as he talked. "That girl's going to kill me." He paced past the table where Sally sat, reached the end of the porch, and retraced his steps. "A camping trip in the woods with some rebel Marine. Getting shot at. Hell, she shot back." He shook his head, stifling a smile by biting his lip, replaying the phone call. "I thought I was listening to a patrol leader's battle debrief. That girl's got more balls than her brother." He sat down hard, pounding his fist into his palm. "We're going down there this weekend and if I get my way, she's coming home."

Sally watched her husband steam. It was Sunday morning. Becca had waited two days to call. "She won't come," Sally said. "She's too much like you, plus I think she's got something going on with that Nate guy."

Michael resumed his pacing. "Well, we're going anyway. If nothing else, I'll put the fear of a real Marine into that history teacher."

"Okay, killer," Sally answered. She began to clear the table. Her hands trembled and her movements were slow. Sleep had proven impossible and the coffee only aggravated her already chafed nerves. Michael paced off without announcing his departure. She sat back down.

It had been a long two days. She'd spent Friday night in Greenville and flown back on Saturday. Michael's lack of interest in her family and his worry about Becca's little adventure made her cover story unnecessary.

She'd comforted him when Becca didn't call on Saturday. She'd begun to think she'd killed them both and that their bodies remained undiscovered. After all, she'd heard them both cry out. Now Becca was alive. Worse yet, that spoiled little child had battled her and won. At least Becca hadn't mentioned her dream. Maybe now, she'd have a new nightmare. She'd fly down with Michael. The trip was pointless, but at least she could check out Becca. Maybe she didn't have to die. She seemed impossible to kill. How many lives could that girl have?

Sally stole quick glances at her husband as they flew south. Michael sat in his traditional window seat. His eyes were focused outside, but she could tell his mind was somewhere else. A flight attendant walked by and she traded magazines. The movement caught Michael's attention.

"I've been thinking," he said, glancing out the window, then turning his gaze back to Sally. "Becca should see a psychologist; maybe even a hypnotist. You know, let him try to find out what that crazy dream really means. Get rid of this nonsense before it drives us both nuts."

The gasp she suppressed came out as a chuckle and she forced a smile to accompany it. Michael gave her a dumbfounded look. "I'm sorry," she said, chuckling again, then pinching his cheek. "I just don't see you as the psychological, hypnotic type. You know what those people are like."

"No," Michael said. "Do you?"

"Well, you know, they're weird. They give people false memories. I've seen things like that on that doctor show. You know, where kids accuse their parents of things they didn't do, because some therapist convinced them they happened."

"Yeah," Michael agreed, "I've heard of stuff like that, but I don't think it would happen with Becca."

"Why not?"

"Because those people are trying to go back to a person's childhood and find out why they're screwed up. We only want to explore one thing that happened a year ago."

Sally shook her head. "I still think it's a bad idea. She seems better and making her relive the accident might make her worse. We've got enough trouble with Staci."

Michael nodded then reached into her carry bag and popped open his copy of the *Wall Street Journal*. She knew the discussion was over. For all his bluster, Michael hated arguing. He just did what he planned to do. "We'll see how Becca's doing," he said, lowering the paper, "but if this crap keeps up, I'm going to do something."

She read for the rest of the flight, alternating between the fluff of the airline's publication and the in-depth analysis of several news magazines. She stole frequent glances at Michael, smiling when caught. He was quiet, but restless, rustling through newspapers, staring out the window, reclining his seat only to pop back up and stare at the headrest. Michael was a man of action. His favorite quote was, "Do something even if it's wrong." A slight shiver slid down her spine. He was about to do something. She couldn't stop him, but maybe she could stop Becca. The alternative wasn't pretty.

Arriving in Savannah, Michael was on his feet before the plane stopped taxiing. Sally sensed his urgency as he nudged her into the aisle, then slid in behind her. His hands were firm on her shoulders as he sped her down the stairs, steering her into the metal tunnel. Whatever plan he'd hatched was about to be sprung. She hoped she'd have time to react. At least Becca wouldn't crumble. She might give in, but that would take a sales job on Michael's part. All she needed was a little time to assess the situation.

Sally spotted Becca first, her blonde hair outlined against the green leaves of a towering corn plant. Nate stood close behind her, his arms encircling her waist. Becca's head was cocked back and her lips tilted upwards in a secret smile.

Sally studied Nate. He looked different now. Jean shorts and a faded safari shirt replaced the crisp cammies and DI hat. His face was softer. His gray eyes were still piercing, but their harshness was gone.

She remembered how Becca had hated him. "Things change," she thought. She pictured them huddled together in the mountain darkness, facing an unknown assailant. She wondered what the outcome would have been if she had pressed on with her attack. It didn't matter. She'd done the right thing. Bullet wounds were hard to explain. She'd lost a skirmish, but the war wasn't over.

Sally tapped Michael on this arm and pointed towards the pair in the corridor. "They don't seem to be looking for us."

Michael shook his head. "I guess there's something about being shot at that draws people together." He waved as they walked, finally catching Becca's attention. She ran towards them, holding Nate's hand, pulling him behind her.

"You're early, Daddy," she said. She released Nate's hand and wrapped her arms around her father's neck. "You look great." She turned and gave Sally a brief hug and an air kiss. "You too, Sally," she said. Becca glanced behind her. Nate waited several steps back.

"This is Nate." She pulled him forward. "I told you about him on the phone and you saw him in action on Parris Island."

Sally hugged Nate tightly. She'd heard about his shoulder wound. War was random. A little higher aim, a totally different outcome. Just like in the mountains.

"Thanks for all you did for Becca," she said. "That must have been horrifying."

Michael extended his hand. "Yeah, thanks," he said. He glanced towards Becca. "You both showed a lot of guts."

"Actually," Nate said, "Becca deserves the medals. We wouldn't have made it without her."

"I was a Marine grunt in Vietnam," Michael added. "Nighttime firefights are rough."

"That's our signal to get moving," Becca said. "We can swap war stories on the way home."

Leaving the airport, Becca drove at her normal quick pace. Nate twisted sideways to talk with Michael and Sally. He replayed the mountain battle for Michael who dug for every detail. Sally listened in silence. Military history fascinated her and this was like hearing an opposing general explain his strategy. The booby trap intrigued her. She should have expected it. In Helmond Province, the Marines were known to booby trap their booby traps. Next time, if there was a next time, she'd be more careful.

"We're going to Nate's parents for dinner tonight," Becca said, when the firefight had been exhausted. "I hope that's okay?"

"Sounds great," Michael said, "though we don't want to be any trouble."

"No trouble," Nate answered. "Mom and Dad didn't think you'd be down very often, so they wanted some time to get to know you."

Michael looked at Sally. She knew this was his opening to broach Becca's coming home.

"You know," Michael said, "with all this trouble Becca's been having, we're not so sure she should be so far from home."

Becca grabbed the rearview mirror and aimed it at her father's face.

"You expect me to come home?" she asked. Michael's eyes lowered. He could intimidate corporate boards, but not his daughter. "If that's why you came, you can just go back to the airport."

"Becca," her father said, "you need to do something. You can't live the rest of your life with some ghost chasing you around. It'll run you crazy."

"So, I guess you know an exorcist?"

"I was thinking more like a hypnotist. Maybe a psychologist."

"We know a root doctor."

"A what?" Sally asked, breaking her silence.

"A root doctor," Becca repeated. "It's like a witch doctor. They have them out on the islands and they can do all sorts of voodoo stuff. Rumor has it, our principal used to be one."

"I'm not kidding," Michael said. His tone was quiet but determined. "I want this thing cleared up."

"Look, Daddy," Becca said, staring hard into the mirror. "I've been thinking about this. There was somebody there the night of the accident and he followed me to Beaufort and then up into the mountains. I've got to find him before he kills me." She shivered at the word kill. "He knows I saw him. Maybe he's not connected to the accident, but he wants me dead."

"Baby," Michael said, in a soft, tired voice, "nobody wants to protect you more than me. That's why I want to get to the bottom of this."

"I don't believe you, Daddy. You want somebody to tell me it's all in my head, so I'll forget everything about it."

"That's not true, Becca. I want to find out what's happening as bad as you do."

"Okay," she said, readjusting the mirror. "I'll think about it. Now, let's change the subject."

Sally glanced at Michael. She'd heard enough. Becca's answer was ambiguous. Michael squeezed her hand in what she was sure was a victory grip. This thing could play out two ways. Maybe a psychologist would convince Becca that her dream was a pure fantasy, or under different circumstances, Becca would remember what she saw. Fifty-fifty wasn't her kind of odds. This was a gamble she couldn't afford to take.

"So this is how you lawyers live?" Michael asked N.B. as they strolled back from N.B.'s Battery Creek dock towards his house, sipping a frosty beer as they walked.

"Well, I do pretty well suing stockbrokers for bad advice."

Michael laughed. He swatted at the unseen gnats that swarmed around them. "You'd have to do pretty good just to keep these guys fed. I remember these monsters from Parris Island."

"Yeah, the no-see-ums can be pretty rough. I think they know the recruits aren't allowed to swat them. You remember that scene from the 'D.I.'?"

Michael laughed. "I remember. They held a funeral for a sand flea that a recruit slapped. That movie made me join the Corps."

"Me too," N.B. said, clinking his beer against Michael's. "Old Jack Webb was probably the best recruiter the Marines ever had."

"Probably was," Michael agreed. "I wish I'd taken my boy to see that movie. He slipped off and joined the Air Force."

"I'm not sure why Nate joined," N.B. said. "He always seemed to lack focus." He pointed towards his house where Nate and Becca stood holding hands next to a steaming outdoor cooker. Bismarck sat wedged between them, ready for handouts. "He seems to have a new focus now."

"I know," Michael said. "Becca too. That mountain firefight must have really changed things."

"I guess," N.B. said, looking back towards the house, "but I do think things were headed in that direction though without the conscious thoughts of the involved parties." He shook his head. "They're quite a pair."

"They are," Michael answered," and I think I hear somebody calling your name." N.B. cuffed his ear and turned towards the house.

"I think I'm being paged." He spotted Peggy on the bank, motioning for him to come up. "That's my signal," N.B said to Michael. "They need the chef to prepare the shrimp."

"Your wife's just what I imagined a true southern lady would be like," Michael said, as they started uphill from the dock. "Sweet, but you can tell there's a real backbone behind that smile."

"The term's 'Steel Magnolia' and you're right. Peggy's a lot tougher than me, though I'll sue you for slander if you quote me."

"Your secret's safe," Michael said. He watched Sally join Peggy beside the cooker. "Just between us two former jarheads, Sally's the same way." He laughed. "Of course, I feel a little guilty not warning Nate about Becca."

Peggy Forrest seated them at a weathered, newspaper-covered table beneath two sprawling oaks. Above them, Spanish moss provided a veil-like cover from the setting sun.

N.B dumped a large pot of steaming food onto the table. "Thought we'd give you a true southern seafood experience. No need to complicate things by using plates and silverware but from now on, it's every man for himself. Just make sure you peel the shrimp."

"What do you call this?" Michael asked. He mixed a bite of sausage, shrimp, and potatoes before chomping down on the corn on the cob. It's a great combination."

"We call it Frogmore Stew," Peggy answered. She'd done most of the cooking, allowing her husband to claim the final glory by boiling the shrimp. "It's a more quaint name, though it's also called Beaufort Stew, Carolina Stew and Low Country Boil. You know, I took some to work one day and the northern doctors though it had frogs in it."

"That's funny," Becca said. "Did you know your son calls us Yankees, not northerners and that he plans to attack us with grits and kudzu?"

She punched Nate on the shoulder, then grabbed a strand of moss from the tree trunk and draped it around his neck. "Of course he also believes in elves."

Nate elbowed her softly in the ribs. "That was our little secret."

"You're out of the closet now, elf man. Might as well confess."

"Well," he said, "at least I don't believe in ghosts." The words were a reflex and he regretted them as they left his lips. Becca's face crumbled. She counted Lizzie and him as her only true allies. "I'm sorry," he said, "I didn't mean that."

"It's okay," Becca said. She patted Nate's arm. "I know it's a strange story."

"Have you told N.B. about your dream?" Michael asked. "I bet he's done some detective work."

"Well," N.B. began in his slow drawl, "Nate's kind of briefed me, and I did talk to some of my police buddies. Of course a firsthand account always fills in some missing details." He turned to Becca. "No time like the present."

"Okay," she said. "I'll give you my New York minute version." She looked at Nate. "It's a lot faster than a South Carolina minute."

Michael listened intently as Becca spoke. He searched her words for something different, a little detail they had all missed that would give them a new direction to go on, but there was nothing new. He glanced at Sally. She sat still, her arms crossed with her head tilted up. Her eyes were locked on Becca.

"So what do you think?" Michael asked N.B. after Becca finished.

"You mean do I think Becca really saw something or if it's all in her mind?"

"Exactly," Michael answered." That's what we need to know. I've suggested a psychologist, maybe even a hypnotist. We need to get to the bottom of this."

N.B smiled at Becca then turned his attention back to Michael. "The police say all crimes have three things in common: means, motivation and opportunity. I always like to look at the facts first. They have to support any theory." He looked around the table. "I feel like I'm Columbo without the cigar, but here goes."

"We all agree there was a car accident that killed Becca's mother. We also agree that somebody tried to break into her apartment, though we can't know his intentions. Then we have the attack up in the mountains. Now what we have to see is if there's a common thread. Who knew where you were in Beaufort and the mountains?" He looked around the table again. "From what I know, only Michael and Sally." Becca nodded in agreement.

"Well, then, it's Sally," Michael said. He patted his belly. "I couldn't climb that damn rope." Nobody laughed. N.B looked at Sally. "Isn't this fun?"

"Not really," Sally answered.

"Give me a minute and I'll get you off." He glanced around at his audience. "Next we must examine motive. Who stands to benefit by Becca's demise? Not our only suspects, Sally or Michael, nor did they have the opportunity." N.B. took a puff on an imaginary cigar, inhaling deeply before exhaling with a sigh. "In conclusion, the available evidence doesn't support a conspiracy theory." N.B. turned to Becca. "I'm sorry, sweetie, but I think you're the victim of three horrible incidents. I just can't see how they could be related."

"What about my dream?" Becca asked. "The person I saw in the mountains is the one I see in my vision?"

N.B shook his head. "That part's always confused me. I mean, how can you be so certain when we're talking about a faceless figure?"

"I just know," Becca said. She took a deep breath and squeezed Nate's hand. "It's like you catch just a glimpse of someone you know; the curve of their chin or the way they walk, and you know it's them before your brain fills in the details. I know this person. I don't know how—I just know— and I believe that someday under the right circumstances, my brain will fill in the details. I just need a way to speed up that process."

"I don't know," N.B said, "but I'll tell you what I'd do."

"What," Becca asked, her voice rising. "Pretend that nothing happened? Don't you think I'd like to?" Nate felt her hand tighten. *You didn't question Becca's dream.*

"No," N.B. said, his voice still slow and relaxed. "You can't do that. I was thinking that maybe you and Nate might fly up over Thanksgiving and give the accident scene a good going over. You could take a bunch of pictures, walk the surrounding area, and make sure there's nothing there."

Becca shook her head. "The cops did that."

"Not really. They weren't looking for anything but skid marks and point of impact. No reason to."

Becca turned to Nate. "Want to give it a shot?"

"Sure," he answered. "Think you could handle it?"

"I guess. I haven't driven down Noyac Road since the accident." She looked at her father. "I think I'm stronger now, and it's about time you let someone see the Jag. We'll give it a good going over too."

"Okay," Michael said. "At least we're making progress." He lifted his beer towards N.B. "Thanks, counselor."

"Wait until you get my bill," N.B said. "There's a lot of New York minutes in a South Carolina hour."

Bile floated up into Sally's throat. She'd never expected this. Michael treated Allison's car like his private shrine. He kept it locked in a monitored storage unit in Greenport. Only he was allowed to visit. She forced herself to swallow, then diluted the bile with half a glass of iced tea. She watched Nate and Becca share a long embrace complete with a too-long kiss. They were going to find them. She'd looked everywhere else. Her dog tags were in that car.

"No cleanup," Peggy said. when they finished eating. She rolled the remains of corn cobs and shrimp peeling up in the newspaper and tossed them into a garbage bag. She turned towards her husband. "Maybe we could take a short boat ride downtown and check out Bay Street from the water."

"Can't," N.B. answered. "Something's wrong with the navigation lights. I think they're on Nate's to-do list."

"We need to get going anyway," Michael said. "I'm spoiling my surprise, but I taking the kids and Sally sailing tomorrow morning. Guy from my yacht club arranged for us to borrow a sailboat at Dataw Island. I hear they just rebuilt their marina."

"They did," N.B. answered, "but let me give you a definition of sailing I once heard. It goes something like this: 'Sailing is the fine art of going nowhere at great expense while being cold, wet, and miserable.' Sorry, but that pretty much summarizes my experiences. Of course I'm an impatient powerboater. What kind of boat did you borrow?"

"It's a Catalina 32 Sport. It's got a funny name. The owner says he named it with his ex-wife in mind." He squeezed Sally's shoulders and let out a loud laugh. "He named it the 'Knot Now.' Get it?" He laughed again. "It's got plenty of room. You and Peggy care to join us? I bet I can change your mind about sailing, plus I'm hoping a relaxing sail might refocus Becca's mind."

"Can't tomorrow. We're driving up to Charleston to see Peggy's sister." N.B took a long look across the marsh. "Weather forecast is a little sketchy. Weatherman's calling for a depression to form south of Jacksonville, then head out to sea. Problem is those storms have a history of sliding north and stalling out right on top of us. Things around here can get real bad, real quick. Almost like a homegrown hurricane."

Michael smiled at the news. "Real sailor's weather," he said, patting Sally on the shoulder. "Adds some excitement to going slowly."

Becca turned to her father and shook her head. "After last weekend, that's just what I need."

"This is fun excitement. Man's skill versus nature's power."

"That's very poetic, Daddy. Suppose nature wins."

"Oh, the deck's stacked, honey," Michael answered. "We just let old mother nature think she might have a chance."

CHAPTER NINETEEN

Nate studied the low-hanging sky as he followed Sally and Becca aboard the *Knot Now*. The warm wind pushed in from the east, chopping the water with its gusts, moving gray clouds across the bright morning sun. He'd listened to the Weather Channel and checked the forecast on his smart phone. Both agreed; cloudy with late morning clearing. He put the small cooler he carried down on the deck. His left shoulder ached. That was never a good sign.

"Red sky in morning, sailor take warning," Becca yelled across the boat to her already busy father. He didn't answer.

Nate watched Michael scurry along the deck. He bounced between the mast and the cockpit, tightening some lines, slackening others, pulling in unused fenders as he worked his way around the boat. Nate sensed an internal checklist.

"Can I help?" he asked, "not that you look like you need it."

Michael turned toward him. "You could throw the port side fenders in the locker. I like a clear deck when I launch. Don't need some landlubber tripping and going overboard."

"Roger that," Nate answered. He stored the fenders and joined Michael on the cabin roof next to the mast.

"I'm no sailor," he said, "but I follow orders real well." Michael gave him a quick glance and began to unfurl the main sail. A white baseball cap with "Captain" embroidered across its bill sat tilted back on his head.

"Then you and Becca make a perfect couple," Michael answered, "because she sure likes to give them." He handed Nate a piece of green yarn.

"Hang on to this for a minute while I store this cover." Nate glanced towards the cockpit. Both women were watching. He turned his attention to the sail.

"Yep," Michael said. "I'm lucky she's not up here right now telling me how to do this." Nate looked back towards the cockpit. Becca caught his eye, smiled, and started towards him. Sally picked up the cooler and headed towards the cabin.

"I think you just ran out of luck," he said to Michael. "The Admiral's heading aft."

Nate watched Becca's approach. Behind her low clouds swept across the sky, skirting the water, dyeing the horizon gray as they hurried before the gusting wind. Michael slid the canvas sail up the mast and cleated its halyard. Beneath them the graveled monotoned voice of NOAA Weather Radio slipped from the cabin. Buoy reports from Tybee Island indicated rapidly increasing wave heights.

"That's still way south of us," Michael said, looking at a coastal chart pinned to the wall, "but we'll monitor the Coast Guard on the VHF radio. They've got some pretty tall towers, though sometimes a bad storm can drown out the signal." He flipped a toggle switch and the VHF radio buzzed to life. "You're always better off with a satellite phone."

Nate offered Becca his hand as she slid across the cabin. She slipped her arm around him, balancing easily on the pitching deck.

"I thought I better see how Captain Bly was treating you," she said. "He's kind of rough on apprentice seamen." She felt good next to him and his arm wrapped naturally around her waist.

"Funny, your Dad said the same thing about you." Nate looked up at the lofted sail. "I've got a question, though."

"Shoot," Michael said. "Looks like I'm going have to train a new crewman."

"Well, why isn't all that wind trying to drag us with it? It's blowing pretty hard, but nothing's happening."

"That's because the sail's let out," Michael answered. "If you just let the sail go, it turns straight into the wind and loses all power. It's the nautical equivalent of a skiing 'aw shit' moment. You know, when you hit your 'aw shit' mode, you just sit down and the laws of physics bring you to a stop. It's the same with a sailboat. We say, 'when in doubt, let it out'. It's almost like having brakes." Michael looked up at the speeding clouds. "There's an exception though."

"What's that?" Nate asked.

"If you release the sail in rough seas, you can broach and capsize."

"I'll keep that in mind," Nate said. He looked up at the billowing sails, "in the unlikely event I'm ever at the helm during rough weather."

Michael laughed. "Sure you'll be. I'm already planning on having you crew for me in Shelter Island's Thanksgiving Frostbite race."

"I don't think so, Daddy," Becca said. She squeezed Nate's hand. "He's got a full schedule in New York and freezing to death with your yacht club buddies isn't on it."

Michael bowed to his daughter. "Okay, Admiral, I'll shanghai another crew. I might even draft your sister. Now, with your permission, I'm going to launch this expedition."

"You may sail when ready." Becca glanced down at the small outboard bolted to the transom. "Want me to start the kicker?"

"Motors are for sissies," Michael said. "If you can't leave a pier under sail, then you're no sailor." He turned to Nate. "Tie that piece of yarn I gave you on the port line. I need to know what the wind's doing." Nate fished the yarn from his pocket. "It's called a 'telltale'," Michael added, as Nate tied the yarn in a square knot. "You two prepare to cast off. I'm going back to the cockpit."

"You go to the bow and I'll go to the stern," Becca said. "You just release the line from the cleat when Daddy says to."

"You sound like a sailor."

"I am." She pointed towards the front of the boat. "The bow's that way. It's the pointy end."

Nate looked towards the cockpit. Michael and Sally were focused on a series of ropes that converged there. Convinced he was unobserved, he slapped Becca's butt. "Get wise and I'll spank your stern."

She smiled up at him. The filtered morning sun danced through her hair and bounced off her face. He shook his head. *How could he have ever thought she wasn't pretty?* "Now," she said, "you sound like a sailor."

"I feel like I've been at sea a long time."

"It's only one more night until they leave. I think you'll survive."

"Maybe," he said, "but I'm not prepared to take that risk. Remember the drones."

She laughed. "I thought they exploded after sex."

"They do, but imagine what would happen if they didn't have that release."

"Prepare to cast off," Michael's voice boomed from the cockpit. Becca waved, then stepped towards Nate, twisting her body so that it blocked the cockpit view. "It'll be worth the wait," she whispered. He felt her hand slide up his leg, her fingers teasing their way under his shorts.

"I'll let you be the admiral, and I'll be a pirate princess you captured while saving the colony from my dastardly crew." Her green eyes flashed and a sly smile slid across her face. "Imagine the possibilities."

"I can," he said, "and you're killing me."

"You can't explode without my permission." He felt her hand go higher, then suddenly jerk away. He'd been caught. She slowly traced the seam of his pocket.

"Either you're super glad to see me or you brought a gun?"

"Your favorite one," Nate answered. She pressed the Colt against his thigh. "You know," he said, "just in case."

"In case what?"

"Well, for example, I heard there'd been a booty-hunting pirate spotted out on Fripp."

She nodded. "That's a coincidence. I heard there'd been a booty-hunting Neanderthal spotted out on Dataw."

"Cro-magnon. You keep forgetting my promotion."

"Whatever," Becca said. She started towards the stern, then turned around. "If I had time I'd take you below and do a strip search." She turned back around before he could respond.

Nate inhaled deeply and watched her walk away. For the week after the mountain trip, he'd stayed at her place, but Sally's and Michael's arrival had forced him back to his apartment. In some ways, Becca was still Daddy's little girl. What would happen long term he wasn't sure, though for now he couldn't imagine a day without her. He looked back at Becca. A wind gust lofted her hair from beneath her Red Sox hat and she pushed it back into place with her fingers. He liked her hair down. How would a pirate princess wear her hair? Probably up, he thought, held in place with a jeweled clip captured from a seized merchant ship.

He visualized the scene: Removing the clip, her hair falling around her bare shoulders. She'd wear the peasant blouse she'd worn at Parris Island, the Princess White Shirt one with the laced front and cinched waist. He shook his head. It was going to be a long day.

Michael ended Nate's fantasy with a loud, "Standby." Nate gave a thumbs-up. Becca did the same. He watched her bend over and uncoil her line. She wore a French sailor shirt over short white shorts.

"Your six looks mighty good," he yelled. She wiggled her hips.

"You're supposed to be protecting it, not ogling it."

"Cast off," Michael yelled.

Nate released the bow line and started towards the cockpit. Becca did the same. They met midship. "You're lucky your father's here," he said.

Becca slowly licked her lips. "You're lucky my father's here."

Once the lines were released, the outflowing tide took possession of the *Knot Now*, carrying her smoothly away from the pier. Michael allowed the boat to run with the wind, gathering speed before heading eastward for open water.

"Come on back here, you two," Michael called from the cockpit. "I want to give Nate a sailing lesson. I've got to undo the propaganda he's been subjected to by the power boat brigade."

"Coming," Becca yelled.

Nate grabbed her elbow. "We meet tonight, pirate wench, or you shall be held accountable for the explosion that sunk his majesty's ship." She stopped and cocked her head. Her eyes searched his face.

"And at what time and place should this admiralty order be executed?"

Her answer surprised him. He'd expected resistance. He thought a moment. "Twenty-three hundred hours on the forward bedroom patio," Nate finally answered. "There shall be lashes for lateness."

Sally met them at the cockpit. "You should feel honored," she said to Nate, "Michael's sailing techniques are closely guarded secrets. Of course, next time he plans a surprise trip, I'm going to drown him. I don't have half my stuff and we've got nothing to snack on."

"I'm only covering the basics," Michael said. He winked at Nate. "Otherwise, I'd have to toss him overboard." He stood up and motioned Nate towards him. "Here, son, take the tiller and get a feel for the boat. I'll explain how everything works."

The tiller reacted like the small outboards Nate had guided through Beaufort's maze of creeks and rivers. The boat moved easily through the waves, riding their crests with a rhythmic pitching motion as they slipped between Harbor Island and Edisto Beach, and into the Atlantic Ocean.

"Isn't this great?" Michael asked. He settled in beside Nate. "No noise, no pollution. Using the wind the way the first sailors did. Hell, if we wanted to, we could cross this ocean."

"I think I'll stay on this side for a while," Nate said. "My last trip across wasn't any fun." He held the tiller tightly. A rogue wave broke sharply across the bow, slapping the boat hard and hurling a stream of salty spray into the cockpit.

"Shouldn't you take the tiller?" Nate asked. He pointed toward the bow. "That one looks like it means business."

Another wave rolled towards them, its foamy crest reaching out like a claw. It lifted the boat, then squeezed it down as it collapsed, rolling along the deck before sloshing across the self-bailing cockpit. Sally ducked down into the cabin, followed by Becca.

"Lesson number one," Michael said. He placed his hand over Nate's and angled the boat into the waves. "Don't hit these big guys head-on. About forty-five degrees is fine." He pulled in on a line, tightening the mainsail. Deprived of its wind, the boat slowed. Sally opened the cabin door and emerged with two towels. Becca followed with an arm full of yellow rain slickers. She stuck her tongue out at her father, and gave Nate a big smile.

The boat was rolling gently now, cutting through the waves with a fluid motion as they headed seaward.

"We won't need those," Michael said, nodding at Becca. "We're hitting deeper water, so it'll stay like this for a while. These are non-cresting waves. Rollers, they call them." He patted Nate's shoulder. "Plus, I've got a natural sailor at the helm." He looked up at the sky. Above the layers of mist and gray clouds, a blue patch emerged.

"Ye of little faith." He smiled at Becca. "Hope Sally packed the sunscreen."

Becca sat down beside Nate. "Now, isn't this better than paddling?"

"I guess," he said, "but when I paddle, I'm in control. Out here you're at the mercy of the wind."

"Not true," Michael said. "We can make the wind carry us in any direction we want."

"Even straight into it?"

"Almost." Michael glanced at the telltale. "Matter of fact, we need to do that now. We're heading too far north. We'll switch from a port tack to a starboard tack." He swiveled his head, checking that another boat hadn't slipped in on them. "Stand by to come about." Michael stood behind Nate.

"That means we're to put the wind on the other side of the boat. Just maintain your course. The boom's going to swing across the boat." Michael glanced over his shoulder. "Now," he said.

Released from the wind, the boom swung violently across. Its power gone, the boat slowed, no longer responsive to the tiller. "We're in irons," Michael said, as he pulled in the sail.

"Is that bad?" Nate asked.

"It's not good," Michael said, "but we'll be out in a second." He loosened a line in the cockpit. The boat gained momentum, again responding to the tiller, picking its way through the rowdy water. "You know," Michael said, settling back into the cockpit, "sailing's a lot like life."

"Sounds deep," Sally said.

"Yeah, Daddy, it does sound deep. Please enlighten us."

Okay," Michael said, "I will and you two pay attention. You kids don't know it all yet." He looked up towards the sky and then focused back on the sail.

"Well, right now we're sailing into the wind." He looked at his telltale. "Just about twenty degrees off the wind, which is all a cruising boat like this can do. We're making headway; using our opponent's strength to reach our objective at a gradual rate, taking what the wind will give us." He paused a moment to check the sail. "But," he continued, "if we get greedy, go too high in the wind, then we'll be stopped; the sails will start luffing, the boat won't respond to the tiller, and we'll be back in irons. Life's like that. If you get greedy, it has a way of knocking you off course." He looked over at Becca. "Your arty friends would call it karma."

"That is deep, Daddy," Becca said from her perch by the cabin door, "and very nautical. Is it original?"

"Original as sin," Michael answered.

"I think that's the original sin you're thinking of," Sally said. She pointed towards the sky, "and I think you're about to be punished."

Nate followed Sally's gaze. Above them the clouds had thickened into a swirling gray mass, their darkness erasing the blue from the sky. To the south, dark, menacing towers rose from the gray water. Silent lightning bolts darted from their anvil tops. He watched the storm cells converge, forming a solid wall as they joined forces and marched towards land.

"That's not good," Michael said, watching the storm strengthen. "Not good at all." He looked at Nate. "Your dad was right. Looks like that depression did move north, and it moved fast."

"Is this when we batten down the hatches?" Nate asked, still looking at the clouds. "Looks like we're going to have some fun."

"Shouldn't we head in?" Sally asked. She rolled her eyes at Nate. "I don't think being lost at sea is fun."

"We'll be fine," Michael said, wrapping his arm around her shoulders, "but it's too late to turn back." Distant thunder punctuated his words. "That storm would beat us in. We're better off out here where we've got room to maneuver."

"So we're stuck?" Becca asked. "Can't we go around it?"

"It's too big and we're fine," Michael answered in a calm voice. "Now everybody quit bitching, and let's get ready."

The waves announced the storm's arrival. They grew steeper, lifting the boat on to their crests before sending it rushing down into their troughs. Michael sent Becca and Sally below with instructions to secure all loose objects and keep their life jackets on. "Keep doing what you're doing," he said to Nate, "I'm going to lower the mainsail and just use the jib. We need to slow down. This boat wasn't designed for this kind of weather."

The *Knot Now* sliced through the waves, pitching, then rolling, her side decking dipped beneath the waves, burying Michael as he sidestepped along its narrow width. He released the halyard, dropping the sail quickly, staggering as he wrestled with the wind for control. He retraced his steps to the cockpit. "That should help," he said, sliding in beside Nate. "It's called dropping canvas."

Nate studied the waves. They developed a pattern, coming in a series of five or six, each one larger than the last, grabbing the boat, shaking it like a toy before spitting it out.

Above them lightning leapt from cloud to cloud. Nate could feel the electricity. A strange tickling sensation traveled up his arms, then the air around him exploded. He looked around. He wasn't hurt and the boat seemed undamaged. He turned towards Michael.

"We can't stay up here," Michael yelled. "We're going to get washed overboard, plus we're a floating lightning rod. You get below. I'm going to lash the tiller and we'll let her make her own way."

"I thought you said that would capsize us."

"It's our best shot for now," Michael answered. "This boat's keel makes it self-righting and we can't stay up top. Now get below. I'll be there when I finish."

Nate started towards the cabin door. A wall of water pounded him from above, collapsing around him. It reformed and rushed rearward to slam into Michael, lifting him with it as it left the boat. He clung to the tiller, battling to stay onboard. Nate turned around to help.

"That was the worst one yet," Becca said. She and Sally sat side by side, their feet braced across the narrow walkway, their backs wedged against the bulkhead. A dull roar inundated the cabin.

Sally studied the cabin door. Water trickled around its seal, dropping to the floor, surging back and forth with the pitch of the boat. Gray duct tape lined every door and drawer. The tape had been a real find and she'd used it down to its cardboard core. The cabin was as secure as she could make it, though she didn't know why she cared. The way things were going, lost at sea would make a fine epitaph.

"Maybe we should check up top," she said. "The guys might need help."

"I'll go," Becca said, "Daddy won't shoot me for disobeying orders."

Sally watched Becca fight for balance, stumbling before grabbing the railing and starting up the stairs. She'd known Becca would volunteer. With a little luck, Mother Nature might take care of her problem. She said a little prayer. God would understand. She didn't want him to calm the sea.

Alone, Sally felt strangely indifferent to her fate, her earlier fear replaced by resignation. Becca's memory became clearer every day and a visit to the accident scene would surely complete it. Of course, Nate and Becca were going to find her dog tags. How else would they get in Allison's car? There was only one explanation. Once the cops got involved, they'd do a DNA sweep of Allison's Jaguar. All Special Ops people were in the system. She remembered the medic swabbing her cheek. "No more unknown soldiers," he'd said. "Even if you're blown to itty bitty pieces."

She looked around the spartan cabin. A fire axe above the hatch looked strangely out of place. Its red blade seemed to bleed as water trickled down its handle, changing color like a chameleon as it worked its way to the cabin floor.

Michael huddled against the cockpit's bulkhead. He studied the coastal charts. Becca hovered over him, shielding him from the wind. Nate battled the tiller.

"What's our heading?" Michael asked.

Nate looked at the compass mounted beside him. Its red arrow swung in a narrow arc. "270 degrees," he answered, "give or take a few for the boat's motion." He looked at the compass again. "Almost due west."

Michael tapped the chart with his finger. "Good," he said. "With any luck, we'll be able to reach Tubman Island in less than an hour."

"Then what?" Becca asked.

"From there, we can improvise. We'll try to use the island to block the wind or if it's too rough, we'll run her aground in some inlet. He unpinned the chart. "Now let's get below." Michael paused at the top of the stairs. "You know," he said. "Some people pay good money for a ride like this."

Below, a narrow passageway divided the two couples. Both men sat next to the door. Michael's eyes flicked around the cabin.

"I'd pay to get off," Sally said, bracing hard as they slid down a wave's crest and rolled in its trough before being lifted by a following wave.

Michael laughed. "Honey, I planned this all for you. You're always saying that you don't have any sailing stories to tell at the club."

"And now I'll be the posthumous subject of one. Maybe they'll give me a plaque."

Michael rubbed his wife's shoulders. "We'll be fine." The boat crested again, thrown from the sea, balancing in the wind until embraced by the waves.

"Of course, we are in the Bermuda Triangle."

Nate studied Michael. He seemed concerned but not frightened, like he'd gotten in just a little over his head, but not beyond his capabilities.

Becca snuggled against Nate. "Aren't you glad you came along?"

"Well," Nate said, "I do like a different adventure every weekend and your family seems capable of providing one." The boat pitched hard, its bow rising before pancaking back into the water. He braced himself and looked at Becca. "Of course, I'm a little concerned about what you've got scheduled for next weekend."

They all laughed. Michael reached across and slapped Nate's knee. "And they say the Corps is getting soft." He looked at Becca. "You ought to hang on to this one for a while. He's a keeper."

Becca sighed. Her father retained his innate ability to embarrass her. He'd perfected it during high school and it hadn't diminished with time. She glanced at Nate, then back at her father.

"I will," she said, giving him an impish smile. "After all, he's quite a stud."

Michael shook his head. "As you young people say, TMI." He was silent for a moment. "Listen," he said, "the waves sound different." Michael looked at his watch. "It's been about an hour. I need to check topside and see how we're doing." He paused at the top of the stairs, listened for a moment then opened the hatch.

The lightning reached out from the clouds like a small sun. Bright and hot, it entered the *Knot Now* through her aluminum mast, its blue tentacles reaching out, searching for ground, exiting the fiberglass hull below the waterline before spending itself in the salty confines of the Atlantic Ocean.

No one moved. The memory of the explosion lingered in their ears and smells of burnt plastic and ozone saturated their nostrils. Warm, salt water rose from the cabin's floor. Michael spoke first.

"We're taking on water and we may be on fire," he said. "The radio's fried so we're on our own for a little while." He flipped a toggle switch. "Bilge pump's gone too. We may have to bail by hand."

He looked at Nate. "The wind sounds like its slackened. Check topside. If it's safe, check the compass in the cockpit, start the kicker, and head us due west. I want to hit Tubman Island before we take on too much water."

"I'll go with him," Becca said.

"Just watch from the hatch, and let me know how things are going. No sense in having both of you exposed."

"What's next?" Sally asked. "Are we going to sink?"

"I don't know." Michael grabbed the fire axe. "I'm going to rip out these sole boards over the bilge and see if I can find where all this water's coming from."

Nate opened the cabin door and climbed out onto the deck. The jib was gone, but the mast looked undamaged. Water splashed across the deck. He wasn't sure how Michael defined safe, but both the rain and wind had slackened. He tightened his hood and started towards the cockpit. It took three steps. Becca slid in beside him.

"You disobeyed your captain."

"My captain overestimated your talents. You need my help. You can't run the outboard and navigate at the same time. The motor and the compass are too far apart." Becca looked at the compass. "We're heading north. What'll we hit if we keep going this way?"

"Probably a big freighter leaving Charleston."

She laughed. "Okay, wise-ass, let's do what Daddy says. You think he's right about that island?"

"Yeah, though according to his original calculations, we ought to be real close. If we miss it and keeping heading west, we'll eventually hit land." He pulled the canvas cover off the motor. "Let's fire this thing up," he said. "I don't want to miss tonight's princess interrogation."

Becca grabbed his arm. "You do realize that we're in a small, leaky boat in a big storm somewhere in the Atlantic Ocean?" Her voice trembled. He pulled her against him. Her slicker felt wet and cold.

"Sorry," she said. "I just looked around and there's nothing here but us. All of a sudden I felt tiny and helpless."

"We're okay. Your Dad's going to fix the leak and we're going to park this baby on a tropical isle filled with cocoa and marshmallows."

"You sure there'll be marshmallows?"

"Positive." He tweaked her nose. "But remember this little princess."

"What?" Becca answered.

"We have ways to make you talk."

"Maybe," she answered, pursing her lips, "but we have ways to make you beg."

Nate primed the gas can and gave the starter rope a tug. The motor started on his third pull. He pointed the bow west and opened up to half-throttle. The small gas can concerned him. How far could they go on three gallons? Michael would know. Pushing a little skiff, you burned about half a gallon per hour, but the *Knot Now* was much heavier with a deep riding hull. His dad had a rule: one-third tank out, one-third back and one-third in reserve. That didn't apply here. His guess was when they reached Tubman Island, they'd be running on fumes.

CHAPTER TWENTY

Nate watched Michael climb out of the hatch. A worried frown crinkled across his face. He wasn't bringing good news. Michael stood still for a minute, his eyes searching the *Knot Now's* deck before doing a slow, up and down appraisal of her mast. Apparently satisfied, he walked over and sat heavily beside Nate.

"Looks good topside," Michael said, raising his voice to be heard over the noisy motor, "but I've stuffed everything but the galley sink into that hole, and we're still taking on more water than we can pump out. Sally just relieved me on the bilge pump. Even superwoman can't stem the flow."

"So we're sinking?" Becca asked.

"Technically yes, though slowly, and I've got an idea that might keep the water out." He turned to Nate. "Let's go to full-throttle. I want to see if we can put that hole above the waterline. It'll be a rough ride, but we need to slow that leak."

Nate twisted the throttle open. The motor whined louder in protest but the boat definitely rode higher in the water. Michael sensed the change. He jumped to his feet.

"A keel boat can't plane," he said, "but I believe this is working. I'll check below."

"It better work fast," Nate said as Michael walked past him. "That tank only holds three gallons."

"That's okay," Michael said. He shielded his eyes from the rain and looked west. "We've got to be close to Tubman Island. I bet we could see it if this mess cleared up. We'll just need enough fuel to power our way ashore."

Nate watched Michael disappear down the cabin steps. He looked over at Becca. She sat with her legs and arms crossed, the oversized slicker's hood covering most of her face. The temperature had fallen and the cold drizzle and blustery wind cast a dampened chill around them. He patted the space beside him.

"I can hold a straight course for a while. Come sit beside me and we can keep each other warm."

A smile slipped from beneath her hood, but Michael popped back out of the hatch before she could answer. He wore a set of binoculars around his neck and a big smile covered his face. "It's working," he said. "We can stay afloat as long as we can maintain this speed." He raised the binoculars. "Just found these. They were hidden under a mattress that we stuffed in the hole." He did a quick scan then focused back on their heading. "I'll be dammed," he said. He lowered the binoculars, but kept his focus dead ahead. Becca climbed out of the cockpit and stood beside him.

"See that?" Michael asked, pointing into the swirling rain. "That's Tubman Island. Just where I said it would be."

He leaned over and high-fived Nate. "Keep that thing running. We're going to storm ashore like old John Wayne at Iwo Jima."

Nate strained to see the island. It came into focus slowly, growing larger as they approached, a green shadow silhouetted against a gray sky.

"It's pretty shallow around these islands," Nate said. "We might run aground a long way out and there's no depth finder on this boat."

Michael dropped down beside him. "See the gap between those tree lines?" He pointed towards the right. A hazy image of gray contrasts rose from the sea. "That's probably an inlet of some sort, so there should be a channel. We'll run up in there and wait out the storm."

Nate aimed the bow towards the inlet. Sheets of rain ripped across the boat, biting at his face. The water churned, pitching the *Knot Now* with a series of crests. "It's getting rougher," he said to Michael.

"It's a confluence of conflicting currents," Michael said. "The storm surge is pushing water in and the island's rejecting it and sending it out. Sort of like a chest bump with us in the middle." He turned to Becca. "Go below and tell Sally to stop pumping and hang on. Don't come up until we stop. We should just settle into the mud, but you never know what kind of junk a storm can wash in. Some guy off Orient Point hit a washing machine after last year's Nor'easter. It wasn't pretty."

"Okay," Becca said. She hugged her father and Nate, then headed towards the cabin. Her steps were short and careful and she grasped the boom for balance pausing at the hatch before looking back at Nate. "I wonder if a pirate treasure chest ever washed up?"

Nate laughed. "Never heard of that happening," he said. "From what I hear, those pirates kept a good eye on their booty."

"You mean treasure."

"They're interchangeable. Check your thesaurus."

She paused and crossed her arms. "Not always," she said, "and besides, you can't learn everything from a book."

Nate watched Becca enter the cabin. Her mood had lightened. That helped. Finding Tubman Island was the key. They'd be okay now; maybe a little uncomfortable for a day or so but not in any real danger. Fresh water was their biggest problem. Overall, it would a happy ending. Sally would have her sailing story and Michael would play the hero. The pirate princess interrogation was the sole casualty. It would have to wait.

Nate focused on the island. Michael had moved back into the cockpit. He stood braced against the bulkhead, the binoculars pointed towards the island. His yellow slicker glistened with rain and seawater filled the wrinkles of his brow. Michael mopped the water away with the back of his hand and squinted into the pelting rain. "Can't be much longer," he said, "otherwise we'll go aground in the marsh."

"Wouldn't it be better to ground it on the beach?" Nate asked, "so we can patch her up and sail her back."

"Nope," Michael answered, "for now I want to get this boat as sheltered as possible. If it ends up as salvage, then that's what insurance is for." Michael looked to the south. The squall lines were reforming. "I'm afraid," he said, "this might have been round one, and I don't want to be blown out to sea by round two." He pointed to their right. A narrow stream of muddy water rushed inland. "Here's our ride," Michael said. "Damn the torpedoes and full speed ahead."

They rode the storm surge into the inlet like a surfer, passing over the sandbars and oyster rakes that blocked its entrance, then settling as the surge dissipated into the inlet's delta.

The *Knot Now's* deep keel carved a slip through the oyster beds as it crunched its way to a stop, settling at a thirty- degree list in the shallow water. Nate killed the motor. Sally and Becca rushed out the cabin door.

"We're taking on water," Sally said. She looked around at the island then back at Michael. The boat groaned with each wave. "Are we going to sink?"

"We're on the bottom now," Michael answered, "though there's no telling where a storm surge could take us. I'll have a look at that leak." He glanced at Nate and Becca.

"We probably need to get some stuff together in case we have to abandon ship."

Michael stepped inside the cabin. Water sloshed beneath his feet. He moved forward into the berthing area and soon spotted the leak; a new two-foot-long crack, open at its center, just above the waterline and taking in water with each wave. The lightning hole remained dry.

"It's not too bad," he said, joining them in the cockpit. "I think we rammed an oyster bed."

"Can we fix it?" Sally asked.

"Maybe. Depends on what I can find onboard. At worst, we can slow it down with some towels and go back to manning the bilge pump."

"You sure this is Tubman Island?" Nate asked Michael. "There're a lot of little islands around here. Though one's probably as good as another."

"Let's see," Michael said. He pulled out his charts and placed his finger on a ribbon-like blue line.

"I think we're here. The shape on the chart seems to match this island. If I'm right, we're within twenty miles of civilization." He looked across the marsh towards the island, then out to sea.

"Here's how I see it: The Coast Guard and rescue services are overwhelmed right now, plus they won't be looking for us. Nobody was at the marina when we left, so only N.B and Peggy know that we went out and they're up in Charleston. I doubt if they will report us missing before tomorrow morning, so it wouldn't hurt if we got ready for a couple of days on our own." He pulled out his smart phone.

"I've got no bars," he said, "but keep checking your phones. You just might catch a signal from a cruise ship. They're like floating cell towers, though there's probably not one between Charleston and Jacksonville."

Becca watched her father. He seemed calm and as usual, in control.

"Are we going to stay on the boat?" she asked.

"Depends on whether or not I can stop that leak from flooding the cabin. It may stop itself when the waves die down." Michael turned to Nate. "Any suggestions?"

"Well, a signal fire would be nice, especially if no one flies over until tomorrow." Nate looked down at the chart. "I could explore the island for fresh water and hike down to Skull Creek. It's part of the Intercoastal so there might be some boat traffic through there."

"Sounds like a plan. I'll go below and get started on that leak." He looked at the sky. "This thing's about finished with us, but I'm afraid she might have a big sister."

"So who won this round?" Becca asked, as she trailed her father down the cabin ladder. "Mother Nature or us?"

"We did, sweetie," Michael answered. "We took old Mother Nature's best punch and we're alive, unhurt, and ready for more. What else could you ask for?" He looked down at the rising water. "Well, maybe a couple of tubes of epoxy and some hull tape. I'll see what I can find."

Michael found a can of putty in a storage locker. He pried it open with a dinner knife and crawled into the forward berthing compartment. The putty wasn't perfect but it might do the job. He pressed it into the crack but the sea fought back. Each wave squirted water, carrying the putty with it.

"I need to get outside," Michael said after a few tries. "Put something over the hole and give the putty a chance to set." He put on his slicker.

"Wait," Sally said, as he started up the stairs. "You won't need that jacket. Listen."

"Listen to what?"

"It's stopped raining."

Nate opened the cabin door. The wind lashed at him but with less fury and it carried no rain. Departing thunder echoed across the gray sky.

Michael popped his head up beside him. "Our storm's saying goodbye." He sniffed the air and looked seaward, "and she might take her big sister with her." He sniffed again. "I smell clear air and sunny skies."

Becca shook her head. "I smell a fake weatherman. What happened to your blue skies forecast?"

"I was just a few hours early. You just wait until you see your old man in action." He leaned down into the cabin. "Sally, bring me that swim ladder and a bailing bucket."

They lowered the ladder off the bow, and Michael climbed down. He stepped carefully onto the soft mud and sank to his knees. "I'm going to load this bucket with pluff mud, then plaster it over the hull crack. It's like cement. It'll give the putty a chance to set. I think they used it down here to build houses."

"Not really," Nate said. "It's pretty strong stuff, but the mortar used to build houses is called tabby. That's sand mixed with lime and oyster shells. They used to mine phosphate here. That's where they got the lime."

"We can make do with this for now," Michael said, "why don't you start on your hike while Sally and Becca grab some firewood?"

"We could all go together," Becca said. She wrapped her arms around Nate. "I'd miss him."

"No," Sally said quickly. "If we split up, we get to see twice as much of the island. You never know when something useful might turn up." She looked at Becca. "Give him a goodbye kiss while I grab the axe and some water bottles."

Sally watched Nate head into the underbrush. He stopped, turned around and waved before he disappeared into the green canopy that ringed the island. She said another silent prayer, shouldered the axe, and followed Becca inland. The storm had given her new hope. She just had to be patient. God would reveal his plan. She'd keep walking until he did. She stepped up beside Becca.

"We'll need some small, dry wood for kindling," she said, "plus some bigger wood to keep the fire going and some wet palms for smoke."

"Sounds good to me," Becca answered. "You're the survival expert. You just show me where."

Sally took the lead. They moved inland, sloshing their way through the marsh grass and onto the island. A natural path curved its way through the palm fronds and water oaks. Sally studied the ground, then knelt down and ran her fingers along a two-pronged track.

"Deer use this trail," she said, leaning on the axe. "That means this path probably leads to fresh water."

Becca pointed towards a hand-sized print. Four claws extended from its muddy center. "What made that track?"

"I'm not sure. Probably an alligator."

"Oh great," Becca said. She stared back into the marsh. "I assume they'll be where we're going?"

"Maybe, but they're more afraid of you than you are of them, and they're easier to catch than a deer." Sally started down the trail. "If we're stuck here for a while, I hear alligator tail is a real delicacy." She licked her lips. "but I bet it's not as good as the snakes we ate during Escape and Evasion Training."

Becca frowned and fell in behind Sally who set a fast pace which Becca struggled to match. Above them the wind moaned; its changing currents painting the sky a whitish gray. She'd heard the snake-eating stories before. She'd starve first.

Nate had snake-eating stories too. Her thoughts drifted to him as she silently followed Sally down the trail. She missed him already. Had it only been a week since the tent event? That's what Nate called it. He'd stayed at her condo all that week. It wasn't planned. He hadn't moved in. Not exactly. The goodbyes just never took and after the second night they'd quit pretending.

They were on a honeymoon, a working honeymoon interrupted by an eight-hour school day. It began with an afternoon run followed by an ocean swim and a desperate bathing suit shedding sprint to the bedroom. She'd texted Lizzie. She had her story. She'd share the details at Thanksgiving. Mojitos at Claudio's.

Lizzie texted back. "Was the magic penis theory still valid and did the earth move?"

"I'll let you know about the theory," she'd answered, "but right now I'm surprised the planet's still in orbit. Maybe Hemingway got it right." She was daydreaming when she almost bumped into Sally. Sally had stopped where the path veered off into a patch of tall, swaying reeds.

"Looks spooky," Becca said. "Something could be right next to you and you wouldn't know it." Sally nodded. Becca turned back towards the boat. She could no longer see its mast. They'd walked a long way, much of it through a pine forest. Dead limbs littered the forest floor. It looked like kindling to her.

"How far do we have to go for wood?" she asked. She pointed at a pile of brush. "Can't we use this?" Sally didn't answer. Apparently, she didn't like having her wilderness skills questioned. Becca spun around. Sally was gone.

Becca hesitated. Sally had probably gone just a few steps ahead but what if she hadn't? Becca looked around. What if something had dragged Sally off into the reeds? What else lived on this island? Panthers, bears, snakes, for sure. Down here, snakes were everywhere. Nate said they wouldn't hurt you, but they'd make you hurt yourself. Something slithered. She froze and called out to Sally, softly at first, then louder. There was no answer. The alligator tracks flashed through her brain as she watched the clouds dip lower, masking the taller trees with their whiteness and casting a shadow across the island.

She couldn't just turn around. *What would she say to her father? 'Sorry Dad, I lost Sally?'* She looked down the path. It opened and closed with the blowing reeds. She sighed and started forward. Sharp reeds scraped across her jacket. The feeling returned. It was like before; a sense of dread that enveloped her like the mist, sending her a warning. She stopped. The reeds closed around her, then opened with the wind. Sally appeared like an apparition. Becca jumped backwards. The apparition laughed.

"You look like you've seen another ghost," Sally said, walking towards her, the axe resting across her shoulders. "Come on; I've found some water." She laughed again. "You first," Sally said. It sounded like a command. "Just follow the path. I don't want you getting lost again, little girl."

Sally watched Becca pick her way along the path. The clouds dipped lower; ghostly swirls danced above the reeds like dust devils, twirling then shooting skyward, disappearing into the clouds that spawned them.

The pond she'd found was a miracle. Like she'd ordered it and it was delivered: Perfect time, perfect place. Just like the deer and the storm. God took care of his people. She felt like Moses, only she didn't need the sea to part. It only needed to remain angry for a few more hours. Sally looked up into the swirling clouds. She was looking into heaven. God had picked out her promised land and now he'd prepared the way for her to claim it. This time it wouldn't take forty years.

Becca stopped just short of the narrow sandy beach that separated the pond from the trail. Four bulky alligators gazed at them from the opposite bank. Sally stared back into lidded eyes that glowed red in the afternoon darkness. They weren't aggressive, but they wouldn't be able to resist a thrashing, bloody body. She walked up behind Becca.

"I need you to taste the water," she said. She wanted Becca's footprints near the water. She could arrange the scene later.

Becca's face scrunched into a frown. She looked down at the murky water then back at Sally. "You want me to taste this?"

"Just a little," Sally answered. "Tell me if you think it's salty. I tried it but I'm not sure and we might have to drink it. There're only four water bottles on the boat and it's too late to trap any rainwater."

"All right," Becca said. "I guess I can take one for the team." She dropped to one knee. The gray sand dug into her skin like coarse gravel. The feeling was still there. She scooped the water with her hand.

"Where's Nate when you need him?" Becca took a mouthful and spit it out on the sand. "This is a bad year for swamp water, but I don't think it's salty." She started to stand. Her eyes focused on the pond. An alligator on the far bank submerged, scattering her reflection. Water swirled around its giant body as it sank into the darkness.

Sally stepped forward. She choked down on the axe, the blunt edge facing Becca. It would be a half-swing, just enough to knock Becca unconscious. Splitting her head open might look suspicious. She didn't know where the alligators would start. Probably somewhere soft.

Becca saw the movement in the pond's dull reflection. She felt the axe fall and dove to her left. She looked up. Sally stood above her, the axe's red hue silhouetted against the dark sky. The image merged with her dream, gradually focusing until they became one.

"It's you!" she screamed. "I remember. You were there that night. You had a knife. You killed my mother!"

Sally stepped closer. Becca trembled at her feet. "I'm sorry," Sally said, "but I've got no choice. You wouldn't give up."

"Please," Becca said. "You don't have to do this. It's not too late." She was playing for time. What would Nate do? He'd do something. The wet sand dug at her skin. Sally stepped closer. She forced Becca's head down with her foot. "Just keep still and close your eyes. You won't feel a thing." Sally's voice sounded soft and calming. Her head was tilted towards the sky and her lips moved silently. It took a second before it sank in: Sally was praying for her soul.

"Let me say my own prayer?" Becca asked. Her voice cracked. Sally's foot made it hard to breathe. "It's been a long time, and I need to make things right."

Sally lowered the axe to her waist and lifted her foot off Becca's throat. Mercy was a virtue. "Make it quick," she said. "God knows what's in your heart."

"Thank you," Becca said. She rose to her knees, then lowered her forehead to the sand. "Our Father," she began. She felt Sally move behind her. Amen was going to be her last word. She squeezed the wet sand in her hands, forming it like a snow ball. "Who art in heaven," she continued, before flinging the sand into Sally's face.

"You're going to die, bitch," Sally yelled. She wiped her eyes and blindly swung the axe. "You've abused God's word."

Becca sprang to her feet. Sally staggered towards her. Her swings were slow and awkward. They could be timed. Sally's vision would soon clear. Becca dove under the axe and slammed into Sally's legs, knocking her backward into the pond. Sally disappeared beneath the brown water, then resurfaced, pushing herself up with the axe, struggling through the waist-deep water.

Becca sprinted towards the path. She heard Sally yell, "It'll be worse if you run."

Becca's arms flailed through the sharp reeds. She stifled a scream that slipped from her throat. There was no one there to hear her. She had to beat Sally back to the boat. They'd run together before. She couldn't match Sally's speed or stamina, but she had had a head start. It had to be enough.

Splashing sounds drifted in behind her. Becca listened for Sally's footsteps, but all she heard was the wind rushing through the trees. She ran faster, her pace a mixture of fear and caution. Falling could prove fatal, but so would being caught from behind.

The reeds' sudden end surprised her. She blasted through them and on to the sandy path. She looked back. The reeds closed behind her like a curtain.

She headed towards the boat, slowing to look behind her, then sprinting ahead. She was running on adrenalin. It all seemed crazy,; like a tropical *Shining* with a female Jack Nicholson. She was afraid, but not panicked. Her calmness surprised her. It came from that night in the mountains, only now she was alone.

The soft sand, drained her energy, absorbing her efforts, giving nothing in return. She couldn't run much further. The boat had to be close. She strained to see through the deep canopy, finally spotting its bare mast through an opening in the trees. The mast rose above the marsh like a giant finger, beckoning her on. She'd be safe there. Sally wouldn't follow her. She'd probably hide and make the cops find her. That shouldn't take long. It was a small island. Splashing sounds came from her right. Becca turned and screamed.

Sally rose from the marsh. Weeds and mud draped her like a ghillie suit, and her dark eyes flickered beneath the crusted mud. She rested the axe against her leg and shook like a wet dog. Mud and water sprayed into the air. A victory smile slowly lit her face. Becca was cut off. Sally had used the pond as a shortcut.

Sally started forward. Becca leapt off the path and into the trees. She headed inland. She'd try to hide, let Sally pass by, then make a sprint for the boat. The wind blew harder, swaying the trees as it pushed its way across the island. A light mist began to fall. She stopped and turned around. Sally wasn't there.

Becca kept running. Heavy brush forced her deeper into the island. She twisted her way through the crowded trees, following openings and ducking under thick, green vines armed with bayonet thorns that ripped at her skin. One snagged her hat. She kept moving. Sally was out there somewhere.

The woods ended in a saltwater marsh. Becca crawled to its edge. Ragged cedars and palms lined its bank. Finally, she could see something. She wiggled under a cluster of palm fronds and looked out across the open marsh. Nate would be proud of her camouflage. She could stay here.

A flimsy fog drifted by, blurring her view. She continued to stare. Something was wrong. She watched the fog lift. It took her a second but there it was; a yellow slicker, peeking out from the trees along the far right bank, nearly a quarter mile away. Her way to the boat was blocked, but she had a clear path to Nate. She took off her slicker and stuffed it under the palms. They were yellow for a reason, but even if Sally spotted her, there was nothing she could do. She was too far away. G.I. Jane had guessed wrong.

Becca flinched as she splashed into the water. It was cold and it stung her scratches, but she felt better in the open. She checked the slicker. Sally hadn't moved.

Becca kept up her pace. No need to take chances. Her shoes slipped across the marsh mud. It was shallow, a dark covering for the firm sand beneath it. The marsh ended in a sand flat which gave way to a tree line of scrawny pines and stubby palms.

She thought back to the chart. She was headed towards Nate. A light rain replaced the mist, blanketing the landscape in a gray curtain. Ahead, a shadowy figure emerged from the wood line. She looked back. The slicker was still there.

"Nate," she yelled; then she saw the axe. Becca sprinted across the sand flat and into the tree line. Sally's footsteps grew louder. She was closing the distance. Becca's lungs burned and her calves ached. She had nothing left. She had to find Nate. She curved through the cedars and oaks, angled towards the beach, then headed back inland. She couldn't let Sally cut her off.

The trees ended in a clearing that gave way to another marsh. Becca searched ahead. A form emerged from the trees. It couldn't be. How'd she get there? Becca tried to turn. The boat became her only option, but her legs buckled and she toppled face down in the soft dirt. She lay still, gulping air and listening. Faint footsteps squished across the sand. She had to get up. She wasn't going to die like this. She rolled onto her side and struggled to her knees, but the world spun around her and she dropped back onto the sand. The spinning became a vortex. She closed her eyes, lying still, listening to the rain plop against the marsh. A hand softly touched her cheek. She looked up.

"Becca," Nate said. He knelt down beside her and pushed back her tangled hair. "My God, what happened to you? Where's Sally?"

She pulled his hand to her face. "You're real," she said, then collapsed back onto the sand.

Sally moved quietly through the trees. God had shown her Nate first. She eased past them and into the marsh grass. Thunder boomed in the distance and the wind's dull moan hid her movements. She stalked them like a lion, dashing from cover to cover, quick and silent, stopping to observe, then creeping closer. Her battle face was on. No feelings, no mercy, a separate person she'd discovered in Afghanistan that lived just below her civilized surface, ready to do her bidding.

Nate was a problem, but she was accustomed to problems. "Improvise, adapt and overcome". That was the motto. She'd take him first. The initial blow would be critical. After that, Becca would be easy. She'd carry their bodies back to the pond. It'd take two trips. Not ideal. She'd have to work fast, but she had her story: An alligator dragged Becca in; Nate dived in after her. It happened so quickly. There was nothing she could do. A tragic ending to a silly adventure. She'd stay by the pond. Michael would find her there, battling the alligators for Becca and Nate's bodies.

She studied her victims. Her muscles twitched, anxious and ready, waiting for her moment. A long strip of sand lay between them. She needed to cross it unseen. She watched Nate help Becca to her feet. His back was turned. She slipped from the grass and broke into a quick, silent stride.

"It's Sally," Becca said. Her arm draped around Nate's shoulder. "She's the figure in my dreams. She murdered my mother and she tried to kill me with that axe." She pointed towards the wood line. "I think she's in there."

"You're sure?" Nate said. "Sally's trying to kill you?" He tried to hide the disbelief in his voice. It all sounded crazy, but crazy shit happened. The Green on Blue attacks he'd seen in Afghanistan proved there wasn't a friend/foe detector for what was in a person's mind. He looked towards the trees where Becca pointed. His eyes moved in short scans, searching for an outline in the misty shadows. It was like being in a sniper hide. You never moved without a 360-degree check. He looked to his rear. Sally was almost on them.

"Run," he yelled to Becca, "run."

Sally was thirty yards away. He tugged at his pistol. It was stuck; the barrel twisted in the mesh pocket liner of his water shorts. He turned to run. Sally was a skilled warrior. He wasn't going to fight her unarmed if he had a choice. Two steps later, he tripped over Becca. She'd collapsed at his feet.

Sally slowed, then circled around him. He sprang up, turning with her, keeping himself between Sally and Becca. She feinted with the axe, then jerked it above her head. He watched Sally's eyes. Becca was her target. He stepped to his left, angled the stuck pistol upward, and pulled the trigger.

The bullet ripped through his shorts, burning his leg as it exited his shorts. Sally froze. Hit or startled; he couldn't tell. He tugged at the pistol, feeling it release from the bullet-ripped liner.

"It's over, Sally," he said. "Put down the axe."

Sally started towards him. Her pace was slow and deliberate. Nate stepped back. He felt Becca with his feet and stopped. Sally kept coming. "Drop the axe," he yelled.

He raised the pistol until its front sight centered on Sally's chest. She stopped. The axe rested on her shoulder. He reached out with his left hand. "Give me the axe."

Sally looked down at Becca and then back up at him. Her feet pawed the sand. Spittle dripped down her chin. She was close, too close. A guttural growl rose from her throat. Nate watched the axe. Sally grunted once, then charged.

He fired twice, the second shot instinctive. Double tap; same point of aim. You always fired twice. Sally seemed to dissolve, the axe falling behind her as she crumpled into the sand. He waited. A wood stork abandoned his perch with beating wings and loud, squawky protests. Nate watched Sally. She'd gone down too easily. Twenty-twos weren't known for their knockdown power. He pulled Becca to her feet. She stared across the sand at Sally.

"Is she dead?"

"Maybe," Nate answered, "but I'm not sure." He stepped towards Sally and kicked the axe away. She didn't move. Becca pulled him back.

"It's okay," he said, wrapping his arm around her shoulder, "she can't hurt you now."

Footsteps splashed in the marsh behind them. Nate turned towards the sound. Michael was sprinting towards them through the marsh.

"He must have heard the gunshots," Nate said. "That's what Marines are trained to do; run towards the battle."

"Poor Daddy," Becca said. She grasped Nate's hand. "I don't know how to tell him. First Mom, and now Sally."

Nate knelt down and placed two fingers on Sally's neck. There was no pulse. Dark, purple blood seeped through her shirt. He'd hit an organ, probably her heart. It must have been the upward angle, the bullet entering beneath her protective ribs. Nate closed Sally's eyes with his fingers and started to rise. Michael hit him at full speed, slamming him hard into the sand.

"You son of a bitch," Michael screamed in his ear. "Why? God damn it. Why?"

It took Nate a second to realize what Michael saw; Sally dead and him standing over Michael's scratched and bleeding daughter, pistol in hand.

"Stop, Daddy," Becca screamed, but Michael used his weight advantage, pressing Nate harder into the ground. Nate felt Becca leap onto her father's back. Michael slung her off. He twisted Nate's right hand. He wanted the gun. They rolled across the sand. Becca followed, screaming at her father to stop.

Nate twisted to his right. He managed to roll Michael off. "You've got it wrong. Sally killed Allison." Michael seemed not to hear. Nate tried to stand, but Michael dived at his legs, dropping him down, then headbutting his chest, both hands now on the gun.

Nate buckled beneath Michael's weight. He couldn't breathe and his hand was crushed against the pistol, his finger on the trigger. Michael squeezed harder. His grip forced the trigger back. Nate ratcheted his hand, but Michael's grip riveted it to the weapon. It was going to fire.

The blast wave slammed against Nate's eardrums. He shook his head. A painful noise echoed through his ears. Becca groaned and Michael's grip went limp. Something warm dripped on his arm. Nate leaped to his feet.

Becca lay on her back, her arms outstretched. Bright, red blood streamed from her forehead. Michael knelt beside her, clutching her hand and whispering her name.

Nate moved around Michael and lifted Becca's head. She was breathing. He removed his slicker and pulled off his shirt. He folded the shirt twice and pressed it against her wound. Blood soaked through. He'd seen headwounds before. They all bled but not like this one. Maybe the internal carotid? He started shaking. She couldn't bleed out. Not Becca; not now.

Nate pressed harder. Warm, sticky blood oozed between his fingers. He continued to press. Michael moved beside him.

"How is she?"

"She's breathing and her skull feels intact." He looked down at his hand. There was no new blood. "And I think the bleeding's stopped."

Becca remained lifeless. Nate wrung out his shirt and mopped the blood from her head. A dark, bloody line angled across her right temple. He'd seen this once; a bullet ricocheting off a skull without penetrating into the brain. He ran his fingers through her hair and probed her scalp. This was the only wound.

Nate turned to Michael. "I think she's going to be okay. It's only a crease." Nate took a deep breath and exhaled slowly.

"It was Sally that Becca saw that night. She killed your wife and she tried to kill Becca."

Michael sat silently, his blank eyes focused on Sally. Nate turned towards Becca. Her breaths came in slow, shallow gasps. Not good. He rolled her onto her side.

"Talk to me, Princess," he said in her ear. She didn't respond. He slapped her cheeks.

"Becca!" he yelled. Her eyes rolled open. "Welcome back," he said. He couldn't stop smiling. Becca looked past him to Sally.

"For a minute I thought I was back in my dream."

"No," Nate answered. "That dream's finished, but I've got a couple of others I'd like to discuss."

"Are they scary?"

"Not unless you're afraid of a booty-hunting Neanderthal."

She sat up. "They're extinct," she said, "but I've developed a real taste for their marshmallow replacements."

"I guess I'll always be a marshmallow?"

Her green eyes smiled. "Remember your options."

Nate heard a familiar noise, thumping through the heavy air. "Sounds like our ride," Nate said, listening to the helicopter approach. It circled the island and came in from the east, a tiny red spot dancing across the gray horizon. "Well," Nate said, picking up his slicker and waving it above his head, "sailing the *Knot Now* home isn't an option, so we better flag this guy down."

The pilot acknowledged Nate's signal by rocking the aircraft. Nate flashed back to his Aircraft Recognition Cards. "It's a Coast Guard Jayhawk," he said, remembering the familiar shape. "It'll have plenty of room and an EMT onboard."

Nate turned to Michael who sat in the sand like a statue, his arms folded and his eyes locked on Sally. He couldn't imagine what Michael felt. He needed closure. Becca could provide some answers, but he felt certain that the truth died with Sally. He reached over and patted Michael's shoulder, "We need to cover her up," he said softly. "There'll be a stretcher onboard the helicopter."

"I'll do it," Michael said. "You go meet the helicopter."

The Jayhawk flared, then touched down along a sandy split about fifty yards away. Its rotor wash peppered them with sand. Nate sprinted forward and slashed his finger across his throat. The engines began to unwind. Nate watched two men dismount and run towards him, probably the crew chief and rescue swimmer, he guessed. One man tossed Nate a jacket.

"We have one dead from a gunshot wound and one with a possible concussion," he told them. "It's a long story but you should notify law enforcement and have them meet us when we land. I'll need to get on the intercom with the pilot to explain what happened."

The flight to Beaufort Memorial Hospital took only a few minutes. Nate had just finished briefing the pilot when they began to descend. The rescue swimmer leaned over towards him. He'd put a sterile dressing on Becca's wound and wrapped a bandage around her head like a sweatband. He'd asked Becca memory questions the entire flight. "I definitely think she's concussed," he shouted in Nate's ear. "She was out for a while and she took quite a hit, plus she keeps getting the months wrong."

The coroner and a Beaufort County detective were waiting at the helipad when they landed. Litter teams carried Becca and Sally inside. The coroner followed, leaving Nate and Michael with the detective.

"Roger Blum," the detective said, holding out his hand. "The pilot explained what you said happened." He switched his eyes back between Nate and Michael. "Sounds like a clear case of self-defense, but, of course, we'll have to do an investigation and that's going to include an autopsy." He looked at Michael. "The deceased lady your wife?" Michael nodded.

"I'm sorry for your loss," Blum said. He pulled a pad from his jacket pocket. "First thing I'm going to do is read you your rights, then I'm going to take you downtown."

"Can't this wait?" Nate asked, before Blum could start. "The hurt girl's my girlfriend and his daughter and she needs somebody with her." Blum gave him a harsh look. "My Dad's N.B Forrest," Nate continued. "He's a local attorney, but he's in Charleston right now and I can't reach him."

Blum laughed. "Well, we won't hold that against you. Matter of fact old N.B was two years ahead of me at the Citadel." He shook his head. "I'll never forget what he did for me during 'Hell Week.'" He nodded like he was agreeing with himself. "You know," he said, "I'd have quit during my Knob year if it wasn't for your dad." Blum looked around. "This violates all kinds of protocols," he said, "but I'm going let you two hang around here until we get some word on the girl." He handed Nate a card. "Call me first thing in the morning. Blum turned around, then turned back. "Oh," he said. "One last thing: Where's the gun she was killed with?"

The question startled Nate. He hadn't thought about the pistol since Becca was shot. "It's in my pocket," he said. "It's loaded with a round in the chamber and it's on safe." Nate sensed Blum stiffen.

"Take it out with your thumb and forefinger," Blum said, "and hand it to me butt first." Nate followed Blum's instructions with exaggerated slowness. Blum unloaded the pistol and slid it into his jacket pocket. "I'll give you a receipt in the morning," he said, "but I doubt if you will see this for a while."

Nate watched Blum walk away, then turned to Michael. "We need to find Becca." Michael nodded. He'd barely spoken since the helicopter flight and his eyes remained blank. Nate guided him towards the lighted entrance. They followed the signs to Patient Registration.

"We were looking for you," the desk clerk said. "Who's Mr. Noble?"

"I am," Michael said.

"The coroner wants to see you." She pointed across the hall. "His office is next to the ER. She turned back to Nate. "We'll be admitting Rebecca when her CAT Scan and MRI are finished." She looked at her computer screen. "She'll be in room four twenty-six. You can wait there if you like."

Nate glanced at Michael. He still looked dazed. "If it's okay," he said, "I'll go with him."

She shook her head. "Sorry, the coroner said *alone*, but there'll be a chaplain there. The coroner will want to talk with you later."

Nate thought about Michael on the elevator ride up. He'd accepted Sally's guilt, but he wasn't ready for an interrogation. Hopefully, the coroner would see that, though he had a job to do. The first step would be to identify the body. Religion wasn't his strong suit, but he was glad the chaplain would be there.

Becca's room was at the end of a hallway. It looked like every hospital room he'd ever seen. A single bed surrounded by robotic-looking machines and plastic tubing occupied most of its space. Two brown Naugahyde chairs sat crowded beneath a rectangular window. Nate walked over and looked out. Beneath him the dull glow of Ribaut Road's streetlights marked the Beaufort River's winding path. His apartment was only a mile down river.

He paced around, walked out into the hallway, then returned to the room. He wasn't worried. Becca was okay. He was sure of that. Well, almost sure. He needed to see her. He walked to the elevator. A trio of nurses exited and headed towards the nursing station. Nate glanced at his watch. Seven p.m. Must be a shift change, he thought. He headed back to the room, flipped on the TV, then turned it off. There was a light knock at the door followed by a gurney's chrome nose. A blue-robed Becca sat on top propelled by a small woman in green scrubs.

"This is Maria," Becca said, "and she drives almost as well as I do."

Maria smiled at Nate. "I learned in Santo Domingo," she said, "and Miss Noble is a bad influence." She wedged the two beds together and helped Becca slide across. "She tried to get me to race another gurney to the elevator."

"You had him," Becca said. "The inside line is always quicker."

Maria pulled the gurney to the door. "Tomorrow," she said, "I'll take you for a wheelchair ride. I am the fourth floor champion."

Nate closed the door behind Maria and walked slowly to Becca's bed, studying her as he walked. Scratches covered her arms and her hair collapsed like a wet mop around her shoulders. She'd never looked prettier. He leaned down and kissed her. Her lips were soft and salty. "You taste like a margarita."

She smiled. "You mean, I'm intoxicating."

He ruffled her blood-matted hair. The EMT's bandage remained in place. "Yeah, that's what I meant. You are intoxicating. The question is, are you bulletproof?"

She took his hands. "Nothing's been read yet, but from what I could get out of the techs, I'm okay. The ER doc's supposed to come up when they know something." She rolled onto her side and propped up on her elbow.

"Where's my father and how's he doing?"

Becca had dominated his thoughts. He'd almost forgotten about Michael.

"He's with the coroner. They wouldn't let me go with him. He's going to have to identify the body and they're going to ask him some questions. At least there's a chaplain with him." Nate pulled a chair over by the bed. Becca lowered the railing and patted the mattress beside her.

"You can sit up here if you promise to behave."

"Too tempting," Nate said. He sat down in the chair. Thoughts of Michael roaming the halls merged with pictures of Sally being slammed back by his bullets. He jumped back up. "I can't just sit here. I need to find your father. The coroner's probably through with him and he shouldn't be alone."

Becca squeezed his hand. "I know I should feel more sympathetic," she said, "but I can't. What I feel is relief. No more dreams; no more doubts about my own sanity. I want to sing, not mourn, and I sense that Mom feels the same way."

"I understand," Nate said, "but it's going to take a while for your father to accept what a monster Sally really was, and even then, he's always going to see me as her killer." He shook his head. "I'll always wonder about that second shot."

"He'll be okay and you had no choice."

"I want to check on him anyway." She caressed his cheek.

"You're a sweet guy," she said. "Tell him I'm fine and hurry back." He leaned down and kissed her. She pulled him down towards her. "Still intoxicating?" she asked, gently nibbling his lips.

"Inebriating," he answered. "Now I've got to go before I get an SWI."

She released his head. "As usual, I know I'm going to regret this, but what's an SWI?"

"Seduced While Inebriated."

She shook her head. "I bet the penalty's worse for repeat offenders. Which reminds me; they did say no sex for six weeks." She fought back a laugh. "Seems they have a lot of trouble with headboard banging."

"Not a problem," he said, walking towards the door; "we'll get you that river helmet you never got to use."

Nate found Michael on the cafeteria patio, sipping a cup of coffee and staring out across the river. "That stuff any good?" he asked.

Michael turned towards him. "Nasty. I think it's some of that chicory left over from the Civil War."

"It's payback for the Union blockade." He sat down. Michael sounded better. The flat monotone was gone and his eyes had lost their zombie deadness.

"Becca's seems okay. She's in her room. You through with the coroner?"

"Just finished. Nice guy, but I couldn't tell him much. I'm trying to talk him out of an autopsy." Michael took a sip of coffee and frowned. "I hate to think of Sally being sliced up that way. Maybe your dad could help?"

"We can try," Nate answered. "You ready to see Becca?"

"Lead the way. That poor girl got the worst out of this deal."

By the time they reached Becca's room, Nate felt better about Michael though they'd only talked about Becca. He'd wait for Michael to bring up

Sally. Describing the shooting would be tough. He'd always wonder which shot was fatal. Michael would wonder too, but there was no way to know and it was pointless to guess.

Becca's door was open. She was sitting by the window.

"Look who I brought," Nate said. Michael seemed to freeze in the doorway. Becca stood up and walked towards him. Her steps were short and slow, and she used the chair back for balance. Michael took her in his arms. "You okay?" he asked. "You're looking a little shaky."

Becca clutched his arm. "They said I might have some dizzy spells. Maybe I better lie down." Michael guided her to the bed and Nate helped her climb in. He fluffed a pillow and stuffed it under her head.

"Comfy?" he asked.

"Yes, thank you, nurse."

Michael moved to the bed's opposite side. He took Becca's hand. "I'm sorry," he said. "Sorry for everything."

"It's okay, Daddy. You couldn't have known. Nobody knew."

Michael pulled a silver chain out of his shirt pocket. "I want to show you something."

"Those look like dog tags," Nate said.

"Yeah," Michael answered, "they're Sally's. I've been hiding them since we left home. She wore them all the time. Thought they were some kind of good luck charm." He ran the chain through his fingers. "Said she rubbed them after every combat mission."

Becca stared at the tags. The letters were blurred. "Where'd you find them?" she asked.

"Some naturalist out at Mashomack brought them by the house last month. Said he found them in an abandoned osprey nest. I told him she used to take them off when she laid out by the pool. Tan line thing. Anyway, this guy thought that maybe a crow stole them. He said crows like to collect shiny things, and they sometimes take over abandoned nests. Funny, she never told me they were missing."

Michael smiled and shook his head. "Anyway, tomorrow's her birthday. They were going to be a surprise. I even got a Tiffany box: The original blue one with the white satin ribbon." He smiled again. "Imagine her expression when she saw what was inside. I could hardly wait." Michael shoved the dog tags back in his shirt pocket. "Now she's lying on a cold metal table with a cardboard tag tied to her big toe with a piece of ratty string." His eyes closed tight, wrinkling with the effort, like he was blotting out the image.

"I asked the coroner if I could fasten the dog tags around her neck but he said no. Some kind of regulation, but I could do it before she's buried."

Michael squeezed Becca's hand. "You two are going to think I'm crazy, but I don't hate her. It's all my fault. Her, Allison, everything. Like my little lesson on the boat. I had it all, but I got greedy. Made her greedy too." He took a deep breath and crossed his arms.

"You know," he continued, "deep down, she stayed a scared little mountain girl. Never could escape her upbringing. Always afraid something bad was going to happen and somebody was going to take it all away." Tears crept down his face.

"I didn't help." He wiped his eyes with his sleeve. "Told her she could have it all. Even did my Gordon Gecko 'greed is good,' impression. Made her do things I knew were wrong. I had my reasons, but I never meant to hurt anybody."

He looked at Becca. His voice broke, and he began to tremble.

"It's okay, Daddy," she said. "She fooled you just like she fooled everybody else." Michael shook his head.

"I should have known," he said. "I'm the one that taught her. I guess you could say I steered her too high in the wind." Michael looked up then returned his gaze to Becca. "Problem was," he said, "I forgot to teach her how to trim her sails."

The End